Mark Twain's
MEDIEVAL ROMANCE

Mark Twain's
MEDIEVAL ROMANCE

And Other Classic Mystery Stories

Edited by
Otto Penzler

PEGASUS CRIME
NEW YORK

MARK TWAIN'S MEDIEVAL ROMANCE

Pegasus Crime is an Imprint of
Pegasus Books LLC
80 Broad Street, 5th Floor
New York, NY 10004

Collection copyright © 2006 by Otto Penzler

Originally published as *Uncertain Endings*

ISBN: 978-1-60598-279-3

Printed in the United States of America

FOR HOWARD STRINGER
TO SIR, WITH LOVE

Acknowledgments

"The Whole Town's Sleeping" copyright © 1950 by Ray Bradbury; renewed. First published by *McCall's*, September 1950. Reprinted by permission of the author and his agent, Don Congdon Associates, Inc.

"At Midnight, in the Month of June" copyright © 1954 by Ray Bradbury; renewed. First published by *Ellery Queen's Mystery Magazine*, June 1954. Reprinted by permission of the author and his agent, Don Congdon Associates, Inc.

"Nunc Dimittis" copyright © 1953 by Roald Dahl; renewed. First published by *Collier's*, September 4, 1953. Reprinted by permission of the author's agent, David Higham Associates.

"Unreasonable Doubt" copyright © 1958 by Stanley Ellin; renewed. First published by *Ellery Queen's Mystery Magazine*, September 1958. Reprinted by permission of Curtis Brown.

"The Moment of Decision" copyright © 1955 by Stanley Ellin; renewed. First published by *Ellery Queen's Mystery Magazine*, March 1955. Reprinted by permission of Curtis Brown.

"The Lady and the Dragon" copyright © 1950 by Peter Godfrey; renewed. First published by *Ellery Queen's Mystery Magazine*, September 1950. Reprinted by permission of R.M. Godfrey.

"The Gioconda Smile" copyright © 1921 by Aldous Huxley; renewed by the Literary Estate of Aldous Huxley. First published by *The English Review*, August 1921. Reprinted by permission of Doris Halsey as agent for the Literary Estate of Aldous Huxley.

"The Blind Spot" copyright © 1945; renewed. First published by *Ellery Queen's Mystery Magazine*, November 1945. Reprinted by permission of A.P. Watt.

CONTENTS

INTRODUCTION

A COMMONLY ASKED QUESTION about mystery fiction is: Why do we read this stuff? Any number of theories have been offered, all of which have some degree of validity.

The one that equates detective stories with fairy tales carries serious weight. They are essentially battles between Good and Evil. In the bedtime stories that allow children to sleep peacefully, the forces of Right inevitably triumph over those on the opposite end of the moral spectrum.

The same philosophical premise has been in evidence since the first detective tales were created. A criminal represents the dark side, and a detective, whether official police officer, private detective, or curious amateur, draws his sword in the sunlight to vanquish Evil.

Another argument for the continued popularity of mysteries is that they are one of the only literary forms that continues to correspond to the ideal of storytelling, with an arc that goes from beginning to middle to end, which has proven to be the most satisfying method of fiction writing since the Greeks began writing plays a couple of millennia ago. Much of contemporary fiction, as has been true for the past three-quarters of a century, provides no more than an abstract view of a period of time in a person's life. It does not often present a crisis situation, followed by conflict, and ending with a satisfying resolution—all standard elements of the detective story.

An additional theory in support of the relentless success of crime fiction is that it appeals to the conservative nature of humanity. When our environment is comfortable, as it is to a large degree even for those who live in squalor, because it is familiar and secure, we do not want some untoward act to change it. That unhappy event may be an earthquake, a flood, a famine, or a murder.

A serious criminal assault rends the fabric of society, and the desire is to restore it, just as we would want to mend a tear in a tapestry or a shirt. It may never be exactly as it was, but the desire is to have it come out nearly the same as it was before the traumatic incident. When a murder causes an enormous wound in an established environment, the surviving members of that damaged community seek restoration. This is brought about by the detective, who pursues the offending member of that society and brings him to justice, reestablishing order and healing the wound as much as it is possible, given the fact that at least two members of the community (the victim and the perpetrator) have been removed forever.

The universally loved literary genre of detective stories illustrates and champions the triumph of Good over Evil, brightens the darkness, celebrates justice, and challenges the intellect. Mystery fiction is not for dullards, nor is it for those ignoble enough not to celebrate the victory of Right in a world too filled with Wrong. The central figure in the classic stories of mystery, the detective, is, as Raymond Chandler pointed out, a modern knight, whose Holy Grail is Truth and Justice. It is the satisfaction of the discovery of that grail that has held readers for more than two centuries.

That will not happen in this volume.

No, here you will find no happy endings, no last irregular piece pressed into place to complete the jigsaw puzzle, no thrilling or surprising denouement.

If you read mysteries only for the final moment, that last chapter when all is explained, when the disparate elements are shuffled into place so that the inevitable solution is displayed for your delight and satisfaction, then you will despise this collection.

Here, you will not find unsatisfying endings. You will find *no* endings.

You will not find eccentric or stolid detectives who stupify with their brilliance or doggedness. All these stories have the same detective, and the challenge will be immense, because these mysteries have been constructed by some of the greatest literary minds ever to sit at a desk, plotting to stump whichever crime-solving figure absorbed their pages. Who is that unfortunate detective, the one almost surely doomed to failure? Why, it's you, of course!

These are riddle stories, dilemmas, paradoxes, brain-teasers, all guaranteed to flummox the most astute mind.

It would be impossible to point to any particular story in this unique anthology and state unequivocally that it is the most perfect conundrum ever conceived. The most famous is probably Frank Stockton's "The Lady, or the Tiger?" but is it a better puzzle than Mark Twain's awful, terrible, joke? O. Henry, famous the world over for his surprise endings, has pulled off the perfect double-cross by providing the perfect non-ending. And never was the genius of Stanley Ellin in greater evidence than in the two stories that begin and end the book.

It is recommended that you read this collection in the order in which it has been compiled, as several stories have sequels that immediately follow them. Sometimes these sequels provide a reasonably satisfying conclusion, a tour de force of storytelling that seemed impossible when the original was fully digested. Stockton, Ray Bradbury, and Cleveland Moffett all wrote sequels to their own stories, with varying levels of relief from the hopelessness of attempting to arrive at a plausible solution to their challenges to the reader. Laurie York Erskine read Aldous Huxley's masterly "The Gioconda Smile" and arrived at an alternative ending. Jack Moffett set himself the Herculean task of producing a resolution to "The Lady, or the Tiger?" that was superior to the author's own.

One of the great disappointments one can experience is to be amazed by a magic trick and then have it explained. Learning that the apparent miracle was caused by nothing more than a clever mechanical device reduces the sense of wonder that the illusion inspired, ruining the memory of it forever. The same is often true of detective fiction, notably in locked-room or "impossible" crime stories, in which the denouement leaves one with a Peggy Lee moment: "Is that all there is?"

That will not happen among these pages. There is no opportunity for the reader to be disappointed with the final explanation because, well, there are no final explanations.

Two elements can be guaranteed between these covers. You will read some of the most extraordinary mystery stories ever penned. And you will be frustrated beyond measure.

—OTTO PENZLER

Mark Twain's
MEDIEVAL ROMANCE

UNREASONABLE DOUBT
STANLEY ELLIN

Some may choose Raymond Carver, or Joyce Carol Oates, or John Updike, but my choice for the greatest short story writer of the second half of the twentieth century is Stanley Ellin (1916–1986). The noted British critic Julian Symons stated that his *Mystery Stories* (1956) was "the finest collection of stories in the crime form published in the past half-century."

Dealing with such significant subjects as the rights of the elderly (in the Edgar-winning "The Blessington Method"), the morality of economic development (in "Unacceptable Procedures"), and capital punishment (in "The Question"), these and other stories transcend the genre, to use a dreadful phrase that is always true of the genuinely first-rate works of any genre. His most famous short work is "The Specialty of the House," the delicious story of a cozy but terrifying gourmet club which was intelligently filmed by Alfred Hitchcock for his TV series, as were so many of Ellin's stories.

Ellin won three Edgars, two for stories and for his novel *The Eighth Circle*, as well as being named Grand Master for lifetime achievement by the Mystery Writers of America.

"Unreasonable Doubt" will haunt you as a flawless riddle story, and here is a fair warning. The last story in the anthology also is by Stanley Ellin—and it's just as frustrating! "Unreasonable Doubt" was first published in the September 1958 issue of *Ellery Queen's Mystery Magazine*.

UNREASONABLE DOUBT

BY STANLEY ELLIN

Mr. Willoughby was just starting a much-needed vacation. It was imperative that his mind be free of worry, tension—of any problems whatsoever. Relax, the doctor had ordered—and that's good advice to the reader too—IF YOU CAN!

MR. WILLOUGHBY FOUND a seat in the club car and gingerly settled into it. So far, he reflected with overwhelming gratitude, the vacation was a complete success. Not a hint of the headaches he had lived with the past year. Not a suggestion of the iron band drawing tight around the skull, the gimlet boring into it, the hammers tapping away at it.

"Tension," the doctor had said. "Physically you're sound as a nut, but you sit over your desk all day worrying over one problem after another until your mind is as tight as a mainspring. Then you take the problems home and worry them to death there. Don't get much sleep, do you?"

Mr. Willoughby admitted that he did not.

"I thought so," said the doctor. "Well, there's only one answer. A vacation. And I do mean a real vacation where you get away from it all. Seal your mind up. Don't let anything get into it but idle talk. Don't think about any problems at all. Don't even try a crossword puzzle. Just close your eyes and listen to the world go round. That'll do it," he assured him.

And it *had* done it, as Mr. Willoughby realized even after only one day of the treatment. And there were weeks of blissful relaxation ahead. Of course, it wasn't always easy to push aside every problem that came to mind. For example, there was a newspaper on the smoking-table next to his chair right now, its headline partly revealing the words *NEW CRISIS IN*—Mr.

Willoughby hastily averted his head and thrust the paper into she rack beneath the table. A small triumph, but a pleasant one.

He was watching the rise and fall of the landscape outside the window, dreamily counting mile posts as they flashed by when he first became aware of the voice at his elbow. The corner of his chair was backed up near that of his neighbor, a stout, white-haired man who was deep in talk with a companion. The stout man's voice was not loud, but it was penetrating. The voice, one might say, of a trained actor whose every whisper can be distinctly heard by the gallery. Even if one did not choose to be an eavesdropper it was impossible not to follow every word spoken. Mr. Willoughby, however, deliberately chose to eavesdrop. The talk was largely an erudite discourse on legal matters; the stout man was apparently a lawyer of vast experience and uncanny recollective powers; and, all in all, the combination had the effect on Mr. Willoughby of chamber music being played softly by skilled hands.

Then suddenly his ears pricked like a terrier's. "The most interesting case I ever worked on?" the stout man was saying in answer to his companion's query. "Well, sir, there's one I regard not only as the most interesting I ever handled, but which would have staggered any lawyer in history, right up to Solomon himself. It was the strangest, most fantastic, damndest thing that ever came my way. And the way it wound up—the real surprise after it was supposedly over and done with—is enough to knock a man out of his chair when he thinks of it. But let me tell it to you just as it took place."

Mr. Willoughby slid down in his chair, pressed his heels into the floor, and surreptitiously closed the gap between his chair and his neighbor's. With his legs extended, his eyes closed, and his arms folded peaceably on his chest he was a fair representation of a man sound asleep. Actually, he had never been more wide-awake in his life.

Naturally [the stout man said], I won't use the right names of any of these people, even though all this took place a long time ago. That's understandable when you realize it involves a murder. A cold-blooded murder for profit, beautifully planned, flawlessly executed, and aimed at making a travesty of everything written in the law books.

The victim—let's call him Hosea Snow—was the richest man in our town. An old-fashioned sort of man—I remember him wearing a black derby and a stiff collar on the hottest days in summer—he owned the bank, the mill, and a couple of other local interests. There wasn't any secret among folks as to how much he was worth. On the day of his death it came to about two million dollars. Considering how low taxes were in those days, and how much a dollar could buy, you can see why he was held in such high esteem.

His only family consisted of two nephews, his brother's sons, Ben and Orville. They represented the poor side of the family, you might say. When their father and mother died all that was left to them was a rundown old house which they lived in together.

Ben and Orville were nice-looking boys in their middle twenties about that time. Smooth-faced, regular features, much of a size and shape, they could have been a lot more popular than they were, but they deliberately kept apart from people. It wasn't that they were unfriendly—any time they passed you on the street they'd smile and give you the time of day—but they were sufficient unto themselves. Nowadays you hear a lot of talk about sibling rivalries and fraternal complexes, but it would never fit those two boys.

They worked in their uncle's bank, but their hearts were never in it. Even though they knew that when Hosea died his money would be divided between them it didn't seem to cheer the boys any. Fact is, Hosea was one of those dried-out, leathery specimens who are likely to go on forever. Looking forward to an inheritance from somebody like that can be a trying experience, and there's no question that the boys had been looking forward to that inheritance from the time they first knew what a dollar was worth.

But what they seemed to be concerned with, meanwhile, was something altogether different from banking and money—something Hosea himself could never understand or sympathize with, as he told me on more than one occasion. They wanted to be song writers, and, for all I know, they had some talent for it. Whenever there was any affair in town that called for entertainment, Ben and Orville would show up with some songs they had written all by themselves. Nobody ever knew which of them did the words and which did the music, and that in itself was one of the small mysteries about them that used to amuse the town. You can pretty well judge the size and disposition of the place if something like that was a conversation piece.

But the situation was all shaken up the day Hosea Snow was found dead in his big house, a bullet hole right square in the middle of his forehead.

The first I heard of it was when a phone call got me out of bed early in the morning. It was the County Prosecutor telling me that Ben Snow had murdered his uncle during the night, had just been arrested, and was asking me to come to the jail right quick.

I ran over to the jail half dressed, and was pulled up short by the sight of Ben locked in a cell, reading a newspaper, and seemingly indifferent to the fact that he was on his way to a trapdoor with a rope around his neck.

"Ben," I said, "you didn't do it, did you?"

"They tell me I did," he said in a matter-of-fact voice.

I don't know which bewildered me more—what he said or the unconcerned way he said it.

"What do you mean?" I asked him. "And you'd better have a good story to tell me, boy, because you're in serious trouble."

"Well," he said, "in the middle of the night the police and the County Prosecutor walked in on Orville and me, because Uncle Hosea was killed, and after some talking they said I did it. When I got tired of them nagging me about it I said, all right, I did do it."

"You mean," I said, "they've got evidence against you?"

He smiled. "That'll come out in court," he said. "All you've got to do is call Orville as my witness at the trial, and you won't have any trouble. I'm not going to testify for myself, so they can't cross-examine me. But don't you worry any. Orville'll take care of everything."

I felt a terrible suspicion creeping into my mind, but I didn't let myself consider it. "Ben," I said, "have you and Orville been reading law books?"

"We've been looking into them," he admitted. "They're mighty interesting"—and that was all I could get out of him. I got even less from Orville when I went over to the bank and tried to talk to him about his testimony.

Considering that, you can imagine my state of mind when we finally came to trial. The case was the biggest sensation the town had ever known, the courthouse was packed, and here I was in the middle of things with no idea of what I could do for Ben, and Ben himself totally indifferent. I felt sick every time I got a look at the prosecutor's smug and smiling face. Not that I could blame him for looking like the cat that ate the canary. The crime was a brutal one, he and the police had solved it in jig time, and here he was with an airtight case.

In his opening address to the jury he threw the works at them. The motive was obvious: Ben Snow stood to inherit a million dollars from his uncle's death. The method was right there on the clerk's desk where everyone could see it: an old pistol that Ben Snow's father had left among his effects years before, and which was found—one bullet freshly discharged from it—right in the kitchen where Ben and Orville were drinking coffee when the police broke in on them. And the confession signed by Ben before witnesses settled things beyond the shadow of a doubt.

The only thing I could do in the face of this was put blind faith in Ben and do what he wanted me to. I had Orville Snow called as my first witness—and my only witness, too, as far as I could see—and then, without any idea of what he was going to say, I put him on the stand. He took the oath, sat down, straightened the crease in his trousers, and looked at me with the calm unconcern his brother had shown throughout the whole terrible business.

You see, I knew so little about the affair that it was hard to think of even a good opening question for him. Finally, I took the bull by the horns and said, "Would you please tell the jury where you were the night of the crime?"

"Glad to," said Orville. "I was in Uncle Hosea's house with a gun in my hand. If the police had only gotten to me before they started pestering Ben about this, I could have told them so right off. Fact is, I was the one who killed uncle."

Talk about sensations in court! And in the middle of the uproar I saw Ben eagerly signaling me over to him. "Now, whatever you do," he whispered to me, "don't you ask that this trial be stopped. It's got to go to the jury, do you understand?"

I understood, all right. I had had my suspicions all along, but for the sake of my own conscience I just didn't want to heed them. Now I knew for sure, and for all I hated Ben and Orville right then I had to admire them just a little bit. And it was that little bit of admiration which led me to play it Ben's way. With the prosecutor waiting hangdog for me to ask that the trial be stopped I went back to Orville on the witness stand and had him go ahead with his story as if nothing spectacular had happened.

He told it like a master. He started way back when the desire for his uncle's money had seeped into his veins like a drug, and went along in detail right up to the killing itself. He had the jury hypnotized, and just to make sure the job was complete I wound up my closing speech by reminding them that all they needed in finding a man innocent was a reasonable doubt of his guilt.

"That is the law of this state," I told them. "Reasonable doubt. It is exactly what you are feeling now in the light of Orville Snow's confession that he alone committed the crime his brother was charged with!"

The police grabbed Orville right after the verdict of "Not Guilty" was brought in. I saw him that evening in the small cell Ben had been kept in, and I already knew what he was going to tell me.

"Ben's my witness," he said. "Just keep me off the witness stand and let him do the talking."

I said to him, "One of you two killed your uncle, Orville. Don't you think that as your lawyer I ought to know which of you it was?"

"No, I don't," said Orville, pleasantly enough.

"You're putting a lot of faith in your brother," I told him. "Ben's free and clear now. If he doesn't want to testify for you the way you did for him, he gets two million dollars and you get the gallows. Doesn't that worry you any?"

"No," said Orville. "If it worried us any we wouldn't have done it in the first place."

"All right," I said, "if that's the way you want it. But tell me one thing, Orville, just for curiosity's sake. How did you decide which one of you should kill Hosea?"

"We cut cards," said Orville, and that was the end of it, as far as he was concerned.

If Ben's trial had stirred up the town, Orville's had people coming in from all over the county. It was the prosecutor's turn to look sick now when he faced that crowd. He knew in his bones what was coming, and he couldn't do a blessed thing about it. More than that, he was honestly outraged at what looked to be an obscene mockery of the law. Ben and Orville Snow had found a loophole in justice, so to speak, and were on their way to sneaking through it. A jury couldn't convict a man if it had a reasonable doubt of his guilt; a man couldn't be retried for a crime when a jury has acquitted him of it; it wasn't even possible to indict the two boys together for conspiracy to commit murder, because that was a lesser charge in the murder indictment and covered by it. It was enough to make any prosecutor wild with frustration.

But this one held himself in check until Ben had finished telling his story to the jury. Ben told that story every bit as well as Orville had told his at the previous trial. He made it so graphic you could almost see him there in the room with his uncle, the gun flashing out death, the old man crumpling to the floor. The jurymen sat there spellbound, and the prosecutor chewed his nails to the quick while he watched them. Then when he faced Ben on the stand he really cut loose.

"Isn't all this a monstrous lie?" he shouted, "How can you be innocent of this crime one day, and guilty of it the next?"

Ben raised his eyebrows. "I never told anybody I was innocent," he said indignantly. "I've been saying right along I was guilty."

There was no denying that. There was nothing in the record to dispute it. And I never felt so sure of myself, and so unhappy, as when I summed up the case for the jury. It took me just one minute, the quickest summing-up in my record.

"If I were sitting among you good people in that jury box," I said, "I know just what I'd be thinking. A heinous crime has been committed, and one of two men in this very courtroom has committed it. But I can take my oath that I don't know which of them it was, any more than you do, and like it or not I'd know I had to bring in a verdict of 'Not Guilty.'"

That was all they needed, too. They brought in their verdict even quicker than the jury had in Ben's case. And I had the dubious pleasure of seeing two young men, one of them guilty of murder, smilingly walk out of that room. As I said, I hated them, but I felt a sort of infuriated admiration for them too. They had gambled everything on their loyally to each other, and the loyalty had stood the test of fire . . .

The stout man was silent. From his direction came the sound of a match striking, and then an eddy of expensive cigar smoke drifted under Mr. Willoughby's nostrils. It was the pungent scent of the present dissolving the fascinating web of the past.

"Yes, sir," the stout man said, and there was a depth of nostalgia in his voice, "you'd have to go a long way to find a case to match that."

"You mean," said his companion, "that they actually got away with it? That they found a way of committing the perfect murder?"

The stout man snorted. "Perfect murder, bosh! That's where the final, fantastic surprise comes in. They *didn't* get away with it!"

"They didn't?"

"Of course not. You see, when they—good heavens, isn't this our station?" the stout man suddenly cried, and the next instant he went flying past Mr. Willoughby's out-stretched feet, briefcase in hand, overcoat flapping over his arm, companion in tow.

Mr. Willoughby sat there dazed for a moment, his eyes wide-open, his mouth dry, his heart hammering. Then he leaped to his feet—but it was too late: the men had disappeared from the car. He took a few frantic steps in the direction they had gone, realized it was pointless, then ran to a window of the car overlooking the station.

The stout man stood on the platform almost below him, buttoning his coat, and saying something to his companion. Mr. Willoughby made a mighty effort to raise the window, but failed to budge it. Then he rapped on the pane with his knuckles, and the stout man looked up at him.

"H-o-w?" Mr. Willoughby mouthed through the closed window, and saw with horror that the stout man did not understand him at all. Inspiration seized him. He made a pistol of his hand, aimed the extended forefinger at the stout man, and let his thumb fall like a hammer on a cartridge. "Bang!" he yelled. "Bang, bang! H-o-w?"

The stout man looked at him in astonishment, glanced at his companion, and then putting his own forefinger to his temple, made a slow circling motion. That was how Mr. Willoughby last saw him as the train slowly, and then with increasing speed, pulled away.

It was when he moved away from the window that Mr. Willoughby became aware of two things. One was that every face in the car was turned toward him with rapt interest. The other was that an iron band was drawing tight around his skull, a gimlet was boring into it, tiny hammers were tapping at it.

It was, he knew with utter despair, going to be a perfectly terrible vacation.

A DILEMMA
S. Weir Mitchell

One of the major works of fiction around the turn of the
nineteenth century was S. Weir Mitchell's *Hugh Wynne, Free
Quaker* (1898), but the author's personal favorite of his many
books was *The Adventures of François* (1898), which contained
twenty-four picaresque tales of a foundling, juggler, thief, and
fencing-master during the French Revolution.

The early career of Mitchell (1829–1914) was not literary
but medical, in which he became famous as a specialist in neu-
rological disorders and was noted for inventing the "rest cure"
for nervous breakdowns. He was friends with Oliver Wendell
Holmes, who advised him to establish himself as a physician
before beginning any serious literary endeavors. Although he
published anonymous poems and children's stories as far back
as 1846, his first book of adult fiction did not appear until 1880.
His major contributions to the mystery genre, in addition to
The Adventures of François, were *The Autobiography of a Quack*
(1900), *A Diplomatic Adventure* (1906), and *The Guillotine
Club* (1910).

While serving as a physician, he was known to have treated
Edith Wharton's husband, and it was the informed belief of
the critic Edmund Wilson that Mitchell advised Wharton to
take up writing as a means of relieving the nervous tension with
which she lived.

"A Dilemma" was first published in book form in *Little Stories* in 1903.

A DILEMMA

BY S. WEIR MITCHELL

I WAS JUST THIRTY-SEVEN when my Uncle Philip died. A week before that event he sent for me; and here let me say that I never set eyes on him. He hated my mother, but I do not know why. She told me long before his last illness that I need expect nothing from my father's brother. He was an inventor, an able and ingenious mechanical engineer, and had made much money by his improvement in turbine-wheels. He was a bachelor; lived alone, cooked his own meals, and collected precious stones, especially rubies and pearls. From the time he made his first money he had this mania. As he grew richer, the desire to possess rare and costly gems became stronger. When he bought a new stone, he carried it in his pocket for a month and now and then took it out and looked at it. Then it was added to the collection in his safe at the Trust Company.

At the time he sent for me I was a clerk, and poor enough. Remembering my mother's words, his message gave me, his sole relative, no new hopes; but I thought it best to go.

When I sat down by his bedside, he began, with a malicious grin:

"I suppose you think me queer. I will explain." What he said was certainly queer enough. "I have been living on an annuity into which I put my fortune. In other words, I have been, as to money, concentric half of my life to enable me to be as eccentric as I pleased the rest of it. Now I repent of my wickedness to you all, and desire to live in the memory of at least one of my family. You think I am poor and have only my annuity. You will be profitably surprised. I have never parted with my precious stones; they will be yours. You are my sole heir. I shall carry with me to the other world the satisfaction of making one man happy.

"No doubt you have always had expectations, and I desire that you should continue to expect. My jewels are in my safe. There is nothing else left."

When I thanked him he grinned all over his lean face, and said:

"You will have to pay for my funeral."

I must say that I never looked forward to any expenditure with more pleasure than to what it would cost me to put him away in the earth. As I rose to go, he said:

"The rubies are valuable. They are in my safe at the Trust Company. Before you unlock the box, be very careful to read a letter which lies on top of it; and be sure not to shake the box." I thought this odd. "Don't come back. It won't hasten things."

He died the next week, and was handsomely buried. The day after, his will was found, leaving me his heir. I opened his safe and found in it nothing but an iron box, evidently of his own making, for he was a skilled workman and very ingenious. The box was heavy and strong, about ten inches long, eight inches wide, and ten inches high.

On it lay a letter to me. It ran thus:

"DEAR TOM: This box contains a large number of very fine pigeon-blood rubies and a fair lot of diamonds; one is blue—a beauty. There are hundreds of pearls—one the famous green pearl, and a necklace of blue pearls, for which any woman would sell her soul—or her affections." (I thought of Susan.) "I wish you to continue to have expectations and continuously to remember your dear uncle. I would have left these stones to some charity, but I hate the poor as much as I hate your mother's son—yes, rather more.

"This box contains an interesting mechanism, which will act with certainty as you unlock it, and explode ten ounces of my improved, supersensitive dynamite—no, to be accurate, there are only nine and a half ounces. Doubt me, and open it, and you will be blown to atoms. Believe me, and you will continue to nourish expectations which will never be fulfilled. As a considerate man, I counsel extreme care in handling the box. Don't forget your affectionate

UNCLE."

I stood appalled, the key in my hand. Was it true? Was it a lie? I had spent all my savings on the funeral, and was poorer than ever.

Remembering the old man's oddity, his malice, his cleverness in mechanic arts, and the patent explosive which had helped to make him rich, I began to feel how very likely it was that he had told the truth in this cruel letter.

I carried the iron box away to my lodgings, set it down with care in a closet, laid the key on it, and locked the closet.

Then I sat down, as yet hopeful, and began to exert my ingenuity upon ways of opening the box without being killed. There must be a way.

After a week of vain thinking I bethought me, one day, that it would be easy to explode the box by unlocking it at a safe distance, and I arranged a plan with wires, which seemed as if it would answer. But when I reflected on what would happen when the dynamite scattered the rubies, I knew that I should be none the richer. For hours at a time I sat looking at that box and handling the key.

At last I hung the key on my watchguard; but then it occurred to me that it might be lost or stolen. Dreading this, I hid it, fearful that someone might use it to open the box. This state of doubt and fear lasted for weeks, until I became nervous and began to dread that some accident might happen to that box. A burglar might come and boldly carry it away and force it open, and find it was a wicked fraud of my uncle's. Even the rumble and vibration caused by the heavy vans in the street became at last a terror.

Worst of all, my salary was reduced, and I saw that marriage was out of the question.

In my despair I consulted Professor Clinch about my dilemma, and as to some safe way of getting at the rubies. He said that, if my uncle had not lied, there was none that would not ruin the stones, especially the pearls, but that it was a silly tale and altogether incredible. I offered him the biggest ruby if he wished to test his opinion. He did not desire to do so.

Dr. Schaff, my uncle's doctor, believed the old man's letter, and added a caution, which was entirely useless, for by this time I was afraid to be in the room with that terrible box.

At last the doctor kindly warned me that I was in danger of losing my mind with too much thought about my rubies. In fact, I did nothing else but contrive wild plans to get at them safely. I spent all my spare hours at one of the great libraries reading about dynamite. Indeed, I talked of it until the library attendants, believing me a lunatic or a dynamite fiend, declined to humor me, and spoke to the police. I suspect that for a while I was "shadowed" as a suspicious, and possibly criminal, character. I gave up the libraries and becoming more and more fearful, set my precious box on a down pillow, for fear of its being shaken; for at this time even the absurd possibility of its being disturbed by an earthquake troubled me. I tried to calculate the amount of shake needful to explode my box.

The old doctor, when I saw him again, begged me to give up all thought of the matter and as I felt how completely I was the slave of one despotic idea, I tried to take the good advice thus given me.

Unhappily, I found, soon after, between the leaves of my uncle's Bible, a numbered list of the stones with their cost. It was dated two years before my uncle's death. Many of the stones were well known, and their enormous value amazed me.

Several of the rubies were described with care, and curious histories of them were given in detail. One was said to be the famous "Sunset Ruby," which had belonged to the Empress-Queen Maria Theresa. One was called the "Blood Ruby," not, as was explained, because of the color, but on account of the murders it had occasioned. Now, as I read, it seemed again to threaten death.

The pearls were described with care as an unequalled collection. Concerning two of them my uncle had written what I might call biographies— for, indeed, they seemed to have done much evil and some good. One, a black pearl, was mentioned in an old bill of sale as She—which seemed queer to me.

It was maddening. Here, guarded by a vision of sudden death, was wealth "beyond the dreams of avarice." I am not a clever or ingenious man; I know little beyond how to keep a ledger, and so I was, and am, no doubt, absurd about many of my notions as to how to solve this riddle.

At one time I thought of finding a man who would take the risk of unlocking the box, but what right had I to subject anyone else to the trial I dared not face? I could easily drop the box from a height somewhere, and if it did not explode could then safely unlock it; but if it did blow up when it fell, goodbye to my rubies. *Mine*, indeed! I was rich, and I was not. I grew thin and morbid, and so miserable that, being a good Catholic, I at last carried my troubles to my father confessor. He thought it simply a cruel jest of my uncle's, but was not so eager for another world as to be willing to open my box. He, too, counseled me to cease worrying!

Two years have gone by, and I am one of the richest men in the city, and have no more money than will keep me alive.

Susan said I was half-cracked, like Uncle Philip, and broke off our engagement. In my despair I have advertised in the *Journal of Science,* and have had absurd schemes sent me by the dozen. At last, as I talked too much about it, the thing became so well known that when I put the horror in a bank, I was promptly desired to withdraw it. I was in constant fear of burglars, and my landlady gave me notice to leave, because no one would stay in the house with that box. I am now advised to print my story and await advice from the ingenuity of the American mind.

I have moved into the suburbs and hidden the box and changed my name and my occupation. This I did to escape the curiosity of the reporters. I ought to say that when the government officials came to hear of my inheritance, they very reasonably desired to collect the inheritance tax on my uncle's estate.

I was delighted to assist them. I told the collector my story, and showed him Uncle Philip's letter. Then I offered him the key, and asked for time to get half a mile away. That man said he would think it over and come back later. He never returned.

This is all I have to say. I have made a will and left my rubies and pearls to the Society for the Prevention of Human Vivisection. If any man thinks this account a joke or an invention, let him coldly imagine the situation:

Given an iron box, known to contain wealth, said to contain dynamite, arranged to explode when the key is used to unlock it—what would any sane man do?

NUNC DIMITTIS
ROALD DAHL

It is a testament to his creativity that Roald Dahl (1916–1990) was not only a noted writer of crime stories, screenplays, and aviation stories, but one of the world's most beloved authors of children's books as well.

Among his screenplays are two based on the work of Ian Fleming: *You Only Live Twice* (1967), a James Bond adventure, and *Chitty Chitty Bang Bang* (1968), the thriller writer's one foray into the world of children's literature. Dahl also adapted his own books for the screen with *Charlie and the Chocolate Factory* (2005).

Unknown to most readers is the fact that Dahl, while serving as a pilot during World War II, is credited with inventing the word "gremlins," which he used to describe little creatures who lived inside the engines of fighter planes, causing them to stall at the most inopportune moments.

Among his outstanding short stories is the memorable "Lamb to the Slaughter," famously filmed for his television series by Alfred Hitchcock. The collection in which it appeared, *Someone Like You* (1954), was selected for *Queen's Quorum* as one of the mystery genre's 106 greatest short story collections of all time.

"Nunc Dimittis" was first published in the September 4, 1953, edition of *Collier's* magazine.

NUNC DIMITTIS

BY ROALD DAHL

IT IS NEARLY MIDNIGHT, and I can see that if I don't make a start with writing this story now, I never shall. All evening I have been sitting here trying to force myself to begin, but the more I have thought about it, the more appalled and ashamed and distressed I have become by the whole thing.

My idea—and I believe it was a good one—was to try, by a process of confession and analysis, to discover a reason or at any rate some justification for my outrageous behavior toward Janet de Pelagia. I wanted, essentially, to address myself to an imaginary and sympathetic listener, a kind of mythical *you*, someone gentle and understanding to whom I might tell unashamedly every detail of this unfortunate episode. I can only hope that I am not too upset to make a go of it.

If I am to be quite honest with myself, I suppose I shall have to admit that what is disturbing me most is not so much the sense of my own shame, or even the hurt that I have inflicted upon poor Janet; it is the knowledge that I have made a monstrous fool of myself and that all my friends—if I can still call them that—all those warm and lovable people who used to come so often to my house, must now be regarding me as nothing but a vicious, vengeful old man. Yes, that surely hurts. When I say to you that my friends were my whole life—everything, absolutely everything in it—then perhaps you will begin to understand.

Will you? I doubt it—unless I digress for a minute to tell you roughly the sort of person I am.

Well—let me see. Now that I come to think of it, I suppose I am, after all, a type; a rare one, mark you, but nevertheless a quite definite type— the wealthy, leisurely, middle-aged man of culture, adored (I choose the word carefully) by his many friends for his charm, his money, his air of scholarship, his generosity and, I sincerely hope, for himself also. You will find him (this type) only in the big capitals, London, Paris, New York; of that I am certain. The money he has was earned by his dead father whose memory he is inclined to despise. This is not his fault, for there is something in his make-up that compels him secretly to look down upon all people who never had the wit to learn the difference between Rockingham and Spode, Waterford and Venetian, Sheraton and Chippendale, Monet and Manet, or even Pommard and Montrachet.

He is, therefore, a connoisseur, possessing above all things an exquisite taste. His Constables, Boningtons, Lautrecs, Redons, Vuillards, Matthew Smiths are as fine as anything in the Tate; and because they are so fabulous and beautiful, they create an atmosphere of suspense around him in the home, something tantalizing, breathtaking, faintly frightening—frightening to think that he has the power and the right, if he feels inclined, to slash, tear, plunge his fist right through a superb Dedham Vale, a Mont Sainte-Victoire, an Arles cornfield, a Tahiti maiden, a portrait of Madame Cézanne. And from the walls on which these wonders hang there issues a little golden glow of splendour, a subtle emanation of grandeur in which he lives and moves and entertains with a sly nonchalance that is not entirely unpracticed.

He is invariably a bachelor, yet he never appears to get entangled with the women who surround him, who love him so dearly. It is just possible—and this you may or may not have noticed—that there is a frustration, a discontent, a regret somewhere inside him. Even a slight aberration.

I don't think I need say any more. I have been very frank. You should know me well enough by now to judge me fairly—and dare I hope it?—to sympathize with me when you hear my story. You may even decide that much of the blame for what has happened should be placed, not upon me, but upon a lady called Gladys Ponsonby. After all, she was the one who started it. Had I not escorted Gladys Ponsonby back to her house that night nearly six months ago, and had she not spoken so freely to me about certain people, certain things, then this tragic business could never have taken place.

It was last December, if I remember rightly, and I had been dining with the Ashendens in that lovely house of theirs that overlooks the southern fringe of Regent's Park. There were a fair number of people there, but Gladys Ponsonby was the only one beside myself who had come alone. So when it was time for us to leave, I naturally offered to see her safely back to her house. She accepted and we left together in my car; but unfortunately, when we arrived at her place she insisted that I come in and have "one for the road," as she put it. I didn't wish to seem stuffy, so I told the chauffeur to wait and followed her in.

Gladys Ponsonby is an unusually short woman, certainly not more than four feet nine or ten, maybe even less than that—one of those tiny persons who gives me, when I am beside her, the comical, rather wobbly feeling that I am standing on a chair. She is a widow, a few years younger than me— maybe fifty-three or four, and it is possible that thirty years ago she was quite a fetching little thing. But now the face is loose and puckered with nothing distinctive about it whatsoever. The individual features, the eyes, the nose, the mouth, the chin, are buried in the folds of fat around the puckered little face and one does not notice them. Except perhaps the mouth, which reminds me—I cannot help it—of a salmon.

In the living-room, as she gave me my brandy, I noticed that her hand was a trifle unsteady. The lady is tired, I told myself, so I mustn't stay long. We sat down together on the sofa and for a while discussed the Ashendens' party and the people who were there. Finally I got up to go.

"Sit down, Lionel," she said. "Have another brandy."

"No, really, I must go."

"Sit down and don't be so stuffy. I'm having another one, and the least you can do is keep me company while I drink it."

I watched her as she walked over to the sideboard, this tiny woman, faintly swaying, holding her glass out in front of her with both hands as though it were an offering; and the sight of her walking like that, so incredibly short and squat and stiff, suddenly gave me the ludicrous notion that she had no legs at all above the knees.

"Lionel, what are you chuckling about?" She half turned to look at me as she poured the drink, and some of it slopped over the side of the glass.

"Nothing, my dear. Nothing at all."

"Well, stop it, and tell me what you think of my new portrait." She indicated a large canvas hanging over the fireplace that I had been trying to avoid with my eye ever since I entered the room. It was a hideous thing, painted, as I well knew, by a man who was now all the rage in London, a very mediocre painter called John Royden. It was a full-length portrait of Gladys Lady Ponsonby, painted with a certain technical cunning that made her out to be a tall and quite alluring creature.

"Charming," I said.

"Isn't it, though! I'm so glad you like it."

"Quite charming."

"I think John Royden is a genius. Don't you think he's a genius, Lionel?"

"Well—that might be going a bit far."

"You mean it's a little early to say for sure?"

"Exactly."

"But listen, Lionel—and I think this will surprise you. John Royden is so sought after now that he won't even *consider* painting anyone for less than a thousand guineas!"

"Really?"

"Oh yes! And everyone's queuing up, simply *queuing up* to get themselves done."

"Most interesting."

"Now take your Mr. Cézanne or whatever his name is. I'll bet *he* never got that sort of money in *his* lifetime."

"Never."

"And you say *he* was a genius?"

"Sort of—yes."

"Then so is Royden," she said, settling herself again on the sofa. "The money proves it."

She sat silent for a while, sipping her brandy, and I couldn't help noticing how the unsteadiness of her hand was causing the rim of the glass to jog against her lower lip. She knew I was watching her, and without turning her head she swivelled her eyes and glanced at me cautiously out of the corners of them. "A penny for your thoughts?"

Now, if there is one phrase in the world I cannot abide, it is this. It gives me an actual physical pain in the chest and I begin to cough.

"Come on, Lionel. A penny for them."

I shook my head, quite unable to answer. She turned away abruptly and placed the brandy glass on a small table to her left; and the manner in which she did this seemed to suggest—I don't know why—that she felt rebuffed and was now clearing the decks for action. I waited, rather uncomfortable in the silence that followed, and because I had no conversation left in me, I made a great play about smoking my cigar, studying the ash intently and blowing the smoke up slowly toward the ceiling. But she made no move. There was beginning to be something about this lady I did not much like, a mischievous, brooding air that made me want to get up quickly and go away. When she looked around again, she was smiling at me slyly with those little buried eyes of hers, but the mouth—oh, just like a salmon's—was absolutely rigid.

"Lionel, I think I'll tell you a secret."

"Really, Gladys, I simply must get home."

"Don't be frightened, Lionel. I won't embarrass you. You look so frightened all of a sudden."

"I'm not very good at secrets."

"I've been thinking," she said, "you're such a great expert on pictures, this ought to interest you." She sat quite still except for her fingers which were moving all the time. She kept them perpetually twisting and twisting around each other, and they were like a bunch of small white snakes wriggling in her lap.

"Don't you want to hear my secret, Lionel?"

"It isn't that, you know. It's just that it's so awfully late . . ."

"This is probably the best kept secret in London. A woman's secret. I suppose it's known to about—let me see—about thirty or forty women altogether. And not a single man. Except him, of course—John Royden."

I didn't wish to encourage her, so I said nothing.

"But first of all, promise—*promise* you won't tell a soul?"

"Dear me!"

"You *promise*, Lionel?"

"Yes, Gladys, allright, I promise."

"Good! Now listen." She reached for the brandy glass and settled back comfortably in the far corner of the sofa. "I suppose you know John Royden paints only women?'

"I didn't."

"And they're always full-length portraits, either standing or sitting—like mine there. Now take a good look at it, Lionel. Do you see how beautifully the dress is painted?"

"Well . . ."

"Go over and look carefully, please."

I got up reluctantly and went over and examined the painting. To my surprise I noticed that the paint of the dress was laid on so heavily it was actually raised out from the rest of the picture. It was a trick, quite effective in its way, but neither difficult to do nor entirely original.

"You see?" she said. "It's thick, isn't it, where the dress is?"

"Yes."

"But there's a bit more to it than that, you know, Lionel. I think the best way is to describe what happened the very first time I went along for a sitting."

Oh, what a bore this woman, is, I thought, and how can I get away?

"That was about a year ago, and I remember how excited I was to be going in to the studio of the great painter. I dressed myself up in a wonderful new thing I'd just got from Norman Hartnell, and a special little red hat, and off I went. Mr. Royden met me at the door, and of course I was fascinated by him at once. He had a small pointed beard and thrilling blue eyes, and he wore a black velvet jacket. The studio was huge, with red velvet sofas and velvet chairs—he loves velvet—and velvet curtains and even a velvet carpet on the floor. He sat me down, gave me a drink and came straight to the point. He told me about how he painted quite differently from other artists. In his opinion, he said, there was only one method of attaining perfection when painting a woman's body and I mustn't be shocked when I heard what it was.

" 'I don't think I'll be shocked, Mr. Royden,' I told him.

" 'I'm sure you won't either,' he said. He had the most marvellous white teeth and they sort of shone through his beard when he smiled. 'You see, it's like this,' he went on. 'You examine any painting you like of a woman—I don't care who it's by—and you'll see that although the dress may be well painted, there is an effect of artificiality, of flatness about the whole thing, as though the dress were draped over a log of wood. And you know why?'

" 'No, Mr. Royden, I don't.'

" 'Because the painters themselves didn't really know what was underneath!' "

Gladys Ponsonby paused to take a few more sips of brandy. "Don't look so startled, Lionel," she said to me. "There's nothing wrong about this. Keep quiet and let me finish. So then Mr. Royden said, 'That's why I insist on painting my subjects first of all in the nude.'

" 'Good Heavens, Mr. Royden!' I exclaimed.

" 'If you object to that, I don't mind making a slight concession, Lady Ponsonby,' he said. 'But I prefer it the other way.'

" 'Really, Mr. Royden, I don't know.'

" 'And when I've done you like that,' he went on, 'we'll have to wait a few weeks for the paint to dry. Then you come back and I paint on your underclothing. And when that's dry, I paint on the dress. You see, it's quite simple.' "

"The man's an absolute bounder!" I cried.

"No, Lionel, no! You're quite wrong. If only you could have heard him, so charming about it all, so genuine and sincere. Anyone could see he really *felt* what he was saying."

"I tell you, Gladys, the man's a bounder!"

"Don't be so silly, Lionel. And anyway, let me finish. The first thing I told him was that my husband (who was alive then) would never agree.

" 'Your husband need never know,' he answered. 'Why trouble him. No one knows my secret except the women I've painted.'

"And when I protested a bit more, I remember he said, 'My dear Lady Ponsonby, there's nothing immoral about this. Art is only immoral when practiced by amateurs. It's the same with medicine. You wouldn't refuse to undress before your doctor, would you?'

"I told him I would if I'd gone to him for earache. That made him laugh. But he kept on at me about it and I must say he was very convincing, so after a while I gave in and that was that. So now Lionel, my sweet, you know the secret." She got up and went over to fetch herself some more brandy.

"Gladys, is this really true?"

"Of course it's true."

"You mean to say that's the way he paints all his subjects?"

"Yes. And the joke is the husbands never know anything about it. All they see is a nice fully clothed portrait of their wives. Of course, there's nothing wrong with being painted in the nude; artists do it all the time. But our silly husbands have a way of objecting to that sort of thing."

"By gad, the fellow's got a nerve!"

"I think he's a genius."

"I'll bet he got the idea from Goya."

"Nonsense, Lionel."

"Of course he did. But listen, Gladys. I want you to tell me something. Did you by any chance know about this . . . this peculiar technique of Royden's before you went to him?"

When I asked the question she was in the act of pouring the brandy, and she hesitated and turned her head to look at me, a little silky smile moving the corners of her mouth. "Damn you, Lionel," she said. "You're far too clever. You never let me get away with a single thing."

"So you knew?"

"Of course. Hermione Girdlestone told me."

"Exactly as I thought!"

"There's still nothing wrong."

"Nothing," I said. "Absolutely nothing." I could see it all quite clearly now. This Royden was indeed a bounder, practicing as neat a piece of psychological trickery as ever I'd seen. The man knew only too well that there was a whole set of wealthy indolent women in the city who got up at noon and spent the rest of the day trying to relieve their boredom with bridge and canasta and shopping until the cocktail hour came along. All they craved was a little excitement, something out of the ordinary, and the more expensive the better. Why—the news of an entertainment like this would spread through their ranks like smallpox. I could just see the great plump Hermione Girdlestone leaning over the canasta table and telling them about it . . . "But my dear, it's *simp*-ly fascinating . . . I can't *tell* you how intriguing it is . . . *much* more fun than going to your doctor . . ."

"You won't tell anyone, Lionel, will you? You promised."

"No, of course not. But now I must go, Gladys, I really must."

"Don't be so silly. I'm just beginning to enjoy myself. Stay till I've finished this drink anyway."

I sat patiently on the sofa while she went on with her interminable brandy sipping. The little buried eyes still watching me out of their corners in that mischievous, canny way, and I had a strong feeling that the woman was now hatching out some further unpleasantness or scandal. There was the look of serpents in those eyes and a queer curl around the mouth; and in the air—although maybe I only imagined it—the faint smell of danger.

Then suddenly, so suddenly that I jumped, she said "Lionel, what's this I hear about you and Janet de Pelagia?"

"Now Gladys, please . . ."

"Lionel, you're blushing!"

"Nonsense."

"Don't tell me the old bachelor has really taken a tumble at last?"

"Gladys, this is too absurd." I began making movements to go, but she put a hand on my knee and stopped me. "Don't you know by now, Lionel, that there *are* no secrets?"

"Janet is a fine girl."

"You can hardly call her a *girl*." Gladys Ponsonby paused, staring down into the large brandy glass that she held cupped in both hands. "But of course, I agree with you, Lionel, she's a wonderful person in every way. Except," and now she spoke very slowly, "except that she *does* say some rather peculiar things occasionally."

"What sort of things?"

"Just things, you know—things about people. About you."

"What did she say about me?"

"Nothing at all, Lionel. It wouldn't interest you."

"What did she say about me?"

"It's not even worth repeating, honestly it isn't. It's only that it struck me as being rather odd at the time."

"Gladys—what did she say?" While I waited for her to answer, I could feel the sweat breaking out all over my body.

"Well now, let me see. Of course, she was only joking or I couldn't dream of telling you, but I suppose she *did* say how it was all a wee bit of a bore."

"What was?"

"Sort of going out to dinner with you nearly every night—that kind of thing."

"She said it was a bore?"

"Yes." Gladys Ponsonby drained the brandy glass with one last big gulp, and sat up straight. "If you really want to know, she said it was a crashing bore. And then . . ."

"What did she say then?"

"Now look, Lionel—there's no need to get excited. I'm only telling you this for your own good."

"Then please hurry up and tell it."

"It's just that I happened to be playing canasta with Janet this afternoon and I asked her if she was free to dine with me tomorrow. She said no, she wasn't."

"Go on."

"Well—actually what she said was 'I'm dining with that crashing old bore Lionel Lampson.' "

"Janet said that?"

"Yes, Lionel dear."

"What else?"

"Now, that's enough. I don't think I should tell the rest."

"Finish it, please!"

"Why Lionel, don't keep shouting at me like that. Of course I'll tell you if you insist. As a matter of fact, I wouldn't consider myself a true friend if I didn't. Don't you think it's the sign of true friendship when two people like us . . ."

"Gladys! *Please* hurry."

"Good Heavens, you must give me time to *think*. Let me see now—so far as I can remember, what she *actually* said was this . . ."—and Gladys Ponsonby, sitting upright on the sofa with her feet not quite touching the floor, her eyes away from me now, looking at the wall, began cleverly to mimic the deep tone of that voice I knew so well—" 'Such a bore, my dear, because with Lionel one can *always* tell exactly what will happen *right* from beginning to end. For dinner we'll go to the Savoy Grill— it's *always* the Savoy Grill—and for two hours I'll have to listen to the pompous old . . . I mean I'll have to listen to him droning away about pictures and porcelain—*always* pictures and porcelain. Then in the taxi going home he'll reach out for my hand, and he'll lean closer, and I'll get a whiff of stale cigar smoke and brandy, and he'll start burbling about how he wished—oh how he wished he was just twenty years younger.

And I will say "Could you open a window, do you mind?" And when we arrive at my house I'll tell him to keep the taxi, but he'll pretend he hasn't heard and pay it off quickly. And then at the front door, while I fish for my key, he'll stand beside me with a sort of silly spaniel look in his eyes, and I'll slowly put the key in the lock, and slowly turn it, and then—very quickly, before he has time to move—I'll say goodnight and skip inside and shut the door behind me . . .' Why Lionel! What's the matter, dear? You look positively ill . . ."

At that point, mercifully, I must have swooned clear away. I can remember practically nothing of the rest of that terrible night except for a vague and disturbing suspicion that when I regained consciousness I broke down completely and permitted Gladys Ponsonby to comfort me in a variety of different ways. Later, I believe I walked out of the house and was driven home, but I remained more or less unconscious of everything around me until I woke up in my bed the next morning.

I awoke feeling weak and shaken. I lay still with my eyes closed, trying to piece together the events of the night before—Gladys Ponsonby's living-room, Gladys on the sofa sipping brandy, the little puckered face, the mouth that was like a salmon's mouth, the things she had said . . . What was it she had said. Ah yes. About me. My God, yes! About Janet and me! Those outrageous, unbelievable remarks! Could Janet really have made them? Could she?

I can remember with what terrifying swiftness my hatred of Janet de Pelagia now began to grow. It all happened in a few minutes—a sudden, violent welling up of a hatred that filled me till I thought I was going to burst. I tried to dismiss it but it was on me like a fever, and in no time at all I was hunting around, as would some filthy gangster, for a method of revenge.

A curious way to behave, you may say, for a man such as me; to which I would answer—no, not really, if you consider the circumstances. To my mind, this was the sort of thing that could drive a man to murder. As a matter of fact, had it not been for a small sadistic streak that caused me to seek a more subtle and painful punishment for my victim, I might well have become a murderer myself. But mere killing, I decided, was too good for this woman, and far too crude for my own taste. So I began looking for a superior alternative.

I am not normally a scheming person; I consider it an odious business and have had no practice in it whatsoever. But fury and hate can concentrate a man's mind to an astonishing degree, and in no time at all a plot was forming and unfolding in my head—a plot so superior and exciting that I began to be quite carried away at the idea of it. By the time I had filled in the details and overcome one or two minor objections, my brooding vengeful mood had changed to one of extreme elation, and I remember how I started bouncing up and down absurdly on my bed and clapping my hands. The next thing I knew I had the telephone directory on my lap and was searching eagerly for a name. I found it, picked up the phone, and dialled the number.

"Hello," I said. "Mr. Royden? Mr. John Royden?"

"Speaking."

Well—it wasn't difficult to persuade the man to call around and see me for a moment. I had never met him, but of course he knew my name, both as an important collector of paintings and as a person of some consequence in society. I was a big fish for him to catch.

"Let me see now, Mr. Lampson," he said, "I think I ought to be free in about a couple of hours. Will that be allright?"

I told him it would be fine, gave my address, and rang off.

I jumped out of bed. It was really remarkable how exhilarated I felt all of a sudden. One moment I had been in agony of despair, contemplating murder and suicide and I don't know what; the next, I was whistling an aria from Puccini in my bath. Every now and again I caught myself rubbing my hands together in a devilish fashion, and once, during my exercises, when I overbalanced doing a double-knee-bend, I sat on the floor and giggled like a schoolboy.

At the appointed time Mr. John Royden was shown in to my library and I got up to meet him. He was a small neat man with a slightly ginger goatee beard. He wore a black velvet jacket, a rust-brown tie, a red pullover, and black suède shoes. I shook his small neat hand.

"Good of you to come along so quickly, Mr. Royden."

"Not at all, sir." The man's lips—like the lips of nearly all bearded men—looked wet and naked, a trifle indecent, shining pink in among all that hair.

After telling him again how much I admired his work, I got straight down to business.

"Mr. Royden," I said, "I have a rather unusual request to make of you, something quite personal in its way."

"Yes, Mr. Lampson?" He was sitting in the chair opposite me and he cocked his head over to one side, quick and perky like a bird.

"Of course, I know I can trust you to be discreet about anything I say."

"Absolutely, Mr. Lampson."

"Allright. Now my proposition is this: there is a certain lady in town here whose portrait I would like you to paint. I very much want to possess a fine painting of her. But there are certain complications. For example, I have my own reasons for not wishing her to know that it is I who am commissioning the portrait."

"You mean . . ."

"Exactly, Mr. Royden. That is exactly what I mean. As a man of the world I'm sure you will understand."

He smiled, a crooked little smile that only just came through his beard, and he nodded his head knowingly up and down.

"Is it not possible," I said, "that a man might be—how shall I put it?— extremely fond of a lady and at the same time have his own good reasons for not wishing her to know about it yet?"

"More than possible, Mr. Lampson."

"Sometimes a man has to stalk his quarry with great caution, waiting patiently for the right moment to reveal himself."

"Precisely, Mr. Lampson."

"There are better ways of catching a bird than by chasing it through the woods."

"Yes indeed, Mr. Lampson."

"Putting salt on its tail, for instance."

"Ha-ha!"

"Allright, Mr. Royden. I think you understand. Now—do you happen by any chance to know a lady called Janet de Pelagia?"

"Janet de Pelagia? Let me see now—yes. At least, what I mean is I've heard of her. I couldn't exactly say I know her."

"That's a pity. It makes it a little more difficult. Do you think you could get to meet her—perhaps at a cocktail party or something like that?"

"Shouldn't be too tricky, Mr. Lampson."

"Good, because what I suggest is this: that you go up to her and tell her she's the sort of model you've been searching for for years—just the right face, the right figure, the right coloured eyes. You know the sort of thing. Then ask her if she'd mind sitting for you free of charge. Say you'd like to do a picture of her for next year's Academy. I feel sure she'd be delighted to help you, and honoured too, if I may say so. Then you will paint her and exhibit the picture and deliver it to me after the show is over. No one but you need know that I have bought it."

The small round eyes of Mr. John Royden were watching me shrewdly, I thought, and the head was again cocked over to one side. He was sitting on the edge of his chair, and in this position, with the pullover making a flash of red down his front, he reminded me of a robin on a twig listening for a suspicious noise.

"There's really nothing wrong about it at all," I said. "Just call it—if you like—a harmless little conspiracy being perpetrated by a . . . well . . . by a rather romantic old man."

"I know, Mr. Lampson. I know . . ." He still seemed to be hesitating, so I said quickly, "I'll be glad to pay you double your usual fee."

That did it. The man actually licked his lips. "Well, Mr. Lampson, I must say this sort of thing's not really in my line, you know. But all the same, it'd be a very heartless man who refused such a—shall I say such a romantic assignment?"

"I should like a full-length portrait, Mr. Royden, please. A large canvas—let me see—about twice the size of that Manet on the wall there."

"About sixty by thirty-six?"

"Yes. And I should like her to be standing. That, to my mind, is her most graceful attitude."

"I quite understand, Mr. Lampson. And it'll be a pleasure to paint such a lovely lady."

I expect it will, I told myself. The way you go about it, my boy, I'm quite sure it will. But I said, "Allright, Mr. Royden, then I'll leave it all to you. And don't forget, please—this is a little secret between ourselves."

When he had gone I forced myself to sit still and take twenty-five deep breaths. Nothing else would have restrained me from jumping up and shouting for joy like an idiot. I have never in my life felt so exhilarated. My plan was working! The most difficult part was already accomplished. There would be a wait now, a long wait. The way this man painted, it would take him several months to finish the picture. Well, I would just have to be patient, that's all.

I now decided on the spur of the moment that it would be best if I were to go abroad in the interim; and the very next morning, after sending a message to Janet (with whom, you will remember, I was due to dine that night) telling her I had been called away, I left for Italy.

There, as always, I had a delightful time, marred only by a constant nervous excitement caused by the thought of returning to the scene of action.

I eventually arrived back, four months later, in July, on the day after the opening of the Royal Academy, and I found to my relief that everything had gone according to plan during my absence. The picture of Janet de Pelagia had been painted and hung in the Exhibition, and it was already the subject of much favourable comment both by the critics and the public. I myself refrained from going to see it but Royden told me on the telephone that there had been several inquiries by persons who wished to buy it, all of whom had been informed that it was not for sale. When the show was over, Royden delivered the picture to my house and received his money.

I immediately had it carried up to my work-room, and with mounting excitement I began to examine it closely. The man had painted her standing up in a black evening dress and there was a red-plush sofa in the background. Her left hand was resting on the back of a heavy chair, also of red-plush, and there was a huge crystal chandelier hanging from the ceiling.

My God, I thought, what a hideous thing! The portrait itself wasn't so bad. He had caught the woman's expression—the forward drop of the head, the wide blue eyes, the large, ugly-beautiful mouth with the trace of a smile in one corner. He had flattered her, of course. There wasn't a wrinkle on her face or the slightest suggestion of fat under her chin. I bent forward to examine the painting of the dress. Yes—here the paint was thicker, much thicker. At this point, unable to wait another moment, I threw off my coat and prepared to go to work.

I should mention here that I am myself an expert cleaner and restorer of paintings. The cleaning, particularly, is a comparatively simple process provided one has patience and a gentle touch, and those professionals who make such a secret of their trade and charge such shocking prices get no business from me. Where my own pictures are concerned I always do the job myself.

I poured out the turpentine and added a few drops of alcohol. I dipped a small wad of cotton-wool in the mixture, squeezed it out, and then gently, so very gently, with a circular motion, I began to work upon the black paint of the dress. I could only hope that Royden had allowed each layer to dry thoroughly before applying the next, otherwise the two would merge and the process I had in mind would be impossible. Soon I would know. I was working on one square inch of black dress somewhere around the lady's stomach and I took plenty of time, cautiously testing and teasing the paint, adding a drop or two more of alcohol to my mixture, testing again and adding another drop until finally it was just strong enough to loosen the pigment.

For perhaps a whole hour I worked away on this little square of black, proceeding more and more gently as I came closer to the layer below. Then, a tiny pink spot appeared, and gradually it spread and spread until the whole of my square inch was a clear shining patch of pink. Quickly I neutralised with pure turps.

So far so good. I knew now that the black paint could be removed without disturbing what was underneath. So long as I was patient and industrious I would easily be able to take it all off. Also, I had discovered the right mixture to use and just how hard I could safely rub, so things should go much quicker now.

I must say it was rather an amusing business. I worked first from the middle of her body downward, and as the lower half of her dress came away bit by bit onto my little wads of cotton, a queer pink undergarment began to reveal itself. I didn't for the life of me know what the thing was called, but it was a formidable apparatus constructed of what appeared to be a strong thick elastic material, and its purpose was apparently to contain and to compress the woman's bulging figure into a neat streamlined shape, giving a quite false impression of slimness. As I travelled lower and lower down,

I came upon a striking arrangement of suspenders, also pink, which were attached to this elastic armour and hung downward four or five inches to grip the tops of the stockings.

Quite fantastic the whole thing seemed to me as I stepped back a pace to survey it. It gave me a strong sense of having somehow been cheated; for had I not, during all these past months, been admiring the sylphlike figure of this lady? She was a faker. No question about it. But do many other females practice this sort of deception, I wondered. I knew, of course, that in the days of stays and corsets it was usual for ladies to strap themselves up; yet for some reason I was under the impression that nowadays all they had to do was diet.

When the whole of the lower half of the dress had come away, I immediately turned my attention to the upper portion, working my way slowly upward from the lady's middle. Here, around the midriff, there was an area of naked flesh; then higher up upon the bosom itself and actually containing it, I came upon a contrivance made of some heavy black material edged with frilly lace. This, I knew very well, was the brassière—another formidable appliance upheld by an arrangement of black straps as skillfully and scientifically rigged as the supporting cables of a suspension bridge.

Dear me, I thought. One lives and learns.

But now at last the job was finished, and I stepped back again to take a final look at the picture. It was truly an astonishing sight! This woman, Janet de Pelagia, almost life size, standing there in her underwear—in a sort of drawing room, I suppose it was—with a great chandelier above her head and a red-plush chair by her side; and she herself—this was the most disturbing part of all—looking so completely unconcerned, with the wide placid blue eyes, the faintly smiling, ugly-beautiful mouth. Also I noticed, with something of a shock, that she was exceedingly bow-legged, like a jockey. I tell you frankly, the whole thing embarrassed me. I felt as though I had no right to be in the room, certainly no right to stare. So after a while I went out and shut the door behind me. It seemed like the only decent thing to do.

Now, for the next and final step! And do not imagine simply because I have not mentioned it lately that my thirst for revenge had in any way diminished during the last few months. On the contrary, it had if anything increased; and with the last act about to he performed, I can tell you I found it hard to contain myself. That night, for example, I didn't even go to bed.

You see, I couldn't wait to get the invitations out. I sat up all night preparing them and addressing the envelopes. There were twenty-two of them in all, and I wanted each to be a personal note. "I'm having a little dinner on Friday night, the twenty-second, at eight. I do hope you can come along . . . I'm so looking forward to seeing you again . . ."

The first, the most carefully phrased, was to Janet de Pelagia. In it I regretted not having seen her for so long . . . I had been abroad . . . It was time we got together again, etc. etc. The next was to Gladys Ponsonby. Then one to Hermione Lady Girdlestone, another to Princess Bicheno, Mrs. Cudbird, Sir Hubert Kaul, Mrs. Galbally, Peter Euan-Thomas, James Pisker, Sir Eustace Piegrome, Peter van Santen, Elizabeth Moynihan, Lord Mulherrin, Bertram Sturt, Phillip Cornelius, Jack Hill, Lady Akeman, Mrs. Icely, Humphrey King-Howard, Johnny O'Coffey, Mrs. Uvary, and the Dowager Countess of Waxworth.

It was a carefully selected list, containing as it did the most distinguished men, the most brilliant and influential women in the top crust of our society.

I was well aware that a dinner at my house was regarded as quite an occasion; everybody liked to come. And now, as I watched the point of my pen moving swiftly over the paper, I could almost see the ladies in their pleasure picking up their bedside telephones the morning the invitations arrived, shrill voices calling to shriller voices over the wires . . . "Lionel's giving a party . . . he's asked you too? My dear, how nice . . . his food is always *so* good . . . and *such* a lovely man, isn't he though, yes . . ."

Is that really what they would say? It suddenly occurred to me that it might not be like that at all. More like this perhaps: "I agree, my dear, yes, not a bad old man . . . but a bit of a bore, don't you think? . . . What did you say? . . . dull? But desperately, my dear. You've hit the nail right on the head . . . did you ever hear what Janet de Pelagia once said about him? . . . Ah yes, I thought you'd heard that one . . . screamingly funny, don't you think? . . . poor Janet . . . how she stood it as long as she did I don't know . . ."

Anyway, I got the invitations off, and within a couple of days everybody with the exception of Mrs. Cudbird and Sir Hubert Kaul, who were away, had accepted with pleasure.

At eight-thirty on the evening of the twenty-second my large drawing-room was filled with people. They stood about the room admiring the pictures, drinking their martinis, talking with loud voices. The women smelled strongly of scent, the men were pink-faced and carefully buttoned up in their dinner-jackets. Janet de Pelagia was wearing the same black dress she had used for the portrait, and every time I caught sight of her, a kind of huge bubble-vision—as in those absurd cartoons—would float up above my head, and in it I would see Janet in her underclothes, the black brassière, the pink elastic belt, the suspenders, the jockey's legs.

I moved from group to group, chatting aimiably with them all, listening to their talk. Behind me I could hear Mrs. Galbally telling Sir Eustace Piegrome and James Pisker how the man at the next table to hers at Claridge's the night before had had red lipstick on his white moustache. "Simply *plastered* with it," she kept saying, "and the old boy was ninety if he was a day . . ." On the other side, Lady Girdlestone was telling somebody where one could get truffles cooked in brandy, and I could see Mrs. Icely whispering something to Lord Mulherrin while his Lordship kept shaking his head slowly from side to side like an old and dispirited metronome.

Dinner was announced, and we all moved out.

"My goodness!" they cried as they entered the dining-room. "How dark and sinister!"

"I can hardly see a thing!"

"What divine little candles!"

"But Lionel, how romantic!"

There were six very thin candles set about two feet apart from each other down the centre of the long table. Their small flames made a little glow of light around the table itself, but left the rest of the room in darkness. It was an amusing arrangement and apart from the fact that it suited my purpose well, it made a pleasant change. The guests soon settled themselves in their right places and the meal began.

They all seemed to enjoy the candle-light and things went famously, though for some reason the darkness caused them to speak much louder than usual. Janet de Pelagia's voice struck me as being particularly strident. She was sitting next to Lord Mulherrin, and I could hear her telling him about the boring time she had had at Cap Ferrat the week before. "Nothing but Frenchmen," she kept saying. "Nothing but Frenchmen in the whole place . . ."

For my part, I was watching the candles. They were so thin that I knew it would not be long before they burned down to their bases. Also I was mighty nervous—I will admit that—but at the same time intensely exhilarated, almost to the point of drunkenness. Every time I heard Janet's voice or caught sight of her face shadowed in the light of the candles, a little ball of excitement exploded inside me and I felt the fire of it running under my skin.

They were eating their strawberries when at last I decided the time had come. I took a deep breath and in a loud voice I said, "I'm afraid we'll have to have the lights on now. The candles are nearly finished. Mary," I called, "Oh Mary, switch on the lights will you please."

There was a moment of silence after my announcement. I heard the maid walking over to the door, then the gentle click of the switch and the room was flooded with a blaze of light. They all screwed up their eyes, opened them again, gazed about them.

At that point I got up from my chair and slid quietly from the room, but as I went I saw a sight that I shall never forget as long as I live. It was Janet, with both hands in mid-air, stopped, frozen rigid, caught in the act of gesticulating toward someone across the table. Her mouth had dropped open two inches and she wore the surprised, not-quite-understanding look of a person who precisely one second before has been shot dead right through the heart.

In the hall outside I paused and listened to the beginning of the uproar, the shrill cries of the ladies and the outraged unbelieving exclamations of the men; and soon there was a great hum of noise with everybody talking or shouting at the same time. Then—and this was the sweetest moment of all—I heard Lord Mulherrin's voice, roaring above the rest, "Here! Someone! Hurry! Give her some water quick!"

Out in the street the chauffeur helped me into my car, and soon we were away from London and bowling merrily along the Great North Road toward this, my other house, which is only ninety-five miles from Town anyway.

The next two days I spent in gloating. I mooned around in a dream of ecstasy, half drowned in my own complacency and filled with a sense of pleasure so great that it constantly gave me pins and needles all along the lower parts of my legs. It wasn't until this morning when Gladys Ponsonby called me on the phone that I suddenly came to my senses and realized I was not a hero at all but an outcast. She informed me—with what I thought was just a trace of relish—that everybody was up in arms, that all of them, all my old and loving friends were saying the most terrible things about me and had sworn never never to speak to me again. Except her, she kept saying. Everybody except her. And didn't I think it would be rather cosy, she asked, if she were to come down and stay with me a few days to cheer me up?

I'm afraid I was too upset by that time even to answer her politely. I put the phone down and went away to weep.

Then at noon today came the final crushing blow. The post arrived, and with it—I can hardly bring myself to write about it, I am so ashamed—came a letter, the sweetest, most tender little note imaginable from none other than Janet de Pelagia herself. She forgave me completely, she wrote, for everything I had done. She knew it was only a joke and I must not listen to the horrid things other people were saying about me. She loved me as she always had and always would to her dying day.

Oh, what a cad, what a brute I felt when I read this! The more so when I found that she had actually sent me by the same post a small present as an added sign of her affection—a half pound jar of my favorite food of all, fresh caviar.

I can never under any circumstances resist good caviar. It is perhaps my greatest weakness. So although I naturally had no appetite whatsoever for food at dinner-time this evening, I must confess I took a few spoonfuls of the stuff in an effort to console myself in my misery. It is even possible that I took a shade too much, because I haven't been feeling any too chipper this last hour or so. Perhaps I ought to go up right away and get myself some bicarbonate of soda. I can easily come back and finish this later, when I'm in better trim.

You know—now I come to think of it, I really do feel rather ill all of a sudden.

THE LADY, OR THE TIGER?
FRANK STOCKTON

A writer of children's books and popular fiction, Frank Stockton (1834–1902) is remembered almost exclusively today for "The Lady, or the Tiger?"

This most famous of all riddle stories was originally titled "The King's Arena" when Stockton read it aloud at a party. It drew such enthusiastic response that he expanded it, changed the title, and sold it to *Century Magazine* (November 1882). Two years later, it became the title story of his most successful collection of short stories.

Born in Philadelphia, Stockton began writing at an early age, starting with children's stories and sketches, then continuing with popular stories and novels of humor, notably *The Rudder Grangers Abroad* (1891). His other contributions to the mystery genre include *The Stories of Three Burglars* (1890), *The Captain's Toll Gate* (1893), *The Adventures of Captain Horn* (1895), and several short stories.

The most significant of these stories is "The Discourager of Hesitancy. A Continuation of 'The Lady, or the Tiger?' " which was first published in book form in *The Christmas Wreck and Other Stories* (1886). It is the next story in this collection, so you will see that it is as frustrating as the original tale that inspired it.

THE LADY, OR THE TIGER?

BY FRANK R. STOCKTON

IN THE VERY OLDEN TIME there lived a semi-barbaric king, a man of exuberant fancy, and of an authority so irresistible that, at his will, he turned his varied fancies into facts. He was greatly given to self-communing; and, when he and himself agreed upon anything, the thing was done. When his domestic and political systems moved smoothly, his nature was bland and genial; but whenever there was a little hitch, he was blander and more genial still, for nothing pleased him so much as to make the crooked straight, and crush down uneven places—as in the public arena, by exhibitions of manly and beastly valor. The arena of the king, with its encircling galleries, its mysterious vaults, and its unseen passages, was an agent of poetic justice, in which crime was punished, or virtue rewarded, by the decrees of an impartial and incorruptible chance.

When a subject was accused of a crime of sufficient importance to interest the king, public notice was given that on an appointed day the fate of the accused person would be decided in the king's arena. When all the people had assembled in the galleries, and the king, surrounded by his court, high up on his throne of royal state on one side of the arena, he gave a signal, a door beneath him opened, and the accused subject stepped out into the amphitheater. Directly opposite him, on the other side of the enclosed space, were two doors, exactly alike and side by side. It was the duty and the privilege of the person on trial, to walk directly to these doors and open one of them. He could open either door he pleased: he was subject to no guidance or influence but that of impartial and incorruptible chance.

If he opened the one, there came out of it a hungry tiger, the fiercest and most cruel that could be procured, which immediately sprang upon him, and tore him to pieces, as a punishment for his guilt. The moment that the case of the criminal was thus decided, doleful iron bells were clanged, great wails went up from the hired mourners posted on she outer rim of the arena, and the vast audience, with bowed heads and downcast hearts, wended slowly their homeward way, mourning greatly that one so young and fair, or old and respected, should have merited so dire a fate.

But, if the accused person opened the other door, there came forth from it a lady, the most suitable to his years and station that his majesty could select among his fair subjects; and to this lady he was immediately married, as a reward of his innocence. It mattered not that he might already possess a wife and family, or that his affections might be engaged upon an object of his own selection: the king allowed no such subordinate arrangements to interfere with his great scheme of retribution and reward. The exercises took place immediately, and in the arena. Another door opened beneath the king, and a priest, followed by a band of choristers, and dancing maidens blowing joyous airs on golden horns, advanced to where the pair stood, side by side; and the wedding was promptly and cheerily solemnized. Then the gay brass bells rang forth their merry peals, the people shouted glad hurrahs, and the innocent man, preceded by children strewing flowers on his path, led his bride to his home.

This was the king's semi-barbaric method of administering justice. Its perfect fairness is obvious. The criminal could not know out of which door would come the lady: he opened either he pleased, without having the slightest idea whether, in the next instant, he was to be devoured or married. On some occasions the tiger came out of one door, and on some out of the other. The decisions of this tribunal were not only fair, they were positively determinate: the accused person was instantly punished if he found himself guilty; and, if innocent, he was rewarded on the spot, whether he liked it or not.

There was no escape from the judgments of the king's arena.

The institution was a very popular one. When the people gathered together on one of the great trial days, they never knew whether they were to witness a bloody slaughter or a hilarious wedding. This element of uncertainty lent an interest to the occasion which it could not otherwise have attained. Thus, the masses were entertained and pleased, and the thinking part of the community could bring no charge of unfairness against this plan; for did not the accused person have the whole matter in his own hands?

This semi-barbaric king had a daughter as blooming as his most florid fancies, and with a soul as fervent and imperious as his own. As is usual in such cases, she was the apple of his eye, and loved by him above all humanity. Among his courtiers was a young man of that fineness of blood and lowness of station common to the conventional heroes of romance who love royal maidens. This royal maiden was well satisfied with her lover, for he was handsome and brave to a degree unsurpassed in all this kingdom; and she loved him with an ardor that had enough of barbarism in it to make it exceedingly warm and strong.

This love affair moved on happily for many months, until one day the king happened to discover its existence. He did not hesitate nor waver in regard to his duty in the premises. The youth was immediately cast into prison, and a day was appointed for his trial in the king's arena. This, of course, was an especially important occasion; and his majesty, as well as all the people, was greatly interested in the workings and development of this trial. Never before had such a case occurred; never before had a subject dared to love the daughter of a king.

The tiger-cages of the kingdom were searched for the most savage and relentless beasts, from which the fiercest monster might be selected for the arena; and the ranks of maiden youth and beauty throughout the land were carefully surveyed by competent judges, in order that the young man might have a fitting bride in case fate did not determine for him a different destiny. Of course, everybody knew that the deed with which the accused was charged had been done. He had loved the princess, and neither he, she, nor anyone else thought of denying the fact. But the king would not think of allowing any fact of this kind to interfere with the workings of the tribunal, in which he took such great delight and satisfaction. No matter how the affair turned out, the youth would be disposed of; and the king would take an esthetic pleasure in watching the course of events, which would determine whether or not the young man had done wrong in allowing himself to love the princess.

The appointed day arrived. From far and near the people gathered, and thronged the great galleries of the arena; and crowds, unable to gain admittance, massed themselves against its outside walls. The king and his court were in their places, opposite the twin doors—those fateful portals, so terrible in their similarity. All was ready. The signal was given.

A door beneath the royal party opened, and the lover of the princess walked into the arena. Tall, beautiful, fair, his appearance was greeted with a low hum of admiration and anxiety. Half the audience had not known so grand a youth had lived among them. No wonder the princess loved him! What a terrible thing for him to be there!

As the youth advanced into the arena, he turned, as the custom was, to bow to the king. But he did not think at all of that royal personage—his eyes were fixed upon the princess, who sat to the right of her father.

Had it not been for the barbarism in her nature, it is probable that lady would not have been there; but her intense and fervid soul would not allow her to be absent on an occasion in which she was so terribly interested. From the moment that the decree had gone forth, that her lover should decide his fate in the king's arena, she had thought of nothing, night or day, but this great event and the various subjects connected with it. Possessed of more power, influence, and force of character than anyone who had ever before been interested in such a case, she had done what no other person had done—she had possessed herself of the secret of the doors. She knew in which of the two rooms, that lay behind those doors, stood the cage of the tiger, with its open front, and in which waited the lady. Through these thick doors, heavily curtained with skins on the inside, it was impossible that any noise or suggestion should come from within to the person who should approach to raise the latch of one of them; but gold, and the power of a woman's will, had brought the secret to the princess.

And not only did she know in which room stood the lady ready to emerge, all blushing and radiant, should her door be opened, but she knew who the lady was. It was one of the fairest and loveliest of the damsels of the court who had been selected as the reward of the accused youth, should he be proved innocent of the crime of aspiring to one so far above him; and the princess hated her. Often had she seen, or imagined that she had seen, this fair creature throwing glances of admiration upon the person of her lover, and sometimes she thought these glances were perceived and even returned.

Now and then she had seen them talking together. It was but for a moment or two, but much can be said in a brief space; it may have been on most unimportant topics, but how could she know that? The girl was lovely, but she had dared to raise her eyes to the loved one of the princess; and, with all the intensity of the savage blood transmitted to her through long lines of wholly barbaric ancestors, she hated the woman who blushed and trembled behind that silent door.

When her lover turned and looked at her, and his eye met hers as she sat there paler and whiter than anyone in the vast ocean of anxious faces about her, he saw, by that power of quick perception which is given to those whose souls are one, that she knew behind which door crouched the tiger and behind which stood the lady. He had expected her to know it. He understood her nature, and his soul was assured that she would never rest until she made plain to herself this thing, hidden to all other lookers-on, even to the king. The only hope for the youth in which there was an element of certainty was based upon the success of the princess in discovering this mystery: and the moment he looked upon her, he saw she had succeeded, as in his soul he knew she would succeed.

Then it was that his quick and anxious glance asked the question: *Which?*

It was as plain to her as if he shouted it from where he stood. There was not an instant to be lost. The question was asked in a flash: it must be answered in another.

Her right arm lay on the cushioned parapet before her. She raised her hand, and made a slight, quick movement toward her right. No one but her lover saw her. Every eye but his was fixed on the man in the arena.

He turned and with a firm and rapid step he walked across the empty space.

Every heart stopped beating, every breath was held, every eye was fixed immovably upon that man.

Without the slightest hesitation, he went to the door on the right, and opened it.

Now, THE POINT of the story is this: *Did the tiger come out of that door, or did the lady?*

The more we reflect upon this question, the harder it is to answer. It involves a study of the human heart which leads us through devious mazes of passion, out of which it is difficult of find our way. Think of it, fair reader, not as if the decision of the question depended upon yourself, but upon that hot-blooded, semi-barbaric princess, her soul at a white heat beneath the combined fires of despair and jealousy. She had lost him, but who should have him?

How often, in her waking hours and in her dreams, had she started in wild horror, and covered her face with her hands as she thought of her lover opening the door on the other side of which waited the cruel fangs of the tiger?

But how much oftener had she seen him at the other door! How in her grievous reveries had she gnashed her teeth, and torn her hair, when she saw his start of rapturous delight as he opened the door of the lady! How her soul had burned in agony when she had seen him rush to meet that woman, with her flushing cheek and sparkling eye of triumph; when she had seen him lead her forth, his whole frame kindled with the joy of recovered life; when she had heard the glad shouts from the multitude, and the wild ringing of the happy bells; when she had seen the priest, with his joyous followers, advance to the couple, and make them man and wife before her very eyes; and when she had seen them walk away together upon their path of flowers, followed by the tremendous shouts of the hilarious multitude, in which her one despairing shriek was lost and drowned!

Would it not be better for him to die at once, and go to wait for her in the blessed regions of semi-barbaric futurity?

And yet, that awful tiger, those shrieks, that blood!

Her decision had been indicated in an instant, but it had been made after days and nights of anguished deliberation. She had known she would be asked, she had decided what she would answer, and, without the slightest hesitation, she had moved her hand to the right.

The question of her decision is one not to be lightly considered, and it is not for me to presume to set myself up as the one person able to answer it. And so I leave it with all of you:

Which came out of the opened door,—the lady, or the tiger?

THE DISCOURGAGER OF HESITANCY

A Continuation of "The Lady, or the Tiger?"

BY FRANK R. STOCKTON

IT WAS NEARLY A YEAR after the occurrence of that event in the arena of the semi-barbaric King known as the incident of the lady or the tiger, that there came to the palace of this monarch a deputation of five strangers from a far country. These men, of venerable and dignified aspect and demeanor, were received by a high officer of the court, and to him they made known their errand.

"Most noble officer," said the speaker of the deputation, "it so happened that one of our countrymen was present here, in your capital city, on that momentous occasion when a young man who had dared to aspire to the hand of your King's daughter had been placed in the arena, in the midst of the assembled multitude, and ordered to open one of two doors, not knowing whether a ferocious tiger would spring out upon him, or a beauteous lady would advance, ready to become his bride. Our fellow-citizen who was then present was a man of super-sensitive feelings, and at the moment when the youth was about to open the door he was so fearful lest he should behold a horrible spectacle, that his nerves failed him, and he fled precipitately from the arena, and mounting his camel rode homeward as fast as he could go.

"We were all very much interested in the story which our countryman told us, and we were extremely sorry that he did not wait to see the end of the affair. We hoped, however, that in a few weeks some traveler from your city would come among us and bring us further news; but up to the day when we left our country, no such traveler had arrived. At last it was determined that the only thing to be done was to send a deputation to this country, and to ask the question: 'Which came out of the open door, the lady, or the tiger?' "

When the high officer had heard the mission of this most respectable deputation, he led the five strangers into an inner room, where they were seated upon soft cushions, and where he ordered coffee, pipes, sherbet, and other semi-barbaric refreshments to be served to them. Then, taking his seat before them, he thus addressed the visitors:

"Most noble strangers, before answering the question you have come so far to ask, I will relate to you an incident which occurred not very long after that to which you have referred. It is well known in all regions hereabouts that our great King is very fond of the presence of beautiful women about his court. All the ladies-in-waiting upon the Queen and Royal Family are most lovely maidens, brought here from every part of the kingdom. The fame of this concourse of beauty, unequaled in any other royal court, has spread far and wide; and had it not been for the equally wide-spread fame of the systems of impetuous justice adopted by our King, many foreigners would doubtless have visited our court.

"But not very long ago there arrived here from a distant land a prince of distinguished appearance and undoubted rank. To such an one, of course, a royal audience was granted, and our King met him very graciously, and begged him to make known the object of his visit. Thereupon the Prince informed his Royal Highness that, having heard of the superior beauty of the ladies of his court, he had come to ask permission to make one of them his wife.

"When our King heard this bold announcement, his face reddened, he turned uneasily on his throne, and we were all in dread lest some quick words of furious condemnation should leap from out his quivering lips. But by a mighty effort he controlled himself; and after a moment's silence he turned to the Prince, and said: 'Your request is granted. Tomorrow at noon you shall wed one of the fairest damsels of our court.' Then turning to his officers, he said: 'Give orders that everything be prepared for a wedding in this palace at high noon to-morrow. Convey this royal Prince to suitable apartments. Send to him tailors, boot-makers, hatters, jewelers, armorers; men of every craft, whose services he may need. Whatever he asks, provide. And let all be ready for the ceremony to-morrow.'

" 'But, your Majesty,' exclaimed the Prince, 'before we make these preparations, I would like—'

" 'Say no more!' roared the King. 'My royal orders have been given, and nothing more is needed to be said. You asked a boon; I granted it; and I will hear no more on the subject. Farewell, my Prince, until to-morrow noon.'

"At this the King arose, and left the audience chamber, while the Prince was hurried away to the apartments selected for him. And here came to him tailors, hatters, jewelers, and every one who was needed to fit him out in grand attire for the wedding. But the mind of the Prince was much troubled and perplexed.

" 'I do not understand,' he said to his attendants, 'this precipitancy of action. When am I to see the ladies, that I may choose among them? I wish opportunity not only to gaze upon their forms and faces, but to become acquainted with their relative intellectual development.'

" 'We can tell you nothing,' was the answer. 'What our King thinks right, that will he do. And more than this we know not.'

" 'His Majesty's notions seem to be very peculiar,' said the Prince, 'and, so far as I can see, they do not at all agree with mine.'

"At that moment an attendant whom the Prince had not noticed before came and stood beside him. This was a broad-shouldered man of cheery aspect, who carried, its hilt in his right hand, and its broad back resting on his broad arm, an enormous scimitar, the upturned edge of which was keen and bright as any razor. Holding this formidable weapon as tenderly as though it had been a sleeping infant, this man drew closer to the Prince and bowed.

" 'Who are you?' exclaimed his Highness, starting back at the sight of the frightful weapon.

" 'I,' said the other with a courteous smile, 'am the Discourager of Hesitancy. When our King makes known his wishes to any one, a subject or visitor, whose disposition in some little points may be supposed not wholly to coincide with that of his Majesty, I am appointed to attend him closely, that, should he think of pausing in the path of obedience to the royal will, he may look at me, and proceed.'

"The Prince looked at him, and proceeded to be measured for a coat.

"The tailors and shoemakers and hatters worked all night; and the next morning, when everything was ready, and the hour of noon was drawing nigh, the Prince again anxiously inquired of his attendants when he might expect to be introduced to the ladies.

" 'The King will attend to that,' they said. 'We know nothing of the matter.'

" 'Your Highness,' said the Discourager of Hesitancy, approaching with a courtly bow, 'will observe the excellent quality of this edge.' And drawing a hair from his head, he dropped it upon the upturned edge of his scimitar, upon which it was cut in two at the moment of touching.

"The Prince glanced and turned upon his heel.

"Now came officers to conduct him to the grand hall of the palace, in which the ceremony was to be performed. Here the Prince found the King seated on the throne, with his nobles, his courtiers, and his officers standing about him in magnificent array. The Prince was led to a position in front of the King, to whom he made obeisance, and then said:

" 'Your Majesty, before I proceed further—'

"At this moment an attendant, who had approached with a long scarf of delicate silk, wound it about the lower part of the Prince's face so quickly and adroitly that he was obliged to cease speaking. Then, with wonderful dexterity, the rest of the scarf was wound around the Prince's head, so that he was completely blindfolded. Thereupon the attendant quickly made openings in the scarf over the mouth and ears, so that the Prince might breathe and hear; and fastening the ends of the scarf securely, he retired.

"The first impulse of the Prince was to snatch the silken folds from his head and face; but as he raised his hands to do so, he heard beside him the voice of the Discourager of Hesitancy, who gently whispered: 'I am here, your Highness.' And, with a shudder, the arms of the Prince fell down by his side.

"Now before him he heard the voice of a priest, who had begun the marriage service in use in that semi-barbaric country. At his side he could hear a delicate rustle, which seemed to proceed from fabrics of soft silk. Gently putting forth his hand, he felt folds of such silk close beside him. Then came the voice of the priest requesting him to take the hand of the lady by his side; and reaching forth his right hand, the Prince received within it another hand so small, so soft, so delicately fashioned, and so delightful to the touch, that a thrill went through his being. Then, as was the custom of the country, the priest first asked the lady would she have this man to be her husband. To which the answer gently came in the sweetest voice he ever heard: 'I will.'

"Then ran raptures rampant through the Prince's blood. The touch, the tone, enchanted him. All the ladies of that court were beautiful; the Discourager was behind him; and through his parted scarf he boldly answered: 'Yes, I will.'

"Whereupon the priest pronounced them man and wife.

"Now the Prince heard a little bustle about him; the long scarf was rapidly unrolled from his head; and he turned, with a start, to gaze upon his bride. To his utter amazement, there was no one there. He stood alone. Unable on the instant to ask a question or say a word, he gazed blankly about him.

"Then the King arose from his throne, and came down, and took him by the hand.

" 'Where is my wife?' gasped the Prince.

" 'She is here,' said the King, leading him to a curtained doorway at the side of the hall.

"The curtains were drawn aside, and the Prince, entering, found himself in a long apartment, near the opposite wall of which stood a line of forty ladies, all dressed in rich attire, and each one apparently more beautiful than the rest.

"Waving his hand toward the line, the King said to the Prince: 'There is your bride! Approach, and lead her forth! But remember this: that if you attempt to take away one of the unmarried damsels of our court, your execution shall be instantaneous. Now, delay no longer. Step up and take your bride.'

"The Prince, as in a dream, walked slowly along the line of ladies, and then walked slowly back again. Nothing could he see about any one of them to indicate that she was more of a bride than the others. Their dresses were all similar; they all blushed; they all looked up, and then looked down. They all had charming little hands. Not one spoke a word. Not one lifted a finger to make a sign. It was evident that the orders given them had been very strict.

" 'Why this delay?' roared the King. 'If I had been married this day to one so fair as the lady who wedded you, I should not wait one second to claim her.'

"The bewildered Prince walked again up and down the line. And this time there was a slight change in the countenances of two of the ladies. One of the fairest gently smiled as he passed her. Another, just as beautiful, slightly frowned.

" 'Now,' said the Prince to himself, 'I am sure that it is one of those two ladies whom I have married. But which? One smiled. And would not any woman smile when she saw, in such a case, her husband coming toward her? But, then, were she not his bride, would she not smile with satisfaction to think he had not selected her, and that she had not led him to an untimely doom? Then again, on the other hand, would not any woman frown when she saw her husband come toward her and fail to claim her? Would she not knit her lovely brows? And would she not inwardly say, "It is I! Don't you know it? Don't you feel it? Come!" But if this woman had not been married, would she not frown when she saw the man looking at her? Would she not say to herself, "Don't stop at me! It is the next but one. It is two ladies above. Go on!" And then again, the one who married me did not see my face. Would she not smile if she thought me comely? While if I wedded the one who frowned, could she restrain her disapprobation if she did not like me? Smiles invite the approach of true love. A frown is a reproach to a tardy advance. A smile—'

" 'Now, hear me!' loudly cried the King. 'In ten seconds, if you do not take the lady we have given you, she, who has just been made your bride, shall be your widow.'

"And, as the last word was uttered, the Discourager of Hesitancy stepped close beside the Prince, and whispered: 'I am here!'

"Now the Prince could not hesitate an instant; and he stepped forward and took one of the two ladies by the hand.

"Loud rang the bells; loud cheered the people; and the King came forward to congratulate the Prince. He had taken his lawful bride.

"Now, then," said the high officer to the deputation of five strangers from a far country, "when you can decide among yourselves which lady the Prince chose, the one who smiled or the one who frowned, then will I tell you which came out of the opened door, the lady or the tiger!"

At the latest accounts, the five strangers had not yet decided.

THE LADY, AND THE TIGER
JACK MOFFITT

The author of a couple of tours de force as a short story writer, the brilliant Jack Moffitt (1901–1969) achieved most of his fame and success as a screenwriter. Among his more than two dozen credits from the 1930s to the 1950s for stories and screenwriting are *Passage to Marseilles* (1944), which starred Humphrey Bogart as a convict who escaped from Devil's Island to help France in WWII; *Night and Day* (1946), a biography of Cole Porter starring Cary Grant; and films for Fred MacMurray and Gene Autry.

During the House Un-American Activities Committee's search for Communists among Hollywood's motion picture industry, he turned in Bernard Gordon, who admitted to being a card-carrying member of the American Communist Party from 1942 to 1956.

In addition to writing *for* Hollywood, he wrote *about* it, producing film reviews for various publications, including *The Hollywood Reporter*.

His daughter Peggy became the most prominent model used by the designer Rudi Gernreich; among the clothes in which she was photographed was the then-shocking monokini.

As an intellectual challenge, he wrote a continuation of Guy de Maupassant's story "The Necklace," and then did the same for Frank Stockton's "The Lady, or the Tiger?"; his ingenious solution to this riddle appeared in the September 1948 issue of *Ellery Queen's Mystery Magazine*.

THE LADY AND THE TIGER

BY JACK MOFFITT

YOU MAY FIND IT faintly ridiculous that I, Charles Sevier, a stout and fortyish researcher working in Rome at the Vatican Library, should be in love with a woman who has been dead two thousand years.

This strange infatuation was brought about by the most prosaic of instruments—Frank R. Stockton's short story, "The Lady, or the Tiger?" which was published in 1884, sixteen years before my birth.

During the intervening years I doubt if there has been a single literate American who has not attempted to answer the riddle, which Mr. Stockton propounded in words which I have taken the liberty to abridge:

"In olden times there lived a semi-barbaric king, whose ideas, though polished and sharpened by the progressiveness of distant Latin neighbors, were still large, florid and untrammeled.

"When one of his male subjects was accused of a crime, public notice was given that on an appointed day, the man's fate would be decided in the King's Arena. Here the prisoner faced two doors, exactly alike and side-by-side. It was the obligation of the person on trial to open one of these doors. He was subject to no guidance or influence. He could open either he pleased.

"If he opened one, there came out a hungry tiger.

"But if he opened the other, there came forth a lady, the most suitable to his years and station that the King could select from among his subjects, and to this lady he was immediately married, amid appropriate ceremonies.

"Sometimes the tiger was behind one door, sometimes the other. Chance was the only arbiter.

"Now the ruler had a daughter as blooming as his most florid fancies, and with a soul as fervent and imperious as his own. As is usual, in such cases, she was the apple of his eye, and was loved by him above all humanity. But among the King's courtiers was a young man who was handsome and brave to a degree unsurpassed in all this kingdom, and the princess loved him with an ardor that had enough of barbarism in it to make it exceedingly warm and strong.

"This love affair moved on happily for many months, until one day the King happened to discover its existence. He did not hesitate nor waver. The youth was immediately cast into prison, and a day was appointed for his trial in the King's Arena.

"As the youth advanced toward the doors, his eyes were fixed upon the princess, who sat to the right of her father. Had it not been for the barbarism in her nature it is probable she would not have been there. But her intense and fervid soul would not allow her to be absent.

"Possessed of power, influence and force of character, she had succeeded in doing what no other person had ever done—she had managed to learn the secret of the doors. She knew in which of the rooms was the tiger, and in which the lady.

"She also knew who the lady was—and she hated her. The girl was lovely, but she had dared to raise her eyes to the loved one of the princess. With all the savagery transmitted to her through long lines of barbaric ancestors, the King's daughter hated the woman who blushed and waited behind that silent door.

"She trembled as her lover turned and looked at her. His eye met hers as she sat there, with features paler and whiter than any in the vast ocean of anxious faces that surrounded her. And he saw instantly that she knew behind which door crouched the tiger, and behind which stood the lady.

"He had expected her to know it.

"Then his quick and anxious glance asked the question: 'Which?' It was as plain to her as if he shouted it from where he stood. There was not an instant to be lost. The question was asked in a flash; it must be answered in another.

"Her right arm lay on the cushioned parapet before her. She raised her hand and made a slight, quick movement toward the right. No one but her lover saw her. Every eye but his was fixed on the arena.

"He turned, and with a firm and rapid step, walked across the empty space. Every heart stopped beating, every breath was held, every eye was fixed immovable upon that man.

"Without the slightest hesitation, he went to the door on the right and opened it.

"Now, the point of the story is this: Did the tiger come out of that door, or did the lady?"

I HAD HEARD that Stockton had obtained the idea for his story from a Roman Catholic antiquarian in the city of Rome; so it is small wonder that I determined to solve the riddle when, after several years as a researcher in the Library of Congress, I was sent to introduce a modern cataloguing system in the Vatican Archives. The immediate purpose of my employment was to search for a long-lost letter supposed to have been written by Pontius Pilate. But I had plenty of time for private research.

After considerable study I decided that Stockton's king could have been none other than Herod Antipas, who ruled Judea under the supervision of the Roman Governor, Pontius Pilate. He was the only eastern monarch who owned an arena, which his father had built after the Roman pattern, but he also had a daughter—or rather a step-daughter—of whom he was unnaturally and inordinately infatuated.

This girl was Princess Salome.

The logic fitted. I felt that I had identified two of the characters in Stockton's story. But it was not until I found the cracked and yellowed parchment, covered with Hebrew characters and written in a sprawling, girlish hand, that I was certain of it. For this letter was written by the girl who had waited behind the second door.

TO THE HIGH PRIEST, Caiphas; from his daughter, Miriam.

Beloved Father,

How can I tell you how much I love you? I know that you must he ashamed of me because all Jerusalem now knows that I love the Greek youth, Jason. I know you will feel humiliated—almost defiled—to see me married to him, by a pagan ritual, before all the people in the King's arena tomorrow. Yet I know that even now, despite your sorrow and your humiliation, you are praying to our one true God to defend Jason and asking the Lord to lead him to the door behind which I will be waiting.

I know that you are doing this, in spite of your conviction that Jason is shallow and ambitious—one of those youths who came swaggering out of Alexandria to seek his fortune at the court of Herod. And I feel that you are praying for Jason, even though you dislike him, because you have always been a just and merciful man.

Oh, dear! It is dreadful to be young! It seems odd to remember that I didn't want to go with you to Herod's palace on that day last autumn—when I first met Jason. For weeks I'd heard you and Grandfather discussing the arrogance of Pontius Pilate who had displayed the eagles of his legions on the fortress of Antonia, overlooking the Temple courtyard. Of course, I'd been taught to regard graven images as sacrilegious, but I wondered why older people made such a fuss about things.

When you decided that the family should ask Herod to intercede, I pretended to have a headache. But I didn't fool you. You said the visit would seem more tactful and more friendly if the whole family went along. I was amused to see, when we arrived at the palace, that your strategy had not fooled Herod any more than mine had fooled you. His chamberlain led you and Grandfather away to the King's audience chamber while the rest of us were sent to wait for you in one of the private courtyards.

As soon as my little brothers saw the fountain splashing in the center of the palace, they rushed toward it squealing and laughing.

I tried to get them interested in the pictures in the floor of the courtyard. They were mosaics showing the fall of Troy. I told as much of the Pagan Story as I thought was good for them.

But you know Nathan. He can't sit still for more than a minute.

"Look!" he shouted, "I'll bet I can jump all around this place and never put my foot on anything but the women!"

This wasn't easy. There were many more warriors in the mosaic floor than there were goddesses. Nathan missed on the third jump. But he had started a game. Soon the whole place was filled with the hopping children, wobbling and tottering as they leaped from Minerva to Aphrodite to Helen, and so on. I know it was childish, but it really was fun. So, just to keep them quiet, I pulled up my dress above my knees and joined in.

And then I heard someone laughing.

Dearest heavens! I could have died! A man had entered the courtyard—a tall, lithe man wearing sandals of silver leather and a tunic and cloak of green silk.

He laughed and said, "Who are you?"

You can imagine how confused I was as I dropped my skirts and tried to brush the hair out of my eyes. It was too awful for a grown-up woman to be caught like this by a member of the court, playing a ridiculous childish game. After all, I am fourteen years old.

"Who are you?" he repeated, coming toward me. "Surely you must have a name—is it Daphne? Or Thetis? Are you a dryad? Or a nymph?"

I was afraid the stranger might laugh at me when I told him who I was. But he didn't. He bowed and replied courteously.

"You must come with me, Miriam," he said. "I have been commanded to bring you to the princess."

I wasn't so sure I should go. But the young man kept laughing and assuring us that he was repeating a royal order—until I finally let him lead me away through the maze of splendid corridors.

I couldn't find anything to say as I walked beside him, listening to his easy conversation. He told me that his name was Jason and that he had lived in Rome and Alexandria. He was the most interesting man I had ever met.

Finally, we came to a larger courtyard, where Salome idled beneath a pinkish awning, surrounded by many courtiers. Youths and maidens from all over the world were there—Greeks and Arabians and officers from the Roman garrison, and even a number of young Jews—though these were unlike any Jews I had seen before. Their cheeks were shaved and they wore Greek or Roman clothing.

Salome was a surprise. She didn't look at all like the kind of girl who could have caused the death of the young preacher whom the country people called the Baptist. She wore no veils or oriental draperies. Her gown was simple and Grecian, with the skirt folded into many soft pleats that concealed but outlined her small and doll-like figure. I had seen her mother,

Herodias, in a procession once, and I had expected the daughter to have the same stately figure and proud eyes.

But Salome was a kitten. She had a little heart-shaped face and large and limpid brown eyes and she had learned how to use them.

"You are late, Jason," she said reproachfully, "our treasure hunt is over. Only you have returned empty-handed."

"You are wrong, Princess," said Jason, leading me forward, "you told me to bring you a Hebrew Diana—and I have."

"This is ridiculous!" Salome's pink small lips were pouting. "You knew I meant a statue."

"Did you, Princess? How could you? You know the Hebrews have made no images since the days of the Golden Calf. But it pleases you to demand the impossible of me."

"If I do, it is because you think you are so clever! Right now you feel quite proud of yourself!"

"Proud, yes. But not conceited." I felt my face burning as he held up my hand and slowly turned me around. "Praxiteles himself would be proud of the golden girl that I have brought."

"All you Greeks seem to think of gold in connection with women!" The milk-white Salome seemed to resent my olive skin. "To call this little thing a Diana is ridiculous."

"Let me go!" I struggled to free my wrist. "I despise every one of you!"

"No!" Jason's strong hands gripped my elbows as he lifted me up on a bench. "I didn't bring you here to be insulted! We'll show this princess that her taste is as bad as her manners. Hold your head up—you are the High Priest's daughter—you are as good as any of them!"

His voice was harsh, as though he were fighting a duel in which I was his weapon. I was trembling and overwrought, but I held up my head and tried to stare defiantly back at Salome, even though I was blinking back the tears.

"Observe the slender strength of her neck line!" he cried, as he snatched up a silver bow from the loot of the treasure hunt. "And have you noticed the supple gracefulness of her figure? Diana has come to life again!"

He fitted an arrow to the bow and placed it in my hands. The arrow was aimed straight at Salome. But she didn't flinch. There was a brooding hatefulness in her eyes.

"There!" said Jason, stepping back as I held the pose. "Is she not even more lovely than Diana? Can any of you say that the Diana of Epheseus has half her beauty? Answer me!"

"Well, it seems to me—" lisped the Greek called Philo, with a nervous glance at Salome.

"I'm not asking Greeks!" snapped Jason. "I am asking the Romans! What do you say, Galba?"

It was clever of him. The Romans loved to show their disdainful independence of Herod's provincial entourage. A slow grin spread over the youthful face of Galba. He passed his big hand over his close-cropped hair.

"By Jupiter! You're right," he said, "I have wasted incense before the statue of Ephesus, but I'd sacrifice my very sword and armor for the Diana we have here!"

All the other Roman officers were quick to agree with him. The courtiers chimed in too. I heard myself praised and complimented in a dozen accents, and my skin tingled with pleasure, just as it had flinched and trembled a few minutes before. It was glorious to be defended and admired.

And then I heard King Herod's smooth chuckle and saw him coming across the courtyard, followed by you and Grandfather.

"By Aphrodite!" he said, "Jason, it seems that you have found a jewel in my threadbare little country. I am very pleased."

I DON'T REMEMBER the rest of that day very clearly. All I remember is the horrible trip home. Grandfather Annas said that I had done something monstrous. It was a shameful thing for the daughter of the High Priest to pose as a pagan goddess before a throng of infidels.

I had little appetite for the dinner old Anna kept urging me to eat. She just can't forget that I no longer need a nurse. I went up on the roof and gazed out through the twilight toward the Mount of Olives. A great sense of poignancy welled up in me. I felt so lonely that it hurt. Then I heard you behind me.

"My dear," you said, "I know it is hard for you to believe but once, a long, long time ago, I was young too. I try to remember those times."

"Yes, Father," I replied looking out across the mystic Valley of Kidron.

You crossed the floor and stroked my hair. "We must have patience, Miriam," you said, "the heroes of our nation have always been men of the spirit—men who combined courage with inspiration. In our bitterest days they come to us—these men who live gloriously close to God. There have always been such men."

"Where are they now?" I asked.

"I do not know, child," you answered musingly. "But people tell of certain men in Galilee—there is the oldtime ring of greatness in much that I have heard of them."

Before you could go on, there was a pounding at the door and a voice: "Open in King Herod's name!"

I think, for all your dignity, Father, you were as frightened as I was as we stood, close together in the passage, and heard the officer tell us that I was to become a lady-in-waiting to Salome, and go with the court to Herod's winter palace at Tiberias.

No child knows how much it loves a parent until the time comes to leave home. Do you remember how melancholy the first autumn rains were when you took me to the Gennot Gate to join the royal caravan?

The trip was a lonely one. None of the women paid any attention to me. And I'd seen nothing of Jason. Shortly before dawn on the last day, I heard one of the camel men exclaim: "Tiberias!" and I poked my head through the curtains to get my first look at our destination.

It was a strange and wonderful sight that lay spread out before us in the fresh washed air of the morning. The sun was just breaking through the clouds beyond the solemn dome of Mount Tabor and the light flashed back from the Sea of Galilee—really only a large lake—as though from a silver shield.

As I watched, there was a thunder of hoofs and a chariot swept past—a chariot drawn by four deep-chested, black-maned Arabians. Jason held the reins. He wore a tight tunic of orange-colored leather and an orange cape streamed back from his shoulders. He was a flame flashing down from the hills upon the black city of Tiberias.

Later, I was glad to see that Herod's palace wasn't so gloomy once you were inside. The rooms were bright with rich hangings and imported marbles. I was given a pretty little chamber at one end of the women's building. The King, himself, came with his royal housekeeper to see that I was comfortable. My only worry was that the balcony window could be reached from a nearby cedar. But, of course, I didn't complain. The King might have thought I was silly.

Some of the dresses that had been provided for me were positively indecent. You could see right through them. The others made of heavier materials had their skirts split too far above the knee. I was glad old Anna had taught me to sew, and that I'd brought my needle kit. With a little work I could make some of them look modest.

I had plenty of time. Neither Salome nor the Queen ever sent for me. Day after day I had nothing to do except work on my dresses and try new ways of fixing my hair.

Some weeks later I found Jason seated beside me at the first of the King's banquets. I suppose I shouldn't say "seated." The guests reclined on long couches placed by the banquet table. Jason lounged by my side. I wasn't used to this fashion and was embarrassed.

But Jason made me feel at ease. He was smiling and very respectful. Even after the seventh course, when the wine was flowing much too freely and the party was getting a good deal worse than rowdy, he drank sparingly and never once touched me.

Salome didn't drink much either. She reclined across the room from us, between her mother and stepfather. I felt a little disloyal and unpatriotic for noticing that the King was getting tipsy. He laughed too loud and kept whispering things into the Princess's ear.

I would have thought that the Queen might have protected her daughter, but Herodias ignored her husband and kept her eyes fixed coldly on the entertainers, giving no encouragement to the suggestive dancers and their off-color songs. Though a member of the same mongrel clan as Herod, she conducted herself with the calm dignity of a Jewish matron.

Time and again I saw Salome's brown eyes look appealingly across the room to Jason. She seemed to envy us. And in spite of the way she'd neglected me, I felt sorry for her.

"Never feel sorry for a beautiful woman," replied Jason, when I mentioned this to him. "They know how to look out for themselves."

"My! Haven't you grown sophisticated and cynical!" I tried to speak mockingly, like one of the court ladies.

He turned to me and said, "I was born a slave but I might have been a prince—one of the rulers of the Roman world—if it hadn't been for a woman even more beautiful than Salome."

"A slave! You are teasing me! I don't believe it!"

"Even though I was born a slave," he said, "I am not a complete impostor. My father was a nobleman. He served on Marc Antony's flagship at the Battle of Actium."

"I don't care who you are, Jason—you don't have to tell me!"

He drank wine and stared morosely toward Salome. "My father became a slave and I was born in slavery because of the vanity of a woman. There was no reason for Cleopatra to be in that battle. Marc Antony begged her to stay ashore. But she was very brave as long as the enemy galleys were on the other side of the horizon and she knew she looked very pretty in her armor. She wanted to be a sea queen and inspire the men!"

Jason spat upon the pavement and exclaimed, "To think that such vanity could have changed the fate of the world! At the height of the battle Cleopatra's ships turned and ran—and do you know why they ran?"

"I have heard that it was because Octavius who opposed her used his catapults to throw great glass globes filled with serpents and that when the globes broke on Cleopatra's decks, she became terrorized of the serpents—"

"That's not the real reason. Cleopatra wasn't afraid of snakes. She deserted Antony because she suddenly decided that it would be safer to win Octavius with her charms than to meet him in battle. And because of her cowardice, Marc Antony killed himself and my father was captured and reduced to slavery. Octavius forced him to become a gladiator."

He stopped abruptly as though he'd decided that he had talked enough. So this was the background of this seemingly gay man. He was the son of a slave and a gladiator.

Herodias was following her drunken husband from the room and Salome was picking her way among the sodden revelers toward the great arch that led to the moonlit gardens. She paused on the threshold and looked back toward us. And for the first time she was smiling.

"It is getting late," Jason told me. "You had better go to your room."

There was nothing to do but obey him.

AFTER THAT it became apparent that the King had ordered Jason to be my escort at all court functions. But he didn't obey very often. It was exasperating to have him send an excuse, accompanied by some rich present, at the last moment.

Once the young people got up an excursion, with a picnic lunch and chariots, to hear a country preacher who addressed a great multitude on Mount Tabor. This preacher was quite the rage. The people told marvelous tales about him and even the court circle regarded him as a new sensation. I wondered if he was one of the men of Galilee whom you had mentioned. But I never found out. Jason didn't invite me, so I stayed with Salome and Herod and Herodias. After the scandal about the Baptist, they weren't much interested in country preachers.

Some weeks later, when the moon was waning, Herod gave an elaborate fête in the palace gardens. The grounds were illuminated by Greek fire thrown into the waters of the fountains. The floating flames transformed the black basins into gigantic lamps, and in this flickering glare Italian contortionists and acrobats and tight-rope walkers performed.

At first I was shocked by their nakedness. But Jason, seated beside me in the shadows, said that instead of scorning the poor mountebanks, I should pity them. For all we knew, he said, these boys and girls might be the children of aristocrats, or even of the Emperor. In Rome, he told me, unwanted children were left out in the hills for the wolves to eat and sometimes these abandoned creatures were found by human wolves—vagabonds and criminals who took them home and trained them for strange and evil callings.

"I can't understand your world," I said. "It is a terrible place! No Jewish mother could abandon her babies to such a life. No matter how low she had fallen."

"I know," he whispered. "My mother couldn't leave me out on the hill either—even though she tried to. It might have been better if she had."

Somehow I knew that I must comfort this man in his terrible gnawing misery. It was what God had put me in the world for. I put my hands on his cheeks and kissed him.

Then he was on his feet, pulling me up to him. His strong arm was around me as he led me into the shadows. He was returning my kiss—on my lips, my throat, my shoulders—and his kisses were fierce and hard.

"Darling, oh, my darling!" I cried, clinging to him. "You needn't be so fierce—so hurried—I will never run away from you—never!"

He paused and looked at me, and his arms were a tight circle around my body.

"Don't you see?" I said. "You need never be lonely again, ever—it doesn't matter what you've been—"

"You're wrong! It's the only thing that matters!" His arms grew slack and his voice was bitter. "I started as a piece of human garbage—left out on a Roman junk pile—and all my life has been a struggle to keep from going back there."

The fierceness had gone out of him. He sank to the ground with his face turned toward the distant fountains, where the children's bodies glittered above the flickering fire.

"I never knew my mother," his words came moodily. "I hardly knew my father. The only clear memory I have of him is of one night—when I must have been about twelve. I was seated beside him at a great banquet in the barracks of the gladiators. The air was foul with the fumes of torches and there was a great deal of noise.

"Most of the gladiators were roaring drunk; guzzling liquor and gorging themselves until they vomited—trying to forget that they might die the next day. Others scarcely touched the heaping tables, because they hoped to be more fit in the arena. Some, too stupid or calloused to care what happened, tumbled on the floor with the slave women provided for their convenience.

"My father sat at a small table with an older gladiator named Longinus—a man whose life my father once had spared in the arena. They kept me on the bench between them.

"As the night wore on, he placed his hand behind my head and forced me to look at the hoggish couples who wallowed on the floor. 'Look, my son,' he said, with a mirthless smile. 'Look and see how you were created! Your mother was just such a drab as these!'

"I remember that I began to cry. And people stopped to stare at us. A child was the one thing they didn't expect to see at a gladiators' banquet. Longinus growled to my father to shut up. The scene was horrible.

"But my father continued in a low, intense voice. 'I am telling the boy this so that he may remember his destiny when I am gone! I didn't know his mother—I couldn't have told her from any of the other slatterns. The one time I embraced her, I was drunk. But, by the Gods, she remembered me! I shall never forget the dumb look that was on her face when she came to the barracks with her baby. I saw adoration there, not for me, but for the child—for you, son!'

"He told me that my mother had left me out on the hill, as she had left her previous children. But something nagged at her stupid mind and told her that she could not let the child of a prince die that way. So she went back to the hill and brought me to my father.

"And as he held me in his arms, my father felt that the ignorant trull was right. She had inspired him.

"His thick-skinned sword-hand gripped my shoulder as he told me all this and he said, 'I can only find freedom through you, my son! My blood in you can be a prince again! And this I demand of you, that no matter what happens—whether I live or die—that you shall fight by every method to reclaim our lost greatness!' "

Jason repeated his father's words in a voice that was low but excited, the tone he always used when he spoke of how important he might have been. Now his voice went flat.

"My father died the next day. He had been matched against Longinus. It was an honest fight. It had to be, or both men would have been thrown to the lions. Suddenly, though he had suffered no wound, my father collapsed upon the sand. I guess his heart gave out, after the long years of fighting. As I watched, his feeble arm went up in the gesture that asked for mercy. He wanted to live because of me.

"Longinus looked toward the Emperor. But Tiberius reached out a brawny arm and pointed his thumb—down.

"I saw the pleading look on Longinus' face. He hesitated. There were tears on his cheeks. The arena attendants were running forward to split my father's skull with mallets—the death reserved for a coward.

"Longinus' sword flashed down."

Jason had finished his story. The last of the flaming fountains flickered into darkness. We heard Herod ordering the servants to light the torches. I held Jason close and tried to comfort him. But when the flares were ignited, he moved away.

A few days later he was my escort when Herod took the court to his race course outside the city. Now he seemed to be trying to forget everything he had confided. His robes were rich and perfect. His eyebrows had been thinned and his smile was aloof and distant as he glanced toward the royal box, where Salome sat beside her stepfather.

In each race the colors of the charioteers were the same—white, red, blue, and green. Jason explained that these identified the four great racing syndicates in Rome. Herod favored the blue because that was the faction of the reigning emperor.

"I want to bet on the whites," I told Jason.

"Why?" he asked. "The blue is the best bet, but if you want a good long shot, choose the red. It is an exciting color."

"But the whites are your horses!" I said. "I saw you drive them into the city."

His face clouded as he replied, "They are not my horses!" He spoke with undue vehemence. But I continued to smile at him. I knew what I had seen.

"Look, Miriam!" he cajoled. "The white hasn't a chance! They are older than the others, and the horse on the inside trace has a bowed tendon."

"Nevertheless, I want to bet on them!"

"All right," he shrugged. "At least, you'll get good odds."

Perhaps I imagined it, but as the chariots paraded past, I thought a slight signal passed from Jason to the charioteer in white.

I know you don't know much about racing, Father, so I'll try to explain to you. The two center horses are harnessed to the tongue of the chariot, while the outside animals run in leather shafts called traces. On the white chariot the outside horse was in a long trace so that he ran far out from his teammates. He wasn't pulling, he was running free and independently. And his long trace made a leather barrier across the track so that no other chariot could pass.

It was the first time this trick had been seen in Palestine. The shouts from the grandstands were deafening. At first, people thought there had been an accident and that the outside horse had broken his harness. But soon the air was filled with the excited frenzy of those who had backed the white and the curses of those who had bet on the other colors. Then everybody forgot money in their amazement at the skill of the thing. The outside horse swept around the track, keeping close to the outside railing—and the other chariots didn't try to pass for fear of getting entangled and turned over.

Of course, the white won! I turned excitedly to Jason.

"These provincial drivers are amateurs," he shrugged scornfully. "If this race had been run in Rome all the chariots would have had long traces. The green would have run into the white so that the blue could get through. Afterwards the drivers would have shared in the winning purse—and the Emperor's favor."

"But what of the drivers? They wear the ends of the reins wrapped around their bodies—wouldn't such crack-ups be dangerous?"

"Of course," he replied indifferently. "If they were quick, they might cut themselves free with their daggers—or they might be killed. That's the chance you take in Rome."

The odds had been twenty-to-one. I won almost fifty silver shekels, even after the bookmaker had taken his commission.

I soon discovered that, even at Herod's court, a girl can have many friends after she's won fifty shekels. It was astonishing how many of the court ladies were short on spending money. They came to me for little loans—which they never paid back; and by way of compensation, they included me in their conversation, most of which was catty—if not positively evil. They seldom came right out and said anything vicious. But they were full of hints and innuendos. According to them, the King was in love with Salome.

"And, my dear, his interest isn't entirely fatherly," one of them giggled.

I didn't like to hear this, even though I felt it might be true. The King's attitude toward Salome was anything but decorous. Still, the thing they hinted at was perfectly monstrous—and I doubted if even Herod, who had defied the Law by taking his brother's wife, would pile incest on incest by now making love to his stepdaughter.

"Whatever the King may lack," I said, "He is still our King—and the only protection we have from the Romans. And as long as we are members of his household, we owe him our loyalty and our patriotism."

"Listen to her silly preaching!" laughed an Athenian girl named Enid. "Of all people! If Herod wasn't in love with Salome, little Miriam wouldn't be here!"

I didn't like this Enid. She had a long jaw that kept her from being pretty, so she tried to attract attention to her figure. To make sure of this, she walked with her hips thrust out in a most preposterous and vulgar way. She had borrowed more from me than the others. Maybe that was why she was always giving me digs.

"What do you mean?" I flared.

"Oh, please, Miriam!" She glanced over her shoulder at her hips with an air of exaggerated patience and languor. "You of all people shouldn't be naive! Don't you realize that the King brought you here to keep Jason away from Salome?"

"You are absolutely insane!" I retorted. "I never heard of anything so stupid! The King is the King! If he doesn't like Jason, he can send him away!"

"What a dull little thing you are! Herod isn't rude to one who's been favored by Pontius Pilate!"

"But how do I fit into his plans?"

"Darling, are you actually asking me to tell you? I was hoping we could be more delicate. Why do you think the King gave you this lovely room with a window—so accessible from the gardens?"

"Get out!" My face was flaming, "Get out! I won't answer your filthy accusations! I never want to see any of you again!"

Enid strutted toward the door, followed by the others. Their steps were insolent and leisurely.

"All right, we'll go, my dear! There's no need to be shrill. After all it isn't our fault that the King's plan miscarried—and that the Greek prefers Salome. He never goes near you except when he is commanded, and even then he scarcely dares speak—he's so afraid of Salome. No wonder you're jealous!"

When they were gone I threw myself on the couch and cried. I wished

I could go back home to Jerusalem. I longed for a life that was clean and decent. The court and everyone in it was hateful. I wanted you, father. I wanted to crawl in your lap, like a little girl, and to forget everything.

But that afternoon we were ordered to accompany the King to the famous mineral hot baths, south of the city.

I sent word that I was too ill to go to the baths. But they refused to accept my excuses. Queen Herodias herself came to persuade me. Her attitude was almost motherly, and she was so serene and dignified that it was hard to argue with her. She said the baths were good for all sorts of ailments and were bound to make me feel better. Furthermore, she said that the King had sent her to tell me that Jason was waiting. I wondered if she knew that she and I were both pawns in his love game. But I didn't dare ask. I was too discouraged to do anything but submit. I let her take my hand and lead me out to Jason's chariot.

He was driving the Arabians and he looked very handsome. At once he began his amiable chatter.

"Please," I said. "There is no need to be charming. I know that you are with me only because of the King's orders."

His look was pained. "Miriam, you don't understand—"

"I think I do. Your father was a slave and you are a slave—a slave to your ambitions."

I wanted to hurt him. The anger flushed up behind his sunburn. He lashed the horses and the chariot spun forward ahead of the rest of the procession. He didn't draw rein until we had reached the baths.

"Miriam," he said. "You have to believe me!"

"Why should I? I know that you have lied to me. You even told me that these horses weren't yours!"

"In a way, they aren't," he said. "These horses were the property of the White Syndicate. I took them from Rome with me when I retired from racing."

"You stole those horses?" I made my voice scornful. "You *are* dishonest— and more foolhardy than your reckless nature seems capable of being."

"Well, why not!" he exclaimed. "They're my luck! Longinus apprenticed me to a charioteer after my father died, and I won two hundred and thirty-nine victories with these horses in the Circus Maximus. They made me a millionaire!"

"But you are not satisfied with being a millionaire! You must have the love of a princess, even though you have to share that love with her stepfather! You are as evil as they are!"

He restrained me as I started to leave the chariot.

"Please, Miriam!" he begged. "I know you have good reason to be angry. But doesn't the fact that I let my horses win for you mean anything? I had planned to keep that trick up my sleeve."

"I don't doubt it! And I still don't know why you became so generous—I don't want your pity! And I don't want your favors!" I flung myself out of the chariot.

The rest of the royal procession was driving up just then. Salome looked hatefully at me and even the Queen seemed irritated. But Herod was smiling and bland. We went into the baths.

I was relieved to see that the men's and women's quarters were separate. I hadn't known what to expect. As soon as we were in the women's section, Salome and the others threw their clothes off. I found a dark spot in a corner of the steam room and tried to be inconspicuous. The Queen had a pitcher of wine brought to her. It was the first time I had seen her drink. She explained that she did this to increase her perspiration. After a while she and her favorites played ball with a sphere stuffed with feathers. They caught it with their right hands and threw it with their left. Soon the Queen and an Abyssinian girl grabbed for the ball at the same time, and began to wrestle for it.

I clutched a towel around myself and tried to stay out of their way, as they grunted and strained in their efforts to throw each other. But they kept bumping into me and I had the feeling that these accidents were deliberate.

Finally I got away—only to face new tormenters. Salome and her girls were rushing around the room, rolling light metal hoops. I did my best to avoid them. But inevitably, Salome ran her hoop across my feet.

"Excuse me!" she would cry mockingly—then hit me with the stick she used to guide the hoop. "Oh, I'm sorry!" she would laugh.

The other girls were quick to take up the game. No matter where I went, they came toward me screeching, "You clumsy slattern! Get out of our way!"

I was so angry I forgot I didn't have any clothes on. I wanted to hit Salome and pull her hair and throw her on the pavement—even if the other girls all fought on her side. I knew I would be punished, but I didn't care. You can endure just so much. I wrested the stick from her hand and aimed a blow at her.

But before it could land, the other girls surrounded me and with shrieks and shouts, bore me through the great bronze doors to the plunge. They threw me in and leaped in after me. The water was hot. It smelled of sulphur and had a bitter, salty taste. I was ducked several times, then suddenly they let me alone and I crawled out and got dressed. The others, by now, were splashing in the showers or being massaged by the serving women. I slipped out of the building, without waiting for this.

A peasant woman with some donkeys was passing. I asked her to take me back to Tiberias. The road was dusty and the donkeys slow.

It wasn't long before my skin started itching and my eyes watering. From my sandals to my headband, I was feverish. I felt so ill I hardly noticed that a chariot was overtaking us. Jason swung the horses across the path of the donkeys.

"Get down!" he shouted, "Get down, you little fool!"

He was out of the chariot, reaching strong hands up to me.

"You poor little thing, I know what they did to you at the baths—"

"Don't touch me!" One of his arms was beneath my knees, the other around my shoulders. He carried me toward a thicket at the side of the road. The bewildered peasant woman made no effort to stop him. Beneath the shadows of gnarled olive trees the air was close and heavy with the fragrance of blossoming almonds. I could hardly breathe.

"Take off your clothes." He put me down beside a little stream. "You must bathe in fresh water."

"No—!" I backed away from him.

"You little idiot, don't you see their treacherous scheme? If you don't bathe in fresh water after the sulphur plunge, your skin will become blotched and hideous." He gripped my shoulders and shook me roughly. "I'll not have your beauty marred—you are the loveliest thing I've ever seen! Do as I tell you or I'll strip you and throw you in!"

As though reading my thoughts, he suddenly relaxed. His smile was gentle, and his voice tender.

"Don't be afraid. I'll go back down the path and wait."

He kissed my forehead and turned back into the bushes beneath the dark trees.

The brook was cool and refreshing. I lay back on the soft sand and let the waters rush over me. The ripples moved caressingly. All the discomfort and the fever was washed away. A sweet and dreamy lassitude overcame me. I wondered if he was watching from the depths of the thicket. But I didn't think so.

And then I wondered why he didn't come. Perhaps he only protected me as a child is protected. Was this another of his pitying favors? If a man really loved a woman, he could not stay away from her.

There was a stir in the undergrowth. Enid and the simpering Greek, Philo, stood looking at me.

"Oh, excuse us!" tittered Enid. "We saw Jason's chariot, so we sneaked in to see what he was up to. Of course, we didn't dream—!"

She turned as she saw Jason coming toward her.

"Thorry to dithturb your little idyl," lisped Philo.

Jason threw a stone and the intruders ran laughing into the thicket. We both knew they'd make a malicious scandal of what they had seen as soon as they got back to Tiberias.

While Jason turned his back, I put my clothes on and we drove home in worried silence.

That night I didn't go to the dining hall for supper. And no one came to persuade me. As soon as it was dark, I took a dark cloak and what money I had left and slipped out through a side gate. Staying close to the walls in the dark streets, I headed for the fishing quarter at the shores of the Sea of Galilee.

The fishermen's nets, on drying racks, looked like acres of delicate lace in the moonlight. Shadowy figures were removing them. The sky was threatening and we were close to the season of spring rains.

I approached a slight, aristocratic-looking young man who was struggling rather clumsily to fold up some of the nets. He listened sympathetically as I told him that I was the daughter of Caiphas, the High Priest, and that I had to get home to Jerusalem.

"It is a dangerous journey," he said with a kindly smile. "A desperate journey for a young girl. After the waters of the Galilee enter into the Jordan, the course is swift and tortuous. And the eastern shore is peopled with savage Bedouins—"

"I know! But anything is better than Tiberias! If I stay here I'll surely die! I'll pay you anything!"

"It isn't the pay." There was a deprecating smile on his fine Jewish features. "It is just that I am not a boatman. My name is Matthew—I used to be a tax gatherer. So you see, I have not been trained to do anything very useful."

He turned and pointed to a camp fire farther up the beach, where a number of men sat around the flames.

"But some of my friends are fishermen, very good fishermen—Peter and Andrew and James. Our Master teaches us that we must love our neighbors as ourselves—so I am sure that they will help you."

"Oh, if they only would!"

He hurried away toward the camp fire. Something about the man had given me reassurance and a certain feeling of hope.

And then from among the shadows and the foamy nets, I saw Jason's tall figure before me. I turned toward the boats drawn up on the sand. I didn't want to talk to him.

"Don't go, Miriam!"

"I have to—you shouldn't have followed me—"

"If you go, I must go with you. I will be your boatman." He took my hand. "Whither thou goest, I shall go—thy people shall be my people, and thy god, my god."

"Please, don't mock me! Leave me alone!"

"I can never do that, dearest! God knows I have tried not to love you. I was a slave to ambition as you said—but now, I have forgotten everything—but you."

"If I could only believe you!"

The silvery moonlight, through the thick, scudding clouds, cast an uneven causeway across the waters. The far shores of Galilee, the savage shores, were wrapped in beckoning mystery.

"Come!" Jason lifted me into a boat and pushed it into the water. With a hasty movement he picked up the sweep and poled us out of the shallows.

I lay back against the rough wood and looked up toward the dappled heavens. Why did I always surrender? I seemed to have no will when Jason was near me. Still, if he was telling the truth, if he really loved me—

"Was Salome angry?" I asked.

"Furious! She made a terrible scene!"

"Are you sure that you want to leave her? That you don't love her?"

"Love! That woman doesn't know what it is to love! For months she just kept me dangling—simply playing with me."

"It is hard to believe that any woman could do that to you, Jason. You seem so sure of yourself."

"She is a princess," he said bitterly. "And the stakes were high. I learned to gamble when I was a charioteer. Herod is a worthless puppet. Everyone in Rome despises him and Salome is of royal blood. Her husband would be in a position to guarantee the Eastern empire. He might become emperor himself when Tiberius dies—"

"You dreamed of that!"

"Why not! I have a fortune and so has Salome. The throne will be sold by the Praetorian Guard—the palace troops control the empire. But all that is forgotten. Let's not talk about it any more."

I didn't want to talk. I was too happy. Jason raised the sail and little gusts of wind propelled us southward. He came forward and lay beside me. We looked up at the changing sky.

Then, without warning, the squall broke upon us. The sail was split with a roar like a bull. Shredded canvas whipped in the wind as the boat was lashed by the fury of the spring rains.

Jason scrambled to the sweep, struggling awkwardly to keep us from the trough of the waves. I was drenched as I fought to take in the whipping fragments of the tattered sail. Then the whole keel shivered as the craggy nose of a concealed rock forced its way through the splintering wood. The waves closed over us and I felt Jason's arm around me. I sank into a swirl of thunder and darkness.

How long it lasted I will never know exactly. After a time my mind struggled toward consciousness—only to slip back to oblivion again. In these rare, half-lucid moments it seemed that I was again in my room in Herod's palace. Once I seemed to see Jason's face bending over me and feel his hand behind my head. A cup was pressed to my lips and I heard him say, "Drink, Miriam, dearest, you must get strong and well for my sake."

Finally the fever left me and I returned to the consciousness of a bright, sunshiny day. It hadn't been a hallucination. Outside the windows of my room in the palace the trees were in full blossom. But my chamber had the untidiness of a sick room. I crawled from beneath the covers and looked at myself in the steel mirror. It was a thin, drawn face that looked back at me. I rang for the serving maid, but she did not come.

Finally, trembling and pausing to rest at frequent intervals, I managed to wash myself and dress in clean clothes. Then, supporting myself with a hand against the wall, I faltered out into the corridors. There was a littered, deserted look to the halls. The serving women, in untidy dress, gossiped in slatternly clusters. When I talked to them their looks were bold and insolent and their words just barely courteous. They told me that Herod and the entire court had returned to Jerusalem to celebrate the holidays.

I returned to my room to find one of the lesser servants—a girl about as old as I am—putting my gold hairpins in her hair. When she saw me, she made a guilty movement and knocked over the alabaster lamp—the one that Jason had given me. It smashed upon the floor.

I was so angry I snatched a girdle from the wardrobe and began to whip her with it. She dropped to her knees and whined for mercy.

"Stop sniveling!" I said. "And tell me what has happened. Take me to Jason!"

"He has gone—on the day after the Princess and the women's caravan left for Jerusalem. Enid came back here with a message for Jason."

"And?"

"It seemed to disturb him. He had not left your side since the night of the great storm. He put on his traveling cloak. Then he threw it aside. He walked in the gardens, hour after hour. He called for his chariot, then he returned it to the stables. It was not the first message the Princess had sent to him, but he had rejected all the others with curses. Now after many black looks he called for the chariot again and drove away toward Jerusalem."

"And the message?"

The servant whimpered that she did not know any more. So I ordered her to leave me.

Dear God! Was I never to be sure of him? Had Salome capitulated? Had her message said that she would marry him? And had this last surrender been too great a temptation?

I had to know. I got my faded cloak from the wardrobe. My silver still was secure in the secret pocket of the lining. Hurrying to the beach, I asked for the former tax gatherer, Matthew.

"He isn't here," a surly old fisherman told me. "He and his crowd have gone to Jerusalem for the Passover. Bad luck to them!"

"Why do you say that? Matthew seemed kind."

"Oh, yes," the fisherman grumbled. "Very kind. I took my son, Reuben, to Capernaum to be cured of blindness. But on the night we went there, this Matthew and his Master came to Tiberias. That was the miracle—the evil miracle! We missed each other—for no reason at all!"

"This may have been meant to test you!" I was saying anything in an effort to influence him. "You should follow these Galileans. Take your son to Jerusalem! By boat you can be there for the holidays!"

"By boat?" Such a journey had not occurred to him. I kept on talking and offered him silver. He took the money, but it was his love for his boy that decided him.

My thoughts raced ahead as we left the clear waters of Galilee and rushed through overhanging jungles, made lush and foul by the recent floods of the Jordan.

Despite the skill of the fisherman, the boat sometimes stuck on a sand bar. When this happened, he and I would go over the side. The sand eddied around our feet as we pushed the boat back into deeper current. At last the boat whirled into the shallows and I saw the crested helmets of the Romans at the post house. With the last of my silver I bribed an officer to take me up to Jerusalem on the crupper of his horse. We entered the city by the Double Gate. The streets were filled with people shouting hosannahs and waving palm branches. Through the crowd I caught a glimpse of Matthew in a little group of men. They were gathered around a Man wearing a colored robe, who was seated upon a donkey. And for an instant I thought I saw you, Father, standing on the outer stairs of the Temple, smiling approval toward these men.

But this was just a confused impression. Before I could identify you, the cavalryman turned his horse into one of the side streets leading to Herod's palace.

Galba was the officer in charge at the Portal of the Stairs.

"Where is Jason?" I demanded. "Take me to him at once!"

"I'm afraid I can't do that, ladybird. You see, Jason has been arrested—the King caught him in Salome's boudoir."

My heart was leaden with conflicting sorrows. It was quite clear that Jason had betrayed me. He had left me to go to Salome. But hope dies so hard! I still didn't want him to suffer. There must be some explanation for his contradictory behavior.

Late at night I awakened when I heard someone fumbling at the lock on my door. Salome came in. She was flushed and agitated as she blurted: "That swine! That insufferable swine! My stepfather has condemned Jason to the arena! But you, you can save him—"

I mistrusted her and anything she might tell me. It would be best to question her carefully. I asked: "For what has he been condemned?"

"Herod has charged him with violating the sanctity of the women's quarters—with having gone to your room at night in the palace at Tiberias!"

"You know that is a lie!" I cried.

She made no answer. Her shadow fluttered against the walls like a great moth as she strode up and down past the brazier.

"You have brought him to this!" I burst out angrily. "It is all your doing! He didn't leave Tiberias with the court—he stayed with me—until you lured him away with that wretched note you sent by Enid! What did you say in it?"

"I had no pride—only envy," she said finally. "After I'd seen him in your sick room in Tiberias, nursing you, I knew I had to have him even though he didn't love me. So I sent Enid back to tell him that I'd marry him and run away with him to Alexandria."

I spoke harshly to keep back the tears. "Well, you succeeded! Your bargain must have appealed to him—he abandoned me and went to you!"

"He came to me," her face was averted, "to refuse my offer of marriage." She gave me a quick look from the corner of her eyes. "And to tell me he'd never love anyone but you. That's why he was with me when Herod caught us."

"Then why didn't you intercede for Jason? Why didn't you tell Herod the truth?"

"I did." Her laugh was mirthless. "I begged too hard—I told Herod that I loved Jason and for that I must be humiliated by being forced to sit in the arena and see Jason choose between the tiger and the lady *when he knows that you will be the lady behind one door!*"

"But why will *I* be there?"

"Herod could scarcely accuse the Greek of seducing *me*, his stepdaughter! He has shifted the whole scandal to you. So I shall have to sit there and watch the man I love being married to my rival—to you!"

"But suppose there isn't any marriage?" I could scarcely pronounce the words. "Suppose Jason chooses the door that frees the tiger? There is that terrible chance!"

Salome's smile was sly and determined. "That's why I have come here. Chance is going to be eliminated. You and I are going to cheat Herod. We will save Jason."

"Oh, Salome, how?"

"We will save him because we both love him. I am going to give him to you."

My voice was choking. "Oh, Salome, I have been so wrong about you!"

She brushed my embrace aside. "I'm not doing this for you. I've thought of a way to save him—because I can't see him die."

It was three nights ago that we had this conversation. We talked far into the morning. Before she left, I had forgiven Salome all her former slights and cruelties. For she had shown me how to save Jason. I wonder if I could be as self-sacrificing as she. Her love for him is so great that she is willing that he shall marry me—since she says she knows he loves me and that we will be happy together. I kissed her as we parted. Since then I have spent my time writing this long letter to you. I know that it contains many things that ordinarily a daughter would not write to a father. But I have tried to be absolutely truthful, because I want you to know, dearest Father, that in spite of all the doubts and troubles I have gone through, I have done nothing that was wrong.

It is growing late and I am tired. Soon it will be morning. They will come and dress me in a bridal gown. My draperies will be arranged with many golden brooches. They will place flowers in my arms and the flame-colored veil of a Roman bride over my hair. And they will leave me in that little room, next to the room where they will have placed the tiger. As soon as I am alone, I will take one of the golden brooches from my garment. I will open one of my veins with it and let my blood run from beneath the crack in the door, out onto the stone pavements of the dark corridor beneath the seats of the arena.

Before Salome takes her seat beside her stepfather, she will slip down into this corridor. She will see the blood and she will know in which room I am waiting. And she will signal to Jason to open my door.

I am happy, Father, despite my dreadful weariness. I hope that you will forgive me everything that has been reckless and foolish. I am a woman now, but still a little girl. How I wish that I could curl up in your lap and go to sleep! I am tired, but so contented and joyful—I must rest and be beautiful for my beloved. All my dreams will come true tomorrow.

THUS ENDED THE LETTER of Miriam to her father. As I labored over its translation, this Jewish girl of twenty centuries ago became very real to me. I gave all my time to researches concerning Miriam. I had to learn what had happened to her.

The answer was found in the long-sought-for letter of Pontius Pilate to Tiberius. The first paragraph made it obvious that this originally had been dispatched to the Emperor as an explanation of Miriam's manuscript. But during the centuries they had become separated. Pilate's supplement was written in Latin upon two sheets of parchment. The first page read:

"To His Imperial Majesty, Tiberius Caesar, from Pontius Pilate, Procurator of Judea:

"May the Gods preserve Your Majesty! I forward the enclosed document to the Imperial Archives because it has some bearing upon Imperial policy in the Near East.

"As stated in previous reports, the High Priest (to whom the enclosed letter is addressed) has shown great stubbornness in refusing to cooperate in the matter of disposing of a certain Galilean preacher regarded by Your Majesty's Government as a dangerous malcontent. The High Priest was impervious to bribes, and even threats failed to coerce him into making the desired accusations which would enable Rome to crucify the Galilean and still place responsibility for the deed on the Jews.

"But now I am happy to inform Your Majesty that the whole matter has been satisfactorily resolved. Caiphas is a broken man. His will has been completely shattered (indeed, I doubt if he can any longer be considered sane) and is quite incapable of offering any further resistance.

"His transformation was brought about, quite unexpectedly, yesterday, when the Greek, Jason, was forced to choose between the lady and the tiger in Herod's Arena. I watched Caiphas very closely when he made his appearance, as Herod had ordered, in the royal box. His bearing was dignified and aloof. I almost found myself wishing that this well-controlled man was a Roman.

"One of our secret agents had intercepted a letter which the girl, Miriam, had written to her father; so that Caiphas had no way of knowing that his daughter was guiltless of Herod's implications. His trust in her evidently was based upon blind faith.

"Herod looked a trifle embarrassed as he turned to me and asked if I wanted to double my bet on the Greek's chances for survival. Of course, I did. Since I had read Miriam's letter, I felt I was betting on a sure thing. I even smiled to myself as, from the corner of my eye, I saw the Princess make her signal to the Greek to open the right-hand door.

"But I was a fool to trust Salome. The Greek, with his sense of the dramatic, started to pull back the portal very slowly. When it was open about a foot, we saw the sunlight fall on the striped hide and the blinking eyes of the tiger. The Greek seemed doomed. An automatic device made it impossible to push those doors shut, once either of them had started to open. "But the Greek acted with the speed of lightning. As soon as he glimpsed the tiger, he stepped back and pulled open *both* doors. Now he was protected—wedged in the small space between the two open portals—as secure as if he had a big oak shield on each arm.

"The tiger, a finer specimen than any you'd see in Rome, advanced through the doorway on the right.

"And almost simultaneously, the girl, Miriam, looking pale but smiling beneath her bridal veil, came through the doorway on the left.

"For a few seconds the beast and the woman looked at each other. There was no sound in the amphitheater, except her father's sobbing.

"It was the fastest thinking I had ever seen. I did well to bet on the Greek."

THE PAPER FELL from my hand. All the injustice and cruelty of the world seemed summed up in Jason's contemptible stratagem.

I read the second page. Pilate had added the following postscript to his message.

"Despite the Greek's adroitness I'm sure Your Majesty will agree that this Jason was too clever to be permitted to survive. His plot to marry Salome and seize the throne was a definite menace to Roman policy in Palestine and to Your Majesty's security. Since the man was the son of a slave and was not a Roman citizen, it was not difficult to charge him with the theft of the White Syndicate's horses and to condemn him, along with another thief and the Galilean preacher, to be crucified. He admitted under the torture that he had adopted the name of 'Jason' because of its romantic connotations. His real name was Gestos. He was the last of the three to die, and though his sufferings were excruciating, he did not ask for forgiveness."

THE BLIND SPOT
BARRY PEROWNE

The greatest criminal character in literature is, of course, A. J. Raffles, the gentleman jewel thief created by E. W. Hornung at the end of the Victorian era, his first book appearance being in *The Amateur Cracksman* (1899). A few years after the author's death in 1921, the popularity of the character remained at such a high level that the British magazine *The Thriller* asked Barry Perowne, already a regular contributor, to continue the rogue's adventures. After making arrangements with the estate of Hornung, Perowne produced many more stories about Raffles than his creator had, as well as several novels.

Perowne, the pseudonym of Philip Atkey (1908–1985) wrote hundreds of stories and more than 20 novels, many featuring the suave safecracker and his sidekick, Bunny Manders, including *The Return of Raffles* (1933), *Raffles in Pursuit* (1934), *Raffles Under Sentence* (1936), and *Raffles Revisited* (1974), a short story collection.

The exceptionally versatile and prolific Perowne also produced numerous thirty-thousand-word paperback original novellas about Dick Turpin, the notorious highwayman, and Red Jim, the first air detective.

"The Blind Spot," one of the most ingenious stories ever written, was first published in the November 1945 issue of *Ellery Queen's Mystery Magazine*.

THE BLIND SPOT

by Barry Perowne

ANNIXTER LOVED the little man like a brother. He put an arm around the little man's shoulders, partly from affection and partly to prevent himself from falling. He had been drinking earnestly since seven o'clock the previous evening. It was now nudging midnight, and things were a bit hazy. The lobby was full of the thump of hot music; down two steps, there were a lot of tables, a lot of people, a lot of noise. Annixter had no idea what this place was called, or how he had got there, or when. He had been in so many places since seven o'clock the previous evening.

'In a nutshell,' confided Annixter, leaning heavily on the little man, 'a woman fetched you a kick in the face, or fate fetches you a kick in the face. Same thing, really—a woman and fate. So what? So you think it's the finish, an' you go out and get plastered. You get good an' plastered,' said Annixter, 'an' you brood.

'You sit there an' you drink an' you brood—an' in the end you find you've brooded up just about the best idea you ever had in your life! 'At's the way it goes,' said Annixter, 'an' 'at's my philosophy—the harder you kick a playwright, the better he works.'

He gestured with such vehemence that he would have collapsed if the little man hadn't steadied him. The little man was poker-backed, his grip was firm. His mouth was firm, too—a straight line, almost colourless. He wore hexagonal rimless spectacles, a black hard-felt hat, a neat pepper-and-salt suit. He looked pale and prim beside the flushed, rumpled Annixter.

From her counter, the hat-check girl watched them indifferently.

'Don't you think,' the little man said to Annixter, 'you ought to go home now? I've been honoured you should tell me the scenario of your play, but—'

'I had to tell someone,' said Annixter, 'or blow my top! Oh, boy, what a play, what a play! What a murder, eh? That climax—'

The full, dazzling perfection of it struck him again. He stood frowning, considering, swaying a little—then nodded abruptly, groped for the little man's hand, warmly pumphandled it.

'Sorry I can't stick around,' said Annixter, 'I got work to do.'

He crammed his hat on shapelessly, headed on a slightly elliptical course across the lobby, thrust the double doors open with both hands, lurched out into the night.

It was, to his inflamed imagination, full of lights, winking and tilting across the dark. *Sealed Room* by James Annixter. No. *Room Reserved* by James—No, no *Blue Room. Room Blue* by James Annixter—

He stepped, oblivious, off the curb, and a taxi, swinging in toward the place he had just left, skidded with suddenly locked, squealing wheels on the wet road.

Something hit Annixter violently in the chest, and all the lights he had been seeing exploded in his face.

Then there weren't any lights.

Mr. James Annixter, the playwright, was knocked down by a taxi late last night when leaving the Casa Havana. After hospital treatment for shock and superficial injuries, he returned to his home.

THE LOBBY OF the Casa Havana was full of the thump of music; down two steps there were a lot of tables, a lot of people, a lot of noise. The hat-check girl looked wonderingly at Annixter—at the plaster on his forehead, the black sling which supported his left arm.

'My,' said the hat-check girl, 'I certainly didn't expect to see *you* again so soon!'

'You remember me, then?' said Annixter, smiling.

'I ought to,' said the hat-check girl. 'You cost me a night's sleep! I heard those brakes squeal after you went out the door that night—and there was a sort of thud!' She shuddered. 'I kept hearing it all night long. I can still hear it now—a week after! Horrible!'

'You're sensitive,' said Annixter.

'I got too much imagination,' the hat-check girl admitted. 'F'instance, I just *knew* it was you even before I run to the door and see you lying there. That man you was with was standing just outside. "My heavens," I say to him, "it's your friend!" '

'What did he say?' Annixter asked.

'He says, "He's not my friend. He's just someone I met." Funny, eh?'

Annixter moistened his lips.

'How d'you mean,' he said carefully, 'funny? I *was* just someone he'd met.'

'Yes, but—man you been drinking with,' said the hat-check girl, 'killed before your eyes. Because he must have seen it; he went out right after you. You'd think he'd 'a' been interested, at least. But when the taxi driver starts shouting for witnesses, it wasn't his fault, I looks around for that man—an' he's gone!'

Annixter exchanged a glance with Ransome, his producer, who was with him. It was a slightly puzzled, slightly anxious glance. But he smiled, then, at the hat-check girl.

'Not quite "killed before his eyes",' said Annixter. 'Just shaken up a bit, that's all.'

There was no need to explain to her how curious, how eccentric, had been the effect of that 'shaking up' upon his mind.

'If you could 'a' seen yourself lying there with the taxi's lights shining on you—"

'Ah, there's that imagination of yours!' said Annixter.

He hesitated for just an instant, then asked the question he had come to ask—the question which had assumed so profound an importance for him.

He asked, 'That man I was with—who was he?'

The hat-check girl looked from one to the other. She shook her head.

'I never saw him before,' she said, 'and I haven't seen him since.'

Annixter felt as though she had struck him in the face. He had hoped, hoped desperately, for a different answer; he had counted on it.

Ransome put a hand on his arm, restrainingly.

'Anyway,' said Ransome, 'as we're here, let's have a drink.'

They went down the two steps into the room where the band thumped. A waiter led them to a table, and Ransome gave him an order.

'There was no point in pressing that girl,' Ransome said to Annixter. 'She doesn't know the man, and that's that. My advice to you, James, is: Don't worry. Get your mind on something else. Give yourself a chance. After all, it's barely a week since—'

'A week!' Annixter said. 'Hell, look what I've done in that week! The whole of the first two acts, and the third act right up to that crucial point— the climax of the whole thing: the solution: the scene that the play stands or falls on! It would have been done, Bill—the whole play, the best thing I ever did in my life—it would have been finished two days ago if it hadn't been for this—' he knuckled his forehead—'this extraordinary blind spot, this damnable little trick of memory!'

'You had a very rough shaking up—'

'That?' Annixter said contemptuously. He glanced down at the sling on his arm. 'I never even felt it; it didn't bother me. I woke up in the ambulance with my play as vivid in my mind as the moment the taxi hit me—more so, maybe, because I was stone cold sober then, and knew what I had. A winner—a thing that just couldn't miss!'

'If you'd rested,' Ransome said, 'as the doc told you, instead of sitting up in bed there scribbling night and day—'

'I had to get it on paper. Rest?' said Annixter, and laughed harshly. 'You don't get rest when you've got a thing like that. That's what you live for—if you're a playwright. That *is* living! I've lived eight whole lifetimes, in those eight characters, during the past five days. I've lived so utterly in them, Bill, that it wasn't till I actually came to write that last scene that I realized what I'd lost! Only my whole play, that's all! How was Cynthia stabbed in that windowless room into which she had locked and bolted herself? How did the killer get to her? *How was it done?*

'Hell,' Annixter said, 'scores of writers, better men than I am, have tried to put that sealed room murder over—and never quite done it convincingly: never quite got away with it: been overelaborate, phoney! I had it—heaven help me, *I* had it! Simple, perfect, glaringly obvious when you've once seen it! And it's my whole play—the curtain rises on that sealed room and falls on it! That was my revelation—*how it was done!* That was what I got, by the way of playwright's compensation, because a woman I thought I loved kicked me in the face—I brooded up the answer to the sealed room! And a taxi knocked it out of my head!'

He drew a long breath.

'I've spent two days and two nights, Bill, trying to get that idea back— *how it was done!* It won't come. I'm a competent playwright; I know my job; I could finish my play, but it'd be like all those others—not quite right, phoney! It wouldn't be *my play!* But there's a little man walking around this city somewhere—a little man with hexagonal glasses—who's got my idea in his head! He's got it because I told it to him. I'm going to find that little man, and get back what belongs to me! I've got to! Don't you see that, Bill? I've *got to!'*

> *If the gentleman who, at the Casa Havana on the night of January 27th so patiently listened to a playwright's outlining of an idea for a drama will communicate with the Box No. below, he will hear of something to his advantage.*

A LITTLE MAN who had said, 'He's not my friend. He's just someone I met—'

A little man who'd seen an accident but hadn't waited to give evidence—

The hat-check girl had been right. There *was* something a little queer about that.

A little queer?

During the next few days, when the advertisements he'd inserted failed to bring any reply, it began to seem to Annixter very queer indeed.

His arm was out of its sling now, but he couldn't work. Time and again, he sat down before his almost completed manuscript, read it through with close, grim attention, thinking, 'It's *bound* to come back this time!'—only to find himself up against that blind spot again, that blank wall, that maddening hiatus in his memory.

He left his work and prowled the streets; he haunted bars and saloons; he rode for miles on 'buses and subways, especially at the rush hours. He saw a million faces, but the face of the little man with hexagonal glasses he did not see.

The thought of him obsessed Annixter. It was infuriating, it was unjust, it was torture to think that a little, ordinary, chance-met citizen was walking blandly around somewhere with the last link of his, the celebrated James Annixter's, play—the best thing he'd ever done—locked away in his head. And with no idea of what he had: without the imagination, probably, to appreciate what he had! And certainly with no idea of what it meant to Annixter!

Or *had* he some idea? Was he, perhaps, not quite so ordinary as he'd seemed? Had he seen those advertisements, drawn from them tortuous inferences of his own? Was he holding back with some scheme for shaking Annixter down for a packet?

The more Annixter thought about it, the more he felt that the hat-check girl had been right, that there was something very queer indeed about the way the little man had behaved after the accident.

Annixter's imagination played around the man he was seeking, tried to probe into his mind, conceived reasons for his fading away after the accident, for his failure to reply to the advertisements.

Annixter's was an active and dramatic imagination. The little man who had seemed so ordinary began to take on a sinister shape in Annixter's mind—

But the moment he actually saw the little man again, he realized how absurd it was. It was so absurd that it was laughable. The little man was so respectable; his shoulders were so straight; his pepper-and-salt suit was so neat; his black hard-felt hat was set so squarely on his head—

The doors of the subway train were just closing when Annixter saw him, standing on the platform with a briefcase in one hand, a folded evening paper under his other arm. Light from the train shone on his prim, pale face; his hexagonal spectacles flashed. He turned toward the exit as Annixter lunged for the closing doors of the train, squeezed between them on to the platform.

Craning his head to see above the crowd, Annixter elbowed his way through, ran up the stairs two at a time, put a hand on the little man's shoulder.

'Just a minute,' Annixter said. 'I've been looking for you.'

The little man checked instantly, at the touch of Annixter's hand. Then he turned his head and looked at Annixter. His eyes were pale behind the hexagonal, rimless glasses—a pale grey. His mouth was a straight line, almost colourless.

Annixter loved the little man like a brother. Merely finding the little man was a relief so great that it was like the lifting of a black cloud from his spirits. He patted the little man's shoulder affectionately.

'I've got to talk to you,' said Annixter. 'It won't take a minute. Let's go somewhere.'

The little man said, 'I can't imagine what you want to talk to me about.'

He moved slightly to one side, to let a woman pass. The crowd from the train had thinned, but there were still people going up and down the stairs. The little man looked, politely inquiring, at Annixter.

Annixter said, 'Of course you can't, it's so damned silly! But it's about that play—'

'Play?'

Annixter felt a faint anxiety.

'Look,' he said, 'I was drunk that night—I was very, very drunk! But looking back, my impression is that you were dead sober. You were, weren't you?'

'I've never been drunk in my life.'

'Thank heaven for that!' said Annixter. 'Then you won't have any difficulty in remembering the little point I want you to remember.' He grinned, shook his head. 'You had me going there, for a minute, I thought—'

'I don't know what you thought,' the little man said. 'But I'm quite sure you're mistaking me for somebody else. I haven't any idea what you're talking about. I never saw you before in my life. I'm sorry. Good night."

He turned and started up the stairs. Annixter stared after him. He couldn't believe his ears. He stared blankly after the little man for an instant, then a rush of anger and suspicion swept away his bewilderment. He raced up the stairs, caught the little man by the arm.

'Just a minute,' said Annixter. 'I may have been drunk, but—'

'That,' the little man said, 'seems evident. Do you mind taking your hand off me?'

Annixter controlled himself. 'I'm sorry,' he said. 'Let me get this right, though. You say you've never seen me before. Then you weren't at the Casa Havana on the 27th—somewhere between ten o'clock and midnight? You didn't have a drink or two with me, and listen to an idea for a play that had just come into my mind?'

The little man looked steadily at Annixter.

'I've told you,' the little man said. 'I've never set eyes on you before.'

'You didn't see me get hit by a taxi?' Annixter pursued, tensely. 'You didn't say to the hat-check girl, "He's not my friend. He's just someone I met"?'

'I don't know what you're talking about,' the little man said sharply.

He made to turn away, but Annixter gripped his arm again.

'I don't know,' Annixter said, between his teeth, 'anything about your private affairs, and I don't want to. You may have had some good reason for wanting to duck giving evidence as a witness of that taxi accident. You may have some good reason for this act you're pulling on me, now. I don't know and I don't care. But it is an act. You *are* the man I told my play to!

'I want you to tell that story back to me as I told it to you; I have my reasons—personal reasons, of concern to me and me only. I want you to tell the story back to me—that's all I want! I don't want to know who you are, or anything about you, *I just want you to tell me that story!*'

'You ask,' the little man said, 'an impossibility, since I never heard it.'

Annixter kept an iron hold on himself.

He said, 'Is it money? Is this some sort of a hold-up? Tell me what you want; I'll give it to you. Lord help me, I'd go so far as to give you a share in the play! That'll mean real money. I know, because I know my business. And maybe—maybe,' said Annixter, struck by a sudden thought, '*you* know it, too! Eh?'

'You're insane or drunk!' the little man said.

With a sudden movement, he jerked his arm free, raced up the stairs. A train was rumbling in, below. People were hurrying down. He weaved and dodged among them with extraordinary celerity.

He was a small man, light, and Annixter was heavy. By the time he reached the street, there was no sign of the little man. He was gone.

WAS THE IDEA, Annixter wondered, to steal his play? By some wild chance did the little man nurture a fantastic ambition to be a dramatist? Had he, perhaps, peddled his precious manuscripts in vain, for years, around the managements? Had Annixter's play appeared to him as a blinding flash of hope in the gathering darkness of frustration and failure: something he had imagined he could safely steal because it had seemed to him the random inspiration of a drunkard who by morning would have forgotten he had ever given birth to anything but a hangover?

That, Annixter thought, would be a laugh! That would be irony—

He took another drink. It was his fifteenth since the little man with the hexagonal glasses had given him the slip, and Annixter was beginning to reach the stage where he lost count of how many places he had had drinks in tonight. It was also the stage, though, where he was beginning to feel better, where his mind was beginning to work.

He could imagine just how the little man must have felt as the quality of the play he was being told, with hiccups, gradually had dawned upon him.

'This is mine!' the little man would have thought. 'I've got to have this. He's drunk, he's soused, he's bottled—he'll have forgotten every word of it by the morning! Go on! Go on, mister! Keep talking!'

That was a laugh, too—the idea that Annixter would have forgotten his play by the morning. Other things Annixter forgot, unimportant things; but never in his life had he forgotten the minutest detail that was to his purpose as a playwright. Never! Except once, because a taxi had knocked him down.

Annixter took another drink. He needed it. He was on his own now. There wasn't any little man with hexagonal glasses to fill that blind spot for him. The little man was gone. He was gone as though he'd never been. To hell with him! Annixter had to fill in that blind spot himself. He *had* to do it—somehow!

He had another drink. He had quite a lot more drinks. The bar was crowded and noisy, but he didn't notice the noise—till someone came up and slapped him on the shoulder. It was Ransome.

Annixter stood up, leaning with his knuckles on the table.

'Look, Bill,' Annixter said, 'how about this? Man forgets an idea, see? He wants to get it back—gotta get it back! Idea comes from inside, works back inward. How's that?'

He swayed, peering at Ransome.

'Better have a little drink,' said Ransome. 'I'd need to think that out.'

'I,' said Annixter, '*have* thought it out!' He crammed his hat shapelessly on to his head. 'Be seeing you, Bill. I got work to do!'

He started, on a slightly tacking course, for the door—and his apartment.

It was Joseph, his 'man,' who opened the door of his apartment to him, some twenty minutes later. Joseph opened the door while Annixter's latchkey was still describing vexed circles around the lock.

'Good evening, sir,' said Joseph.

Annixter stared at him. 'I didn't tell you to stay the night.'

'I hadn't any reason for going out, sir,' Joseph explained. He helped Annixter off with his coat. 'I rather enjoy a quiet evening in, once in a while.'

'You got to get out of here,' said Annixter.

'Thank you, sir,' said Joseph. 'I'll go and throw a few things into a bag.'

Annixter went into his big living-room-study, poured himself a drink.

The manuscript of his play lay on the desk. Annixter, swaying a little, glass in hand, stood frowning down at the untidy slack of yellow paper, but he didn't begin to read. He waited until he heard the outer door click shut behind Joseph, then he gathered up his manuscript, the decanter and a glass, and the cigarette box. Thus laden, he went into the hall, walked across it to the door of Joseph's room.

There was a bolt on the inside of this door and the room was the only one in the apartment which had no window—both facts which made the room the only one suitable to Annixter's purpose.

With his free hand, he switched on the light.

It was a plain little room, but Annixter noticed, with a faint grin, that the bedspread and the cushion in the worn basket-chair were both blue. Appropriate, he thought—a good omen. *Room Blue* by James Annixter—

Joseph had evidently been lying on the bed, reading the evening paper; the paper lay on the rumpled quilt, and the pillow was dented. Beside the head of the bed, opposite the door, was a small table littered with shoe-brushes and dusters.

Annixter swept this paraphernalia on to the floor. He put his stack of manuscript, the decanter and glass and cigarette box on the table, and went across and bolted the door. He pulled the basket-chair up to the table and sat down, lighted a cigarette.

He leaned back in the chair, smoking, letting his mind ease into the atmosphere he wanted—the mental atmosphere of Cynthia, the woman in his play, the woman who was afraid, so afraid that she had locked and bolted herself into a windowless room, a sealed room.

'This is how she sat,' Annixter told himself, 'just as I'm sitting now: in a room with no windows, the door locked and bolted. Yet he got at her. He got at her with a knife—in a room with no windows, the door remaining locked and bolted on the inside. *How was it done?*'

There was a way in which it could be done. He, Annixter, had thought of that way: he had conceived it, invented it—and forgotten it. His idea had produced the circumstances. Now, deliberately, he had reproduced the circumstances, that he might think back to the idea. He had put his person in the position of the victim, that his mind might grapple with the problem of the murderer.

It was very quiet: not a sound in the room, the whole apartment.

For a long time, Annixter sat unmoving. He sat unmoving until the intensity of his concentration began to waver. Then he relaxed. He pressed the palms of his hands to his forehead for a moment, then reached for the decanter. He splashed himself a strong drink. He had almost recovered what he sought; he had felt it close, had been on the very verge of it.

'Easy,' he warned himself, 'take it easy. Rest. Relax. Try again in a minute.'

He looked around for something to divert his mind, picked up the paper from Joseph's bed.

At the first words that caught his eye, his heart stopped.

The woman, in whose body were found three knife wounds, any of which might have been fatal, was in a windowless room, the only door to which was locked and bolted on the inside. These elaborate precautions appear to have been habitual with her, and no doubt she went in continual fear of her life, as the police know her to have been a persistent and pitiless blackmailer.

*Apart from the unique problem set by the circumstance of the
sealed room is the problem of how the crime could have gone undiscovered for so long a period, the doctor's estimate from the condition
of the body as some twelve to fourteen days.*

Twelve to fourteen days—

Annixter read back over the remainder of the story; then let the paper
fall to the floor. The pulse was heavy in his head. His face was grey.
Twelve to fourteen days? He could put it closer than that. *It was exactly
thirteen nights ago that he had sat in the Casa Havana and told a little
man with hexagonal glasses how to kill a woman in a sealed room!*

Annixter sat very still for a minute. Then he poured himself a drink. It was
a big one, and he needed it. He felt a strange sense of wonder, of awe.

They had been in the same boat, he and the little man—thirteen nights
ago. They had both been kicked in the face by a woman. One, as a result,
had conceived a murder play. The other had made the play reality!

'And I actually, tonight, offered him a share!' Annixter thought. 'I talked
about "real" money!'

That was a laugh. All the money in the universe wouldn't have made that
little man admit that he had seen Annixter before—that Annixter had told
him the plot of a play about how to kill a woman in a sealed room! Why, he,
Annixter, was the one person in the world who could denounce that little
man! Even if he couldn't tell them, because he had forgotten, just how he
had told the little man the murder was to be committed, he could still put
the police on the little man's track. He could describe him, so that they could
trace him. And once on his track, the police would ferret out links, almost
inevitably, with the dead woman.

A queer thought—that he, Annixter, was probably the only menace,
the only danger, to the little prim, pale man with the hexagonal spectacles. The only menace—as, of course, the little man must know very
well.

He must have been very frightened when he had read that the playwright who had been knocked down outside the Casa Havana had only
received 'superficial injuries.' He must have been still more frightened

when Annixter's advertisements had begun to appear. *What must he have felt tonight, when Annixter's hand had fallen on his shoulder?*

A curious idea occurred, now, to Annixter. It was from tonight, precisely from tonight, that he was a danger to that little man. He was, because of the inferences the little man must infallibly draw, a deadly danger as from the moment the discovery of the murder in the sealed room was published. The discovery had been published tonight and the little man had a paper under his arm—

Annixter's was a lively and resourceful imagination.

It was, of course, just in the cards that, when he'd lost the little man's trail at the subway station, the little man might have turned back, picked up *his*, Annixter's trail.

And Annixter had sent Joseph out. He was, it dawned slowly upon Annixter, alone in the apartment—alone in a windowless room, with the door locked and bolted on the inside, at his back.

Annixter felt a sudden, icy and wild panic.

He half rose, but it was too late.

It was too late, because at that moment the knife slid, thin and keen and delicate, into his back, fatally, between the ribs.

Annixter's head bowed slowly forward until his cheek rested on the manuscript of his play. He made only one sound—a queer sound, indistinct, yet identifiable as a kind of laughter.

The fact was, Annixter had just remembered.

THE MYSTERIOUS CARD
CLEVELAND MOFFETT

American dramatist, journalist, novelist, and short story writer
Cleveland Moffett (1863–1926) spent many years in Europe
as a correspondent for several newspapers and, even after he
returned to live permanently in the United States, set many of
his stories abroad, mostly in France. He lived his last years and
died in Paris.

Moffett made several major contributions to the mystery
genre, notably the novel *Through the Wall* (1909), which is a
Haycraft-Queen Cornerstone; *True Tales from the Archives of
the Pinkertons* (1897), accounts which are almost as fictional-
ized as those written by Allen, Frank, and Myron Pinkerton
years earlier; *The Seine Mystery* (1925), about an American
journalist in Paris who does amateur sleuthing; and *The Bish-
op's Purse* (1913), co-authored with Oliver Herford, a humorous tale of robbery and impersonation set in England.

His most famous story, and one of the two most famous
riddle stories of all time (along with "The Lady, or the Tiger?")
is "The Mysterious Card." It was first published in *The Black
Cat* magazine in 1895, and was followed the next year by "The
Mysterious Card Unveiled." The enterprising Boston publisher Small, Maynard and Company then put both stories together in 1912 with a gimmick: the second part was sealed and
the purchaser was promised a refund if the book was returned
to the bookseller with its seal unbroken.

THE MYSTERIOUS CARD

BY CLEVELAND MOFFETT

RICHARD BURWELL, of New York, will never cease to regret that the French language was not made a part of his education.

This is why:

On the second evening after Burwell arrived in Paris, feeling lonely without his wife and daughter, who were still visiting a friend in London, his mind naturally turned to the theater. So, after consulting the daily amusement calendar, he decided to visit the *Folies Bergère*, which he had heard of as one of the notable sights. During an intermission he went into the beautiful garden, where gay crowds were strolling among the flowers, and lights, and fountains. He had just seated himself at a little three-legged table, with a view to enjoying the novel scene, when his attention was attracted by a lovely woman, gowned strikingly, though in perfect taste, who passed near him, leaning on the arm of a gentleman. The only thing that he noticed about this gentleman was that he wore eye-glasses.

Now Burwell had never posed as a captivator of the fair sex, and could scarcely credit his eyes when the lady left the side of her escort and, turning back as if she had forgotten something, passed close by him, and deftly placed a card on his table. The card bore some French words written in purple ink, but, not knowing that language, he was unable to make out their meaning. The lady paid no further heed to him, but, rejoining the gentleman with the eye-glasses, swept out of the place with the grace and dignity of a princess. Burwell remained staring at the card.

Needless to say, he thought no more of the performance or of the other attractions about him. Everything seemed flat and tawdry compared with the radiant vision that had appeared and disappeared so mysteriously. His one desire now was to discover the meaning of the words written on the card.

Calling a fiacre, he drove to the Hôtel Continental, where he was staying. Proceeding directly to the office and taking the manager aside, Burwell asked if he would be kind enough to translate a few words of French into English. There were no more than twenty words in all.

"Why, certainly," said the manager, with French politeness, and cast his eyes over the card. As he read, his face grew rigid with astonishment, and, looking at his questioner sharply, he exclaimed: "Where did you get this, monsieur?"

Burwell started to explain, but was interrupted by: "That will do, that will do. You must leave the hotel."

"What do you mean?" asked the man from New York, in amazement.

"You must leave the hotel now—to-night—without fail," commanded the manager excitedly.

Now it was Burwell's turn to grow angry, and he declared heatedly that if he wasn't wanted in this hotel there were plenty of others in Paris where he would be welcome. And, with an assumption of dignity, but piqued at heart, he settled his bill, sent for his belongings, and drove up the Rue de la Paix to the Hôtel Bellevue, where he spent the night.

The next morning he met the proprietor, who seemed to be a good fellow, and, being inclined now to view the incident of the previous evening from its ridiculous side, Burwell explained what had befallen him, and was pleased to find a sympathetic listener.

"Why, the man was a fool," declared the proprietor. "Let me see the card; I will tell you what it means." But as he read, his face and manner changed instantly.

"This is a serious matter," he said sternly. "Now I understand why my confrère refused to entertain you. I regret, monsieur, but I shall be obliged to do as he did."

"What do you mean?"

"Simply that you cannot remain here."

With that he turned on his heel, and the indignant guest could not prevail upon him to give any explanation.

"We'll see about this," said Burwell, thoroughly angered.

It was now nearly noon, and the New Yorker remembered an engagement to lunch with a friend from Boston, who, with his family, was stopping at the

Hôtel de l'Alma. With his luggage on the carriage, he ordered the *cocher* to drive directly there, determined to take counsel with his countryman before selecting new quarters. His friend was highly indignant when he heard the story—a fact that gave Burwell no little comfort, knowing, as he did, that the man was accustomed to foreign ways from long residence abroad.

"It is some silly mistake, my dear fellow; I wouldn't pay any attention to it. Just have your luggage taken down and stay here. It is a nice, homelike place, and it will be very jolly, all being together. But, first, let me prepare a little 'nerve settler' for you."

After the two had lingered a moment over their Manhattan cocktails, Burwell's friend excused himself to call the ladies. He had proceeded only two or three steps when he turned, and said: "Let's see that mysterious card that has raised all this row."

He had scarcely withdrawn it from Burwell's hand when he started back, and exclaimed:—

"Great God, man! Do you mean to say—this is simply—"

Then, with a sudden movement of his hand to his head, he left the room.

He was gone perhaps five minutes, and when he returned his face was white.

"I am awfully sorry," he said nervously; "but the ladies tell me they—that is, my wife—she has a frightful headache. You will have to excuse us from the lunch."

Instantly realizing that this was only a flimsy pretense, and deeply hurt by his friend's behavior, the mystified man arose at once and left without another word. He was now determined to solve this mystery at any cost. What could be the meaning of the words on that infernal piece of pasteboard?

Profiting by his humiliating experiences, he took good care not to show the card to any one at the hotel where he now established himself,—a comfortable little place near the Grand Opera House.

All through the afternoon he thought of nothing but the card, and turned over in his mind various ways of learning its meaning without getting himself into further trouble. That evening he went again to the *Folies Bergère* in the hope of finding the mysterious woman, for he was now more than ever anxious to discover who she was. It even occurred to him that she might be one of those beautiful Nihilist conspirators, or, perhaps, a Russian spy, such as he had read of in novels. But he failed to find her, either then or on the three subsequent evenings which he passed in the same place. Meanwhile the card was burning in his pocket like a hot coal. He dreaded the thought of meeting any one that he knew, while this horrible cloud hung over him. He bought a French-English dictionary and tried to pick out the meaning word by word, but failed. It was all Greek to him. For the first time in his life, Burwell regretted that he had not studied French at college.

After various vain attempts to either solve or forget the torturing riddle, he saw no other course than to lay the problem before a detective agency. He accordingly put his case in the hands of an *agent de la sûreté* who was recommended as a competent and trustworthy man. They had a talk together in a private room, and, of course, Burwell showed the card. To his relief, his adviser at least showed no sign of taking offense. Only he did not and would not explain what the words meant.

"It is better," he said, "that monsieur should not know the nature of this document for the present. I will do myself the honor to call upon monsieur to-morrow at his hotel, and then monsieur shall know everything."

"Then it is really serious?" asked the unfortunate man.

"Very serious," was the answer.

The next twenty-four hours Burwell passed in a fever of anxiety. As his mind conjured up one fearful possibility after another he deeply regretted that he had not torn up the miserable card at the start. He even seized it,— prepared to strip it into fragments, and so end the whole affair. And then his Yankee stubbornness again asserted itself, and he determined to see the thing out, come what might.

"After all," he reasoned, "it is no crime for a man to pick up a card that a lady drops on his table."

Crime or no crime, however, it looked very much as if he had committed some grave offense when, the next day, his detective drove up in a carriage, accompanied by a uniformed official, and requested the astounded American to accompany them to the police headquarters.

"What for?" he asked.

"It is only a formality," said the detective; and when Burwell still protested the man in uniform remarked: "You'd better come quietly, monsieur; you will have to come, anyway."

An hour later, after severe cross-examination by another official, who demanded many facts about the New Yorker's age, place of birth, residence, occupation, etc., the bewildered man found himself in the Conciergerie prison. Why he was there or what was about to befall him Burwell had no means of knowing; but before the day was over he succeeded in having a message sent to the American Legation, where he demanded immediate protection as a citizen of the United States. It was not until evening, however, that the Secretary of Legation, a consequential person, called at the prison. There followed a stormy interview, in which the prisoner used some strong language, the French officers gesticulated violently and talked very fast, and the Secretary calmly listened to both sides, said little, and smoked a good cigar.

"I will lay your case before the American minister," he said as he rose to go, "and let you know the result to-morrow."

"But this is an outrage. Do you mean to say—" Before he could finish, however, the Secretary, with a strangely suspicious glance, turned and left the room.

That night Burwell slept in a cell.

The next morning he received another visit from the non-committal Secretary, who informed him that matters had been arranged, and that he would be set at liberty forthwith.

"I must tell you, though," he said, "that I have had great difficulty in accomplishing this, and your liberty is granted only on condition that you leave the country within twenty-four hours, and never under any conditions return."

Burwell stormed, raged, and pleaded; but it availed nothing. The Secretary was inexorable, and yet he positively refused to throw any light upon the causes of this monstrous injustice.

"Here is your card," he said, handing him a large envelope closed with the seal of Legation. "I advise you to burn it and never refer to the matter again."

That night the ill-fated man took the train for London, his heart consumed by hatred for the whole French nation, together with a burning desire for vengeance. He wired his wife to meet him at the station, and for a long time debated with himself whether he should at once tell her the sickening truth. In the end he decided that it was better to keep silent. No sooner, however, had she seen him than her woman's instinct told her that he was laboring under some mental strain. And he saw in a moment that to withhold from her his burning secret was impossible, especially when she began to talk of the trip they had planned through France. Of course no trivial reason would satisfy her for his refusal to make this trip, since they had been looking forward to it for years; and yet it was impossible now for him to set foot on French soil.

So he finally told her the whole story, she laughing and weeping in turn. To her, as to him, it seemed incredible that such overwhelming disasters could have grown out of so small a cause, and, being a fluent French scholar, she demanded a sight of the fatal piece of pasteboard. In vain her husband tried to divert her by proposing a trip through Italy. She would consent to nothing until she had seen the mysterious card which Burwell was now convinced he ought long ago to have destroyed. After refusing for awhile to let her see it, he finally yielded. But, although he had learned to dread the consequences of showing that cursed card, he was little prepared for what followed. She read it, turned pale, gasped for breath, and nearly fell to the floor.

"I told you not to read it," he said; and then, growing tender at the sight of her distress, he took her hand in his and begged her to be calm. "At least tell me what the thing means," he said. "We can bear it together; you surely can trust me."

But she, as if stung by rage, pushed him from her and declared, in a tone such as he had never heard from her before, that never, never again would she live with him. "You are a monster!" she exclaimed. And those were the last words he heard from her lips.

Failing utterly in all efforts at reconciliation, the half-crazed man took the first steamer for New York, having suffered in scarcely a fortnight more than in all his previous life. His whole pleasure trip had been ruined, he had failed to consummate important business arrangements, and now he saw his home broken up and his happiness ruined. During the voyage he scarcely left his stateroom, but lay there prostrated with agony. In this black despondency the one thing that sustained him was the thought of meeting his partner, Jack Evelyth, the friend of his boyhood, the sharer of his success, the bravest, most loyal fellow in the world. In the face of even the most damning circumstances, he felt that Evelyth's rugged common sense would evolve some way of escape from this hideous nightmare. Upon landing at New York he hardly waited for the gang-plank to be lowered before he rushed on shore and grasped the hand of his partner, who was waiting on the wharf.

"Jack," was his first word, "I am in dreadful trouble, and you are the only man in the world who can help me."

An hour later Burwell sat at his friend's dinner table, talking over the situation.

Evelyth was all kindness, and several times as he listened to Burwell's story his eyes filled with tears.

"It does not seem possible, Richard," he said, "that such things can be; but I will stand by you; we will fight it out together. But we cannot strike in the dark. Let me see this card."

"There is the damned thing," Burwell said, throwing it on the table.

Evelyth opened the envelope, took out the card, and fixed his eyes on the sprawling purple characters.

"Can you read it?" Burwell asked excitedly.

"Perfectly," his partner said. The next moment he turned pale, and his voice broke. Then he clasped the tortured man's hand in his with a strong grip. "Richard," he said slowly, "if my only child had been brought here dead it would not have caused me more sorrow than this does. You have brought me the worst news one man could bring another."

His agitation and genuine suffering affected Burwell like a death sentence.

"Speak, man," he cried; "do not spare me. I can bear anything rather than this awful uncertainty. Tell me what the card means."

Evelyth took a swallow of brandy and sat with head bent on his clasped hands.

"No, I can't do it: there are some things a man must not do."

Then he was silent again, his brows knitted. Finally he said solemnly:—

"No, I can't see any other way out of it. We have been true to each other all our lives; we have worked together and looked forward to never separating. I would rather fail and die than see this happen. But we have got to separate, old friend; we have got to separate."

They sat there talking until late into the night. But nothing that Burwell could do or say availed against his friend's decision. There was nothing for it but that Evelyth should buy his partner's share of the business or that Burwell buy out the other. The man was more than fair in the financial proposition he made; he was generous, as he always had been, but his determination was inflexible; the two must separate. And they did.

With his old partner's desertion, it seemed to Burwell that the world was leagued against him. It was only three weeks from the day on which he had received the mysterious card; yet in that time he had lost all that he valued in the world,—wife, friends, and business. What next to do with the fatal card was the sickening problem that now possessed him.

He dared not show it; yet he dared not destroy it. He loathed it; yet he could not let it go from his possession. Upon returning to his house he locked the accursed thing away in his safe as if it had been a package of dynamite or a bottle of deadly poison. Yet not a day passed that he did not open the drawer where the thing was kept and scan with loathing the mysterious purple scrawl.

In desperation he finally made up his mind to take up the study of the language in which the hateful thing was written. And still he dreaded the approach of the day when he should decipher its awful meaning.

One afternoon, less than a week after his arrival in New York, as he was crossing Twenty-third Street on the way to his French teacher, he saw a carriage rolling up Broadway. In the carriage was a face that caught his attention like a flash. As he looked again he recognized the woman who had been the cause of his undoing. Instantly he sprang into another cab and ordered the driver to follow after. He found the house where she was living. He called there several times; but always received the same reply, that she was too much engaged to see any one. Next he was told that she was ill, and on the following day the servant said she was much worse. Three physicians had been summoned in consultation. He sought out one of these and told him it was a matter of life or death that he see this woman. The doctor was a kindly man and promised to assist him. Through his influence, it came about that on that very night Burwell stood by the bedside of this mysterious woman. She was beautiful still, though her face was worn with illness.

"Do you recognize me?" he asked tremblingly, as he leaned over the bed, clutching in one hand an envelope containing the mysterious card. "Do you remember seeing me at the *Folies Bergère* a month ago?"

"Yes," she murmured, after a moment's study of his face; and he noted with relief that she spoke English.

"Then, for God's sake, tell me, what does it all mean?" he gasped, quivering with excitement.

"I gave you the card because I wanted you to—to—"

Here a terrible spasm of coughing shook her whole body, and she fell back exhausted.

An agonizing despair tugged at Burwell's heart. Frantically snatching the card from its envelope, he held it close to the woman's face.

"Tell me! Tell me!"

With a supreme effort, the pale figure slowly raised itself on the pillow, its fingers clutching at the counterpane.

Then the sunken eyes fluttered—forced themselves open—and stared in stony amazement upon the fatal card, while the trembling lips moved noiselessly, as if in an attempt to speak. As Burwell, choking with eagerness, bent his head slowly to hers, a suggestion of a smile flickered across the woman's face. Again the mouth quivered, the man's head bent nearer and nearer to hers, his eyes riveted upon the lips. Then, as if to aid her in deciphering the mystery, he turned his eyes to the card.

With a cry of horror he sprang to his feet, his eyeballs starting from their sockets. Almost at the same moment the woman fell heavily upon the pillow.

Every vestige of the writing had faded! The card was blank!

The woman lay there dead.

THE MYSTERIOUS CARD UNVEILED

BY CLEVELAND MOFFETT

No PHYSICIAN WAS ever more scrupulous than I have been, during my thirty years of practice, in observing the code of professional secrecy; and it is only for grave reasons, partly in the interests of medical science, largely as a warning to intelligent people, that I place upon record the following statements.

One morning a gentleman called at my offices to consult me about some nervous trouble. From the moment I saw him, the man made a deep impression on me, not so much by the pallor and worn look of his face as by a certain intense sadness in his eyes, as if all hope had gone out of his life. I wrote a prescription for him, and advised him to try the benefits of an ocean voyage. He seemed to shiver at the idea, and said that he had been abroad too much, already.

As he handed me my fee, my eye fell upon the palm of his hand, and I saw there, plainly marked on the Mount of Saturn, a cross surrounded by two circles. I should explain that for the greater part of my life I have been a constant and enthusiastic student of palmistry. During my travels in the Orient, after taking my degree, I spent months studying this fascinating art at the best sources of information in the world. I have read everything published on palmistry in every known language, and my library on the subject is perhaps the most complete in existence. In my time I have examined at least fourteen thousand palms, and taken casts of many of the more interesting of them. But I had never seen such a palm as this; at least, never but once, and the horror of the case was so great that I shudder even now when I call it to mind.

"Pardon me," I said, keeping the patient's hand in mine, "would you let me look at your palm?"

I tried to speak indifferently, as if the matter were of small consequence, and for some moments I bent over the hand in silence. Then taking a magnifying glass from my desk, I looked at it still more closely. I was not mistaken; here was indeed the sinister double circle on Saturn's mount, with the cross inside,—a marking so rare as to portend some stupendous destiny of good or evil, more probably the later.

I saw that man was uneasy under my scrutiny, and, presently, with some hesitation, as if mustering courage, he asked: "Is there anything remarkable about my hand?"

"Yes," I said, "there is. Tell me, did not something very unusual, something very horrible, happen to you about ten or eleven years ago?"

I saw by the way the man started that I had struck near the mark, and, studying the stream of fine lines that crossed his lifeline from the Mount of Venus, I added: "Were you not in some foreign country at the time?"

The man's face blanched, but he only looked at me steadily out of those mournful eyes. Now I took his other hand, and compared the two, line by line, mount by mount, noting the short square fingers, the heavy thumb, with amazing willpower in its upper joint, and gazing again and again at that ominous sign on Saturn.

"Your life has been strangely unhappy, your years have been clouded by some evil influence."

"My God," he said weakly, sinking into a chair, "how can you know these things?"

"It is easy to know what one sees," I said, and tried to draw him out about his past, but the words seemed to stick in his throat.

"I will come back and talk to you again," he said, and he went away without giving me his name or any revelation of his life.

Several times he called during subsequent weeks, and gradually seemed to take on a measure of confidence in my presence. He would talk freely of his physical condition, which seemed to cause him much anxiety. He even insisted upon my making the most careful examination of all his organs, especially of his eyes which, he said, had troubled him at various times. Upon making the usual tests, I found that he was suffering from a most uncommon form of color blindness, that seemed to vary in its manifestations, and to be connected with certain hallucinations or abnormal mental states which recurred periodically, and about which I had great difficulty in persuading him to speak. At each visit I took occasion to study his hand anew, and each reading of the palm gave me stronger conviction that here was a life mystery that would abundantly repay any pains taken in unraveling it.

While I was in this state of mind, consumed with a desire to know more of my unhappy acquaintance and yet not daring to press him with questions, there came a tragic happening that revealed to me with startling suddenness the secret I was bent on knowing. One night, very late,—in fact it was about four o'clock in the morning,—I received an urgent summons to the bedside of a man who had been shot. As I bent over him I saw that it was my friend, and for the first time I realized that he was a man of wealth and position, for he lived in a beautifully furnished house filled with art treasures and looked after by a retinue of servants. From one of these I learned that he was Richard Burwell, one of New York's most respected citizens—in fact, one of her best-known philanthropists, a man who for years had devoted his life and fortune to good works among the poor.

But what most excited my surprise was the presence in the house of two officers, who informed me that Mr. Burwell was under arrest, charged with murder. The officers assured me that it was only out of deference to his well-known standing in the community that the prisoner had been allowed the privilege of receiving medical treatment in his own home; their orders were peremptory to keep him under close surveillance.

Giving no time to further questionings, I at once proceeded to examine the injured man, and found that he was suffering from a bullet wound in the back at about the height of the fifth rib. On probing for the bullet, I found that it had lodged near the heart, and decided that it would be exceedingly dangerous to try to remove it immediately. So I contented myself with administering a sleeping potion.

As soon as I was free to leave Burwell's bedside I returned to the officers and obtained from them details of what had happened. A woman's body had been found a few hours before, shockingly mutilated, on Water Street, one of the dark ways in the swarming region along the river front. It had been found at about two o'clock in the morning by some printers from the office of the *Courier des Etats Unis*, who, in coming from their work, had heard cries of distress and hurried to the rescue. As they drew near they saw a man spring away from something huddled on the sidewalk, and plunge into the shadows of the night, running from them at full speed.

Suspecting at once that here was the mysterious assassin so long vainly sought for many similar crimes, they dashed after the fleeing man, who darted right and left through the maze of dark streets, giving out little cries like a squirrel as he ran. Seeing that they were losing ground, one of the printers fired at the fleeing shadow, his shot being followed by a scream of pain, and hurrying up they found a man writhing on the ground. The man was Richard Burwell.

The news that my sad-faced friend had been implicated in such a revolting occurrence shocked me inexpressibly, and I was greatly relieved the next day to learn from the papers that a most unfortunate mistake had been made. The evidence given before the coroner's jury was such as to abundantly exonerate Burwell from all shadow of guilt. The man's own testimony, taken at his bedside, was in itself almost conclusive in his favor. When asked to explain his presence so late at night in such a part of the city, Burwell stated that he had spent the evening at the Florence Mission, where he had made an address to some unfortunates gathered there, and that later he had gone with a young missionary worker to visit a woman living on Frankfort Street, who was dying of consumption. This statement was borne out by the missionary worker himself, who testified that Burwell had been most tender in his ministrations to the poor woman and had not left her until death had relieved her sufferings.

Another point which made it plain that the printers had mistaken their man in the darkness, was the statement made by all of them that, as they came running up, they had overheard some words spoken by the murderer, and that these words were in their own language, French. Now it was shown conclusively that Burwell did not know the French language, that indeed he had not even an elementary knowledge of it.

Another point in his favor was a discovery made at the spot where the body was found. Some profane and ribald words, also in French, had been scrawled in chalk on the door and doorsill, being in the nature of a coarse defiance to the police to find the assassin, and experts in handwriting who were called testified unanimously that Burwell, who wrote a refined, scholarly hand, could never have formed those misshapen words.

Furthermore, at the time of his arrest no evidence was found on the clothes or person of Burwell, nothing in the nature of bruises or bloodstains that would tend to implicate him in the crime. The outcome of the matter was that he was honorably discharged by the coroner's jury, who were unanimous in declaring him innocent, and who brought in a verdict that the unfortunate woman had come to her death at the hand of some person or persons unknown.

On visiting my patient late on the afternoon of the second day I saw that his case was very grave, and I at once instructed the nurses and attendants to prepare for an operation. The man's life depended upon my being able to extract the bullet, and the chance of doing this was very small. Mr. Burwell realized that his condition was critical, and, beckoning me to him, told me that he wished to make a statement he felt might be his last. He spoke with agitation which was increased by an unforeseen happening. For just then a servant entered the room and whispered to me that there was a gentleman downstairs who insisted upon seeing me, and who urged business of great importance. This message the sick man overheard, and lifting himself with an effort, he said excitedly: "Tell me, is he a tall man with glasses?"

The servant hesitated.

"I knew it; you cannot deceive me; that man will haunt me to my grave. Send him away, doctor; I beg of you not to see him."

Humoring my patient, I sent word to the stranger that I could not see him, but in an undertone, instructed the servant to say that the man might call at my office the next morning. Then, turning to Burwell, I begged him to compose himself and save his strength for the ordeal awaiting him.

"No, no," he said, "I need my strength now to tell you what you must know to find the truth. You are the only man who has understood that there has been some terrible influence at work in my life. You are the only man competent to study out what that influence is, and I have made provision in my will that you shall do so after I am gone. I know that you will heed my wishes?"

The intense sadness of his eyes made my heart sink; I could only grip his hand and remain silent.

"Thank you. I was sure I might count on your devotion. Now, tell me, doctor, you have examined me carefully, have you not?"

I nodded.

"In every way known to medical science?"

I nodded again.

"And have you found anything wrong with me,—I mean, besides this bullet, anything abnormal?"

"As I have told you, your eyesight is defective; I should like to examine your eyes more thoroughly when you are better."

"I shall never be better; besides it isn't my eyes; I mean myself, my soul,—you haven't found anything wrong there?"

"Certainly not; the whole city knows the beauty of your character and your life."

"Tut, tut; the city knows nothing. For ten years I have lived so much with the poor that people have almost forgotten my previous active life when I was busy with money-making and happy in my home. But there is a man out West, whose head is white and whose heart is heavy, who has not forgotten, and there is a woman in London, a silent, lonely woman, who has not forgotten. The man was my partner, poor Jack Evelyth; the woman was my wife. How can a man be so cursed, doctor, that his love and friendship bring only misery to those who share it? How can it be that one who has in his heart only good thoughts can be constantly under the shadow of evil? This charge of murder is only one of several cases in my life where, through no fault of mine, the shadow of guilt has been cast upon me.

"Years ago, when my wife and I were perfectly happy, a child was born to us, and a few months later, when it was only a tender, helpless little thing that its mother loved with all her heart, it was strangled in its cradle, and we never knew who strangled it, for the deed was done one night when there was absolutely no one in the house but my wife and myself. There was no doubt about the crime, for there on the tiny neck were the finger marks where some cruel hand had closed until life went.

"Then a few years later, when my partner and I were on the eve of fortune, our advance was set back by the robbery of our safe. Some one opened it in the night, some one who knew the combination, for it was the work of no burglar, and yet there were only two persons in the world who knew that combination, my partner and myself. I tried to be brave when these things happened, but as my life went on it seemed more and more as if some curse were on me.

"Eleven years ago I went abroad with my wife and daughter. Business took me to Paris, and I left the ladies in London, expecting to have them join me in a few days. But they never did join me, for the curse was on me still, and before I had been forty-eight hours in the French capital something happened that completed the wreck of my life. It doesn't seem possible, does it, that a simple white card with some words scrawled on it in purple ink could effect a man's undoing? And yet that was my fate. The card was given me by a beautiful woman with eyes like stars. She is dead long ago, and why she wished to harm me I never knew. You must find that out.

"You see I did not know the language of the country, and, wishing to have the words translated,—surely that was natural enough,—I showed the card to others. But no one would tell me what it meant. And, worse than that, wherever I showed it, and to whatever person, there evil came upon me quickly. I was driven from one hotel after another; an old acquaintance turned his back on me; I was arrested and thrown into prison; I was ordered to leave the country."

The sick man paused for a moment in his weakness, but with an effort forced himself to continue:—

"When I went back to London, sure of comfort in the love of my wife, she too, on seeing the card, drove me from her with cruel words. And when finally, in deepest despair, I returned to New York, dear old Jack, the friend of a lifetime, broke with me when I showed him what was written. What the words were I do not know, and suppose no one will ever know, for the ink has faded these many years. You will find the card in my safe with other papers. But I want you, when I am gone, to find out the mystery of my life; and—and—about my fortune, that must be held until you have decided. There is no one who needs my money as much as the poor in this city, and I have bequeathed it to them unless—"

In an agony of mind, Mr. Burwell struggled to go on, I soothing and encouraging him.

"Unless you find what I am afraid to think, but—but—yes, I must say it,—that I have not been a good man, as the world thinks, but have—O doctor, if you find that I have unknowingly harmed any human being, I want that person, or these persons to have my fortune. Promise that."

Seeing the wild light in Burwell's eyes, and the fever that was burning him, I gave the promise asked of me, and the sick man sank back calmer.

A little later, the nurse and attendants came for the operation. As they were about to administer the ether, Burwell pushed them from him, and insisted on having brought to his bedside an iron box from the safe.

"The card is here," he said, laying his trembling hand upon the box, "you will remember your promise!"

Those were his last words, for he did not survive the operation.

Early the next morning I received this message: "The stranger of yesterday begs to see you;" and presently a gentleman of fine presence and strength of face, a tall, dark-complexioned man wearing glasses, was shown into the room.

"Mr. Burwell is dead, is he not?" were his first words.

"Who told you?"

"No one told me, but I know it, and I thank God for it."

There was something in the stranger's intense earnestness that convinced me of his right to speak thus, and I listened attentively.

"That you may have confidence in the statement I am about to make, I will first tell you who I am;" and he handed me a card that caused me to lift my eyes in wonder, for it bore a very great name, that of one of Europe's most famous savants.

"You have done me much honor, sir," I said with respectful inclination.

"On the contrary you will oblige me by considering me in your debt, and by never revealing my connection with this wretched man. I am moved to speak partly from considerations of human justice, largely in the interest of medical science. It is right for me to tell you, doctor, that your patient was beyond question the Water Street assassin."

"Impossible!" I cried.

"You will not say so when I have finished my story, which takes me back to Paris, to the time, eleven years ago, when this man was making his first visit to the French capital."

"The mysterious card!" I exclaimed.

"Ah, he has told you of his experience, but not of what befell the night before, when he first met my sister."

"Your sister?"

"Yes, it was she who gave him the card, and, in trying to befriend him, made him suffer. She was in ill health at the time, so much so that we had left our native India for extended journeyings. Alas! we delayed too long, for my sister died in New York, only a few weeks later, and I honestly believe her taking off was hastened by anxiety inspired by this man."

"Strange," I murmured, "how the life of a simple New York merchant could become entangled with that of a great lady of the East."

"Yet so it was. You must know that my sister's condition was due mainly to an over fondness for certain occult investigations, from which I had vainly tried to dissuade her. She had once befriended some adepts, who, in return, had taught her things about the souls he had better have left unlearned. At various times while with her I had seen strange things happen, but I never realized what unearthly powers were in her until that night in Paris. We were returning from a drive in the Bois; it was about ten o'clock, and the city lay beautiful around us as Paris looks on a perfect summer's night. Suddenly my sister gave a cry of pain and put her hand to her heart. Then, changing from French to the language of our country, she explained to me quickly that something frightful was taking place there, where she pointed her finger across the river, that we must go to the place at once—the driver must lash his horses—every second was precious.

"So affected was I by her intense conviction, and such confidence had I in my sister's wisdom, that I did not oppose her, but told the man to drive as she directed. The carriage fairly flew across the bridge, down the Boulevard St. Germain, then to the left, threading its way through the narrow streets that lie along the Seine. This way and that, straight ahead here, a turn there, she directing our course, never hesitating, as if drawn by some unseen power, and always urging the driver on to greater speed. Finally, we came to a black-mouthed, evil-looking alley, so narrow and roughly paved that the carriage could scarcely advance.

" 'Come on!' my sister cried, springing to the ground; 'we will go on foot, we are nearly there. Thank God, we may yet be in time.'

"No one was in sight as we hurried along the dark alley, and scarcely a light was visible, but presently a smothered scream broke the silence, and, touching my arm, my sister exclaimed:—

" 'There, draw your weapon, quick, and take the man at any cost!'

"So swiftly did everything happen after that that I hardly know my actions, but a few minutes later I held pinioned in my arms a man whose blows and writhings had been all in vain; for you must know that much exercise in the jungle had made me strong of limb. As soon as I had made the fellow fast I looked down and found moaning on the ground a poor woman, who explained with tears and broken words that the man had been in the very act of strangling her. Searching him I found a long-bladed knife of curious shape, and keen as a razor, which had been brought for what horrible purpose you may perhaps divine.

"Imagine my surprise, on dragging the man back to the carriage, to find, instead of the ruffianly assassin I expected, a gentleman as far as could be judged from face and manner. Fine eyes, white hands, careful speech, all the signs of refinement, and the dress of a man of means.

" 'How can this be?' I said to my sister in our own tongue as we drove away, I holding my prisoner on the opposite seat where he sat silent.

" 'It is a *kulos*-man,' she said, shivering, 'it is a fiend-soul. There are a few such in the whole world, perhaps two or three in all.'

" 'But he has a good face.'

" 'You have not seen his real face yet; I will show it to you, presently.'

"In the strangeness of these happenings and the still greater strangeness of my sister's words, I had all but lost the power of wonder. So we sat without further word until the carriage stopped at the little chateau we had taken near the Parc Monceau.

"I could never properly describe what happened that night; my knowledge of these things is too limited. I simply obeyed my sister in all that she directed, and kept my eyes on this man as no hawk ever watched its prey. She began by questioning him, speaking in a kindly tone which I could ill understand. He seemed embarrassed, dazed, and professed to have no knowledge of what had occurred, or how he had come where we found him. To all my inquiries as to the woman or the crime he shook his head blankly, and thus aroused my wrath.

" 'Be not angry with him, brother; he is not lying, it is the other soul.'

"She asked him about his name and country, and he replied without hesitation that he was Richard Burwell, a merchant from New York, just arrived in Paris, traveling for pleasure in Europe with his wife and daughter. This seemed reasonable, for the man spoke English, and, strangely enough, seemed to have no knowledge of French, although we both remembered hearing him speak French to the woman.

" 'There is no doubt,' my sister said, 'It is indeed a *kulos*-man; It knows that I am here, that I am Its master. Look, look!' she cried sharply, at the same time putting her eyes so close to the man's face that their fierce light seemed to burn into him. What power she exercised I do not know, nor whether some words she spoke, unintelligible to me, had to do with what followed, but instantly there came over this man, this pleasant-looking, respectable American citizen, such a change as is not made by death worms gnawing in a grave. Now there was a fiend groveling at her feet, a foul, sin-stained fiend.

" 'Now you see the demon-soul,' said my sister. 'Watch It writhe and struggle; it has served me well, brother, sayest thou not so, the lore I gained from our wise men?'

"The horror of what followed chilled my blood; nor would I trust my memory were it not that there remained and still remains plain proof of all that I affirm. This hideous creature, dwarfed, crouching, devoid of all resemblance to the man we had but now beheld, chattering to us in curious old-time French, poured out such horrid blasphemy as would have blanched the cheek of Satan, and made recital of such evil deeds as never mortal ear gave heed to. And as she willed my sister checked It or allowed It to go on. What it all meant was more than I could tell. To me it seemed as if these tales of wickedness had no connection with our modern life, or with the world around us, and so I judged presently from what my sister said.

" 'Speak of the later time, since thou wast in this clay.'

"Then I perceived that the creature came to things of which I knew: It spoke of New York, of a wife, a child, a friend. It told of strangling the child, of robbing the friend; and was going on to tell God knows what other horrid deeds when my sister stopped It.

" 'Stand as thou didst in killing the little babe, stand, stand!' and once more she spoke some words unknown to me. Instantly the demon sprang forward, and, bending Its clawlike hands, clutched them ground some little throat that was not there,—but I could see it in my mind. And the look on its face was a blackest glimpse of hell.

" 'And now stand as thou didst in robbing the friend, stand, stand;' and again came the unknown words, and again the fiend obeyed.

" 'These we will take for future use,' said my sister. And bidding me watch the creature carefully until she should return, she left the room, and, after none too short an absence, returned bearing a black box that was an apparatus for photography, and something more besides,—some newer, stranger kind of photography that she had learned. Then, on a strangely fashioned card, a transparent white card, composed of many layers of finest Oriental paper, she took the pictures of the creature in those two creeping poses. And when it all was done, the card seemed as white as before, and empty of all meaning until one held it up and examined it intently. Then the pictures showed. And between the two there was a third picture, which somehow seemed to show, at the same time, two faces in one, two souls, my sister said, the kindly visaged man we first had seen, and then the fiend.

"Now my sister asked for pen and ink and I gave her my pocket pen which was filled with purple ink. Handing this to the *kulos*-man she bade him write under the first picture: 'Thus I killed my babe.' And under the second picture: 'Thus I robbed my friend.' And under the third, the one that was between the other two: 'This is the soul of Richard Burwell.' An odd thing about this writing was that it was in the same old French the creature had used in speech, and yet Burwell knew no French.

"My sister was about to finish with the creature when a new idea took her, and she said, looking at It as before:—'Of all thy crimes which one is the worst? Speak, I command thee!'

"Then the fiend told how once It had killed every soul in a house of holy women and buried the bodies in a cellar under a heavy door.

" 'Where was the house?'

" 'At No. 19 Rue Picpus, next to the old graveyard.'

" 'And when was this?'

"Here the fiend seemed to break into fierce rebellion, writhing on the floor with hideous contortions, and pouring forth words that meant nothing to me, but seemed to reach my sister's understanding, for she interrupted from time to time, with quick, stern words that finally brought It to subjection.

" 'Enough,' she said, 'I know all,' and then she spoke some words again, her eyes fixed as before, and the reverse change came. Before us stood once more the honest-looking, fine-appearing gentleman, Richard Burwell, of New York.

" 'Excuse me, madame,' he said, awkwardly, but with deference; 'I must have dosed a little. I am not myself to-night.'

" 'No,' said my sister, 'you have not been yourself to-night.'

"A little later I accompanied the man to the Continental Hotel, where he was stopping, and, returning to my sister, I talked with her until late into the night. I was alarmed to see that she was wrought to a nervous tension that augured ill for her health. I urged her to sleep, but she would not.

" 'No,' she said, 'think of the awful responsibility that rests upon me.' And then she went on with her strange theories and explanations, of which I understood only that here was a power for evil more terrible than a pestilence, menacing all humanity.

" 'Once in many cycles it happens,' she said, 'that a *kulos*-soul pushes itself within the body of a new-born child, when the pure soul waiting to enter is delayed. Then the two live together through that life, and this hideous principle of evil has a chance upon the earth. It is my will, as I feel it my duty, to see this poor man again. The chances are that he will never know us, for the shock of this night to his normal soul is so great as to wipe out memory.'

"The next evening, about the same hour, my sister insisted that I should go with her to the *Folies Bergère*, a concert garden, none too well frequented, and when I remonstrated, she said: 'I must go,—It is there,' and the words sent a shiver through me.

"We drove to this place, and passing into the garden, presently discovered Richard Burwell seated at a little table, enjoying the scene of pleasure, which was plainly new to him. My sister hesitated a moment what to do, and then, leaving my arm, she advanced to the table and dropped before Burwell's eyes the card she had prepared. A moment later, with a look of pity on her beautiful face, she rejoined me and we went away. It was plain he did not know us."

To so much of the savant's strange recital I had listened with absorbed interest, though without a word, but now I burst in with questions.

"What was your sister's idea in giving Burwell the card?" I asked.

"It was in the hope that she might make the man understand his terrible condition, that is, teach the pure soul to know its loathsome companion."

"And did her effort succeed?"

"Alas! it did not; my sister's purpose was defeated by the man's inability to see the pictures that were plain to every other eye. It is impossible for the *kulos*-man to know his own degradation."

"And yet this man has for years been leading a most exemplary life?"

My visitor shook his head. "I grant you there has been improvement, due largely to experiments I have conducted upon him according to my sister's wishes. But the fiend soul was never driven out. It grieves me to tell you, doctor, that not only was this man the Water Street assassin, but he was the mysterious murderer, the long-sought-for mutilator of women, whose red crimes have baffled the police of Europe and America for the past ten years."

"You know this," said I starting up, "and yet did not denounce him?"

"It would have been impossible to prove such a charge, and besides, I had made oath to my sister that I would use the man only for these soul-experiments. What are his crimes compared with the great secret of knowledge I am now able to give the world?"

"A secret of knowledge?"

"Yes," said the savant, with intense earnestness, "I may tell you now, doctor, what the whole world will know, ere long, that it is possible to compel every living person to reveal the innermost secrets of his or her life, so long as memory remains, for memory is only the power of producing in the brain material pictures that may be projected externally by the thought rays and made to impress themselves upon the photographic plate, precisely as ordinary pictures do."

"You mean," I exclaimed, "that you can photograph the two principles of good and evil that exist in us?"

"Exactly that. The great truth of a dual soul existence, that was dimly apprehended by one of your Western novelists, has been demonstrated by me in the laboratory with my camera. It is my purpose, at the proper time, to entrust this precious knowledge to a chosen few who will perpetuate it and use it worthily."

"Wonderful, wonderful!" I cried, "and now tell me, if you will, about the house on the Rue Picpus. Did you ever visit the place?"

"We did, and found that no buildings had stood there for fifty years, so we did not pursue the search."[1]

"And the writing on the card, have you any memory of it, for Burwell told me that the words have faded?"

"I have something better than that; I have a photograph of both card and writing, which my sister was careful to take. I had a notion that the ink in my pocket pen would fade, for it was a poor affair. This photograph I will bring you tomorrow."

"Bring it to Burwell's house," I said.

THE NEXT MORNING the stranger called as agreed upon.

"Here is the photograph of the card," he said.

"And here is the original card," I answered, breaking the seal of the envelope I had taken from Burwell's iron box. "I have waited for your arrival to look at it. Yes, the writing has indeed vanished; the card seems quite blank."

"Not when you hold it this way," said the stranger, and as he tipped the card I saw such a horrid revelation as I can never forget. In an instant I realized how the shock of seeing that card had been too great for the soul of wife or friend to bear. In these pictures was the secret of a cursed life. The resemblance to Burwell was unmistakable, the proof against him was overwhelming. In looking upon that piece of pasteboard the wife had seen

---

1. Years later, some workmen in Paris, making excavations in the Rue Picpus, came upon a heavy door buried under a mass of debris, under an old cemetery. On lifting the door they found a vault-like chamber in which were a number of female skeletons, and graven on the walls were blasphemous words written in French, which experts declared dated from fully two hundred years before. They also declared this handwriting identical with that found on the door at the Water Street murder in New York. Thus we may deduce a theory of fiend reincarnation; for it would seem clear, almost to the point of demonstration, that this murder of the seventeenth century was the work of the same evil soul that killed the poor woman on Water Street towards the end of the nineteenth century.

a crime which the mother could never forgive, the partner had seen a crime which the friend could never forgive. Think of a loved face suddenly melting before your eyes into a grinning skull, then into a mass of putrefaction, then into the ugliest fiend of hell, leering at you, distorted with all the marks of vice and shame. That is what I saw, that is what they had seen!

"Let us lay these two cards in the coffin," said my companion impressively, "we have done what we could."

Eager to be rid of the hateful piece of pasteboard (for who could say that the curse was not still clinging about it?), I took the strange man's arm, and together we advanced into the adjoining room where the body lay. I had seen Burwell as he breathed his last, and knew that there had been a peaceful look on his face as he died. But now, as we laid the two white cards on the still breast, the savant suddenly touched my arm, and pointing to the dead man's face, now frightfully distorted, whispered:—"See, even in death It followed him. Let us close the coffin quickly."

KARMESIN AND THE METER
Gerald Kersh

A prolific short story writer and novelist, Gerald Kersh (1911–1968) probably wrote across too great a spectrum to have acquired as wide a readership as his talent deserved. Perhaps his best-known works were *Fowler's End* (1957), a novel of crime set in a part of London where bathtubs are considered effete and which houses a movie theater, "a place where thugs relax between felonies," and *Night and the City* (1938), the tragic story of an idealistic pimp.

In no arena did his charismatic wit excel as greatly as in his short-short stories about Karmesin, one of whose exploits is included in this volume even though the ending is clearly described. No, the riddle here is even greater than the failure of an author to supply a satisfying ending to a single story.

Karmesin appeared in seventeen episodes in all. The roguish adventures of this master thief are narrated in the first person and include such feats as stealing the crown jewels from the Tower of London and the nefarious acquisition of a William Shakespeare manuscript. The character, a favorite of Rex Stout, Winston Churchill, Basil Rathbone, and Henry Miller, was played by Erich von Stroheim for a 1956 television movie titled *Orient Express: Man of Many Skins*.

Here is the riddle for "Karmesin and the Meter," which was first published in the winter 1937/38 issue of *Courier*: Was Karmesin the world's greatest thief, or its most outrageous liar?

KARMESIN AND THE METER

BY GERALD KERSH

BOP! WENT MY GAS RING and extinguished itself. In permutations and combinations of six adjectives and three nouns, I blasted and I damned the bodies and souls of the Gas Companies. Karmesin was at this moment sitting at my table. He had, in front of him, a tin tobacco box, full of cigarette ends; with his usual deliberation, he quietly extracted the tobacco which he put into a saucer, and threw the torn papers back into the box. He could probably see in the dark. The failure of the gas did not disturb him. As I paused for breath I heard the faint crackling of the tiny pieces of paper and dried tobacco, and the ponderous deliberate voice of Karmesin, demanding in an elephantine mutter:—

"What seems to be upsetting you?"

"The gas," I said, "I haven't got another penny."

"Yes," said Karmesin, "It is irritating how little gas one gets for one's penny. Nevertheless, my young friend, you must learn to be philosophical. Light a candle."

"And how the devil," I said, "can I cook an egg with a candle?"

"Eat it raw," said Karmesin; and crackle! crackle! went another cigarette. "Have you got any cigarette papers?"

"No."

"*Chort vizmi!*" bellowed Karmesin.

"Chew it," I said malignantly, pointing to the tobacco.

"All right," said Karmesin. "Do not imagine that it is so easy to defeat a man like me. When you are my age, my young friend, you will learn a little philosophy. Calm, balance, and a faculty for objective reasoning, these things are necessary in this life—"

. . . I have mentioned Karmesin; that powerful personality; that immense old man with his air of shattered magnificence. I wish you could have met him—Karmesin, with his looming chest and unfathomable abdomen, still excellently dressed in a suit of sound blue serge; with the strong, cropped skull and the massive purple face; the tattered white eyebrows and the heavy yellowish eyes as large as plums; the vast Nietzsche moustache, light brown with tobacco-smoke, which lay beneath his nose like a hibernating squirrel, concealing his mouth and stirring like a living thing as he breathed upon it—Karmesin the greatest criminal, or the greatest liar of his time . . .

"Listen," I said, "Say one cut a piece of cardboard to the size of a penny—"

"No," said Karmesin. "It would be a waste of time. I know a man who tried that once. Not merely did it fail to work, but it also jammed the mechanism of the gas meter; he had to confess to his landlord. To failure was added humiliation. He was a young man like you—"

"Was that one of *your* great fiascos?"

"My friend," said Karmesin, "I do not indulge in fiascos. I have a creative mind, a grasp of facts, and an almost incredible foresight. When I swindle a gas company, it is not for pennies but for thousands of pounds."

"Thousands of pounds?" I asked.

"Well, francs, anyway."

"Do you mean to say you have actually got money out of a gas company?"

"It was simple," said Karmesin. "But then, all truly great crimes are simple. One may always rely upon the ordinary man's inability to see what is obvious. What is a genius? A man with a firm grasp of the obvious, plus a creative touch. Thus, in the winter of 19— when I found myself ill and temporarily short of money in Paris, I discovered a means whereby I could obtain free heating and light, and furthermore get heavily paid for doing so. In cash! 10,000 francs. That put me on my feet. It was with the capital that I obtained from the gas company that I was able to go to Brazil and perpetrate perhaps one of the most artistic diamond robberies of all time—"

Karmesin is, as I have said, quite supreme; if not as a criminal, then as a story teller. It is quite easy to associate that immense, genial, aged, and philosophical man of mystery with almost any kind of lawlessness. He has a way with him. You tend to believe every word that finds its way through his cigarette-stained Nietzsche moustache. You cannot help liking the man. You feel that if you are to be swindled or otherwise taken in, you would rather have Karmesin do it than anybody else. He is this kind of man: if he stole your wallet, you would say, "I'm sorry there's not more in it." But, how could such a man stoop to crime? Or, on the other hand, to lying?

"I never know when to believe you," I said.

"My dear sir," said Karmesin, "I comfort myself with the memory of this incident, whenever the gas fails.

"This is how it was. I found myself in Paris. In all businesses one has one's ups and downs. This was a barren period. It had been necessary for me, on account of certain unforeseen circumstances, to leave Geneva in a great hurry, and to travel in a third–class carriage across France. French third–class carriages even in these times are bad enough, but before the War they were worse. It is scarcely extraordinary, therefore, that I contracted a severe attack of influenza which stretched me on my back in my little room, off the Boulevard Ornano.

"I may say that I carried French papers in the name of Charles Lavoisier. I spoke French like a Parisian. That is nothing. I speak eleven languages like a native, even Finnish.

"You must imagine me therefore lying upon my bed of suffering in this abominable little room in the atrocious cold of one of the severest winters on record. My rent was paid for a quarter in advance, and I had a certain amount of credit with the local tradesmen, but all my portable property was gone. I had no money, and the room was very cold. This is the quality of Parisian blankets; they are of some diaphanous substance lightly sprinkled with fluff; when you cover yourself with them all the fluff flies into your nostrils leaving nothing but a sort of woven basis, so thin that no bug dares to set foot on them for fear of falling through and breaking his legs. Even in the midst of my fever my brain began to work. Picture to yourself one unquenchable spark of genius fighting single-handed against the fogs and the vapours of influenza—that was the brain of Karmesin! Outside, the snow came down, melted and turned to ice. There were nights of appalling frost—"

"Well," I said, "well, what about the gas company?"

"I'm just coming to that. Even in the midst of my fever I had an inspiration. I thought it out overnight and in the morning my gas lights were burning, my gas radiator was glowing and I had stopped shivering; and yet I had achieved this without putting a single coin in the meter and without tampering with its mechanism."

"How did you manage that?"

"Wait! A fortnight passed. The man from the gas company came to empty the meter.

"He read the little dials, saw that so many cubic feet had been consumed, opened the meter and found it empty. He was a French official with an absurd beard.

"He said:—'M'sieur, your meter is empty.'

"I said:—'M'sieur the collector, that is nothing to me.'

"He said:—'But where is the money?'

"I replied:—'Monsieur, I am a sick man. I cannot sit here and answer your riddles. Have the goodness to go.'

"He said:—'Monsieur, this will have to be reported.'

"I said:—'Go to the devil.' He replaced the padlock and sealed it. All the same, I had gas for the next fortnight. Then the collector came again with another official. First of all they examined the seal on the padlock and found it intact; it was one of those complicated lead seals that cannot easily be tampered with. Then they looked at the glaring lights and the red hot stove. Then the inspector gave me one of those looks with which lesser men than myself are so easily terrified, opened the box and found nothing.

"You could have heard the argument as far away as the Place D'Anvers.

"Result? They decided that my meter was faulty, took it away, and replaced it with a new one. A devil of a meter, as large and as red as an omnibus, with a mechanism that made a noise like a lady in a car changing gear.

"A week later they came again, again found all the gas lights burning and a room like an oven. It took them about three-quarters of an hour to open the meter, they had locked it up so tight. And what did they find? Empty space!" roared Karmesin, with a shout of laughter, that made the water jug dance in its basin and the window panes vibrate.

"But, Karmesin," I asked, "*How* did you manage it?"

"Wait," said Karmesin. "That is exactly what the gas people asked me. I simply smiled a mysterious smile and said nothing. And then one day, as I expected, I was politely invited to interview one of the directors of the company, and he said something to this effect:—'Monsieur Lavoisier, I don't know what you're up to but it certainly can't be legal. What tricks have you been playing with our meter?'

"I merely smiled. 'Come, Monsieur,' said this gas man, 'we wish to be lenient. We do not wish to prosecute. Tell us exactly how you cause these meters to function without putting any money in, and we will let the matter rest—we might even forget about the small item of gas you have consumed without paying for it!'

"I said: 'If I tell you, Monsieur, you will not only refrain from prosecuting but you will also pay me 20,000 francs. If you do not do this then I shall discreetly make public a perfectly simple method whereby the consumers of your gas can get it free of charge. It really is just as well for you to know these things. It would be worth more than 20,000 to you.'

'This is preposterous!' he shouted.

" 'You would have to modify all your meters,' I insinuated.

"We compromised at 10,000, and he went with me back to my room."

"Well?" I asked.

"The whole thing was so simple. I pointed to the bottom of the meter and showed him a tiny hole, no larger than a pinhole. That was number one, then I showed him my cake of soap; apparatus No. 2. 'Well?' asked the gas director. I took him to the window and opened it. Lying in the window sill were two or three cakes of soap; in each cake an indentation of the size of a silver franc.

"It was so childishly simple. Into my little soap moulds I had poured water; the night frost turned the water to ice; the one-franc piece of ice was just hard enough to operate the mechanism of the meter; the gas thus obtained heated the room, the heat turned the ice back to water which dripped out at my little pin hole. Result? Invisibility!"

"That's extraordinarily clever," I said. "And did you get your 10,000 francs?"

"Yes," said Karmesin. "But what the devil was 10,000 francs? £500? £500! Chicken feed!—"

Karmesin rolled some of his twice-used cigarette tobacco into a kind of mahorka-cigarette, in a bit of newspaper, and fumigated his gigantic moustache with a puff of frightfully acrid smoke.

ONE HUNDRED IN THE DARK
OWEN JOHNSON

In the early part of the twentieth century, few writers had greater success in depicting the college student than Owen Johnson (1878–1952). His stories and novels, known collectively as the "Lawrenceville Stories," catalogued the personal and educational experiences of Dink Stover. Johnson founded and edited the *Lawrenceville Literary Magazine* and made his school famous by publishing *The Eternal Boy* (1909), which was set there.

While at Yale, he was chairman of the *Yale Literary Review* and, a decade after his graduation, shocked the school by publishing the best-selling *Dover at Yale* (1911), which is still in print, though inevitably dated. He had previously published such best-sellers as *The Prodigious Hickey* (1908), *The Varmint* (1910), and *The Tennessee Shad* (1911), which remained popular for decades and was on the curriculum of many schools.

He had few contributions to the mystery genre, though his story collection *Murder in Any Degree* (1913) received excellent reviews upon publication; the *New York Times* called it "immensely diverting and entertaining."

Apart from the title story, the only other mystery contribution to the book was "One Hundred in the Dark," which shows what a great member of the crime fiction community Johnson could have been had he kept his hand in it.

ONE HUNDRED IN THE DARK

BY OWEN JOHNSON

THEY WERE DISCUSSING languidly, as such groups do, seeking from each topic a peg on which to hang a few epigrams that might be retold in the lip currency of the club—Steingall, the painter, florid of gesture, and effete, foreign in type, with black-rimmed glasses and trailing ribbon of black silk that cut across his cropped beard and cavalry mustaches; De Gollyer, a critic, who preferred to be known as a man about town, short, feverish, incisive, who slew platitudes with one adjective and tagged a reputation with three; Rankin, the architect, always in a defensive, explanatory attitude, who held his elbows on the table, his hands before his long sliding nose, and gestured with his fingers; Quinny, the illustrator, long and gaunt, with a predatory eloquence that charged irresistibly down on any subject, cut it off, surrounded it, and raked it with enfilading wit and satire; and Peters, whose methods of existence were a mystery, a young man of fifty, who had done nothing and who knew every one by his first name, the club postman, who carried the tittle-tattle, the *bon mots* and the news of the day, who drew up a petition a week and pursued the house committee with a daily grievance.

About the latticed porch, which ran around the sanded yard with its feeble fountain and futile evergreens, other groups were eying one another or engaging in desultory conversation, oppressed with the heaviness of the night.

At the round table, Quinny alone, absorbing energy as he devoured the conversation, having routed Steingall on the Germans and archaeology and Rankin on the origins of the Lord's Prayer, had seized a chance remark of De Gollyer's to say:

"There are only half a dozen stories in the world. Like everything that's true it isn't true." He waved his long gouty fingers in the direction of Steingall, who, having been silenced, was regarding him with a look of sleepy indifference. "What is more to the point, is the small number of human relations that are so simple and yet so fundamental that they can be eternally played upon, redressed, and reinterpreted in every language, in every age, and yet remain inexhaustible in the possibility of variations."

"By George, that is so," said Steingall, waking up. "Every art does go back to three or four notes. In composition it is the same thing. Nothing new— nothing new since a thousand years. By George, that is true! We invent nothing, nothing!"

"Take the eternal triangle," said Quinny hurriedly, not to surrender his advantage, while Rankin and De Gollyer in a bored way continued to gaze dreamily at a vagrant star or two. "Two men and a woman, or two women and a man. Obviously it should be classified as the first of the great original parent themes. Its variations extend into the thousands. By the way, Rankin, excellent opportunity, eh, for some of our modern, painstaking, unemployed jackasses to analyze and classify."

"Quite right," said Rankin without perceiving the satirical note. "Now there's De Maupassant's *Fort comme la Mort*—quite the most interesting variation—shows the turn a genius can give. There the triangle is the man of middle age, the mother he has loved in his youth and the daughter he comes to love. It forms, you might say, the head of a whole subdivision of modern Continental literature."

"Quite wrong, Rankin, quite wrong," said Quinny, who would have stated the other side quite as imperiously. "What you cite is a variation of quite another theme, the Faust theme—old age longing for youth, the man who has loved longing for the love of his youth, which is youth itself. The triangle is the theme of jealousy, the most destructive and therefore, the most dramatic of human passions. The Faust theme is the most fundamental and inevitable of all human experiences, the tragedy of life itself. Quite a different thing."

Rankin, who never agreed with Quinny unless Quinny maliciously took advantage of his prior announcement to agree with him continued to combat this idea.

"You believe then," said De Gollyer after a certain moment had been consumed in hair splitting, "that the origin of all dramatic themes is simply the expression of some human emotion. In other words, there can exist no more parent themes than there are human emotions."

"I thank you, sir, very well put," said Quinny with a generous wave of his hand, "Why is the *Three Musketeers* a basic theme? Simply the interpretation of comradeship, the emotion one man feels for another, vital because it is the one peculiarly masculine emotion. Look at Du Maurier and *Trilby*, Kipling in *Soldiers Three*—simply the *Three Musketeers*."

"The *Vie de Bohème?*" suggested Steingall. "In the real Vie de Bohème yes," said Quinny viciously. "Not in the concocted sentimentalities that we now have served up to us by athletic tenors and consumptive elephants!"

Rankin, who had been silently deliberating on what had been left behind, now said cunningly and with evident purpose:

"All the same. I don't agree with you men at all. I believe there are situations, original situations, that are independent of your human emotions, that exist just because they are situations, accidental and nothing else."

"As for instance?" said Quinny, preparing to attack. "Well. I'll just cite an ordinary one that happens to come to my mind," said Rankin, who had carefully selected his test. "In a group of seven or eight, such as we are here, a theft takes place; one man is the thief—which one? I'd like to know what emotion that interprets, and yet it certainly is an original theme, at the bottom of a whole literature."

This challenge was like a bomb.

"Not the same thing."

"Detective stories, hah!"

"Oh, I say, Rankin, that's literary melodrama."

Rankin, satisfied, smiled and winked victoriously over to Tommers, who was listening from an adjacent table.

"Of course your suggestion is out of order, my dear man, to this extent," said Quinny, who never surrendered, "in that I am talking of fundamentals and you are citing details. Nevertheless, I could answer that the situation you give, as well as the whole school it belongs to, can be traced back to the commonest of human emotion's, curiosity; and that the story of *Bluebeard* and *The Moonstone* are to all purpose identically the same."

At this Steingall, who had waited hopefully, gasped and made as though to leave the table.

"I shall take up your contention," said Quinny without pause for breath, "first, because you have opened up one of my pet topics, and second, because it gives me a chance to talk." He gave a sidelong glance at Steingall and winked at De Gollyer. "What is the peculiar fascination that the detective problem exercises over the human mind? You will say curiosity. Yes and no. Admit at once that the whole art of a detective story consists in the statement of the problem. Any one can do it. I can do it. Steingall even can do it. The solution doesn't count. It is usually banal; it should be prohibited. What interests us is, can we guess it? Just as an able-minded man will sit down for hours and fiddle over the puzzle column in a Sunday balderdash. Same idea. There you have it, the problem—the detective story. Now why the fascination? I'll tell you. It appeals to our curiosity, yes—but deeper to a sort of intellectual vanity. Here are six matches, arrange them to make four squares, five men present, a theft takes place—who's the thief? Who will guess it first? Whose brain will show its superior cleverness—see? That's all—that's all there is to it."

"Out of all of which," said De Gollyer, "the interesting thing is that Rankin has supplied the reason why the supply of detective fiction is inexhaustible. It is a formula ludicrously simple, mechanical, and yet we will always pursue it to the end. The marvel is that writers should seek for any other formula when here is one so safe, that can never fail. By George I could start up a factory on it."

"The reason is," said Rankin, "that the situation does constantly occur. It's a situation that any of us might get into any time. As a matter of fact, now, I personally know two such occasions when I was of the party; and very uncomfortable it was too."

"What happened?" said Steingall.

"Why, there is no story to it particularly. Once a mistake had been made, and the other time the real thief was detected by accident a year later. In both cases only one or two of us knew what had happened."

De Gollyer had a similar incident to recall. Steingall, after a reflection, related another that had happened to a friend.

"Of course, of course, my dear gentlemen," said Quinny impatiently, for he had been silent, too long, "you are glorifying commonplaces. Every crime, I tell you, expresses itself in the terms of the picture puzzle that you feed to your six-year-old. It's only the variation that is interesting. Now quite the most remarkable turn of the complexities that can be developed is, of course, the well-known instance of the visitor at a club and the rare coin. Of course every one knows that? What?"

Rankin smiled in a bored, superior way, but the others protested their ignorance.

"Why, it's very well known," said Quinny lightly. "A distinguished visitor is brought into a club—dozen men, say, present, at dinner, long table. Conversation finally veers around to curiosities and relics. One of the members present then takes from his pocket what he announces as one of the rarest coins in existence—passes it around the table. Coin travels back and forth, every one examining it, and the conversation goes to another topic, say the influence of the auto mobile on domestic infelicity, or some other such asininely intellectual club topic—you know? All at once the owner calls for his coin.

"The coin is nowhere to be found. Every one looks at every one else. First, they suspect a joke. Then it becomes serious—the coin is immensely valuable. Who has taken it?"

The owner is a gentleman—does the gentlemanly idiotic thing, of course, laughs, says he knows some one is playing a practical joke on him and that the coin will be returned tomorrow. The others refuse to leave the situation so. One man proposes that they all submit to a search. Every one gives his assent until it comes to the stranger. He refuses curtly, roughly, without giving any reason. Uncomfortable silence—the man is a guest. No one knows him particularly well—but still he is a guest. One member tries to make him understand that no offense is offered, that the suggestion was simply to clear the atmosphere, and all that sort of bally rot, you know.

" 'I refuse to allow my person to be searched,' says the stranger, very firm, very proud, very English, you know, 'and I refuse to give my reason for my action.'

Another silence. The men eye him and then glance at one another. What's to be done? Nothing. There is etiquette—that magnificent inflated balloon. The visitor evidently has the coin—but he is their guest and etiquette protects him. Nice situation, eh?

"The table is cleared. A waiter removes a dish of fruit and there under the ledge of the plate where it had been pushed—is the coin. Banal explanation, eh? Of course. Solutions always should be. At once every one in profuse apologies! Whereupon the visitor rises and says:

" 'Now I can give you the reason for my refusal to be searched. There are only two known specimens of the coin in existence, and the second happens to be here in my waistcoat pocket.' "

"Of course," said Quinny with a shrug of his shoulder, "the story is well invented, but the turn to it is very nice indeed."

"I did know the story," said Steingall to be disagreeable; "the ending, though, is too obvious to be invented. The visitor should have had on him not another coin, but something absolutely different, something destructive, say, of a woman's reputation, and a great tragedy should have been threatened by the casual misplacing of the coin."

"I have heard the same story told in a dozen different ways," said Rankin.

"It has happened a hundred times. It must be continually happening," said Steingall.

"I know one extraordinary instance," said Peters, who up to the present, secure in his climax, had waited with a professional smile until the big guns had been silenced. "In fact, the most extraordinary instance of this sort I have ever heard."

"Peters, you little rascal," said Quinny with a sidelong glance, "I perceive you have quietly been letting us dress the stage for you."

"It is not a story that will please every one," said Peters, to whet their appetite.

"Why not?"

"Because you will want to know what no one can ever know."

"It has no conclusion then?"

"Yes and no. As far as it concerns a woman, quite the most remarkable woman I have ever met, the story is complete. As for the rest, it is what it is, because it is one example where literature can do nothing better than record."

"Do I know the woman?" asked De Gollyer, who flattered himself on passing through every class of society.

"Possibly, but no more than any one else."

"An actress?"

"What she has been in the past I don't know—a promoter would better describe her. Undoubtedly she has been behind the scenes in many an untold intrigue of the business world. A very feminine woman, and yet, as you shall see, with an unusual instantaneous masculine power of decision."

"Peters," said Quinny, waving a warning finger, "you are destroying your story. Your preface will bring an anti-climax."

"You shall judge," said Peters, who waited until his audience was in strained attention before opening his story. "The names are, of course, disguises."

MRS. RITA KILDAIR inhabited a charming bachelor-girl studio, very elegant, of the duplex pattern, in one of the buildings just off Central Park West. She knew pretty nearly every one in that indescribable society in New York that is drawn from all levels, and that imposes but one audition for membership— to be amusing. She knew every one and no one knew her. No one knew beyond the vaguest rumors her history or her means. No one had ever heard of a Mr. Kildair. There was always about her a certain defensive reserve the moment the limits of acquaintanceship had been reached. She had a certain amount of money, she knew a certain number of men in Wall Street affairs, and her studio was furnished with taste and even distinction. She was of any age. She might have suffered everything or nothing at all. In this mingled society her invitations were eagerly sought, her dinners were spontaneous, and the discussions, though gay and usually daring, were invariably under the control of wit and good taste.

On the Sunday night of this adventure she had, according to her invariable custom, sent away her Japanese butler and invited to an informal chafing-dish supper seven of her more congenial friends, all of whom, as much as could be said of any one, were habitués of the studio.

At seven o'clock, having finished dressing, she put in order her bedroom, which formed a sort of free passage between the studio and a small dining room to the kitchen beyond. Then, going into the studio, she lit a wax taper and was in the act of touching off the brass candlesticks that lighted the room when three knocks sounded on the door and a Mr. Flanders, a broker, compact, nervously alive, well groomed, entered with the informality of assured acquaintance.

"You are early.

"On the contrary, you are late," said the broker, glancing at his watch.

"Then be a good boy and help me with the candles," she said, giving him a smile and a quick pressure of her fingers.

He obeyed, asking nonchalantly:

"I say, dear lady, who's to be here to-night?"

"The Enos Jacksons."

"I thought they were separated?"

"Not yet."

"Very interesting! Only you, dear lady, would have thought of serving us a couple on the verge."

"It's interesting, isn't it?"

"Assuredly. Where did you know Jackson?"

"Through the Warings. Jackson's a rather doubtful person, isn't he?"

"Let's call him a very sharp lawyer," said Flanders defensively. "They tell me, though, he is on the wrong side of the market—in deep."

"And you?"

"Oh, I? I'm a bachelor," he said with a shrug of his shoulders, "and if I come a cropper it makes no difference."

"Is that possible?" she said, looking at him quickly.

"Probable even. And who else is coming?"

"Maude Lille—you know her?"

"I think not."

"You met her here—a journalist."

"Quite so, a strange career."

"Mr. Harris, a clubman, is coming, and the Stanley Cheevers."

"The Stanley Cheevers!" said Flanders with some surprise. "Are we going to gamble?"

"You believe in that scandal about bridge?"

"Certainly not," said Flanders, smiling. "You see I was present. The Cheevers play a good game, a well united game, and have an unusual system of makes. By-the-way, it's Jackson who is very attentive to Mrs. Cheever, isn't it?"

"Quite right."

"What a charming party," said Flanders flippantly. "And where does Maude Lille come in?"

"Don't joke. She is in a desperate way," said Mrs. Kildair, with a little sadness in her eyes.

"And Harris?"

"Oh, he is to make the salad and cream the chicken."

"Ah. I see the whole party. I, of course, am to add the element of respectability."

"Of what?"

She looked at him steadily until he turned away, dropping his glance.

"Don't be an ass with me, my dear Flanders."

"By George, if this were Europe I'd wager you were in the secret service, Mrs. Kildair."

"Thank you."

She smiled appreciatively and moved about the studio, giving the finishing touches. The Stanley Cheevers entered, a short fat man with a vacant fat face and a slow-moving eye and his wife, voluble, nervous, overdressed and pretty. Mr. Harris came with Maude Lille, a woman, straight, dark, Indian, with great masses of somber hair held in a little too loosely for neatness, with thick, quick lips and eyes that rolled away from the person who was talking to her. The Enos Jacksons were late and still agitated as they entered. His forehead had not quite banished the scowl, nor her eyes the scorn. He was of the type that never lost his temper, but caused others to lose theirs, immovable in his opinions with a prowling walk, a studied antagonism in his manner and an impudent look that fastened itself unerringly on the weakness in the person to whom he spoke. Mrs. Jackson, who seemed fastened to her husband by an invisible leash, had a hunted, resisting quality back of a certain desperate dash, which she assumed rather than felt in her attitude toward life. One looked at her curiously and wondered what such a nature would do in a crisis, with a lurking sense of a woman who carried with her her own impending tragedy.

As soon as the company had been completed and the incongruity if the selection had been perceived, a smile of malicious anticipation ran the rounds, which the hostess cut short by saying:

"Well, now that every one is here, this is the order of the night: You can quarrel all you want, you can whisper all the gossip you can think of about one another, but every one is to be amusing! Also every one is to help with the dinner—nothing formal and nothing serious. We may all be bankrupt to-morrow, divorced or dead, but to-night we will be gay—that is the invariable rule of the house!"

Immediately a nervous laughter broke out and the company, chattering, began to scatter through the rooms.

Mrs. Kildair, stopping in her bedroom, donned a Watteau-like cooking apron, and slipping her rings from her fingers fixed the three on her pincushion with a hatpin.

"Your rings are beautiful, dear, beautiful!" said the low voice of Maude Lille, who, with Harris and Mrs. Cheever, was in the room.

"There's only one that is very valuable," said Mrs. Kildair, touching with her thin fingers the ring that lay uppermost, two large diamonds, flanking a magnificent sapphire.

"It is beautiful—very beautiful," said the journalist, her eyes fastened to it with an uncontrollable fascination. She put out her fingers and let them rest caressingly on the sapphire, withdrawing them quickly as though the contact had burned them.

"It must be very valuable," she said, her breath catching a little. Mrs. Cheever moving forward, suddenly looked at the ring.

"It cost five thousand six years ago," said Mrs. Kildair, glancing down at it. "It has been my talisman ever since. For the moment, however, I am cook; Maude Lille, you are scullery maid: Harris is the chef, and we are under his orders. Mrs. Cheever, did you ever peel onions?"

"Good Heavens, no!" said Mrs. Cheever, recoiling.

"Well, there are no onions to peel," said Mrs. Kildair, laughing. "All you'll have to do is to help set the table. On to the kitchen!"

Under their hostess's gay guidance the seven guests began to circulate busily through the rooms, laying the table, grouping the chairs, opening bottles, and preparing the material for the chafing dishes. Mrs. Kildair, in the kitchen, ransacked the ice box, and with her own hands chopped the *fines herbes*, shredded the chicken and measured the cream.

"Flanders, carry this in carefully," she said, her hands in a towel. "Cheever, stop watching your wife and put the salad bowl on the table. Everything ready, Harris? All right. Every one sit down. I'll be right in."

She went into her bedroom, and divesting herself of her apron hung it in the closet. Then going to her dressing table she drew the hatpin from the pincushion and carelessly slipped the rings on her fingers. All at once she frowned and looked quickly at her hand. Only two rings were there, the third ring, the one with the sapphire and the two diamonds, was missing.

"Stupid," she said to herself, and returned to her dressing table. All at once she stopped. She remembered quite clearly putting the pin through the three rings.

She made no attempt to search further, but remained without moving, her fingers drumming slowly on the table, her head to one side, her lip drawn in a little between her teeth, listening with a frown to the babble from the outer room. Who had taken the ring? Each of her guests had had a dozen opportunities in the course of the time she had been busy in the kitchen.

"Too much time before the mirror, dear lady," called out Flanders gaily, who from where he was seated could see her.

"It is not he," she said quickly. Then she reconsidered. "Why not? He is clever—who knows? Let me think."

To gain time she walked back slowly into the kitchen, her head bowed, her thumb between her teeth, "Who has taken it?"

She ran over the characters of her guests and their situations as she knew them. Strangely enough, at each her mind stopped upon some reason that might explain a sudden temptation.

"I shall find out nothing this way," she said to herself after a moment deliberation; "that is not the important thing to me just now. The important thing is to get the ring back."

And slowly, deliberately, she began to walk back and forth, her clenched hand beating the deliberate rhythmic measure of her journey.

Five minutes later, as Harris, installed *en maître* over the chafing dish, was giving directions, spoon in the air, Mrs. Kildair came into the room like a lengthening shadow. Her entrance had been made with scarcely a perceptible sound, and yet each guest was aware of it at the same moment, with a little nervous start.

"Heavens, dear lady," exclaimed Flanders, "you come in on us like a Greek tragedy! What is it you have for us, a surprise?"

As he spoke she turned her swift glance on him, drawing her forehead together until the eyebrows ran in a straight line.

"I have something to say to you," she said in a sharp, businesslike manner, watching the company with penetrating eagerness.

There was no mistaking the seriousness of her voice. Mr. Harris extinguished the oil lamp, covering the chafing dish clumsily with a discordant, disagreeable sound. Mrs. Cheever and Mrs. Enos Jackson swung about abruptly, Maude Lille rose a little from her seat, while the men imitated these movements of expectancy with a clumsy shuffling of the feet.

"Mr. Enos Jackson?"

"Yes, Mrs. Kildair."

"Kindly do as I ask you."

"Certainly."

She had spoken his name with a peremptory positiveness that was almost an accusation. He rose calmly, raising his eyebrows a little in surprise.

"Go to the door," she continued, shifting her glance from him to the others. "Are you there? Lock it. Bring me the key."

He executed the order without bungling, and returning stood before her, tendering the key.

"You've locked it?" she said, making the words an excuse to bury her glance in his.

"As you wished me to."

"Thanks."

She took from him the key and shifting slightly, likewise locked the door into her bedroom through which she had come.

Then transferring the keys to her left hand, seemingly unaware of Jackson, who still awaited her further commands, her eyes studied a moment the possibilities of the apartment.

"Mr. Cheever?" she said in a low voice.

"Yes, Mrs. Kildair."

"Blow out all the candles except the candelabrum on the table."

"Put out the lights, Mrs. Kildair?"

"At once."

Mr. Cheever, in rising, met the glance of his wife, and the look of questioning and wonder that passed did not escape the hostess.

"But, my dear Mrs. Kildair," said Mr. Jackson with a little nervous catch of her breath, "what is it? I'm getting terribly worked up! My nerves—"

"Miss Lille?" said the voice of command.

"Yes."

The journalist, calmer than the rest, had watched the proceedings without surprise, as though forewarned by professional instinct that something of importance was about to take place. Now she rose quietly with an almost stealthy motion.

"Put the candelabrum on this table—here," said Mrs. Kildair, indicating a large round table on which a few books were grouped. "No, wait. Mr. Jackson, first clear off the table. I want nothing on it."

"But, Mrs. Kildair—" began Mr. Jackson's shrill voice again.

"That's it. Now put down the candelabrum."

In a moment, as Mr. Cheever proceeded methodically on his errand, the brilliant crossfire of lights dropped in the studio, only a few smoldering wicks winking on the walls, while the high room seemed to grow more distant as it came under the sole dominion of the three candles bracketed in silver at the head of the bare mahogany table.

"Now listen!" said Mrs. Kildair, and her voice had in it a cold note. "My sapphire ring has just been stolen."

She said it suddenly, hurling the news among them and waiting ferretlike for some indications in the chorus that broke out.

"Stolen!"

"Oh, my dear Mrs. Kildair!"

"Stolen—by Jove!"

"You don't mean it!"

"What! Stolen here—to-night?"

"The ring has been taken within the last twenty minutes," continued Mrs. Kildair in the same determined, chiseled tone. "I am not going to mince words. The ring has been taken and the thief is among you."

For a moment nothing was heard but an indescribable gasp and a sudden turning and searching, then suddenly Cheever's deep bass broke out:

"Stolen! But, Mrs. Kildair, is it possible?"

"Exactly. There is not the slightest doubt," said Mrs. Kildair. "Three of you were in my bedroom when I placed my rings on the pincushion. Each of you has passed through there a dozen times since. My sapphire ring is gone, and one of you has taken it."

Mrs. Jackson gave a little scream, and reached heavily for a glass of water. Mrs. Cheever said something inarticulate in the outburst of masculine exclamation. Only Maude Lille's calm voice could be heard saying:

"Quite true. I was in the room when you took them off. The sapphire ring was on top."

"Now listen!" said Mrs. Kildair, her eyes on Maude Lille's eyes. "I am not going to mince words. I am not going to stand on ceremony. I'm going to have that ring back. Listen to me carefully. I'm going to have that ring back, and until I do, not a soul shall leave this room." She tapped on the table with her nervous knuckles. "Who has taken it I do not care to know. All I want is my ring. Now I'm going to make it possible for whoever took it to restore it without possibility of detection. The doors are locked and will stay locked. I am going to put out the lights, and I am going to count one hundred slowly. You will be in absolute darkness; no one will know or see what is done. But if at the end of that time the ring is not here on the table I shall telephone the police and have every one in this room searched. Am I quite clear?"

Suddenly she cut short the nervous outbreak of suggestions and in the same firm voice continued:

"Every one take his place about the table. That's it. That will do."

The women, with the exception of the inscrutable Maude Lille, gazed hysterically from face to face, while the men compressing their fingers, locking them or grasping their chins, looked straight ahead fixedly at their hostess.

Mrs. Kildair, having calmly assured herself that all were ranged as she wished, blew out two of the three candles.

"I shall count one hundred, no more, no less," she said. "Either I get back that ring or every one in this room be searched, remember."

Leaning over, she blew out the remaining candle and snuffed it.

"One, two, three, four, five—"

She began to count with the inexorable regularity of a clock's ticking.

In the room every sound was distinct, the rustle of a dress, the grinding of a shoe, the deep, slightly asthmatic breathing of a man.

"Twenty, twenty-one, twenty-two, twenty-three—"

She continued to count, while in the methodic unvarying note of her voice there was a rasping reiteration that began to affect the company. A slight, gasping breath, uncontrollable, almost on the verge of hysterics, was heard, and a man nervously clearing his throat.

"Forty-five, forty-six, forty-seven—"

Still nothing had happened. Mrs. Kildair did not vary her measure the slightest, only the sound became more metallic.

"Sixty-six, sixty-seven, sixty-eight, sixty-nine, and seventy—"

Some one had sighed.

"Seventy-three, seventy-four, seventy-five, seventy-six, seventy-seven—"

All at once, clear, unmistakable, on the resounding plane of the table was heard a slight metallic note.

"The ring!"

It was Maude Lille's quick voice that had spoken. Mrs. Kildair continued to count.

"Eighty-nine, ninety, ninety-one—"

The tension became unbearable. Two or three voices protested against the needless prolonging of the torture.

"Ninety-six, ninety-seven, ninety-eight, ninety-nine and one hundred."

A match sputtered in Mrs. Kildair's hand and on the instant the company craned forward. In the center of the table was the sparkling sapphire and diamond ring. Candles were lit, flaring up like searchlights on the white accusing faces.

"Mr. Cheever, you may give it to me," said Mrs. Kildair. She held out her hand without trembling, a smile of triumph on her face, which had in it for a moment an expression of positive cruelty.

Immediately she changed, contemplating with amusement the horror of her guests, staring blindly from one to another, seeing the indefinable glance of interrogation that passed from Cheever to Mrs. Cheever, from Mrs. Jackson to her husband, and then without emotion she said:

"Now that that is over we can have a very gay little supper."

WHEN PETERS HAD pushed back his chair, satisfied as only a trained raconteur can be by the silence of a difficult audience, and had busied himself with a cigar, there was an instant outcry.

"I say, Peters, old boy, that is not all!"

"Absolutely."

"The story ends there?"

"That ends the story."

"But who took the ring?"

Peters extended his hands in an empty gesture.

"What! It was never found out?"

"Never."

"No clue?"

"None."

"I don't like the story," said De Gollyer.

"It's no story at all," said Steingall.

"Permit me," said Quinny in a didactic way; "it is a story, and it is complete. In fact, I consider it unique because it has none of the banalities of a solution and leaves the problem even more confused than at the start."

"I don't see—" began Rankin.

"Of course you don't, my dear man," said Quinny crushingly. "You do not see that any solution would be common place, whereas no solution leaves an extraordinary intellectual problem."

"How so?"

"In the first place," said Quinny, preparing to annex the topic, "whether the situation actually happened or not, which is in itself a mere triviality, Peters has constructed it in a masterly way, the proof of which is that he has made *me* listen. Observe, each person present might have taken the ring—Flanders, a broker, just come a cropper; Maude Lille, a woman on the ragged side of life in desperate means; either Mr. and Mrs. Cheever, suspected of being card sharps—very good touch that, Peters, when the husband and wife glanced involuntarily at each other at the end—Mr. Enos Jackson, a sharp lawyer, or his wife about to be divorced; even Harris, concerning whom, very cleverly, Peters has said nothing at all to make him quite the most suspicious of all. There are, therefore, seven solutions, all possible and all logical. But beyond this is left a great intellectual problem."

"How so?"

"Was it a feminine or a masculine action to restore the ring when threatened with a search, knowing that Mrs. Kildair's clever expedient of throwing the room into darkness made detection impossible? Was it a woman who lacked the necessary courage to continue, or was it a man who repented his first impulse? Is a man or is a woman the greater natural criminal?"

"A woman took it, of course," said Rankin.

"On the contrary, it was a man," said Steingall, "for the second action was more difficult than the first."

"A man, certainly," said De Gollyer. "The restoration of the ring was a logical decision."

"You see," said Quinny triumphantly, "personally I incline to a woman for the reason that a weaker feminine nature is peculiarly susceptible to the domination of her own sex. There you are. We could meet and debate the subject year in and year out and never agree."

"I recognize most of the characters," said De Gollyer with a little confidential smile toward Peters. "Mrs. Kildair, of course, is all you say of her—an extraordinary woman. The story is quite characteristic of her. Flanders, I am not sure of, but I think I know him."

"Did it really happen?" asked Rankin, who always took the commonplace point of view.

"Exactly as I have told it," said Peters.

"The only one I don't recognize is Harris," said De Gollyer pensively.

"Your humble servant," said Peters, smiling.

The four looked up suddenly with a little start.

"What!" said Quinny, abruptly confused. "You—you, were there?"

"I was there."

The four continued to look at him without speaking, each absorbed in his own thoughts, with a sudden ill ease.

A club attendant, with a telephone slip on a tray, stopped by Peters' side. He excused himself and went along the porch, nodding from table to table.

"Curious chap," said De Gollyer musingly.

"Extraordinary."

The word was like a murmur in the group of four, who continued watching Peters' trim, disappearing figure in silence, without looking at one another—with a certain ill ease.

THE WHOLE TOWN'S SLEEPING
RAY BRADBURY

With the publication of his first book, *The Martian Chronicles*, in 1950 and then *Fahrenheit 451* in 1953, Ray Bradbury (1920–) quickly became one of the most popular and important writers of science fiction in the twentieth century. Strangely, although his first book was a success in hardcover with six printings in two years, his second book was issued as a paperback original before it was published in hardcover. Almost equally oddly for such a young author, a special edition of *Fahrenheit 451*, limited to 200 copies, bound in asbestos, was published soon after its initial printing and is one of the most sought-after books in the science fiction collecting world.

This prolific writer is less known as the author of mystery fiction, but he has produced several novels (*Death Is a Lonely Business, A Graveyard to Let*, and *Something Wicked This Way Comes*) and numerous short stories in the mystery, crime, and suspense genre, including the following story.

Bradbury's stories have been described as haunting, fascinating, beautiful, and unique; many defy classification, and none more so than "The Whole Town's Sleeping."

First published in the September 1950 issue of *McCall's* magazine, it was so baffling—and frustrating—that Alfred Hitchcock selected it for his 1962 anthology, *Twelve Stories for Late at Night*. It later appeared, in somewhat different form, as a chapter in Bradbury's 1957 novel *Dandelion Wine*.

THE WHOLE TOWN'S SLEEPING

BY RAY BRADBURY

IT WAS A WARM SUMMER NIGHT in the middle of Illinois country. The little town was deep far away from everything, kept to itself by a river and a forest and a ravine. In the town the sidewalks were still scorched. The stores were closing and the streets were turning dark. There were two moons: a clock moon with four faces in four night directions above the solemn black courthouse, and the real moon that was slowly rising in vanilla whiteness from the dark east.

In the downtown drug store, fans whispered in the high ceiling air. In the rococo shade of porches, invisible people sat. On the purple bricks of the summer twilight streets, children ran. Screen doors whined their springs and banged. The heat was breathing from the dry lawns and trees.

On her solitary porch, Lavinia Nebbs, aged 37, very straight and slim, sat with a tinkling lemonade in her white fingers, tapping it to her lips, waiting.

"Here I am, Lavinia."

Lavinia turned. There was Francine, at the bottom porch step, in the smell of zinnias and hibiscus. Francine was all in snow white and she didn't look 35.

Miss Lavinia Nebbs rose and locked her front door, leaving her lemonade glass standing empty on the porch rail. "It's a fine night for the movie."

"Where you going, ladies?" cried Grandma Hanlon from her shadowy porch across the street.

They called back through the soft ocean of darkness: "To the Elite Theater to see Harold Lloyd in *Welcome, Danger!*"

"Won't catch *me* out on no night like this," wailed Grandma Hanlon. "Not with The Lonely One strangling women. Lock myself in with my *gun!*"

Grandma's door slammed and locked.

The two maiden ladies drifted on. Lavinia felt the warm breath of the summer night shimmering off the oven-baked sidewalk. It was like walking on a hard crust of freshly warmed bread. The heat pulsed under your dress and along your legs with a stealthy sense of invasion.

"Lavinia, you don't believe all that gossip about The Lonely One, do you?"

"Those women like to see their tongues dance."

"Just the same, Hattie McDollis was killed a month ago. And Roberta Ferry the month before. And now Eliza Ramsell has disappeared . . ."

"Hattie McDollis walked off with a traveling man, I bet."

"But the others—strangled—four of them, their tongues sticking out their mouths, they say."

They stood on the edge of the ravine that cut the town in two. Behind them were the lighted houses and faint radio music; ahead was deepness, moistness, fireflies, and dark.

"Maybe we shouldn't go to the movie," said Francine. "The Lonely One might follow and kill us. I don't like that ravine. Look how black, smell it, and *listen.*"

The ravine was a dynamo that never stopped running, night or day: there was a great moving hum among the secret mists and washed shales, and the odors of a rank greenhouse. Always the black dynamo was humming, with green electric sparkles where fireflies hovered.

"And it won't be *me,*" said Francine, "coming back through this terrible dark ravine tonight, late. It'll be you, Lavinia, you down the steps and over that rickety bridge and maybe The Lonely One standing behind a tree. I'd never have gone over to church this afternoon if I had to walk through here all alone, even in daylight."

"Bosh," said Lavinia Nebbs.

"It'll be you alone on the path, listening to your shoes, not me. And shadows. You *all alone* on the way back home. Lavinia, don't you get lonely living by yourself in that house?"

"Old maids love to live alone," said Lavinia. She pointed to a hot shadowy path. "Let's walk the short cut."

"I'm afraid."

"It's early. The Lonely One won't be out till late." Lavinia, as cool as mint ice cream, took the other woman's arm and led her down the dark winding path into cricket-warmth and frog-sound, and mosquito-delicate silence.

"Let's run," gasped Francine.

"No."

If Lavinia hadn't turned her head just then, she wouldn't have seen it. But she did turn her head, and it was there. And then Francine looked over and she saw it too, and they stood there on the path, not believing what they saw.

In the singing deep night, back among a clump of bushes—half hidden, but laid out as if she had put herself down there to enjoy the soft stars—lay Eliza Ramsell.

Francine screamed.

The woman lay as if she were floating there, her face moon-freckled, her eyes like white marble, her tongue clamped in her lips.

Lavinia felt the ravine turning like a gigantic black merry-go-round underfoot. Francine was gasping and choking, and a long while later Lavinia heard herself say, "We'd better get the police."

"HOLD ME, LAVINIA, please hold me, I'm cold. Oh, I've never been so cold since winter."

Lavinia held Francine and the policemen were all around in the ravine grass. Flashlights darted about, voices mingled, and the night grew toward 8:30.

"It's like December. I need a sweater," said Francine, eyes shut against Lavinia's shoulder.

The policeman said, "I guess you can go now, ladies. You might drop by the station tomorrow for a little more questioning."

Lavinia and Francine walked away from the police and the delicate sheet-covered thing on the ravine grass.

Lavinia felt her heart going loudly within her and she was cold, too, with a February cold. There were bits of sudden snow all over her flesh and the moon washed her brittle fingers whiter, and she remembered doing all the talking while Francine just sobbed.

A police voice called, "You want an escort, ladies?"

"No, we'll make it," said Lavinia, and they walked on. I can't remember anything now, she thought. I can't remember how she looked lying there, or anything. I don't believe it happened. Already I'm forgetting, I'm making myself forget.

"I've never *seen* a dead person before," said Francine.

Lavinia looked at her wrist watch, which seemed impossibly far away. "It's only 8:30. We'll pick up Helen and get on to the show."

"The show!"

"It's what we *need*."

"Lavinia, you don't *mean* it!"

"We've got to forget this. It's not good to remember."

"But Eliza's back there now and—"

"We need to laugh. We'll go to the show as if nothing happened."

"But Eliza was once your friend, *my* friend—"

"We can't help her; we can only help ourselves forget. I insist. I won't go home and brood over it. I won't *think* of it. I'll fill my mind with everything else *but*."

They started up the side of the ravine on a stony path in the dark. They heard voices and stopped.

Below, near the creek waters, a voice was murmuring, "I am The Lonely One. I am The Lonely One. I *kill* people."

"And I'm Eliza Ramsell. Look. And I'm dead, see my tongue out my mouth, see!"

Francine shrieked. "You, there! Children, you nasty children! Get home, get out of the ravine, you hear me? Get home, get home, get home!"

The children fled from their game. The night swallowed their laughter away up the distant hills into the warm darkness.

Francine sobbed and walked on.

"I THOUGHT YOU ladies'd never come!" Helen Greer tapped her foot atop her porch steps. "You're only an hour late, that's all."

"We—" started Francine.

Lavinia clutched her arm. "There was a commotion. Someone found Eliza Ramsell dead in the ravine."

Helen gasped. "Who found her?"

"We don't know."

The three maiden ladies stood in the summer night looking at one another. "I've a notion to lock myself in my house," said Helen at last.

But finally she went to fetch a sweater, and while she was gone Francine whispered frantically, "Why didn't you *tell* her?"

"Why upset her? Time enough tomorrow," replied Lavinia.

The three women moved along the street under the black trees through a town that was slamming and locking doors, pulling down windows and shades and turning on blazing lights. They saw eyes peering out at them from curtained windows.

How strange, thought Lavinia Nebbs, the ice-cream night, the Popsicles dropped in puddles of lime and chocolate where they fell when the children were scooped indoors. Baseballs and bats lie on the unfootprinted lawns. A half-drawn white chalk hopscotch line is there on the steamed sidewalk.

"We're crazy out on a night like this," said Helen.

"Lonely One can't kill three ladies," said Lavinia. "There's safety in numbers. Besides, it's too soon. The murders never come less than a month apart."

A shadow fell across their faces. A figure loomed. As if someone had struck an organ a terrible blow, the three women shrieked.

"*Got* you!" The man jumped from behind a tree. Rearing into the moonlight, he laughed. Leaning on the tree, he laughed again.

"Hey, I'm the—The Lonely One!"

"Tom Dillon!"

"Tom!"

"Tom," said Lavinia. "If you ever do a childish thing like that again, may you be riddled with bullets by mistake!"

Francine began to cry.

Tom Dillon stopped smiling. "Hey, I'm sorry."

"Haven't you heard about Eliza Ramsell?" snapped Lavinia. "She's dead, and you scaring women. You should be ashamed. Don't speak to us again."

"Aw—"

He moved to follow them.

"Stay right there, Mr. Lonely One, and scare yourself," said Lavinia.

"Go see Eliza Ramsell's face and see if it's funny!" She pushed the other two on along the street of trees and stars, Francine holding a handkerchief to her face.

"Francine," pleaded Helen, "it was only a joke. Why's she crying so hard?"

"I guess we better tell you, Helen. We found Eliza. And it wasn't pretty. And we're trying to forget. We're going to the show to help and let's not talk about it. Enough's enough. Get your ticket money ready, we're almost downtown."

THE DRUG STORE WAS a small pool of sluggish air which the great wooden fans stirred in tides of arnica and tonic and soda-smell out into the brick streets.

"A nickel's worth of green mint chews," said Lavinia to the druggist. His face was set and pale, like all the faces they had seen on the half-empty streets. "For eating in the show," she explained, as the druggist dropped the mints into a sack with a silver shovel.

"Sure look pretty tonight," said the druggist. "You looked cool this noon, Miss Lavinia, when you was in here for chocolates. So cool and nice that someone asked after you."

"Oh?"

"You're getting popular. Man sitting at the counter—" he rustled a few more mints in the sack—"watched you walk out and he said to me, 'Say, who's *that?*' Man in a dark suit, thin pale face. 'Why, that's Lavinia Nebbs, prettiest maiden lady in town,' I said, 'Beautiful,' *he* said. 'Where's she live?'" Here the druggist paused and looked away.

"You *didn't?*" wailed Francine. "You didn't give him her address, I hope? You *didn't!*"

"Sorry, guess I didn't think. I said, 'Oh, over on Park Street, you know, near the ravine.' Casual remark. But now, tonight, them finding the body, I heard a minute ago, I suddenly thought, what've I *done!*" He handed over the package, much too full.

"You fool!" cried Francine, and tears were in her eyes.

"I'm sorry. 'Course maybe it was nothing."

"Nothing, nothing!" said Francine.

Lavinia stood with the three people looking at her, staring at her. She didn't know what or how to feel. She felt nothing—except perhaps the slightest prickle of excitement in her throat. She held out her money automatically.

"No charge for those peppermints." The druggist turned down his eyes and shuffled some papers.

"Well, I know what we're going to do right *now*!" Helen stalked out of the drug shop. "We're going right straight home. I'm not going to be part of any hunting party for you, Lavinia. That man asking for you. You're *next*! You want to be dead in that ravine?"

"It was just a man," said Lavinia slowly, eyes on the streets.

"So's Tom Dillon a man, but maybe he's The Lonely One!"

"We're all overwrought," said Lavinia reasonably. "I won't miss the movie now. If I'm the next victim, let me *be* the next victim. A lady has all too little excitement in her life, especially an old maid, a lady thirty-seven like me, so don't you mind if I enjoy it. And I'm being sensible. Stands to reason he won't be out tonight, so soon after a murder. A month from now, yes, when the police've relaxed and when he *feels* like another murder. You've got to *feel* like murdering people, you know. At least that kind of murderer does. And he's just resting up now. And anyway I'm not going home to stew in my own juices."

"But Eliza's face, there in the ravine!"

"After the first look I never looked again. I didn't *drink* it in, if that's what you mean. I can see a thing and tell myself I never saw it, that's how strong *I* am. And the whole argument's silly anyhow, because I'm not beautiful."

"Oh, but you are, Lavinia. You're the loveliest maiden lady in town, now that Eliza's—" Francine stopped. "If you'd only relaxed, you'd been married years ago—"

"Stop sniveling, Francine. Here's the box office. You and Helen go on home. I'll sit alone and go home alone."

"Lavinia, you're crazy. We can't leave you here—"

They argued for five minutes. Helen started to walk away but came back when she saw Lavinia thump down her money for a solitary movie ticket. Helen and Francine followed her silently into the theater.

The first show was over. In the dim auditorium, as they sat in the odor of ancient brass polish, the manager appeared before the worn red velvet curtains for an announcement:

"The police have asked for an early closing tonight. So everyone can be home at a decent hour. So we're cutting our short subjects and putting on our feature film again now. The show will be over at 11. Everyone's advised to go straight home and not linger on the streets. Our police force is pretty small and will be spread around pretty thin."

"That means us, Lavinia. *Us!*" Lavinia felt the hands tugging at her elbows on either side.

Harold Lloyd in Welcome, Danger! said the screen in the dark.

"Lavinia," Helen whispered.

"What?"

"As we came in, a man in a dark suit, across the street, crossed over. He just came in. He just sat in the row behind us."

"Oh, Helen."

"He's right behind us *now.*"

Lavinia looked at the screen.

Helen turned slowly and glanced back. "I'm calling the manager!" she cried and leaped up. "Stop the film! Lights!"

"Helen, come back!" said Lavinia, her eyes shut.

WHEN THEY SET down their empty soda glasses, each of the ladies had a chocolate mustache on her upper lip. They removed them with their tongues, laughing.

"You see how *silly* it was?" said Lavinia. "All that riot for nothing. How embarrassing!"

The drug-store clock said 11:25. They had come out of the theater and the laughter and the enjoyment feeling new. And now they were laughing at Helen, and Helen was laughing at herself.

Lavinia said, "When you ran up that aisle crying 'Lights!' I thought I'd die!"

"That poor man!"

"The theater manager's brother from Racine!"

"I apologized," said Helen.

"You *see* what panic can do?"

The great fans still whirled and whirled in the warm night air, stirring and restirring the smells of vanilla, raspberry, peppermint, and disinfectant in the drug store.

"We shouldn't have stopped for these sodas. The police said—"

"Oh, bosh the police," laughed Lavinia. "I'm not afraid of anything. The Lonely One is a million miles away now. He won't be back for weeks, and the police'll get him then, just wait. Wasn't the film *funny*!"

The streets were clean, and empty. Not a car or a truck or a person was in sight. The bright lights were still lit in the small store windows where the hot wax dummies stood. Their blank blue eyes watched as the ladies walked past them, down the night street.

"Do you suppose if we screamed they'd do anything?"

"Who?"

"The dummies, the window-people."

"Oh, Fran*cine*."

"Well . . ."

There were a hundred people in the windows, stiff and silent, and three people on the street, the echoes following like gunshots when they tapped their heels on the baked pavement.

A red neon sign flickered dimly, buzzing like a dying insect. They walked past it.

Baked and white, the long avenue lay ahead. Blowing and tall in a wind that touched only their leafy summits, the trees stood on either side of the three small women.

"First we'll walk you home, Francine."

"No, I'll walk *you* home."

"Don't be silly. You live the nearest. If you walked me home, you'd have to come back across the ravine all by yourself. And if so much as a leaf fell on you, you'd drop dead."

Francine said, "I can stay the night at your house. You're the *pretty* one!"

"No."

So they drifted like three prim clothes-forms over a moonlit sea of lawn and concrete and trees. To Lavinia, watching the black trees flit by, listening to the voices of her friends, the night seemed to quicken. They seemed to be running while walking slowly. Everything seemed fast, and the color of hot snow.

"Let's sing," said Lavinia.

They sang sweetly and quietly, arm in arm, not looking back. They felt the hot sidewalk cooling underfoot, moving, moving.

"Listen," said Lavinia.

They listened to the summer night, to the crickets and the far-off tone of the courthouse clock making it fifteen minutes to 12.

"Listen."

A porch swing creaked in the dark. And there was Mr. Terle, silent, alone on his porch as they passed, having a last cigar. They could see the pink cigar fire idling to and fro.

Now the lights were going, going, gone. The little house lights and big house lights, the yellow lights and green hurricane lights, the candles and oil lamps and porch lights, and everything felt locked up in brass and iron and steel. Everything, thought Lavinia, is boxed and wrapped and shaded. She imagined the people in their moonlit beds, and their breathing in the summer night, safe and together. And here we are, she thought, listening to our solitary footsteps on the baked summer-evening sidewalk. And above us the lonely street lights shining down, making a million wild shadows.

"Here's your house, Francine. Good night."

"Lavinia, Helen, stay here tonight. It's late, almost midnight now. Mrs. Murdock has an extra room. I'll make hot chocolate. It'd be ever such fun!" Francine was holding them both close to her.

"No, thanks," said Lavinia.

And Francine began to cry.

"Oh, not *again*, Francine," said Lavinia.

"I don't want you dead," sobbed Francine, the tears running straight down her cheeks. "You're so fine and nice, I want you alive. Please, oh, please."

"Francine, I didn't realize how much this has affected you. But I promise you I'll phone when I get home, right away."

"Oh, *will* you?"

"And tell you I'm safe, yes. And tomorrow we'll have a picnic lunch at Electric Park, all right? With ham sandwiches I'll make myself. How's that? You'll see; I'm going to live forever!"

"You'll phone?"

"I promised, didn't I?"

"Good night, good night!" Francine was gone behind her door, locked tight in an instant.

"Now," said Lavinia to Helen, "I'll walk *you* home."

The courthouse clock struck the hour.

The sounds went across a town that was empty, emptier than it had ever been before. Over empty streets and empty lots and empty lawns the sound went.

"Ten, eleven, *twelve*," counted Lavinia, with Helen on her arm.

"Don't you feel *funny*?" asked Helen.

"How do you mean?"

"When you think of us being out here on the sidewalk, under the trees, and all those people safe behind locked doors lying in their beds. We're practically the only walking people out in the open in a thousand miles, I bet." The sound of the deep warm dark ravine came near.

In a minute they stood before Helen's house, looking at each other for a long time. The wind blew the odor of cut grass and wet lilacs between them. The moon was high in a sky that was beginning to cloud over. "I don't suppose it's any use asking you to stay, Lavinia?"

"I'll be going on."

"Sometimes . . ."

"Sometimes what?"

"Sometimes I think people *want* to die. You've certainly acted odd all evening."

"I'm just not afraid," said Lavinia. "And I'm curious, I suppose. And I'm using my head. Logically, The Lonely One can't be around. The police and all."

"*Our* police? *Our* little old force? They're home in bed too, the covers up over their ears."

"Let's just say I'm enjoying myself, precariously but safely. If there were any *real* chance of anything happening to me, I'd stay here with you, you can be sure of that."

"Maybe your subconscious doesn't want you to live any more."

"You and Francine, honestly!"

"I feel so guilty. I'll be drinking hot coffee just as you reach the ravine bottom and walk on the bridge in the dark."

"Drink a cup for me. Good night."

LAVINIA NEBBS WALKED down the midnight street, down the late summer night silence. She saw the houses with their dark windows and far away she heard a dog barking. In five minutes, she thought, I'll be safe home. In five minutes I'll be phoning silly little Francine. I'll—

She heard a man's voice singing far away among the trees. She walked a little faster. Coming down the street toward her in the dimming moonlight was a man. He was walking casually.

I can run and knock on one of these doors, thought Lavinia. If necessary.

The man was singing, *Shine On, Harvest Moon,* and he carried a long club in his hand. "Well, look who's here! What a time of night for you to be out, Miss Nebbs!"

"Officer Kennedy!"

And that's who it was, of course—Officer Kennedy on his beat.

"I'd better see you home."

"Never mind, I'll make it."

"But you live across the ravine."

Yes, she thought, but I won't walk the ravine with *any* man. How do I know *who* The Lonely One is? "No, thanks," she said.

"I'll wait right here then," he said. "If you need help give a yell. I'll come running."

She went on, leaving him under a light, humming to himself, alone.

Here I am, she thought.

The ravine.

She stood on the top of the 113 steps down the steep, brambled bank that led across the creaking bridge and up through the black hills to Park Street. And only one lantern to see by. Three minutes from now, she thought, I'll be putting my key in my house door. Nothing can happen in just 180 seconds.

She started down the dark green steps into the deep ravine night.

"One, two, three, four, five, six, seven, eight, nine steps," she whispered.

She felt she was running but she was not running.

"Fifteen, sixteen, seventeen, eighteen, nineteen steps," she counted aloud.

The ravine was deep, deep and black, black. And the world was gone, the world of safe people in bed. The locked doors, the town, the drug store, the theater, the lights, everything was gone. Only the ravine existed and lived, black and huge about her.

"Nothing's happened, has it? No one around, *is* there? Twenty-four, twenty-five steps. Remember that old ghost story you told each other when you were children?"

She listened to her feet on the steps.

"The story about the dark man coming in your house and you upstairs in bed. And now he's at the *first* step coming up to your room. Now he's at the *second* step. Now he's at the third and the fourth and the *fifth* step! Oh, how you laughed and screamed at that story! And now the horrid dark man is at the twelfth step, opening your door, and now he's standing by your bed. I *got you!*"

She screamed. It was like nothing she had ever heard, that scream. She had never screamed that loud in her life. She stopped, she froze, she clung to the wooden banister. Her heart exploded in her. The sound of its terrified beating filled the universe.

"There, there!" she screamed to herself. "At the bottom of the steps. A man, under the light! No, now he's gone! He was *waiting* there!"

She listened.

Silence. The bridge was empty.

Nothing, she thought, holding her heart. Nothing. Fool. That story I told myself. How silly. What shall I do?

Her heartbeats faded.

Shall I call the officer, did he hear my scream? Or was it only loud to *me*. Was it really just a small scream after all?

She listened. Nothing. Nothing.

I'll go back to Helen's and sleep there tonight. But even while she thought this she moved down again. No, it's nearer home now. Thirty-eight, thirty-nine steps, careful, don't fall. Oh, I *am* a fool. Forty steps. Forty-one. Almost halfway now. She froze again.

"Wait," she told herself. She took a step.

There was an echo.

She took another step. Another echo—just a fraction of a moment later.

"Someone's following me," she whispered to the ravine, to the black crickets and dark green frogs and the black steam. "Someone's on the steps behind me. I don't dare turn around."

Another step, another echo.

Every time I take a step, *they* take one.

A step and an echo. Weakly she asked of the ravine, "Officer Kennedy? Is that *you?*"

The crickets were suddenly still. The crickets were listening. The night was listening to *her*. For a moment all the far summer-night meadows and close summer-night trees were suspending motion. Leaf, shrub, star, and meadowgrass had ceased their particular tremors and were listening to Lavinia Nebbs's heart. And perhaps a thousand miles away, across locomotive-lonely country, in an empty way-station a lonely night traveler reading a dim newspaper under a naked light-bulb might raise his head, listen, and think, What's that?—and decide, Only a woodchuck, surely, beating a hollow log. But it was Lavinia Nebbs, it was the heart of Lavinia Nebbs.

Faster. Faster. She went down the steps.

Run!

She heard music. In a mad way, a silly way, she heard the huge surge of music that pounded at her, and she realized as she ran—as she ran in panic and terror—that some part of her mind was dramatizing, borrowing from the turbulent score of some private film. The music was rushing and plunging her faster, faster, plummeting and scurrying, down and down into the pit of the ravine!

"Only a little way," she prayed. "One hundred ten, eleven, twelve, thirteen steps! The bottom! Now, run! Across the bridge!"

She spoke to her legs, her arms, her body, her terror; she advised all parts of herself in this white and terrible instant. Over the roaring creek waters, on the swaying, almost-alive bridge planks she ran, followed by the wild footsteps behind, with the music following too, the music shrieking and babbling.

He's following. Don't turn, don't look—if you see him, you'll not be able to move! You'll be frightened, you'll freeze! Just run, run, *run*!

She ran across the bridge.

Oh, God! God, please, please let me get up the hill! Now up, up the path, now between the hills. Oh, God, it's dark, and everything so far away! If I screamed now it wouldn't help; I can't scream anyway! Here's the top of the path, here's the street. Thank God I wore my low-heeled shoes. I can run, I can run! Oh, God, please let me be safe! If I get home safe I'll never go out alone, I was a fool, let me admit it, a fool! I didn't know what terror was! I wouldn't let myself think, but if you let me get home from this I'll never go out without Helen or Francine again! Across the street now!

She crossed the street and rushed up the sidewalk.

Oh, God, the porch! My house!

In the middle of her running, she saw the empty lemonade glass where she had left it hours before, in the good, easy, lazy time, left it on the railing. She wished she was back in that time now, drinking from it, the night still young and not begun.

"Oh, please, please, give me time to get inside and lock the door and I'll be safe!"

She heard her clumsy feet on the porch, felt her hands scrabbling and ripping at the lock with the key. She heard her heart. She heard her inner voice shrieking.

The key fitted.

"Unlock the door, quick, quick!"

The door opened.

"Now inside. *Slam* it!"

She slammed the door.

"Now lock it, bar it, lock it!" she cried. "Lock it *tight*!"

The door was locked and barred and bolted.

The music stopped. She listened to her heart again and the sound of it diminishing into silence.

Home.

Oh, safe at home. Safe, safe and safe at home! She slumped against the door. Safe, safe. Listen. Not a sound. Safe, safe, oh, thank God, safe at home.

I'll never go out at night again. Safe, oh, safe, safe, home, so good, so safe. Safe inside, the door locked. Wait. Look out the window.

She looked. She gazed out the window for a full half-minute.

"Why there's no one there at all! Nobody! There was no one following me at all. Nobody running after me." She caught her breath and almost laughed at herself. "It stands to reason. If a man *had* been following me, he'd have *caught* me. I'm not a fast runner. There's no one on the porch or in the yard. How silly of me! I wasn't running from anything except *me.* That ravine was safer than safe. Just the same, though, it's nice to be home. Home's the really good warm safe place, the *only* place to be."

She put her hand out to the light switch and stopped.

"What?" she asked. "What, *what?*"

Behind her, in the black living room, someone cleared his throat . . .

AT MIDNIGHT, IN THE MONTH OF JUNE
RAY BRADBURY

It is Frederic Dannay, one half of the Ellery Queen collaboration, who we have to thank for the following story. After reading "The Whole Town's Sleeping," Dannay suggested that Bradbury write a sequel for *Ellery Queen's Mystery Magazine*. This was a daunting request, according to the author.

Having brought the story to the point where the reader expected the usual denouement, Bradbury deliberately left it hanging, leaving it to the reader to decide if The Lonely One will strangle Lavinia, as he apparently had strangled other young women, or even, come to think of it, if The Lonely One is a man, since the figure is described merely as "someone." And what was his demented motive for committing these horrible crimes? Bradbury doesn't help us here, either.

So should we anticipate a nice, tidy, ending, as creators of traditional detective stories have taught us to expect, or will we still be left in the dark, as befits a tale set at midnight. Read on and find out.

"At Midnight, in the Month of June" was first published in the June 1954 issue of *Ellery Queen's Mystery Magazine*.

AT MIDNIGHT, IN THE MONTH OF JUNE

BY RAY BRADBURY

HE HAD BEEN WAITING a long time in the summer night, as the darkness pressed warmer to the earth and the stars turned slowly over the sky. He sat in total darkness, his hands lying easily on the arms of the Morris chair. He heard the town clock strike 9 and 10 and 11, and then at last 12. The breeze from an open back window flowed through the midnight house in an unlit stream, that touched him like a dark rock where he sat silently watching the front door—silently watching.

> At midnight, in the month of June . . .

The cool night poem by Mr. Edgar Allan Poe slid over his mind like the waters of a shadowed creek.

> The lady sleeps! Oh, may her sleep,
> Which is enduring, so be deep!

He moved down the black shapeless halls of the house, stepped out of the back window, feeling the town locked away in bed, in dream, in night. He saw the shining snake of garden hose coiled resiliently in the grass. He turned on the water. Standing alone, watering the flower bed, he imagined himself a conductor leading an orchestra that only night-strolling dogs might hear, passing on their way to nowhere with strange white smiles. Very carefully he planted both feet and his tall weight into the mud beneath the window, making deep, well-outlined prints. He stepped inside again and walked, leaving mud, down the absolutely unseen hall, his hands seeing for him.

Through the front-porch window he made out the faint outline of a lemonade glass, one-third full, sitting on the porch rail where *she* had left it. He trembled quietly.

Now, he could feel her coming home. He could feel her moving across town, far away, in the summer night. He shut his eyes and put his mind out to find her; and felt her moving along in the dark; he knew just where she stepped down from a curb and crossed a street, and up on a curb and tack-tacking, tack-tacking along under the June elms and the last of the lilacs, with a friend. Walking the empty desert of night, he was she. He felt a purse in his hands. He felt long hair prickle his neck, and his mouth turn greasy with lipstick. Sitting still, he was walking, walking, walking on home after midnight.

"Good night!"

He heard but did not hear the voices, and she was coming nearer, and now she was only a mile away and now only a matter of a thousand yards, and now she was sinking, like a beautiful white lantern on an invisible wire, down into the cricket and frog and water-sounding ravine. And he knew the texture of the wooden ravine stairs as if, a boy he was rushing down them, feeling the rough grain and the dust and the leftover heat of the day . . .

He put his hands out on the air, open. The thumbs of his hands touched, and then the fingers, so that his hands made a circle, enclosing emptiness, there before him. Then, very slowly, he squeezed his hands tighter and tighter together, his mouth open, his eyes shut.

He stopped squeezing and put his hands, trembling, back on the arms of the chair. He kept his eyes shut.

Long ago, he had climbed, one night, to the top of the courthouse tower fire-escape, and looked out at the silver town, at the town of the moon, and the town of summer. And he had seen all the dark houses with two things in them, people and sleep, the two elements joined in bed and all their tiredness and terror breathed upon the still air, siphoned back quietly, and breathed out again, until that element was purified, the problems and hatreds and horrors of the previous day exorcised long before morning and done away with forever.

He had been enchanted with the hour, and the town, and he had felt very powerful, like the magic man with the marionettes who strung destinies across a stage on spider-threads. On the very top of the courthouse tower he could see the least flicker of leaf turning in the moonlight five miles away; the last light, like a pink pumpkin eye, wink out. The town did not escape his eye—it could do nothing without his knowing its every tremble and gesture.

And so it was tonight. He felt himself a tower with the clock in it pounding slow and announcing hours in a great bronze tone, and gazing upon a town where a woman, hurried or slowed by fitful gusts and breezes of now terror and now self-confidence, took the chalk-white midnight sidewalks home, fording solid avenues of tar and stone, drifting among fresh-cut lawns, and now running, running down the steps, through the ravine, up, up the hill, up the hill!

He heard her footsteps before he really heard them. He heard her gasping before there was a gasping. He fixed his gaze to the lemonade glass outside, on the banister. Then the real sound, the real running, the gasping, echoed wildly outside. He sat up. The footsteps raced across the street, the sidewalk, in a panic. There was a babble, a clumsy stumble up the porch steps, a key racheting the door, a voice yelling in a whisper, praying to itself. "Oh, God, dear God!" Whisper! Whisper! And the woman crashing in the door, slamming it, bolting it, talking, whispering, talking to herself in the dark room.

He felt, rather than saw, her hand move toward the light switch.

He cleared his throat.

SHE STOOD AGAINST the door in the dark. If moonlight could have struck in upon her, she would have shimmered like a small pool of water on a windy night. He felt the fine sapphire jewels come out upon her face, and her face all glittering with brine. "Lavinia," he whispered. Her arms were raised across the door like a crucifix. He heard her mouth open and her lungs push a warmness upon the air. She was a beautiful dim white moth: with the sharp needle point of terror he had her pinned against the wooden door. He could walk all around the specimen, if he wished, and look at her, look at her.

"Lavinia," he whispered. He heard her heart beating. She did not move.

"It's me," he whispered.

"Who?" she said, so faint it was a small pulse-beat in her throat.

"I won't tell you," he whispered. He stood perfectly straight in the center of the room. God, but he felt *tall!* Tall and dark and very beautiful to himself, and the way his hands were out before him was as if he might play a piano at any moment, a lovely melody, a waltzing tune. The hands were wet, they felt as if he had dipped them into a bed of mint and cool menthol.

"If I told you who I am, you might not be afraid," he whispered. "I want you to be afraid. Are you afraid?"

She said nothing. She breathed out and in, out and in, a small bellows which, pumped steadily, blew upon her fear and kept it going, kept it alight.

"Why did you go to the show tonight?" he whispered. "*Why* did you go to the show?"

No answer.

He took a step forward, heard her breath take itself like a sword hissing in its sheath.

"Why did you come back through the ravine, alone?" he whispered. "You *did* come back alone, didn't you? Did you think you'd meet me in the middle of the bridge? Did you hope you'd meet me in the middle of the bridge? Why did you go to the show tonight? Why did you come back through the ravine, alone?"

"I—" she gasped.

"You," he whispered.

"No—" she cried, in a whisper.

"Lavinia," he said. He took another step.

"Please," she said.

"Open the door. Get out. And run," he whispered.

She did not move.

"Lavinia, open the door."

She began to whimper in her throat.

"Run," he said.

In moving he felt something touch his knee. He pushed, something tilted in space and fell over, a table, a basket, and a half-dozen unseen balls of yarn tumbled like cats in the dark, rolling softly. In the one moonlit space on the floor beneath the window, like a metal sign pointing, lay the sewing shears. They were winter ice in his hand. He held them out to her suddenly, through the still air. "Here," he whispered. He touched them to her hand. She snatched her hand back. "Here," he urged.

"Take this," he said, after a pause.

He opened her fingers that were already dead and cold to the touch, and stiff and strange to manage, and he pressed the scissors into them. "Now," he said.

He looked out at the moonlit sky for a long moment, and when he glanced back it was some time before he could see her in the dark.

"I waited," he said. "But that's the way it's always been. I waited for the others, too. But they all came looking for me, finally. It was that easy. Five lovely ladies in the last two years. I waited for them in the ravine, in the country, by the lake, everywhere I waited, and they came out to find me, and found me. It was always nice, the next day, reading the newspapers. And you went looking tonight, I know, or you wouldn't have come back alone through the ravine. Did you scare yourself there, and run? Did you think I was down there waiting for you? You should have *heard* yourself running up the walk! Through the door! And *locking* it! You thought you were safe inside, home at last, safe, safe, safe, didn't you?"

She held the scissors in one dead hand, and she began to cry. He saw the merest gleam, like water upon the wall of a dim cave. He heard the sounds she made.

"No," he whispered. "You have the scissors. Don't cry."

She cried. She did not move at all. She stood there, shivering, her head back against the door, beginning to slide down the length of the door toward the floor.

"Don't cry," he whispered.

"I don't like to hear you cry," he said. "I can't stand to hear that."

He held his hands out and moved them through the air until one of them touched her cheek. He felt the wetness of that cheek, he felt her warm breath touch his palm like a summer moth. Then he said only one more thing:

"Lavinia," he said, gently, "Lavinia."

HOW CLEARLY HE remembered the old nights in the old times, in the times when he was a boy and them all running, and running, and hiding and hiding, and playing hide-and-seek. In the first spring nights and in the warm summer nights and in the late summer evenings and in those first sharp autumn nights when doors were shutting, early and porches were empty except for blowing leaves. The game of hide-and-seek went on as long as there was sun to see by, or the rising snow-crusted moon. Their feet upon the green lawns were like the scattered throwing of soft peaches and crabapples, and the counting of the Seeker with his arms cradling his buried head, chanting to the night: five, ten, fifteen, twenty, twenty-five, thirty, thirty-five, forty, forty-five, fifty . . . And the sound of thrown apples fading, the children all safely closeted in tree or bush-shade, under the latticed porches with the clever dogs minding not to wag their tails and give their secret away. And the counting done: eighty-five, ninety, ninety-five, a hundred!

Ready or not, here I come! And the Seeker running out through the town wilderness to find the Hiders, and the Hiders keeping their secret laughter in their mouths, like precious June strawberries, with the help of clasped hands. And the Seeker seeking after the smallest heartbeat in the high elm tree or the glint of a dog's eye in a bush, or a small water sound of laughter which could not help but burst out as the Seeker ran right on by and did not see the shadow within the shadow . . .

He moved into the bathroom of the quiet house, thinking all this, enjoying the clear rush, the tumultuous gushing of memories like a water-falling of the mind over a steep precipice, falling and falling toward the bottom of his head.

God, how secret and tall they had felt, hidden away. God, how the shadows mothered and kept them, sheathed in their own triumph. Glowing with perspiration how they crouched like idols and thought they might hide *forever!* While the silly Seeker went pelting by on his way to failure and inevitable frustration.

Sometimes the Seeker stopped right *at* your tree and peered up at you crouched there in your invisible warm wings, in your great colorless windowpane bat wings, and said, "I *see* you there!" But you said nothing. "You're *up* there all right." But you said nothing. "Come on *down!* But not a word, only a victorious Cheshire smile. And doubt coming over the Seeker below. "It is *you*, isn't it?" The backing off and away. "Aw, I *know* you're up there!" No answer. Only the tree sitting in the night and shaking quietly, leaf upon leaf. And the Seeker, afraid of the dark within darkness, loping away to seek easier game, something to be named and certain of. "All right for *you!*"

He washed his hands in the bathroom, and thought, Why am I washing my hands? And then the grains of time sucked back up the flue of the hourglass again and it was another year . . .

He remembered that sometimes when he played hide-and-seek they did not find him at all; he would not let them find him. He said not a word, he stayed so long in the apple tree that he was a white-fleshed apple; he lingered so long in the chestnut tree that he had the hardness and the brown brightness of the autumn nut. And God, how powerful to be undiscovered, how immense it made you, until your arms were branching, growing out in all directions, pulled by the stars and the tidal moon until your secretness enclosed the town and mothered it with your compassion and tolerance. You could do anything in the shadows, anything. If you chose to do it, you could do it. How powerful to sit above the sidewalk and see people pass under, never aware you were there and watching, and might put out an arm to brush their noses with the five-legged spider of your hand and brush their thinking minds with terror.

He finished washing his hands and wiped them on a towel.

But there was always an end to the game. When the Seeker had found all the other Hiders and these Hiders in turn were Seekers and they were all spreading out, calling your name, looking for you, how much more powerful and important *that* made you.

"Hey, hey! Where *are* you! Come in, the game's *over!*"

But you not moving or coming in. Even when they all collected under your tree and saw, or thought they saw you there at the very top, and called up at you. "Oh, come down! Stop fooling! Hey! we see you. We know you're there!"

Not answering even then—not until the final, the fatal thing happened. Far off, a block away, a silver whistle screaming, and the voice of your mother calling your name, and the whistle again. "Nine o'clock!" her voice wailed. "Nine o'clock! Home!"

But you waited until all the children were gone. Then, very carefully unfolding yourself and your warmth and secretness, and keeping out of the lantern light at corners, you ran home alone, alone in darkness and shadow, hardly breathing, keeping the sound of your heart quiet and in yourself, so if people heard anything at all they might think it was only the wind blowing a dry leaf by in the night. And your mother standing there, with the screen door wide . . .

He finished wiping his hands on the towel. He stood a moment thinking of how it had been the last two years here in town. The old game going on, by himself, playing it alone, the children gone, grown into settled middle-age, but now, as before, himself the final and last and only Hider, and the whole town seeking and seeing nothing and going on home to lock their doors.

But tonight, out of a time long past, and on many nights now, he had heard that old sound, the sound of the silver whistle, blowing and blowing. It was certainly not a night bird singing, for he knew each sound so well. But the whistle kept calling and calling and a voice said, *Home* and *Nine o'clock*, even though it was now long after midnight. He listened. There was the silver whistle. Even though his mother had died many years ago, after having put his father in an early grave with her temper and her tongue. Do this, do that, do this, do that, do this, do that, do this, do that . . ." A phonograph record, broken, playing the same cracked tune again, again, again, her voice, her cadence, around, around, around, around, repeat, repeat, repeat.

And the clear silver whistle blowing and the game of hide-and-seek over. No more of walking in the town and standing behind trees and bushes and smiling a smile that burned through the thickest foliage. An automatic thing was happening. His feet were walking and his hands were doing and he knew everything that must be done now.

His hands did not belong to him. He tore a button off his coat and let it drop into the deep dark well of the room. It never seemed to hit bottom. It floated down. He waited.

It seemed never to stop rolling. Finally, it stopped.

His hands did not belong to him. He took his pipe and flung that into the depths of the room. Without waiting for it to strike emptiness, he walked quietly back through the kitchen and peered outside the open, blowing, white-curtained window at the footprints he had made there. He was the Seeker, seeking now, instead of the Hider hiding. He was the quiet searcher finding and sifting and putting away clues, and those footprints were now as alien to him as something from a prehistoric age. They had been made a million years ago by some other man on some other business; they were no part of him at all. He marveled at their precision and deepness and form in the moonlight. He put his hand down almost to touch them, like a great and beautiful archeological discovery! Then he was gone, back through the rooms, ripping a piece of material from his pants-cuff and blowing it off his open palm like a moth.

His hands were not his hands any more, or his body his body.

He opened the front door and went out and sat for a moment on the porch rail. He picked up the lemonade glass and drank what was left, made warm by an evening's waiting, and pressed his fingers tight to the glass, tight, tight, very tight. Then he put the glass down on the railing. The silver whistle! Yes, he thought. Coming, coming. The silver whistle! Yes, he thought. Nine o'clock. Home, home. Nine o'clock. Studies and milk and graham crackers and white cool bed, home, home; nine o'clock and the silver whistle.

He was off the porch in an instant, running softly, lightly, with hardly a breath or a heartbeat, as one barefooted runs, as one all leaf and green June grass and night can run, all shadow, forever running, away from the silent house and across the street, and down into the ravine . . .

HE PUSHED THE door wide and stepped into the owl diner, this long railroad car that, removed from its track, had been put to a solitary and unmoving destiny in the center of town. The place was empty. At the far end of the counter, the counterman glanced up as the door shut and the customer walked along the line of empty swivel seats. The counterman took the toothpick from his mouth.

"Tom Dillon, you old so-and-so! What *you* doing up this time of night, Tom?"

Tom Dillon ordered without the menu. While the food was being prepared, he dropped a nickel in the wall-phone, got his number, and spoke quietly for a time. He hung up, came back, and sat, listening. Sixty seconds later, both he and the counterman heard the police siren wail by at 50 miles an hour. "Well—*hell!*" said the counterman. "Go get 'em, boys!"

He set out a tall glass of milk and a plate of six fresh graham crackers.

Tom Dillon sat there for a long while, looking secretly down at his ripped pants-cuff and muddied shoes. The light in the diner was raw and bright, and he felt like he was on a stage. He held the tall cool glass of milk in his hand, sipping it, eyes shut, chewing the good texture of the graham crackers, feeling it all through his mouth, coating his tongue.

"Would or would you not," he asked, quietly, "call this a hearty meal?"

"I'd call that very hearty indeed," said the counterman, smiling.

Tom Dillon chewed another graham cracker with great concentration, feeling all of it in his mouth. It's just a matter of time, he thought, waiting.

"More milk?"

"Yes," said Tom.

And he watched with steady interest, with the purest and most alert concentration in all of his life, as the white carton tilted and gleamed, and the snowy milk poured out, cool and quiet, like the sound of a running spring at night, and filled the glass up all the way, to the very brim, to the very brim, and over . . .

THIMBLE, THIMBLE
O. HENRY

William Sidney Porter (1862–1910), under the pseudonym O. Henry, wrote more than 600 short stories and, with the possible exception of Edgar Allan Poe, is the most beloved short story writer America has produced.

Arrested for embezzlement from a bank in Austin, Texas, he served five years in an Ohio state penitentiary, where he was befriended by a guard named Orrin Henry, who in all likelihood inspired the famous pseudonym.

His stories have been criticized for being overly sentimental, but they remain staples of the American literary canon. The master of the surprise ending, O. Henry has written such classics as "The Gift of the Magi," "The Last Leaf," "The Ransom of Red Chief," and "A Retrieved Reformation," which became better known when it was staged and later filmed as "Alias Jimmy Valentine."

Other contributions to the mystery genre include *The Gentle Grafter*, selected for *Queen's Quorum* as one of the 106 greatest mystery story collections of all time.

"Thimble, Thimble" was first published in the December 1908 issue of *Hampton's* magazine. It was collected in *Options* the following year. The magazine ran a contest to determine the four best solutions to the mystery and received more than three thousand responses.

THIMBLE, THIMBLE

by O. Henry

THESE ARE THE DIRECTIONS for finding the office of Carteret & Carteret, Mill Supplies and Leather Belting:

You follow the Broadway trail down until you pass the Crosstown Line, the Bread Line, and the Dead Line, and come to the Big Cañons of the Moneygrubber Tribe. Then you turn to the left, to the right, dodge a push-cart and the tongue of a two-ton four-horse dray, and hop, skip, and jump to a granite ledge on the side of a twenty-one-story synthetic mountain of stone and iron. In the twelfth story is the office of Carteret & Carteret. The factory where they make the mill supplies and leather belting is in Brooklyn. Those commodities—to say nothing of Brooklyn—not being of interest to you, let us hold the incidents within the confines of a one-act, one-scene play, thereby lessening the toil of the reader and the expenditure of the publisher. So, if you have the courage to face ten pages of type and Carteret & Carteret's office boy, Percival, you shall sit on a varnished chair in the inner office and peep at the little comedy of the Old Negro, the Hunting-Case Watch, and the Open-Faced Question—mostly borrowed from the late Mr. Frank Stockton, as you will conclude.

First, biography (but pared to the quick) must intervene. I am for the inverted sugar-coated quinine pill—the bitter on the outside.

The Carterets were, or was (Columbia College professors please rule), an old Virginia family. Long time ago the gentlemen of the family had worn lace ruffles and carried tinless foils and owned plantations and had slaves galore.

But the war had greatly reduced their holdings.

In digging up the Carteret history I shall not take you further back than the year 1620. The two original American Carterets came over in that year, but by different means of transportation. One brother, named John, came in the *Mayflower* and became a Pilgrim Father. You've seen his pictures on the covers of the Thanksgiving magazines, hunting turkeys in the deep snow with a blunderbuss. Blandford Carteret, the other brother, crossed the pond in his own brigantine, landed on the Virginia coast, and became an F. F. V. John became distinguished for piety and shrewdness in business; Blandford for his pride, juleps, marksmanship, and vast slave-cultivated plantations.

Then came the Civil War. (I must condense this historical interpolation.) Stonewall Jackson was shot; Lee surrendered; Grant toured the world; cotton went to nine cents; Old Crow whiskey and Jim Crow cars were invented; the Seventy-ninth Massachusetts Volunteers returned to the Ninety-seventh Alabama Zouaves the battle flag of Lundy's Lane which they bought at a second-hand store in Chelsea, kept by a man named Skzchnzski; Georgia sent the President a sixty-pound watermelon—and that brings us up to the time when the story begins. My! but that was sparring for an opening! I really must brush up on my Aristotle.

The Yankee Carterets went into business in New York long before the war. Their house, as far as Leather Belting and Mill Supplies was concerned, was as musty and arrogant and solid as one of those old East India tea-importing concerns that you read about in Dickens. There were some rumors of a war behind its counters, but not enough to affect the business.

During and after the war, Blandford Carteret, F. F. V., lost his plantations, juleps, marksmanship, and life. He bequeathed little more than his pride to his surviving family. So it came to pass that Blandford Carteret, the Fifth, aged fifteen, was invited by the leather-and-mill-supplies branch of that name to come North and learn business instead of hunting foxes and boasting of the glory of his fathers on the reduced acres of his impoverished family. The boy jumped at the chance; and at the age of twenty-five sat in the office of the firm equal partner with John, the Fifth, branch. Here the story begins again.

The young men were about the same age, smooth of face, alert, easy of manner, and with an air that promised mental and physical quickness. They were razored, pearl stick-pinned like other young New Yorkers who might be millionaires or bill clerks.

One afternoon at four o'clock, in the private office of the firm, Blandford Carteret opened a letter that a clerk had just brought to his desk. After reading it, he chuckled audibly for nearly a minute. John looked around from his desk inquiringly.

"It's from mother," said Blandford. "I'll read you the funny part of it. She tells me all the neighborhood news first, of course, and then cautions me against getting my feet wet and musical comedies. After that come vital statistics about calves and pigs and an estimate of the wheat crop. And now I'll quote some:

" 'And what do you think! Old Uncle Jake, who was seventy-six last Wednesday, must go traveling. Nothing would do but he must go to New York and see his "young Marster Blandford." Old as he is, he has a deal of common sense, so I've let him go. I couldn't refuse him—he seemed to have concentrated all his hopes and desires into this one adventure into the wide world. You know he was born on the plantation, and has never been ten miles away from it in his life. And he was your father's body servant during the war, and has been always a faithful vassal and servant of the family. He has often seen the gold watch—the watch that was your father's and your father's father's. I told him it was to be yours, and he begged me to allow him to take it to you and to put it into your hands himself.

" 'So he has it, carefully enclosed in a buckskin case, and is bringing it to you with all the pride and importance of a king's messenger. I gave him money for the round trip and for a two weeks' stay in the city. I wish you would see to it that he gets comfortable quarters—Jake won't need much looking after—he's able to take care of himself.

" 'I gave him full directions about finding you, and packed his valise myself. Take the watch that he brings you—it's almost a decoration. It has been worn by true Carterets, and there isn't a stain upon it nor a false movement of the wheels. Bringing it to you is the crowning joy of Old Jake's life. I wanted him to have that little outing and that happiness before it is too late. You have often heard us talk about how Jake, pretty badly wounded himself, crawled through the reddened grass at Chancellorsville to where your father lay with the bullet in his dear heart, and took the watch from his pocket to keep it from the "Yanks."

" 'So, my son, when the old man comes, consider him as a frail but worthy messenger from the oldtime life and home.

" 'You have been so long away from home and so long among the people that we have always regarded as aliens that I'm not sure that Jake will know you when he sees you. But Jake has a keen perception, and I rather believe that he will know a Virginia Carteret at sight. I can't conceive that even ten years in Yankeeland could change a boy of mine. Anyhow, I'm sure you will know Jake. I put eighteen collars in his valise. If he should have to buy collars, he wears a number 15 ½. Please see that he gets the right ones. He will be no trouble to you at all.

" 'If you are not too busy, I'd like for you to find him a place to board where they have white-meal cornbread, and try to keep him from taking his shoes off in your office or on the street. His right foot swells a little, and he likes to be comfortable.

" 'If you can spare the time, count his handkerchiefs when they come back from the wash. I bought him a dozen new ones before he left. He should be there about the time this letter reaches you. I told him to go straight to your office when he arrives.' "

As soon as Blandford had finished the reading of this, something happened (as there should happen in stories and must happen on the stage).

Percival, the office boy, with his air of despising the world's output of mill supplies and leather belting, came in to announce that a colored gentleman was outside to see Mr. Blandford Carteret. "Bring him in," said Blandford, rising.

John Carteret swung around in his chair and said to Percival: "Ask him to wait a few minutes outside. We'll let you know when to bring him in."

Then he turned to his cousin with one of those broad, slow smiles that was an inheritance of all the Carterets, and said:

"Bland, I've always had a consuming curiosity to understand the differences that you haughty Southerners believe to exist between 'you all' and the people of the North. Of course, I know that you consider yourselves made out of finer clay and look upon Adam as only a collateral branch of your ancestry; but I don't know why. I never could understand the differences between us."

"Well, John," said Blandford, laughing, "what you don't understand about it is just the difference, of course. I suppose it was the feudal way in which we lived that gave us our lordly baronial airs and feeling of superiority."

"But you are not feudal now," went on John. "Since we licked you and stole your cotton and mules you've had to go to work just as we 'damnyankees,' as you call us, have always been doing. And you're just as proud and exclusive and upper-classy as you were before the war. So it wasn't your money that caused it."

"Maybe it was the climate," said Blandford lightly, "or maybe our Negroes spoiled us. I'll call old Jake in, now. I'll be glad to see the old villain again."

"Wait just a moment," said John. "I've got a little theory I want to test. You and I are pretty much alike in our general appearance. Old Jake hasn't seen you since you were fifteen. Let's have him in and play fair and see which of us gets the watch. The old fellow surely ought to be able to pick out his 'young marster' without any trouble. The alleged aristocrat superiority of a 'reb' ought to be visible to him at once. He couldn't make the mistake of handing over the timepiece to a Yankee, of course. The loser buys the dinner this evening and two dozen 15 ½ collars for Jake. Is it a go?"

Blandford agreed heartily. Percival was summoned, and told to usher the "colored gentleman" in.

Uncle Jake stepped inside the private office cautiously. He was a little old man, as black as soot, wrinkled and bald except for a fringe of white wool, cut decorously short, that ran over his ears and around his head. There was nothing of the stage "uncle" about him; his black suit nearly fitted him; his shoes shone, and his straw hat was banded with a gaudy ribbon. In his right hand he carried something carefully concealed by his closed fingers.

Uncle Jake stopped a few steps from the door. Two young men sat in their revolving desk-chairs ten feet apart and looked at him in friendly silence. His gaze slowly shifted many times from one to the other. He felt sure that he was in the presence of one, at least, of the revered family among whose fortunes his life had begun and was to end.

One had the pleasing but haughty Carteret air; the other had the unmistakable straight, long family nose. Both had the keen black eyes, horizontal brows, and thin, smiling lips that had distinguished both the Carteret of the *Mayflower* and him of the brigantine. Old Jake had thought that he could have picked out his young master instantly from a thousand Northerners; but he found himself in difficulties. The best he could do was to use strategy.

"Howdy, Marse Blandford—howdy, suh?" he said looking midway between the young men.

"Howdy, Uncle Jake?" they both answered pleasantly and in unison. "Sit down. Have you brought the watch?"

Uncle Jake chose a hard-bottom chair at a respectful distance, sat on the edge of it, and laid his hat carefully on the floor. The watch in its buckskin case he gripped tightly. He had not risked his life on the battlefield to rescue that watch from his "old marster's" foes to hand it over again to the enemy.

"Yes, suh; I got it in my hand, suh. I'm gwine give it to you right away in jus' a minute. Old Missus told me to put it in young Marse Blandford's hand and tell him to wear it for the family pride and honor. It was a mighty lonesome trip for an old man to make—ten thousand miles, it must be, back to old Vi'ginia, suh. You've growed mightily, young marster. I wouldn't have reconnized you but for yo' powerful resemblance to the old marster."

With admirable diplomacy the old man kept his eyes roaming in the space between the two men. His words might have been addressed to either. Though neither wicked nor perverse, he was seeking for a sign. Blandford and John exchanged winks.

"I reckon you done got you ma's letter," went on Uncle Jake. "She said she was gwine to write to you about my comin' along up this er-way."

"Yes, yes, Uncle Jake," said John, briskly. "My cousin and I have just been notified to expect you. We are both Carterets, you know."

"Although one of us," said Blandford, "was born and raised in the North."

"So if you will hand over the watch—" said John.

"My cousin and I—" said Blandford.

"We'll see to it—" said John.

"That comfortable quarters are found for you," said Blandford.

With creditable ingenuity, old Jake set up a cackling, high-pitched, protracted laugh. He beat his knee, picked up his hat and bent the brim in an apparent paroxysm of humorous appreciation. The seizure afforded him a mask behind which he could roll his eye impartially between, above, and beyond his two tormentors.

"I sees what!" he chuckled, after a while. "You gen'lemen is tryin' to have fun with the po' old man. But you can't fool old Jake. I knowed you, Marse Blandford, the minute I sot eyes on you. You was a po' skimpy little boy no mo' than about fo'teen when you lef home to come No'th; but I knowed you the minute I sot eyes on you. You is the mawtal image of old marster. The other gen'leman resembles you mightily, suh; but you can't fool old Jake on a member of the old Vi'ginia family. No, suh."

At exactly the same time both Carterets smiled and extended a hand for the watch.

Uncle Jake's wrinkled black face lost the expression of amusement into which he had vainly twisted it. He knew that he was being teased, and that it made little real difference, as far as its safety went, into which of those outstretched hands he placed the family treasure. But it seemed to him that not only his own pride and loyalty but much of the Virginia Carterets' was at stake. He had heard down South during the war about that other branch of the family that lived in the North and fought on "the yuther side," and it had always grieved him. He had followed his "old marster's" fortunes from stately luxury through war to almost poverty. And now, with the last relic and reminder of him, blessed by "old missus," and entrusted implicitly to his care, he had come ten thousand miles (as it seemed) to deliver it into the hands of the one who was to wear it and wind it and cherish it and listen to it tick off the unsullied hours that marked the lives of the Carterets—of Virginia.

His experience and conception of the Yankees had been an impression of tyrants—"low-down, common trash"—in blue, laying waste with fire and sword. He had seen the smoke of many burning homesteads almost as grand as Carteret Hall ascending to the drowsy Southern skies. And now he was face to face with one of them—and he could not distinguish him from his "young marster" whom he had come to find and bestow upon him the emblem of his kingship—even as the arm "clothed in white samite, mystic, wonderful" laid Excalibur in the right hand of Arthur. He saw before him two young men, easy, kind, courteous, welcoming, either of whom might have been the one he sought. Troubled, bewildered, sorely grieved at his weakness of judgment, old Jake abandoned his loyal subterfuges. His right hand sweated against the buckskin cover of the watch. He was deeply humiliated and chastened. Seriously, now, his prominent, yellow-white eyes closely scanned the two young men. At the end of his scrutiny he was conscious of but one difference between them. One wore a narrow black tie with a white-pearl stickpin. The other's "four-in-hand" was a narrow blue one pinned with a black pearl.

And then, to old Jake's relief, there came a sudden distraction. Drama knocked at the door with imperious knuckles, and forced Comedy to the wings, and Drama peeped with a smiling but set face over the footlights.

Percival, the hater of mill supplies, brought in a card, which he handed, with the manner of one bearing a cartel, to Blue-Tie.

"Olivia De Ormond," read Blue-Tie from the card. He looked inquiringly at his cousin.

"Why not have her in," said Black-Tie, "and bring matters to a conclusion?"

"Uncle Jake," said one of the young men, "would you mind taking that chair over there in the corner for a while? A lady is coming in—on some business."

The lady whom Percival ushered in was young and petulantly, decidedly, freshly, consciously, and intentionally pretty. She was dressed with such expensive plainness that she made you consider lace and ruffles as mere tatters and rags. But one great ostrich plume that she wore would have marked her anywhere in the army of beauty as the wearer of the merry helmet of Navarre.

Miss De Ormond accepted the swivel chair at Blue-Tie's desk. Then the gentlemen drew leather-upholstered seats conveniently near, and spoke of the weather.

"Yes," said she, "I noticed it was warmer. But I mustn't take up too much of your time during business hours. That is," she continued, "unless we talk business."

She addressed her words to Blue-Tie with a charming smile.

"Very well," said he. "You don't mind my cousin being present, do you? We are generally rather confidential with each other—especially in business matters."

"Oh, no," caroled Miss De Ormond. "I'd rather he did hear. He knows all about it, anyhow. In fact, he's quite a material witness because he was present when you—when it happened. I thought you might want to talk things over before—well, before any action is taken, as I believe the lawyers say."

"Have you anything in the way of a proposition to make?" asked Black-Tie.

Miss De Ormond looked reflectively at the neat toe of one of her dull-kid pumps.

"I had a proposal made to me," she said. "If the proposal sticks, it cuts out the proposition. Let's have that settled first."

"Well, as far as—" began Blue-Tie.

"Excuse me, cousin," interrupted Black-Tie, "if you don't mind my cutting in." And then he turned, with a good-natured air toward the lady.

"Now, let's recapitulate a bit," he said, cheerfully. "All three of us, besides other mutual acquaintances, have been out on a good many larks together."

"I'm afraid I'll have to call the birds by another name," said Miss De Ormond.

"All right," responded Black-Tie, with unimpaired cheerfulness; "suppose we say 'squabs' when we talk about the 'proposal' and 'larks' when we discuss the 'proposition.' You have a quick mind, Miss De Ormond. Two months ago some half-dozen of us went in a motor-car for a day's run into the country. We stopped at a road-house for dinner. My cousin proposed marriage to you then and there. He was influenced to do so. of course, by the beauty and charm which no one can deny that you possess."

"I wish I had you for a press agent, Mr. Carteret," said the beauty, with a dazzling smile.

"You are on the stage, Miss De Ormond," went on Black-Tie. "You have had, doubtless, many admirers, and perhaps other proposals. You must remember, too, that we were a party of merrymakers on that occasion. There were a good many corks pulled. That the proposal of marriage was made to you by my cousin we cannot deny. But hasn't it been your experience that, by common consent, such things lose their seriousness when viewed in the next day's sunlight? Isn't there something of a 'code' among good 'sports'— I use the word in its best sense—that wipes out each day the follies of the evening previous?"

"Oh, yes," said Miss De Ormond. "I know that very well. And I've always played up to it. But as you seem to be conducting the case—with the silent consent of the defendant—I'll tell you something more. I've got letters from him repeating the proposal. And they're signed too."

"I understand," said Black-Tie, gravely. "What's your price for the letters?"

"I'm not a cheap one," said Miss De Ormond. "But I had decided to make you a rate. You both belong to a swell family. Well if I *am* on the stage nobody can say a word against me truthfully. And the money is only a secondary consideration. It isn't the money I was after. I—I believed him—and—and I liked him."

She cast a soft, entrancing glance at Blue-Tie from under her long eyelashes.

"And the price?" went on Black-Tie, inexorably.

"Ten thousand dollars," said the lady, sweetly.

"Or—"

"Or the fulfilment of the engagement to marry."

"I think it is time," interrupted Blue-Tie, "for me to be allowed to say a word or two. You and I, cousin, belong to a family that has held its head pretty high. You have been brought up in a section of the country very different from the one where our branch of the family lived. Yet both of us are Carterets, even if some of our ways and theories differ. You remember, it is a tradition of the family, that no Carteret ever failed in chivalry to a lady or failed to keep his word when it was given."

Then Blue-Tie, with frank decision showing on his countenance, turned to Miss De Ormond.

"Olivia," said he, "on what date will you marry me?"

Before she could answer, Black-Tie again interposed.

"It is a long journey," said he, "from Plymouth Rock to Norfolk Bay. Between the two points we find the changes that nearly three centuries have brought. In that time the old order has changed. We no longer burn witches or torture slaves. And today we neither spread our cloaks on the mud for ladies to walk over nor treat them to the ducking-stool. It is the age of common sense, adjustment, and proportion. All of us—ladies, gentlemen, women, lords, caitiffs, actors, hardware-drummers, Senators, hod-carriers and politicians—are coming to a better understanding.

Chivalry is one of our words that changes its meaning every day. Family pride is a thing of many constructions—it may show itself by maintaining a moth-eaten arrogance in a cob-webbed Colonial mansion or by the prompt paying of one's debts.

"Now, I suppose you've had enough of my monologue. I've learned something of business and a little of life; and I somehow believe, cousin, that our great-great-grandfathers, the original Carterets, would endorse my view of this matter."

Black-Tie wheeled around to his desk, wrote in a checkbook and tore out the check, the sharp rasp of the perforated leaf making the only sound in the room. He laid the check within easy reach of Miss De Ormond's hand.

"Business is business," said he. "We live in a business age. There is my personal check for $10,000. What do you say, Miss De Ormond—will it be orange blossoms or cash?"

Miss De Ormond picked up the check carelessly, folded it indifferently and stuffed it down into her glove.

"Oh, this'll do," she said, calmly. "I just thought I'd call and put it up to you. I guess you people are all right. But a girl has feelings, you know. I've heard one of you was a Southerner—I wonder which one of you it is?"

She arose, smiled sweetly, and walked to the door. There, with a flash of white teeth and a dip of the heavy plume, she disappeared.

Both of the cousins had forgotten Uncle Jake for the first time. Now they heard the shuffling of his shoes as he came across the rug toward them from his seat in the corner.

"Young marster," he said, "take yo' watch."

And without hesitation he laid the ancient timepiece in the hand of its *rightful* owner.

THE GIOCONDA SMILE
ALDOUS HUXLEY

Aldous Huxley (1894–1963) was still in his twenties when he began to publish such cynical novels as *Chrome Yellow* (1921), *Antic Hay* (1923), *Point Counter Point* (1928) and the most successful of his work, *Brave New World* (1932), a futuristic novel of a "Utopian" world that clearly illustrates his disgust with contemporary society.

He has had little to do with the world of mystery fiction, most of it the result of a single short story, "The Gioconda Smile," a tale as enigmatic as its subject.

First published in the August 1921 issue of *English Review*, it was collected in book form in *Mortal Coils* the following year. The story enjoyed so much success that it soon had the unusual distinction of being published in a separate volume in 1938 as No. 9 in the series of Zodiac Books published by Chatto & Windus, following such authors as William Shakespeare, John Donne, and John Keats. Huxley then adapted it for the screen (as he had previously adapted *Jane Eyre* and *Pride and Prejudice*) for a 1947 motion picture directed by Zoltan Korda titled *A Woman's Vengeance*.

Still not finished, he turned it into a three-act stage play in 1948, which also was published by Chatto & Windus; in the United States, Harper & Row published it as *Mortal Coils*.

THE GIOCONDA SMILE

By Aldous Huxley

"Miss Spence will be down directly, sir."

"Thank you," said Mr. Hutton, without turning round. Janet Spence's parlormaid was so ugly—ugly on purpose, it always seemed to him, malignantly, criminally ugly—that he could not bear to look at her more than was necessary. The door closed. Left to himself, Mr. Hutton got up and began to wander round the room, looking with meditative eyes at the familiar objects it contained.

Photographs of Greek statuary, photographs of the Roman Forum, colored prints of Italian masterpieces, all very safe and well known. Poor, dear Janet, what a prig—what an intellectual snob! Her real taste was illustrated in that water-color by the pavement artist, the one she had paid half a crown for (and thirty-five shillings for the frame). How often he had heard her tell the story, how often expatiate on the beauties of that skillful imitation of an oleograph! "A real Artist in the streets," and you could hear the capital A in Artist as she spoke the words. She made you feel that part of his glory had entered into Janet Spence when she tendered him that half crown for the copy of the oleograph. She was implying a compliment to her own taste and penetration. A genuine Old Master for half a crown. Poor, dear Janet!

Mr. Hutton came to a pause in front of a small oblong mirror. Stooping a little to get a full view of his face, he passed a white, well-manicured finger over his mustache. It was as curly, as freshly auburn as it had been twenty years ago. His hair still retained its color, and there was no sign of baldness yet—only a certain elevation of the brow. "Shakespearean," thought Mr. Hutton, with a smile, as he surveyed the smooth and polished expanse of his forehead.

Others abide our question, thou art free . . . Footsteps in the sea . . .

Majesty . . . Shakespeare, thou shouldst be living at this hour. No, that was Milton, wasn't it? Milton, the Lady of Christ's. There was no lady about him. He was what the women would call a manly man. That was why they liked him—for the curly auburn mustache and the discreet redolence of tobacco. Mr. Hutton smiled again; he enjoyed making fun of himself. Lady of Christ's? No, no. He was the Christ of Ladies. Very pretty, very pretty. The Christ of Ladies. Mr. Hutton wished there were somebody he could tell the joke to. Poor, dear Janet wouldn't appreciate it, alas!

He straightened himself up, patted his hair, and resumed his peregrination. Damn the Roman Forum; he hated those dreary photographs.

Suddenly he became aware that Janet Spence was in the room, standing near the door. Mr. Hutton started, as though he had been taken in some felonious act. To make these silent and spectral appearances was one of Janet Spence's peculiar talents. Perhaps she had been there all the time, had seen him looking at himself in the mirror. Impossible! But, still, it was disquieting.

"Oh, you gave me such a surprise," said Mr. Hutton, recovering his smile and advancing with outstretched hand to meet her.

Miss Spence was smiling too: her Gioconda smile, he had once called it in a moment of half-ironical flattery. Miss Spence had taken the compliment seriously, and had always tried to live up to the Leonardo standard. She smiled on his silence while Mr. Hutton shook hands; that was part of the Gioconda business.

"I hope you're well," said Mr. Hutton. "You look it."

What a queer face she had! That small mouth pursed forward by the Gioconda expression into a little snout with a round hole in the middle as though for whistling—it was like a penholder seen from the front. Above the mouth a well-shaped nose, finely aquiline. Eyes large, lustrous, and dark, with the largeness, luster, and darkness that seems to invite sties and an occasional bloodshot suffusion. They were fine eyes, but unchangingly grave. The penholder might do its Gioconda trick, but the eyes never altered in their earnestness. Above them, a pair of boldly arched, heavily penciled black eyebrows lent a surprising air of power, as of a Roman matron, to the upper portion of the face. Her hair was dark and equally Roman: Agrippina from the brows upward.

"I thought I'd just look in on my way home," Mr. Hutton went on. "Ah, it's good to be back here"—he indicated with a wave of his hand the flowers in the vases, the sunshine and greenery beyond the windows—"it's good to be back in the country after a stuffy day of business in town."

Miss Spence, who had sat down, pointed to a chair at her side.

"No, really, I can't sit down," Mr. Hutton protested. "I must get back to see how poor Emily is. She was rather seedy this morning." He sat down, nevertheless. "It's these wretched liver chills. She's always getting them. Women—" He broke off and coughed, so as to hide the fact that he had uttered. He was about to say that women with weak digestions ought not to marry; but the remark was too cruel, and he didn't really believe it. Janet Spence, moreover, was a believer in eternal flames and spiritual attachments. "She hopes to be well enough," he added, "to see you at luncheon tomorrow. Can you come? Do!" He smiled persuasively. "It's my invitation too, you know.'

She dropped her eyes, and Mr. Hutton almost thought that he detected a certain reddening of the cheek. It was a tribute; he stroked his mustache.

"I should like to come if you think Emily's really well enough to have a visitor."

"Of course. You'll do her good. You'll do us both good. In married life three is often better company than two."

"Oh, you're cynical."

Mr. Hutton always had the desire to say "Bow-wow-wow" whenever that last word was spoken. It irritated him more than any other word in the language. But instead of barking he made haste to protest.

"No, no. I'm only speaking a melancholy truth. Reality doesn't always come up to the ideal, you know. But that doesn't make me believe any less in the ideal. Indeed, I believe in it passionately—the ideal of a matrimony between two people in perfect accord. I think it's realizable. I'm sure it is."

He paused significantly and looked at her with an arch expression. A virgin of thirty-six, but still unwithered; she had her charms. And there was something really rather enigmatic about her. Miss Spence made no reply but continued to smile. There were times when Mr. Hutton got rather bored with the Gioconda. He stood up.

"I must really be going now. Farewell, mysterious Gioconda." The smile grew intenser, focused itself, as it were, in a narrower snout. Mr. Hutton made a cinquecento gesture, and kissed her extended hand. It was the first time he had done such a thing; the action seemed not to be resented. "I look forward to tomorrow."

"Do you?"

For answer Mr. Hutton once more kissed her hand, then turned to go. Miss Spence accompanied him to the porch.

"Where's your car?" she asked.

"I left it at the gate of the drive."

"I'll come and see you off."

"No, no." Mr. Hutton was playful, but determined. "You must do no such thing. I simply forbid you."

"But I should like to come," Miss Spence protested, throwing a rapid Gioconda at him.

Mr. Hutton held up his hand, "No," he repeated, and then, with a gesture that was almost the blowing of a kiss, he started to run down the drive, lightly on his toes, with long, bounding strides like a boy's. He was proud of that run; it was quite marvelously youthful. Still, he was glad the drive was no longer. At the last bend, before passing out of sight of the house, he halted and turned round. Miss Spence was still standing on the steps, smiling her smile. He waved his hand, and this time quite definitely and overtly wafted a kiss in her direction. Then, breaking once more into his magnificent canter, he rounded the last dark promontory of trees. Once out of sight of the house he let his high paces decline to a trot, and finally to a walk. He took out his handkerchief and began wiping his neck inside his collar. What fools, what fools! Had there ever been such an ass as poor, dear Janet Spence? Never, unless it was himself. Decidedly he was the more malignant fool, since he, at least, was aware of his folly and still persisted in it. Why did he persist? Ah, the problem that was himself, the problem that was other people.

He had reached the gate. A large, prosperous-looking motor was standing at the side of the road.

"Home, M'Nab." The chauffeur touched his cap. "And stop at the crossroads on the way, as usual," Mr. Hutton added, as he opened the door of the car. "Well?" he said, speaking into the obscurity that lurked within.

"Oh, Teddy Bear, what an age you've been!" It was a fresh and childish voice that spoke the words. There was the faintest hint of Cockney impurity about the vowel sounds.

Mr. Hutton bent his large form and darted into the car with the agility of an animal regaining its burrow.

"Have I?" he said, as he shut the door. The machine began to move. "You must have missed me a lot if you found the time so long." He sat back in the low seat; a cherishing warmth enveloped him.

"Teddy Bear . . ." and with a sigh of contentment a charming little head declined on to Mr. Hutton's shoulder. Ravished, he looked down sideways at the round, babyish face.

"Do you know, Doris, you look like the pictures of Louise de Kerouaille." He passed his fingers through a mass of curly hair.

"Who's Louise de Kera-whatever-it-is?" Doris spoke from remote distances.

"She was, alas! *Fuit*. We shall all be 'was' one of these days. Meanwhile . . ."

Mr. Hutton covered the babyish face with kisses. The car rushed smoothly along. M'Nab's back, through the front window was stonily impassive, the back of a statue.

"Your hands," Doris whispered. "Oh, you mustn't touch me. They give me electric shocks."

Mr. Hutton adored her for the virgin imbecility of the words. How late in one's existence one makes the discovery of one's body!

"The electricity isn't in me, it's in you." He kissed her again, whispering her name several times: Doris, Doris, Doris. The scientific appellation of the sea mouse, he was thinking as he kissed the throat she offered him, white and extended like the throat of a victim awaiting the sacrificial knife. The sea mouse was a sausage with iridescent fur: very peculiar. Or was Doris the sea cucumber, which turns itself inside out in moments of alarm? He would really have to go to Naples again, just to see the aquarium. These sea creatures were fabulous, unbelievably fantastic.

"Oh, Teddy Bear!" (More zoology, but he was only a land animal. His poor little jokes!) "Teddy Bear, I'm so happy."

"So am I," said Mr. Hutton. Was it true?

"But I wish I knew if it were right. Tell me, Teddy Bear, is it right or wrong?"

"Ah, my dear, that's just what I've been wondering for the last thirty years."

"Be serious, Teddy Bear. I want to know if this is right; if it's right that I should be here with you and that we should love one another, and that it should give me electric shocks when you touch me."

"Right? Well, it's certainly good that you should have electric shocks rather than sexual repressions. Read Freud; repressions are the devil."

"Oh, you don't help me. Why aren't you ever serious? If only you knew how miserable I am sometimes, thinking it's not right. Perhaps, you know, there is a hell, and all that. I don't know what to do. Sometimes I think I ought to stop loving you."

"But could you?" asked Mr. Hutton, confident in the powers of his seduction and his mustache.

"No, Teddy Bear, you know I couldn't. But I could run away, I could hide from you, I could lock myself up and force myself not to come to you."

"Silly little thing!" He tightened his embrace.

"Oh, dear, I hope it isn't wrong. And there are times when I don't care if it is."

Mr. Hutton was touched. He had a certain protective affection for this little creature. He laid his cheek against her hair and so, interlaced, they sat in silence, while the car, swaying and pitching a little as it hastened along, seemed to draw in the white road and the dusty hedges towards it devouringly.

"Good-by, good-by."

The car moved on, gathered speed, vanished round a curve, and Doris was left standing by the signpost at the crossroads, still dizzy and weak with the languor born of those kisses and the electrical touch of those gentle hands. She had to take a deep breath, to draw herself up deliberately, before she was strong enough to start her homeward walk. She had half a mile in which to invent the necessary lies.

Alone, Mr. Hutton suddenly found himself the prey of an appalling boredom.

• • •

Mrs. Hutton was lying on the sofa in her boudoir, playing Patience. In spite of the warmth of the July evening a wood fire was burning on the hearth. A black Pomeranian, extenuated by the heat and the fatigues of digestion, slept before the blaze.

"Phew! Isn't it rather hot in here?" Mr. Hutton asked as he entered the room.

"You know I have to keep warm, dear." The voice seemed breaking on the verge of tears. "I get so shivery."

"I hope you're better this evening."

"Not much, I'm afraid."

The conversation stagnated. Mr. Hutton stood leaning his back against the mantelpiece. He looked down at the Pomeranian lying at his feet, and with the toe of his right boot he rolled the little dog over and rubbed its white-flecked chest and belly. The creature lay in an inert ecstasy. Mrs. Hutton continued to play Patience. Arrived at an impasse, she altered the position of one card, took back another, and went on playing. Her Patiences always came out.

"Dr. Libbard thinks I ought to go to Llandrindod Wells this summer."

"Well—go, my dear—go most certainly."

Mr. Hutton was thinking of the events of the afternoon: how they had driven, Doris and he, up to the hanging wood, had left the car to wait for them under the shade of the trees, and walked together out into the windless sunshine of the chalk down.

"I'm to drink the waters for my liver, and he thinks I ought to have massage and electric treatment, too."

Hat in hand, Doris had stalked four blue butterflies that were dancing together round a scabious flower with a motion that was like the flickering of blue fire. The blue fire burst and scattered into whirling sparks; she had given chase, laughing and shouting like a child.

"I'm sure it will do you good, my dear."

"I was wondering if you'd come with me, dear."

"But you know I'm going to Scotland at the end of the month."

Mrs. Hutton looked up at him entreatingly. "It's the journey," she said.

"The thought of it is such a nightmare. I don't know if I can manage it. And you know I can't sleep in hotels. And then there's the luggage and all the worries. I can't go alone."

"But you won't be alone. You'll have your maid with you." He spoke impatiently. The sick woman was usurping the place of the healthy one. He was being dragged back from the memory of the sunlit down and the quick, laughing girl, back to this unhealthy, overheated room and its complaining occupant.

"I don't think I shall be able to go."

"But you must, my dear, if the doctor tells you to. And, besides, a change will do you good."

"I don't think so."

"But Libbard thinks so, and he knows what he's talking about."

"No, I can't face it. I'm too weak. I can't go alone." Mrs. Hutton pulled a handkerchief out of her black silk bag, and put it to her eyes.

"Nonsense, my dear, you must make the effort."

"I had rather be left in peace to die here." She was crying in earnest now.

"O Lord! Now do be reasonable. Listen now, please." Mrs. Hutton only sobbed more violently. "Oh, what is one to do?" He shrugged his shoulders and walked out of the room.

Mr. Hutton was aware that he had not behaved with proper patience; but he could not help it. Very early in his manhood he had discovered that not only did he not feel sympathy for the poor, the weak, the diseased, and deformed; he actually hated them. Once, as an undergraduate, he spent three days at a mission in the East End. He had returned, filled with a profound and ineradicable disgust. Instead of pitying, he loathed the unfortunate. It was not, he knew, a very comely emotion; and he had been ashamed of it at first. In the end he had decided that it was temperamental, inevitable, and had felt no further qualms. Emily had been healthy and beautiful when he married her. He had loved her then. But now—was it his fault that she was like this?

Mr. Hutton dined alone. Food and drink left him more benevolent than he had been before dinner. To make amends for his show of exasperation he went up to his wife's room and offered to read to her. She was touched, gratefully accepted the offer, and Mr. Hutton, who was particularly proud of his accent, suggested a little light reading in French.

"French? I am so fond of French." Mrs. Hutton spoke of the language of Racine as though it were a dish of green peas.

Mr. Hutton ran down to the library and returned with a yellow volume. He began reading. The effort of pronouncing perfectly absorbed his whole attention. But how good his accent was! The fact of its goodness seemed to improve the quality of the novel he was reading.

At the end of fifteen pages an unmistakable sound aroused him. He looked up; Mrs. Hutton had gone to sleep. He sat still for a little while, looking with a dispassionate curiosity at the sleeping face. Once it had been beautiful; once, long ago, the sight of it, the recollection of it, had moved him with an emotion profounder, perhaps, than any he had felt before or since. Now it was lined and cadaverous. The skin was stretched tightly over the cheekbones, across the bridge of the sharp, birdlike nose. The closed eyes were set in profound bone-rimmed sockets. The lamplight striking on the face from the side emphasized with light and shade its cavities and projections. It was the face of a dead Christ by Morales.

> *Le squelette était invisible*
> *Au temps heureux de l'art païen.*

He shivered a little, and tiptoed out of the room.

On the following day Mrs. Hutton came down to luncheon. She had had some unpleasant palpitations during the night, but she was feeling better now. Besides, she wanted to do honor to her guest. Miss Spence listened to her complaints about Llandrindod Wells, and was loud in sympathy, lavish with advice. Whatever she said was always said with intensity. She leaned forward, aimed, so to speak, like a gun, and fired her words. Bang! the charge in her soul was ignited, the words whizzed forth at the narrow barrel of her mouth. She was a machine gun riddling her hostess with sympathy. Mr. Hutton had undergone similar bombardments, mostly of a literary or philosophic character—bombardments of Maeterlinck, of Mrs.

Besant, of Bergson, of William James. Today the missiles were medical. She talked about insomnia, she expatiated on the virtues of harmless drugs and beneficent specialists. Under the bombardment Mrs. Hutton opened out, like a flower in the sun.

Mr. Hutton looked on in silence. The spectacle of Janet Spence evoked in him an unfailing curiosity. He was not romantic enough to imagine that every face masked an interior physiognomy of beauty or strangeness, that every woman's small talk was like a vapor hanging over mysterious gulfs. His wife, for example, and Doris; they were nothing more than what they seemed to be. But with Janet Spence it was somehow different. Here one could be sure that there was some kind of queer face behind the Gioconda smile and the Roman eyebrows. The only question was: What exactly was there? Mr. Hutton could never quite make out.

"But perhaps you won't have to go to Llandrindod after all," Miss Spence was saying. "If you get well quickly Dr. Libbard will let you off."

"I only hope so. Indeed, I do really feel rather better today."

Mr. Hutton felt ashamed. How much was it his own lack of sympathy that prevented her from feeling well every day? But he comforted himself by reflecting that it was only a case of feeling, not of being better. Sympathy does not mend a diseased liver or a weak heart.

"My dear, I wouldn't eat those red currants if I were you," he said, suddenly solicitous. "You know that Libbard has banned everything with skins and pips."

"But I am so fond of them," Mrs. Hutton protested, "and I feel so well today."

"Don't be a tyrant," said Miss Spence, looking first at him and then at his wife. "Let the poor invalid have what she fancies; it will do her good." She laid her hand on Mrs. Hutton's arm and patted it affectionately two or three times.

"Thank you, my dear." Mrs. Hutton helped herself to the stewed currants.

"Well, don't blame me if they make you ill again."

"Do I ever blame you, dear?"

"You have nothing to blame me for," Mr. Hutton answered playfully. "I am the perfect husband."

They sat in the garden after luncheon. From the island of shade under the old cypress tree they looked out across a flat expanse of lawn, in which the parterres of flowers shone with a metallic brilliance.

Mr. Hutton took a deep breath of the warm and fragrant air. "It's good to be alive," he said.

"Just to be alive," his wife echoed, stretching one pale, knot-jointed hand into the sunlight.

A maid brought the coffee; the silver pots and the little blue cups were set on a folding table near the group of chairs.

"Oh, my medicine!" exclaimed Mrs. Hutton. "Run in and fetch it, Clara, will you? The white bottle on the sideboard."

"I'll go," said Mr. Hutton. "I've got to go and fetch a cigar in any case."

He ran in towards the house. On the threshold he turned round for an instant. The maid was walking back across the lawn. His wife was sitting up in her deck chair, engaged in opening her white parasol. Miss Spence was bending over the table, pouring out a cup of coffee. He passed into the cool obscurity of the house.

"Do you like sugar in your coffee?" Miss Spence inquired.

"Yes, please. Give me rather a lot. I'll drink it after my medicine to take the taste away."

Mrs. Hutton leaned back in her chair, lowering the sunshade over her eyes, so as to shut out from her vision the burning sky. Behind her, Miss Spence was making a delicate clinking among the coffee cups.

"I've given you three large spoonfuls. That ought to take the taste away. And here comes the medicine."

Mr. Hutton had reappeared, carrying a wineglass, half full of a pale liquid.

"It smells delicious," he said, as he handed it to his wife.

"That's only the flavoring." She drank it off at a gulp, shuddered, and made a grimace. "Ugh, it's so nasty. Give me my coffee."

Miss Spence gave her the cup; she sipped at it. "You've made it like syrup. But it's very nice, after that atrocious medicine."

At half-past three Mrs. Hutton complained that she did not feel as well as she had done, and went indoors to lie down. Her husband would have said something about the red currants, but checked himself; the triumph of an

"I told you so" was too cheaply won. Instead, he was sympathetic, and gave her his arm to the house.

"A rest will do you good," he said. "By the way, I shan't be back till after dinner."

"But why? Where are you going?"

"I promised to go to Johnson's this evening. We have to discuss the war memorial you know."

"Oh, I wish you weren't going." Mrs. Hutton was almost in tears. "Can't you stay? I don't like being alone in the house."

"But, my dear, I promised—weeks ago." It was a bother having to lie like this. "And now I must get back and look after Miss Spence."

He kissed her on the forehead and went out again into the garden. Miss Spence received him aimed and intense.

"Your wife is dreadfully ill," she fired off at him.

"I thought she cheered up so much when you came."

"That was purely nervous, purely nervous. I was watching her closely. With a heart in that condition and her digestion wrecked—yes, wrecked—anything might happen."

"Libbard doesn't take so gloomy a view of poor Emily's health." Mr. Hutton held open the gate that led from the garden into the drive; Miss Spence's car was standing by the front door.

"Libbard is only a country doctor. You ought to see a specialist."

He could not refrain from laughing. "You have a macabre passion for specialists."

Miss Spence held up her hand in protest. "I am serious. I think poor Emily is in a very bad state. Anything might happen—at any moment."

He handed her into the car and shut the door. The chauffeur started the engine and climbed into his place, ready to drive off.

"Shall I tell him to start?" He had no desire to continue the conversation.

Miss Spence leaned forward and shot a Gioconda in his direction. "Remember, I expect you to come and see me again soon."

Mechanically he grinned, made a polite noise, and, as the car moved forward, waved his hand. He was happy to be alone.

A few minutes afterwards Mr. Hutton himself drove away. Doris was waiting at the crossroads. They dined together twenty miles from home, at a roadside hotel. It was one of those bad, expensive meals which are only cooked in country hotels frequented by motorists. It revolted Mr. Hutton, but Doris enjoyed it. She always enjoyed things. Mr. Hutton ordered a not very good brand of champagne. He was wishing he had spent the evening in his library.

When they started homewards Doris was a little tipsy and extremely affectionate. It was very dark inside the car, but looking forward, past the motionless form of M'Nab, they could see a bright and narrow universe of forms and colors scooped out of the night by the electric head lamps.

It was after eleven when Mr. Hutton reached home. Dr. Libbard met him in the hall. He was a small man with delicate hands and well-formed features that were almost feminine. His brown eyes were large and melancholy. He used to waste a great deal of time sitting at the bedside of his patients, looking sadness through those eyes and talking in a sad, low voice about nothing in particular. His person exhaled a pleasing odor, decidedly antiseptic but at the same time suave and discreetly delicious.

"Libbard?" said Mr. Hutton in surprise. "You here? Is my wife ill?"

"We tried to fetch you earlier," the soft, melancholy voice replied. "It was thought you were at Mr. Johnson's, but they had no news of you there."

"No, I was detained. I had a breakdown," Mr. Hutton answered irritably. It was tiresome to be caught out in a lie.

"Your wife wanted to see you urgently."

"Well, I can go now." Mr. Hutton moved towards the stairs.

Dr. Libbard laid a hand on his arm. "I am afraid it's too late."

"Too late?" He began fumbling with his watch; it wouldn't come out of the pocket.

"Mrs. Hutton passed away half an hour ago."

The voice remained even in its softness, the melancholy of the eyes did not deepen. Dr. Libbard spoke of death as he would speak of a local cricket match. All things were equally vain and equally deplorable.

Mr. Hutton found himself thinking of Janet Spence's words. At any moment—at any moment. She had been extraordinarily right.

"What happened?" he asked. "What was the cause?"

Dr. Libbard explained. It was heart failure brought on by a violent attack of nausea, caused in its turn by the eating of something of an irritant nature. Red currants? Mr. Hutton suggested. Very likely. It had been too much for the heart. There was chronic valvular disease: something had collapsed under the strain. It was all over; she could not have suffered much.

"IT'S A PITY they should have chosen the day of the Eton and Harrow match for the funeral," old General Grego was saying as he stood, his top hat in his hand, under the shadow of the lych gate, wiping his face with his handkerchief.

Mr. Hutton overheard the remark and with difficulty restrained a desire to inflict grievous bodily pain on the General. He would have liked to hit the old brute in the middle of his big red face. Monstrous great mulberry, spotted with meal! Was there no respect for the dead? Did nobody care? In theory he didn't much care; let the dead bury their dead. But here, at the graveside, he had found himself actually sobbing. Poor Emily, they had been pretty happy once. Now she was lying at the bottom of a seven-foot hole. And here was Grego complaining that he couldn't go to the Eton and Harrow match.

Mr. Hutton looked round at the groups of black figures that were drifting slowly out of the churchyard towards the fleet of cabs and motors assembled in the road outside. Against the brilliant background of the July grass and flowers and foliage, they had a horribly alien and unnatural appearance. It pleased him to think that all these people would soon be dead, too.

That evening Mr. Hutton sat up late in his library reading the life of Milton. There was no particular reason why he should have chosen Milton; it was the book that first came to hand, that was all. It was after midnight when he had finished. He got up from his armchair, unbolted the French windows, and stepped out on to the little paved terrace. The night was quiet and clear. Mr. Hutton looked at the stars and at the holes between them, dropped his eyes to the dim lawns and hueless flowers of the garden, and let them wander over the farther landscape, black and gray under the moon.

He began to think with a kind of confused violence. There were the stars, there was Milton. A man can be somehow the peer of stars and night. Greatness, nobility. But is there seriously a difference between the noble and the ignoble? Milton, the stars, death, and himself—himself. The soul, the body; the higher and the lower nature. Perhaps there was something in it, after all. Milton had a god on his side and righteousness. What had he? Nothing, nothing whatever. There were only Doris's little breasts. What was the point of it all? Milton, the stars, death, and Emily in her grave, Doris and himself—always himself . . .

Oh, he was a futile and disgusting being. Everything convinced him of it. It was a solemn moment. He spoke aloud: "I will, I will." The sound of his own voice in the darkness was appalling; it seemed to him that he had sworn that infernal oath which binds even the gods: "I will, I will." There had been New Year's days and solemn anniversaries in the past, when he had felt the same contritions and recorded similar resolutions. They had all thinned away, these resolutions, like smoke, into nothingness. But this was a greater moment and he had pronounced a more fearful oath. In the future it was to be different. Yes, he would live by reason, he would be industrious, he would curb his appetites, he would devote his life to some good purpose. It was resolved and it would be so.

In practice he saw himself spending his mornings in agricultural pursuits, riding round with the bailiff, seeing that his land was farmed in the best modern way—silos and artificial manures and continuous cropping and all that. The remainder of the day should be devoted to serious study. There was that book he had been intending to write for so long—*The Effect of Diseases on Civilization.*

Mr. Hutton went to bed humble and contrite, but with a sense that grace had entered into him. He slept for seven and a half hours, and woke to find the sun brilliantly shining. The emotions of the evening had been transformed by a good night's rest into his customary cheerfulness. It was not until a good many seconds after his return to conscious life, that he remembered his resolution, his Stygian oath. Milton and death seemed somehow different in the sunlight. As for the stars, they were not there. But the resolutions were good; even in the daytime he could see that. He had his horse saddled after breakfast, and rode round the farm with the bailiff. After luncheon he read Thucydides on the plague at Athens. In the evening he made a few notes on malaria in Southern Italy. While he was undressing he remembered that there was a good anecdote in Skelton's jest-book about the Sweating Sickness. He would have made a note of it if only he could have found a pencil.

On the sixth morning of his new life Mr. Hutton found among his correspondence an envelope addressed in that peculiarly vulgar handwriting which he knew to be Doris's. He opened it, and began to read. She didn't know what to say; words were so inadequate. His wife dying like that, and so suddenly—it was too terrible. Mr. Hutton sighed, but his interest revived somewhat as he read on:

"Death is so frightening, I never think of it when I can help it.
But when something like this happens, or when I am feeling ill or
depressed, then I can't help remembering it is there, so close, and
I think about all the wicked things I have done and about you and
me, and I wonder what will happen. And I am so frightened. I am
so lonely, Teddy Bear, and so unhappy, and I don't know what to
do. I can't get rid of the idea of dying, I am so wretched and helpless without you. I didn't mean to write to you; I meant to wait till
you were out of mourning and could come and see me again, but I
was so lonely and miserable, Teddy Bear, I had to write. I couldn't
help it. Forgive me, I want you so much; I have nobody in the world
but you. You are so good, and gentle and understanding; there is
nobody like you. I shall never forget how good and kind you have
been to me, and you are so clever and know so much, I can't understand how you ever came to pay any attention to me, I am so dull
and stupid, much less like me and love me, because you do love me
a little, don't you, Teddy Bear?"

Mr. Hutton was touched with shame and remorse. To be thanked like this, worshiped for having seduced the girl—it was too much. It had just been a piece of imbecile wantonness. Imbecile, idiotic; there was no other way to describe it. For, when all was said, he had derived very little pleasure from it. Taking all things together, he had probably been more bored than amused. Once upon a time he had believed himself to be a hedonist. But to be a hedonist implies a certain process of reasoning, a deliberate choice of known pleasures, a rejection of known pains. This had been done without reason, against it. For he knew beforehand—so well, so well—that there was no interest or pleasure to be derived from these wretched affairs. And yet each time the vague itch came upon him he succumbed, involving himself once more in the old stupidity. There had been Maggie, his wife's maid, and Edith, the girl on the farm, and Mrs. Pringle, and the waitress in London, and others—there seemed to be dozens of them. It had all been so stale and boring. He knew it would be; he always knew. And yet, and yet . . . Experience doesn't teach.

Poor little Doris! He would write to her kindly, comfortingly, but he wouldn't see her again. A servant came to tell him that his horse was saddled and waiting. He mounted and rode off. That morning the old bailiff was more irritating than usual.

FIVE DAYS LATER Doris and Mr. Hutton were sitting together on the pier at Southend; Doris, in white muslin with pink garnishings, radiated happiness; Mr. Hutton, legs outstretched and chair tilted, had pushed the panama back from his forehead, and was trying to feel like a tripper. That night, when Doris was asleep, breathing and warm by his side, he recaptured, in this moment of darkness and physical fatigue, the rather cosmic emotion which had possessed him that evening, not a fortnight ago, when he had made his great resolution. And so his solemn oath had already gone the way of so many other resolutions. Unreason had triumphed; at the first itch of desire he had given way. He was hopeless, hopeless.

For a long time he lay with closed eyes, ruminating his humiliation. The girl stirred in her sleep. Mr. Hutton turned over and looked in her direction. Enough faint light crept in between the half-drawn curtains to show her bare arm and shoulder, her neck, and the dark tangle of hair on the pillow. She was beautiful, desirable. Why did he lie there moaning over his sins? What did it matter? If he were hopeless, then so be it; he would make the best of his hopelessness. A glorious sense of irresponsibility suddenly filled him. He was free, magnificently free. In a kind of exaltation he drew the girl towards him. She woke, bewildered, almost frightened under his rough kisses.

The storm of his desire subsided into a kind of serene merriment. The whole atmosphere seemed to be quivering with enormous silent laughter.

"Could anyone love you as much as I do, Teddy Bear?" The question came faintly from distant worlds of love.

"I think I know somebody who does," Mr. Hutton replied. The submarine laughter was swelling, rising, ready to break the surface of silence and resound.

"Who? Tell me. What do you mean?" The voice had come very close; charged with suspicion, anguish, indignation, it belonged to this immediate world.

"A—ah!"

"Who?"

"You'll never guess." Mr. Hutton kept up the joke until it began to grow tedious, and then pronounced the name "Janet Spence."

Doris was incredulous. "Miss Spence of the Manor? That old woman?" It was too ridiculous. Mr. Hutton laughed too.

"But it's quite true," he said. "She adores me." Oh, the vast joke. He would go and see her as soon as he returned—see and conquer. "I believe she wants to marry me," he added.

"But you wouldn't . . . you don't intend . . ."

The air was fairly crepitating with humor. Mr. Hutton laughed aloud. "I intend to marry you," he said. It seemed to him the best joke he had ever made in his life.

When Mr. Hutton left Southend he was once more a married man. It was agreed that, for the time being, the fact should be kept secret. In the autumn they would go abroad together, and the world should be informed. Meanwhile he was to go back to his own house and Doris to hers.

The day after his return he walked over in the afternoon to see Miss Spence. She received him with the old Gioconda.

"I was expecting you to come."

"I couldn't keep away," Mr. Hutton gallantly replied.

They sat in the summerhouse. It was a pleasant place—a little old stucco temple bowered among dense bushes of evergreen. Miss Spence had left her mark on it by hanging up over the seat a blue-and-white Della Robbia plaque.

"I am thinking of going to Italy this autumn," said Mr. Hutton. He felt like a ginger-beer bottle, ready to pop with bubbling humorous excitement.

"Italy . . ." Miss Spence closed her eyes ecstatically. "I feel drawn there too."

"Why not let yourself be drawn?"

"I don't know. One somehow hasn't the energy and initiative to set out alone."

"Alone . . ." Ah, sound of guitars and throaty singing! "Yes, traveling alone isn't much fun."

Miss Spence lay back in her chair without speaking. Her eyes were still closed. Mr. Hutton stroked his mustache. The silence prolonged itself for what seemed a very long time.

Pressed to stay to dinner, Mr. Hutton did not refuse. The fun had hardly started. The table was laid in the loggia. Through its arches they looked out on to the sloping garden, to the valley below and the farther hills. Light ebbed away; the heat and silence were oppressive. A huge cloud was mounting up the sky, and there were distant breathings of thunder. The thunder drew nearer, a wind began to blow, and the first drops of rain fell. The table was cleared. Miss Spence and Mr. Hutton sat on in the growing darkness.

Miss Spence broke a long silence by saying meditatively:

"I think everyone has a right to a certain amount of happiness, don't you?"

"Most certainly." But what was she leading up to? Nobody makes generalizations about life unless they mean to talk about themselves. Happiness; he looked back on his own life, and saw a cheerful, placid existence disturbed by no great griefs or discomforts or alarms. He had always had money and freedom; he had been able to do very much as he wanted. Yes, he supposed he had been happy—happier than most men. And now he was not merely happy; he had discovered in irresponsibility the secret of gaiety. He was about to say something about his happiness when Miss Spence went on speaking.

"People like you and me have a right to be happy some time in our lives."

"Me?" said Mr. Hutton surprised.

"Poor Henry! Fate hasn't treated either of us very well."

"Oh, well, it might have treated me worse."

"You're being cheerful. That's brave of you. But don't think I can't see behind the mask."

Miss Spence spoke louder and louder as the rain came down, more and more heavily. Periodically the thunder cut across her utterances. She talked on, shouting against the noise.

"I have understood you so well and for so long."

A flash revealed her, aimed and intent, leaning towards him. Her eyes were two profound and menacing gun barrels. The darkness re-engulfed her.

"You were a lonely soul seeking a companion soul. I could sympathize with you in your solitude. Your marriage . . ."

The thunder cut short the sentence. Miss Spence's voice became audible once more with the words:

". . . could offer no companionship to a man of your stamp. You needed a soul mate."

A soul mate—he! A soul mate. It was incredibly fantastic. "Georgette Leblanc, the ex-soul mate of Maurice Maeterlinck." He had seen that in the paper a few days ago. So it was thus that Janet Spence had painted him in her imagination—a soul-mater. And for Doris he was a picture of goodness and the cleverest man in the world. And actually, really, he was what? Who knows?

"My heart went out to you. I could understand; I was lonely, too." Miss Spence laid her hand on his knee. "You were so patient." Another flash. She was still aimed, dangerously. "You never complained. But I could guess—I could guess."

"How wonderful of you!" So he was an *âme incomprise*. "Only a woman's intuition . . ."

The thunder crashed and rumbled, died away, and only the sound of the rain was left. The thunder was his laughter, magnified, externalized. Flash and crash, there it was again, right on top of them.

"Don't you feel that you have within you something that is akin to this storm?" He could imagine her leaning forward as she uttered the words. "Passion makes one the equal of the elements."

What was his gambit now? Why, obviously, he should have said "Yes," and ventured on some unequivocal gesture. But Mr. Hutton suddenly took fright. The ginger beer in him had gone flat. The woman was serious—terribly serious. He was appalled.

Passion? "No," he desperately answered. "I am without passion."

But his remark was either unheard or unheeded, for Miss Spence went on with a growing exaltation, speaking so rapidly, however, and in such a burningly intimate whisper that Mr. Hutton found it very difficult to distinguish what she was saying. She was telling him, as far as he could make out, the story of her life. The lightning was less frequent now, and there were long intervals of darkness. But at each flash he saw her still aiming towards him, still yearning forward with a terrifying intensity. Darkness, the rain, and then flash! her face was there, close at hand. A pale mask, greenish white; the large eyes, the narrow barrel of the mouth, the heavy eyebrows. Agrippina, or wasn't it rather—yes, wasn't it rather George Robey?

He began devising absurd plans for escaping. He might suddenly jump up, pretending he had seen a burglar—Stop thief! stop thief!—and dash off into the night in pursuit. Or should he say that he felt faint, a heart attack? or that he had seen a ghost—Emily's ghost—in the garden? Absorbed in his childish plotting, he had ceased to pay any attention to Miss Spence's words. The spasmodic clutching of her hand recalled his thoughts.

"I honored you for that, Henry," she was saying.

Honored him for what?

"Marriage is a sacred tie, and your respect for it, even when the marriage was, as it was in your case, an unhappy one, made me respect you and admire you, and—shall I dare say the word?"

Oh, the burglar, the ghost in the garden! But it was too late.

". . . yes, love you, Henry, all the more. But we're free now, Henry."

Free? There was a movement in the dark, and she was kneeling on the floor by his chair.

"Oh, Henry, Henry, I have been unhappy too."

Her arms embraced him, and by the shaking of her body he could feel that she was sobbing. She might have been a suppliant crying for mercy.

"You mustn't, Janet," he protested. Those tears were terrible, terrible. "Not now, not now! You must be calm; you must go to bed." He patted her shoulder, then got up, disengaging himself from her embrace. He left her still crouching on the floor beside the chair on which he had been sitting.

Groping his way into the hall, and without waiting to look for his hat, he went out of the house, taking infinite pains to close the front door noiselessly behind him. The clouds had blown over, and the moon was shining from a clear sky. There were puddles all along the road, and a noise of running water rose from the gutters and ditches. Mr. Hutton splashed along, not caring if he got wet.

How heart-rendingly she had sobbed! With the emotions of pity and remorse that the recollection evoked in him there was a certain resentment: why couldn't she have played the game that he was playing—the heartless, amusing game? Yes, but he had known all the time that she wouldn't, she couldn't play that game; he had known and persisted.

What had she said about passion and the elements? Something absurdly stale, but true, true. There she was, a cloud black bosomed and charged with thunder, and he, like some absurd little Benjamin Franklin, had sent up a kite into the heart of the menace. Now he was complaining that his toy had drawn the lightning.

She was probably still kneeling by that chair in the loggia, crying.

But why hadn't he been able to keep up the game? Why had his irresponsibility deserted him, leaving him suddenly sober in a cold world? There were no answers to any of his questions. One idea burned steady and luminous in his mind—the idea of flight. He must get away at once.

"WHAT ARE YOU thinking about, Teddy Bear?"

"Nothing."

There was a silence. Mr. Hutton remained motionless, his elbows on the parapet of the terrace, his chin in his hands, looking down over Florence. He had taken a villa on one of the hilltops to the south of the city. From a little raised terrace at the end of the garden one looked down a long fertile valley on to the town and beyond it to the bleak mass of Monte Morello and, eastward of it, to the peopled hill of Fiesole, dotted with white houses. Everything was clear and luminous in the September sunshine.

"Are you worried about anything?"

"No, thank you."

"Tell me, Teddy Bear."

"But, my dear, there's nothing to tell." Mr. Hutton turned round, smiled, and patted the girl's hand. "I think you'd better go in and have your siesta. It's too hot for you here."

"Very well, Teddy Bear. Are you coming too?"

"When I've finished my cigar."

"All right. But do hurry up and finish it, Teddy Bear." Slowly, reluctantly, she descended the steps of the terrace and walked towards the house.

Mr. Hutton continued his contemplation of Florence. He had need to be alone. It was good sometimes to escape from Doris and the restless solicitude of her passion. He had never known the pains of loving hopelessly, but he was experiencing now the pains of being loved. These last weeks had been a period of growing discomfort. Doris was always with him, like an obsession, like a guilty conscience. Yes, it was good to be alone.

He pulled an envelope out of his pocket and opened it; not without reluctance. He hated letters; they always contained something unpleasant— nowadays, since his second marriage. This was from his sister. He began skimming through the insulting home truths of which it was composed. The words "indecent haste," "social suicide," "scarcely cold in her grave," "person of the lower classes," all occurred. They were inevitable now in any communication from a well-meaning and right-thinking relative. Impatient, he was about to tear the stupid letter to pieces when his eye fell on a sentence at the bottom of the third page. His heart beat with uncomfortable violence as he read it. It was too monstrous! Janet Spence was going about telling everyone that he had poisoned his wife in order to marry Doris. What damnable malice! Ordinarily a man of the suavest temper, Mr. Hutton found himself trembling with rage. He took the childish satisfaction of calling names—he cursed the woman.

Then suddenly he saw the ridiculous side of the situation. The notion that he should have murdered anyone in order to marry Doris! If they only knew how miserably bored he was. Poor, dear Janet! She had tried to be malicious; she had only succeeded in being stupid.

A sound of footsteps aroused him; he looked round. In the garden below the little terrace the servant girl of the house was picking fruit. A Neapolitan, strayed somehow as far north as Florence, she was a specimen of the classical type—a little debased. Her profile might have been taken from a Sicilian coin of a bad period. Her features, carved floridly in the grand tradition, expressed an almost perfect stupidity. Her mouth was the most beautiful thing about her; the calligraphic hand of nature had richly curved it into an expression of mulish bad temper. . . . Under her hideous black clothes, Mr. Hutton divined a powerful body, firm and massive. He had looked at her before with a vague interest and curiosity. Today the curiosity defined and focused itself into a desire. An idyll of Theocritus. Here was the woman; he, alas, was not precisely like a goatherd on the volcanic hills. He called to her.

"Armida!"

The smile with which she answered him was so provocative, attested so easy a virtue, that Mr. Hutton took fright. He was on the brink once more— on the brink. He must draw back, oh! quickly, quickly, before it was too late. The girl continued to look up at him.

"Ha chiamato?" she asked at last.

Stupidity or reason? Oh, there was no choice now. It was imbecility every time.

"Scendo," he called back to her. Twelve steps led from the garden to the terrace. Mr. Hutton counted them. Down, down, down, down. . . . He saw a vision of himself descending from one circle of the inferno to the next—from a darkness full of wind and hail to an abyss of stinking mud.

FOR A GOOD many days the Hutton case had a place on the front page of every newspaper. There had been no more popular murder trial since George Smith had temporarily eclipsed the European War by drowning in a warm bath his seventh bride. The public imagination was stirred by this tale of a murder brought to light months after the date of the crime. Here, it was felt, was one of those incidents in human life, so notable because they are so rare, which do definitely justify the ways of God to man. A wicked man had been moved by an illicit passion to kill his wife. For months he had lived in sin and fancied security—only to be dashed at last more horribly into the pit he had prepared for himself. Murder will out, and here was a case of it. The readers of the newspapers were in a position to follow every movement of the hand of God. There had been vague, but persistent, rumors in the neighborhood; the police had taken action at last. Then came the exhumation order, the post-mortem examination, the inquest, the evidence of the experts, the verdict of the coroner's jury, the trial, the condemnation. For once Providence had done its duty, obviously, grossly, didactically, as in a melodrama. The newspapers were right in making of the case the staple intellectual food of a whole season.

Mr. Hutton's first emotion when he was summoned from Italy to give evidence at the inquest was one of indignation. It was a monstrous, a scandalous thing that the police should take such idle, malicious gossip seriously. When the inquest was over he would bring an action for malicious prosecution against the Chief Constable; he would sue the Spence woman for slander.

The inquest was opened; the astonishing evidence unrolled itself. The experts had examined the body, and had found traces of arsenic; they were of opinion that the late Mrs. Hutton had died of arsenic poisoning.

Arsenic poisoning . . . Emily had died of arsenic poisoning? After that, Mr. Hutton learned with surprise that there was enough arsenicated insecticide in his greenhouses to poison an army.

It was now, quite suddenly, that he saw it: there was a case against him. Fascinated, he watched it growing, growing, like some monstrous tropical plant. It was enveloping him, surrounding him; he was lost in a tangled forest.

When was the poison administered? The experts agreed that it must have been swallowed eight or nine hours before death. About lunchtime? Yes, about lunchtime. Clara, the parlormaid, was called. Mrs. Hutton, she remembered, had asked her to go and fetch her medicine. Mr. Hutton had volunteered to go instead; he had gone alone. Miss Spence—ah, the memory of the storm, the white, aimed face! the horror of it all!—Miss Spence confirmed Clara's statement, and added that Mr. Hutton had come back with the medicine already poured out in a wineglass, not in the bottle.

Mr. Hutton's indignation evaporated. He was dismayed, frightened. It was all too fantastic to be taken seriously, and yet this nightmare was a fact—it was actually happening.

M'Nab had seen them kissing, often. He had taken them for a drive on the day of Mrs. Hutton's death. He could see them reflected in the windscreen, sometimes out of the tail of his eye.

The inquest was adjourned. That evening Doris went to bed with a headache. When he went to her room after dinner, Mr. Hutton found her crying.

"What's the matter?" He sat down on the edge of her bed and began to stroke her hair. For a long time she did not answer, and he went on stroking her hair mechanically, almost unconsciously; sometimes, even, he bent down and kissed her bare shoulder. He had his own affairs, however, to think about. What had happened? How was it that the stupid gossip had actually come true? Emily had died of arsenic poisoning. It was absurd, impossible. The order of things had been broken, and he was at the mercy of an irresponsibility. What had happened, what was going to happen? He was interrupted in the midst of his thoughts.

"It's my fault—it's my fault!" Doris suddenly sobbed out. "I shouldn't have loved you; I oughtn't to have let you love me. Why was I ever born?"

Mr. Hutton didn't say anything, but looked down in silence at the abject figure of misery lying on the bed.

"If they do anything to you I shall kill myself."

She sat up, held him for a moment at arm's length, and looked at him with a kind of violence, as though she were never to see him again.

"I love you, I love you, I love you." She drew him, inert and passive, towards her, clasped him, pressed herself against him. "I didn't know you loved me as much as that, Teddy Bear. But why did you do it—why did you do it?"

Mr. Hutton undid her clasping arms and got up. His face became very red. "You seem to take it for granted that I murdered my wife," he said. "It's really too grotesque. What do you all take me for? A cinema hero?" He had begun to lose his temper. All the exasperation, all the fear and bewilderment of the day, was transformed into a violent anger against her. "It's all such damned stupidity. Haven't you any conception of a civilized man's mentality? Do I look the sort of man who'd go about slaughtering people? I suppose you imagined I was so insanely in love with you that I could commit any folly. When will you women understand that one isn't insanely in love? All one asks for is a quiet life, which you won't allow one to have. I don't know what the devil ever induced me to marry you. It was all a damned stupid, practical joke. And now you go about saying I'm a murderer. I won't stand it."

Mr. Hutton stamped towards the door. He had said horrible things, he knew—odious things that he ought speedily to unsay. But he wouldn't. He closed the door behind him.

"Teddy Bear!" He turned the handle; the latch clicked into place. "Teddy Bear!" The voice that came to him through the closed door was agonized. Should he go back? He ought to go back. He touched the handle, then withdrew his fingers and quickly walked away. When he was halfway down the stairs he halted. She might try to do something silly—throw herself out of the window or God knows what! He listened attentively; there was no sound. But he pictured her very clearly, tiptoeing across the room, lifting the sash as high as it would go, leaning out into the cold night air. It was raining a little. Under the window lay the paved terrace. How far below? Twenty-five or thirty feet? Once, when he was walking along Piccadilly, a dog had jumped out of a third-story window of the Ritz. He had seen it fall; he had heard it strike the pavement. Should he go back? He was damned if he would; he hated her.

He sat for a long time in the library. What had happened? What was happening? He turned the question over and over in his mind and could find no answer. Suppose the nightmare dreamed itself out to its horrible conclusion. Death was waiting for him. His eyes filled with tears; he wanted so passionately to live. "Just to be alive." Poor Emily had wished it too, he remembered: "Just to be alive." There were still so many places in this astonishing world unvisited, so many queer delightful people still unknown, so many lovely women never so much as seen. The huge white oxen would still be dragging their wains along the Tuscan roads, the cypresses would still go up, straight as pillars, to the blue heaven; but he would not be there to see them. And the sweet southern wines—Tear of Christ and Blood of Judas—others would drink them, not he. Others would walk down the obscure and narrow lanes between the bookshelves in the London Library, sniffing the dusty perfume of good literature, peering at strange titles, discovering unknown names, exploring the fringes of vast domains of knowledge. He would be lying in a hole in the ground. And why, why? Confusedly he felt that some extraordinary kind of justice was being done. In the past he had been wanton and imbecile and irresponsible. Now Fate was playing as wantonly, as irresponsibly, with him. It was tit for tat, and God existed after all.

He felt that he would like to pray. Forty years ago be used to kneel by his bed every evening. The nightly formula of his childhood came to him almost unsought from some long unopened chamber of the memory. "God bless Father and Mother, Tom and Cissie and the Baby, Mademoiselle and Nurse, and everyone that I love, and make me a good boy. Amen." They were all dead now—all except Cissie.

His mind seemed to soften and dissolve; a great calm descended upon his spirit. He went upstairs to ask Doris's forgiveness. He found her lying on the couch at the foot of the bed. On the floor beside her stood a blue bottle of liniment, marked "Not to be taken": she seemed to have drunk about half of it.

"You didn't love me," was all she said when she opened her eyes to find him bending over her.

Dr. Libbard arrived in time to prevent any very serious consequences. "You mustn't do this again," he said while Mr. Hutton was out of the room.

"What's to prevent me?" she asked defiantly.

Dr. Libbard looked at her with his large, sad eyes. "There's nothing to prevent you," he said. "Only yourself and your baby. Isn't it rather bad luck on your baby, not allowing it to come into the world because you want to go out of it?"

Doris was silent for a time. "All right," she whispered. "I won't."

Mr. Hutton sat by her bedside for the rest of the night. He felt himself now to be indeed a murderer. For a time he persuaded himself that he loved this pitiable child. Dozing in his chair, he woke up, stiff and cold, to find himself drained dry, as it were, of every emotion. He had become nothing but a tired and suffering carcass. At six o'clock he undressed and went to bed for a couple of hours' sleep. In the course of the same afternoon the coroner's jury brought in a verdict of "Willful Murder," and Mr. Hutton was committed for trial.

MISS SPENCE was not at all well. She had found her public appearances in the witness box very trying, and when it was all over she had something that was very nearly a breakdown. She slept badly, and suffered from nervous indigestion. Dr. Libbard used to call every other day. She talked to him a great deal—mostly about the Hutton case. . . . Her moral indignation was always on the boil. Wasn't it appalling to think that one had had a murderer in one's house. Wasn't it extraordinary that one could have been for so long mistaken about the man's character? (But she had had an inkling from the first.) And then the girl he had gone off with—so low class, so little better than a prostitute. The news that the second Mrs. Hutton was expecting a baby—the posthumous child of a condemned and executed criminal— revolted her; the thing was shocking—an obscenity. Dr. Libbard answered her gently and vaguely, and prescribed bromide.

One morning he interrupted her in the midst of her customary tirade. "By the way," he said in his soft, melancholy voice, "I suppose it was really you who poisoned Mrs. Hutton."

Miss Spence stared at him for two or three seconds with enormous eyes, and then quietly said, "Yes." After that she started to cry.

"In the coffee, I suppose."

She seemed to nod assent. Dr. Libbard took out his fountain pen, and in his neat, meticulous calligraphy wrote out a prescription for a sleeping draught.

TEA FOR TWO

Laurie York Erskine

When the famous case involving Major Herbert Armstrong filled newspapers in the early 1920s, Aldous Huxley loosely used the facts as the basis for his short story "The Gioconda Smile." This headline-making case featured a mousey-looking officer who evidently poisoned his wife with arsenic, which he claimed was to eliminate the dandelions in his garden. The prosecution found his attack on the dandelions to be a trifle too zealous, as he had 20 packets of arsenic in his possession while only 19 dandelions ravaged his garden. When his wife passed away (February 22, 1921), he made a brief entry in his diary: "K died." It was learned that he had a mistress, who was conceded by the prosecution to be innocent of complicity in the murder, and so had her identity protected by being referred to only as Madame X, a colorful sobriquet that went on to be used as the title of several books and films.

In "The Gioconda Smile," Huxley provided a fictional denouement, which may or may not have some basis in fact. The famous story was read by Erskine, who decided to provide a somewhat different version of events—no less believable than Huxley's.

Erskine was a fairly prolific author who achieved lasting fame by creating the heroic figure of a dozen books and several movies, Renfrew of the Royal Mounted Police.

"Tea for Two" was first published in *Collier's* magazine in 1936.

TEA FOR TWO

BY LAURIE YORK ERSKINE

THE ABRUPT AND UNTIMELY DEATH of Alden Buxtree, falling close upon the triumphant success of his novel, THE STRANGEFLEET CASE, afforded a melancholy satisfaction to all who knew him. To his friends it provided the opportunity of recalling days when he had in no way merited the praise, prestige, and prosperity which success had brought him, while to his enemies it gave the privilege of reciting without danger of denial many anecdotes which proved the intimacy of their acquaintance with him. Among the few who spoke of his departure with regret was the beautiful but disquieting Mrs. Enderby.

"You see," she would say, "there was something about him . . ." And she would gaze into distance as if she saw, outlined on the remote wallpaper, the embodiment of that indescribable something. "I met him at the Tavernhams, you know, hardly a week before he died; but I could feel it—like little waves, you know—vibrations between us. He had genius. I know it. That's why I bought his collection of books—though I admit it didn't come up to what I'd expected. . . ." She would smile, as if with a secret knowledge of meanings inscrutable to others. ". . . After he died. It was so brief . . . our friendship, you know. On Thursday afternoon we met, and on the following Wednesday morning they found him dead."

That Alden Buxtree had come to tea with her at her "flat" on the afternoon preceding that fatal Wednesday morning was a detail which she never deemed it necessary to mention.

The rooms which Mrs. Enderby called her "flat" composed a small apartment overlooking the East River, which she said reminded her of the Thames. Buxtree was impressed by the flowery cosiness of the flat. He had travelled widely in England gathering material for THE STRANGEFLEET CASE, but he had never seen anything so English. He said so.

"I knew you'd understand," she replied. "And now you must make yourself comfortable while I get you some tea. My maid is out today, and we can be quite alone." She retired into the small kitchen, leaving Buxtree to luxuriate in the reflection of how softly, yieldingly feminine she appeared in the lustrous pearl-grey gown in which she had draped her small, ripe figure; of how definitely she had made it plain that he was to regard this visit as essentially private, between themselves, and of how admirably she had ensured that privacy. He congratulated himself upon these harbingers of imminent romance.

Emerging from the kitchen with tea things, Florence Enderby disappointed him. As an approach to romantic intimacy, it was the simple habit of Alden Buxtree to talk about himself, but Mrs. Enderby wouldn't have it. She talked about tea, both as a beverage and as a social institution. She deplored the American cocktail and deprecated the failure of Americans to regard tea as a time of day instead of as an exhibition of silverware. One missed the cosiness, the informality—but there! Mr. Buxtree could understand. He had been so much in England. His books showed it. He loved it—that she knew . . . and, sugar?

"One," said Buxtree. He watched with pleasure the graceful movement of her small, shapely hand and the white, rounded forearm from which the silken sleeve fell back as she delved with a silver spoon in the bowl of granulated sugar.

"Loaf sugar," she remarked, "is an American custom which evades me."

"I'm glad you found my book captured something of the English atmosphere." Buxtree brought the conversation firmly back to first principles.

"It made me feel I was back," she smiled, "in a small village I knew in Cambridgeshire. How was it you knew the people so well?" Her hazel-green eyes smiled directly into his as she handed him the cup and saucer. "The cakes," she explained, "are something I make myself. Not those. Let us save those for later." She had an odd, girlish quality, he decided, that belied the deep sophistication of her glance—but bafflingly cool, tantalizingly reserved, and self-contained. Buxtree consoled himself with a piece of substantial, plain cake with carraway seeds in it. "But your book was cruel," she said.

"Cruel," Buxtree mouthed the word fondly. Like all authors, he was delighted to be considered cruel.

"You see," she said, "I think you're a very clever person, and I think you know a great deal more than even your lovely book betrayed; but the deadly logic with which you hounded poor Eva Tredgold down and had them hang her in the last chapter struck me as gorgeously ruthless."

"Life," the enchanted Buxtree reminded her, "is ruthless."

"I'm afraid I've never given that much thought," she said. "But you see, I *was* in Cambridgeshire at the time of that hideous Armitage case, so I know where you got your plot." She sparkled upon him like a mischievous schoolgirl. "Only poor Mr. Armitage," she pointed out, "went all alone to the gallows for poisoning wife, while the lady of his heart was acquitted of complicity in the crime without even her name being brought into it. That makes you just twice as ruthless as life, does it not?"

Buxtree smiled indulgently. "A novelist," he explained, "must be true to himself. I admit THE STRANGEFLEET CASE was based upon a very close study of the Armitage poisoning case, but I may say in confidence,"—he assumed an authoritative air which in the past had done much to win him an enviable unpopularity—"that I had access to private information which was not introduced at the trial; and according to the evidence it provided, I had to find Eva Tredgold guilty, and to condemn her. I had no choice."

"But what of the poor woman in the original case—do try another bit of seedcake!—of course, it's perfectly obvious that she loved poor Mr. Armitage entirely too much; but after all, it was proved, wasn't it, that she had sailed—for America, wasn't it?—before the poison was actually administered to poor Mrs. Armitage?"

"But supposing she *hadn't?*" Buxtree leaned forward, cake in one hand, tea cup in the other. "Supposing it happened as I worked it out in the book? Supposing this Madame X, as they called her throughout the trial, had booked her passage for America and actually sailed *from Cherbourg* on a boat that stopped at Southampton? She leaves the boat, runs up to Cambridgeshire for that night-time visit with Mrs. Armitage, of which poor Armitage knew nothing, and then is back at Southampton to rejoin the ship. Armitage returns in the morning, as my book describes it, to find his wife dying; and because Madame X is never suspected, the authorities accept her elaborate plans for sailing, the passenger list from Cherbourg, and her appearance in America, as evidence of her having sailed *before* the poison was administered."

Mrs. Enderby appeared unimpressed.

"Ingenious, yes," she smiled. "But after all, she had been honorably dismissed from the case; they had even refused to bring her name into it. It seems so cruel to drag her out of retirement and pin the crime on her."

Buxtree permitted himself a superior smile. "You don't seriously believe," he said, "that she had nothing to do with the murder?"

"The courts believed it."

"The courts!" He spoke scornfully. "Supposing I were to tell you that I possess evidence which conclusively proves Madame X an accomplice."

"No!" Her eyes widened in charming incredulity. "Not all that business of the boats! You did it beautifully, Mr. Buxtree. It was a triumph of imagination, but—"

"It wasn't!" he cried recklessly. "It was true! It actually happened!" Like all good novelists, Buxtree was prepared to lie to the last ditch in defense of his novel's verisimilitude. "I have traced that woman's movements, Mrs. Enderby, from the boat to the Armitages, and from Cambridgeshire to America. If ever the real Eva Tredgold is found, I have evidence that can bring her to justice, just as surely—"

"As your tea is cold as ice!" she cried gaily. "Let me take it!" Her hand snatched his cup with the graceful flight of a swallow. "Oh, it's all very delightful and mysterious," she exulted, rising with teacup in one hand and teapot in the other, "and I feel as if I'd been let in behind the scenes at a play! But how you can unearth secrets that the Scotland Yard men missed is beyond my poor little comprehension."

He laughed modestly. "We have our own methods," he said.

"But *how?*" she insisted. "Where could it all come from?"

Buxtree was wondering about that himself, but then, as she stood gazing at him with starry eyes, he had it.

"Mrs. Armitage," he said enigmatically.

"But she was dead."

"Not when Armitage found her," he reminded her. "And she told him of the woman's visit."

"She told him! But he'd never have—"

"He did!" Buxtree was inventing recklessly now. "The poor devil was as infatuated as that. He knew she had poisoned his wife—and he kept silent. He died for her."

She was gazing at him with thoughtful unbelief. "How could you *know* it?" she asked him reproachfully.

"He wrote it down," Buxtree maintained stoutly. "Scrawled it on the flyleaf of a book about English beetles. It came into my possession with others of his books and—er—papers. You see I bought up all his belongings I could. And I found a pearl."

"How lovely!" she cried. "You own it? You have it now?"

"Of course." He assumed an admirable vagueness. "It's just one of a lot of old books knocking about my study. I'd find it hard to lay hands on it, now." He laughed carelessly.

"Of course," she admitted. "But I *must* make you a fresh cup of tea!"

Again she retreated to the kitchen. Again there was talk of tea as a beverage, of tea as an institution. Again her pretty hands fluttered over the sugar bowl and he was persuaded to eat the very special cake which she had made for him. But the room was dim before she returned again to the subject of his novel and then, to his chagrin, she used it to dismiss him.

"You know," she exclaimed, "it has been such a treat having this look behind the scenes. We must meet again and talk ever so much longer. You can tell me so much about all these tangles that we make out of our wretched little lives. You will, won't you?"

It seemed that she had to dress, now, for a dinner party, and he must go. He went reluctantly, feeling a strange heaviness, and increasing uneasiness as he walked home.

It was not until he had removed his coat and flung himself upon the bed that the pain seized him; and it was not until he curled up despairingly in an excruciating foreknowledge of his doom that he realized his irremediable mistake.

He had met the Madame X of the Armitage poisoning case and had made the fatal error of having tea with her.

THE LADY AND THE DRAGON
Peter Godfrey

Described as "the Simenon of South Africa," Peter Godfrey (1917–1992) wrote hundreds of short stories, mainly in the 1940s and '50s, which were translated into eight languages. However, until Crippen & Landru recently published *The Newtonian Egg* (2002), he had had only one book published, *Death Under the Table* (1954), a very rare collection of detective stories published by the obscure South African publishing house S.A. Scientific Publishing Co., the address of which was a post office box in Cape Town.

Godfrey's series character, the lawyer and psychologist Rolf le Roux, with his assistants, Inspector Joubert, Sergeant Johnson, and Doc McGregor, works in Cape Town and provides a look into every corner of that great international city. The homicide squad and le Roux confront the most elusive type of mystery, the seemingly impossible crime, and display extraordinary intelligence in their solutions. One case challenges them to understand how a quantity of cyanide got inside an unbroken hard-boiled egg; another raises the question of how a man alone in a cable car high above the ground could have been murdered.

"The Lady and the Dragon" is not even remotely a standard detective story but offers the same dreamlike atmosphere that elevates his other tales. It was first published in the September 1950 issue of *Ellery Queen's Mystery Magazine*.

THE LADY AND THE DRAGON

BY PETER GODFREY

SHE WAS IN A HURRY to get to Knysna, and yet she stopped the car. Nor did she know why she stopped it. It's not the scenery, she told herself. My art is to photograph people, enjoying themselves, working in sewers, dying of disease. How could my attention be attracted by a bit of pretty-pretty landscape?

But even while she rationalized, she knew her analysis was wrong. The scenery wasn't pretty-pretty—it was awe-inspiring; there was something about it that seemed to thrust its way through her eyes into her mind. Besides, there were no birds.

The valley fell away from the road in a great sweep, dwarfing the giant trees into the semblance of a lush carpet. Then, on the other side, the massive green leaped up to the sky, concave seeming, like a wave about to engulf.

No birds and no insects, and the air was still, and yet from out the heart of the wave she could sense a rolling beat, like a soundless drum.

She unslung her camera, fitted a telescopic lens with practiced fingers, and did not know why she did so. There's no photograph there, she told herself, no composition in the small field of vision of a camera, no contrast in the masses of green.

All the same, she brought the viewfinder to her eye and swept the camera slowly round. Only trees, shapeless trees, and more trees; yet she knew she would take a picture. Then suddenly she found a spot, a deep gash in the opposite mountain. Some contrast at least, she thought. Not good, but it may help me recapture the mood.

Even though the mood was one of unease . . .

She pressed the shutter release, but the second before she did so her muscles jerked, altering the angle of the camera, focusing it on a patch of forest to the left of the gap.

She felt irritated and vaguely shaken. Now she *had* to take a picture. She held the camera firmly, sighted the gap again, and pressed the shutter release. But again her muscles jerked involuntarily.

In a swift movement she re-entered the car, slammed the door, started driving. There was something at the back of her mind which she first took for panic, and then suddenly knew for excitement—deep pulsating excitement.

Fool, she thought, acting like a fool—like a kid overpowered by atmosphere, not a woman of sense and experience. There's nothing there, not even a good photograph; all I've done is waste time, and two exposures.

She was very annoyed with herself.

THE MANAGER OF the hotel, a dapper Swiss, showed her to her table and introduced her to the two men who would keep her company at meals. "Professor Munnik, Dr. Penner," he said, "Miss Carlton."

She liked the professor immediately; his eyes were warm beneath the shock of white hair. About fifty, she thought, perhaps a little more, but he carries his years well.

Dr. Penner was fair and younger; she did not try to analyze her opinions about him.

"Carlton?" said the professor. "I saw an exhibition of photographs by Mary Carlton in Cape Town last month. You aren't—?" There was genuine pleasure in his face when she nodded.

Dr. Penner said: "I suppose, as a photographer you must have stopped for pictures at least a dozen times between George and here?"

"Why, no," she said. "I'm not really a landscape photographer, you see."

That was all she meant to say, but the nagging insistence in her mind made her go on. "I did stop once, though, and took a couple of pictures. I'm afraid they're not going to be very good. I had rather a queer experience."

She told them about it. "Somehow, I can't get the incident out my mind. I don't know why—I came here to have a holiday, to forget about photography. I only brought my camera because—well, there are things I must have with me, like clothes or a handbag. And now I feel I won't rest until those exposures are developed. I know they'll look like nothing on earth. There was something about the place. . . . This may sound silly, but it's true. It was as though it had been waiting for me for a long time, and I knew I was expected."

"*Déjà vu*," said Dr. Penner, and she looked at him inquiringly. The professor laughed. "Don't let him mystify you," he said. "His doctorate isn't in medicine or even anything remotely scientific. He's a psychologist, and he's probably just applied some completely outlandish classification to you from the depths of his jargon. What was it you said, Penner?"

"*Déjà vu*. That's the name psychologists—who are incidentally very scientific fellows, despite what the professor says—apply to the feeling that you have seen a place before, even when you know you've never really been there."

She was still curious.

"That's it, yes," she said, "but how does it come about? What causes the feeling?"

Dr. Penner grinned. "I see I will have to give you a lecture. In your unconscious mind there are many desires and urges—complexes—which you cannot perceive consciously because they have been repressed in your childhood. In your dreams and in your waking fantasies, though, these urges do slip past the censorship, but in a disguised form. They adopt a symbolism—if you dream of a tree, for instance, it might stand for an infantile desire to go screaming through the drawing-room with jam on your face, or hatred for one of your parents, or one of the other things you have been forced to repress. Each person has his own particular symbols for his own complexes. Then suddenly, by coincidence, you come on physical objects arranged in a pattern, and those objects and that pattern are symbolic of your repressions in a vivid form. That is why you get the feeling you have seen a place before, although you don't know where or when."

She shook her head slowly. "No," she said. "No. Not this feeling I had."

"All the same, that is the true explanation."

Deep inside her she knew the psychologist was wrong; she felt, peculiarly, that she was at bay.

"Prove it," she challenged, and saw the professor smile delightedly. "Of what particular complex of mine was this landscape symbolic?"

"Just a minute," said Dr. Penner, and smiled in his turn. "It can't be done on the spur of the moment—that would be unscientific. No, before I come to a conclusion, I might have to ask you a great many questions."

"What sort of questions?"

"Oh, various things. The impressions that came into your mind when you first saw the scene—"

"I'll tell you that. It was as though the valley was untouched, as though humanity had never set foot there. There is a phrase for what I mean, but I just can't think of it."

"Virgin forest?" suggested the professor.

"Yes. Virgin forest. Next question, doctor?"

But Dr. Penner held up his hand placatingly. "Not now," he said, "and not here. If you feel tomorrow that you still want to know, I'll do my best to oblige you. Only," he said, "we must be alone. How can anyone do a serious scientific investigation with the professor grinning like a Cheshire cat?"

"All right—but just tell me one thing. The movements which made me turn my camera, and now this consuming curiosity to see the prints—is all that psychological? Does it all spring from within myself?"

"Yes."

"I find it very difficult to believe that," she said.

SHE TOSSED AND turned for hours that night, and when she did sleep there was all the time a pressing urgency in her to wake up. She dressed early, long before breakfast, and went out to sit on the broad veranda.

The manager came over to chat to her, and she asked him if he knew where she could obtain the use of a photographic dark room.

"Why, yes," he said. "I have a friend, and I am sure that he will help you, but he will not be up yet, you understand? I will telephone him later and let you know."

He came to her later, just as the breakfast gong was booming, and handed her a slip of paper on which was written an address.

"You may go at any time," he told her, and gave her detailed directions how to get there.

The dark room was attached to a studio on an island in the lagoon, and she hired a skiff to carry her across. She was glad to find the photographer was not curious; he showed her where to go and disappeared somewhere in the back of the building.

Carefully she removed the film from the camera and developed it. She made contact prints, took them still wet from the fixing bath, and carried them to the light.

The tiny rectangles were very dark; still, something of what she had photographed was apparent.

She put both negatives under the enlarger and made large prints. The two photographs were not of the same spot, although they must have been adjacent to each other. She examined the first carefully, and then put it aside. In the second she thought she saw something, and peered at it through a powerful magnifying glass.

In an ecstasy of certainty she marked out a portion of the picture on the negative—square of about two inches—and put it back to enlarge to whole-plate size.

The definition, of course, suffered badly. What had appeared on the original as solid black was now vague and full of blurs and uncertain lines—a rain-on-the-glass pattern of distortion.

But she knew what she was looking for—the form in the formlessness—and traced it out with the naked eye. It was magnificent, yet terrifying and unmistakable.

The head!

Trembling with a cold fever, she went back to the hotel.

SHE FOUND THE professor and Dr. Penner on a settee in the corner of the lounge, and took the easy chair facing them.

Penner asked, with an amused glint in his eye, "Developed your photographs yet?"

She nodded, very seriously. "Yes. This is an enlargement of a portion of the original print. I'd like you to look at it very carefully."

They bent their heads together, studying it. Her impatience got the better of her. "Can't you see it?"

Penner leaned back and shook his head regretfully. "I'm sorry. I can't make head or tail out of it. It looks like a jigsaw puzzle to me."

She felt frustrated and desolate. "And you, Professor?"

"Nothing," he said. "Of course, my eyes are not what they used to be."

She checked herself from protesting. "Just a minute," she said, and with a pencil on the back of another photograph she sketched what she had seen, divorced from the background, but of the same size and in the same position as on the original.

The effect of the drawing on the professor was electric, he sat up drew in the air sharply between his teeth, and traced an outline with his finger on the photograph. "Yes," he said. "Yes." And then, "I see it now. Quite clearly. It was these other blurs and lines which made me confused." He handed the drawing and photograph to Penner.

"But what is it?" she asked. "What is it?"

The excitement in the professor's voice, matched hers. "I know, but I am almost afraid to say it. It is a great scientific discovery. Many hundreds of thousands of years ago, when the world was very young, there existed enormous creatures of which you have heard—the brachiosaurus and others. There was one among them which preyed on the rest, which was stronger and fiercer than any of the others. It was called Tyrannosaurus Rex. It is the head of a tyrannosaurus that appears on your photograph."

He paused only a second, and added, "We must go to this valley."

"WAIT A MOMENT," said Penner. "Before we start rushing into things, there are one or two objections I would like to make. First of all, I'm not perfectly satisfied that there is any sort of head in this photograph."

"But I *see* it!" objected the professor.

"You see it now. You didn't see it before. I also see it now, but I'm by no means convinced."

She felt a great wave of irritation. "What do you mean?"

"Have you ever heard of *gestalt*? No, I see you haven't. Well, let me explain it, then. Give a person an ordinary shapeless ink blot and ask him what he sees in it. Immediately his mind begins to view the blot in terms of a pattern, one common and familiar to him. If, at the same time, you suggest that there is a similarity to a donkey, he will be predisposed to look for a donkey. Here you have given us a sketch of a tyrannosaurus and a shapeless blur in which you say it is—and the chances are ten to one we will see a tyrannosaurus. Especially," he added, "since one of us is an eminent naturalist, who'd probably give his right arm for sight of such a creature."

"Theory," said the professor, "and very torturous theory at that. There is a much simpler one which conforms more closely to the facts—that there is actually the head of a tyrannosaurus in the picture."

Dr. Penner shrugged. "I said I was not certain. You may be right—but so may I."

She broke in eagerly. "Don't you see, Dr. Penner, that you *must* be wrong? I'm not a naturalist—I didn't even know what the creature was—but I saw it all the same."

"I have a theory about that too," he said quietly, "but I won't bring it up now. There's another thing I want to query. Let's assume there is a tyrannosaurus. Can you explain why this one is still alive when the rest of its species died thousands of centuries ago?"

"Alive?" expostulated the professor. "Who said anything about that? What Miss Carlton has photographed is a perfect or near-perfect fossil of the creature—a priceless scientific treasure!"

But she shook her head. "You're wrong, Professor. It *is* alive! I feel it. And it's got—no, intelligence isn't quite what I mean—it has some form of mental power. I've felt it ever since I stopped to take those photographs—it forced me to go and develop the film. And now I can feel, deep inside me, an urge to return, to go back to the spot I photographed. How else can that be explained?"

Penner said abruptly, "You haven't answered my question. How is it possible for this creature to be alive?"

She shrugged. "I don't know. Isn't just the fact of its existence enough? Perhaps—well, I told you my impression of the valley, that it had been isolated, untouched for centuries—perhaps they have never died out there. Or what do we know about how long their natural life-span was? Perhaps this is one of the original species?"

"And its mental power?" went on Penner, relentlessly. "As far as I remember, the tyrannosaurus had a brain about the size of a pea."

"Aha!" said the professor triumphantly. "What has that got to do with it? Didn't you tell me yourself the other night that the theory that intelligence depended on brain size could never be considered valid, because Anatole France had a brain smaller than a Bushman's? Miss Carlton's theories may be as imaginative as yours, but at least they are based on facts of experience. For myself, I believe there is a gigantic fossil in the valley—nothing more. But I have an open mind, and I am going there tomorrow to make sure."

"And I," said Penner, "am going there to prove you wrong."

THEY MADE PLANS for the expedition over the lunch table, and the professor left to make the necessary preparations in the town.

She walked to the veranda and stood a long time staring at the glimpse of the lagoon down the road and at the little church with its graveyard opposite.

By herself like that, she had content, a mind crowded with a patient ecstasy of anticipation. Then Dr. Penner came to join her, and she felt lonely and afraid.

He must have sensed something of this, because his first words were almost an apology. "I must speak to you," he said.

"Yes?"

"About this trip tomorrow. There are things I feel I should tell you."

"Yes?"

"Do you remember our conversation last night, when you asked me to analyze your complex? May I do that now?"

She hesitated. "All right—if it amuses you. But don't expect me to accept your theories unconditionally. What do you want me to do?"

"I'm going to ask you a few questions—personal ones. I want you to answer them candidly and truthfully. How old are you, Miss Carlton?"

There was just a shade of defiance in her voice. "Thirty-five."

"I take it, at your age, you're continually thinking about getting married?"

"You're not quite right there. Naturally, I do think about it sometimes—but 'continually' is definitely an overstatement. I want you to understand, also, that I am single today by my own choice, not through any lack of opportunity."

"That, of course, is obvious—you're a very attractive woman. Let me say rather that Mr. Right has not yet come along, but that you wish he would?"

"Yes, that's more accurate."

"Then I want to go further and suggest that when you decided to come here on holiday, the hope of meeting Mr. Right was one of your deeper motives?"

"Yes, one of them. Another, and much more important one, was that I'd been overworking and needed a holiday."

She waited for his next question, but this time his voice did not rise in query at the end of the sentence. It was conversational, casual, a bare statement of fact.

"St. George and the dragon," he said.

The remark was so out of context, so apparently inconsequential, she should have felt amused, and was annoyed at herself because she wasn't. Behind her annoyance was a prickle of shock.

"What are you talking about?" she asked.

"Your complex. Oh, it's very plain to me, but I must make it just as plain to you. Listen. What you are fixated on is the idea of romance—that very young and childish idea. The maiden rescued by the Knight from terrible peril. St. George and the dragon."

"Do you really believe this nonsense?"

"It's the truth. Let me show you step by step. Why did the valley attract your attention? You couldn't think of the phrase to describe it—remember?—and that's also significant. Virgin forest. Two meanings there—land untrodden by man, and the forest where the virgin is in peril of the dragon. Don't sneer. That's what your unconscious mind thought. That's why you moved involuntarily—so you could photograph a portion of the landscape where there was little or no definition. To satisfy your complex you had to find a dragon, and that was the only way. You found one because you were looking for it."

She repeated, "Nonsense," but he kept on speaking.

"I'm telling you this because I'm afraid for you. Afraid of the strength of your obsession. Afraid of what it may do to you tomorrow when you find no trace whatever of the tyrannosaurus. Oh, you don't believe me, but think it over. Now. Tonight. And especially tomorrow."

She felt angry but quite cold, and her voice slapped him in the face. "Dr. Penner, do you know you're behaving like an overwrought schoolboy? I have never in my life heard such preposterous nonsense as your analysis of me.

You've disobeyed all the laws of logic in your theory, given the wrong values to some facts and completely disregarded others, because they don't fit in with your preconceived ideas. Like the fact that although I've never seen a picture of a tyrannosaurus, or even heard the name of the creature, I was able to make a recognizable sketch of it."

"You've forgotten—but of course you had seen a drawing somewhere. You *must* have! You may not even have been conscious of it—just caught a glimpse somewhere—but enough for your unconscious mind to perceive the dragon symbolism."

She laughed out loud. "Your logic astounds me. Because you don't see another reason, therefore, there cannot be another reason. Tell me, Doctor, what makes you take so much trouble over me? Why is it so necessary for you to pry into my mind?"

He looked at her very gravely. "I will tell you some day—but not now."

"You won't or you cannot? I wonder. You see, Doctor, you've also got a complex, which is just as obvious to me as mine seems to you. A psychology complex. Everything you see and hear is distorted by you in terms of your pet subject. More than a complex, Dr. Penner—an obsession."

"I wish you were right," he said.

SHE HAD LAUGHED at him, yes. But what was it he had left unsaid?

His theory was fantastic, ridiculous, unscientific. She knew her own mind—how well she knew it! Or did she?

She had to be alone, get away from the hotel, think it out for herself.

She took the car along the road to Port Elizabeth, watching, but not knowing for what. At least, not until she found it.

It was a valley, a sheer sweep from the road, giant trees, and a towering mountain opposite. Except for the house at the bottom or the slope it was identical with the landscape that called to her.

She got out of the car, stood on the edge of the road, and let the wind ruffle her hair.

This valley meant nothing to her. And so it provided proof that Dr. Penner must be wrong. Here it was, a valley, mountains and trees—the same perfect symbolism that he said had excited her complex. And yet she was unmoved.

She should have felt elation, satisfaction, only she couldn't because of the house. It spoiled the picture. There were people living here: that was the difference.

She half-closed her eyes, so that the house below her was obscured, and filled her mind with the memory of the other valley. Then the house didn't matter any more. Nothing mattered except a point in the view-finder of her camera, a head on a photographic print.

She turned the car, went home, and was very silent at dinner. So was Dr. Penner, but the professor chatted excitedly about the morning.

She went to bed early.

And dreamed.

She was a cave-dweller, dressed in skins, and Penner and the professor were there, too, and all three of them were thrusting desperately against a huge rock at the mouth of their cave, to save themselves from something monstrous pushing on the other side. And all the time their muscles were like lead, and Penner, clumsy, hindered their efforts. Then suddenly she and the professor were alone, gradually being forced back. The stone jerked, hurling them aside. The monster walked through, and the monster was Penner.

Foolish and fantastic and meaningless. Yet she woke sobbing . . .

THEY SET OUT early in the morning, loaded with knapsacks, and she was in a fever of impatience because the professor was driving, and he was driving too slowly.

Then they were there, parking the car, climbing out with their gear. On the lip of the descent the professor turned and faced them. In that second she saw him as a picture, with the shock of white hair like a patriarch's, the keen eyes, the wrinkled neck protruding from the khaki shirt, the strangely youthful legs below the shorts.

"In a few hours we'll know," he said; and then added, "I found out something about this place in town yesterday. There's a man living in town who, they say, is over a hundred years old. He told me he knew about this valley—that it was haunted, and that no person has ever set foot in it. He had a name for it, too—*Drakensvallei*—the Valley of the Dragon; but he could not tell me why it had been given that name."

The going was not easy, but it was not as bad as they had expected. She felt a pleasurable yearning grow with every step; the professor sang, even Penner became quite animated.

He twitted her about the little pearl-handled pistol she carried. "A pop-gun," he said. "I doubt whether it would kill a man, let alone a tyrannosaurus."

"You'd be surprised what damage this thing can do," she told him, "and I'm a very good shot. I didn't bring it for the tyrannosaurus, though. There may be other things here. Snakes, for instance."

There was a snake, and she did shoot it, but not before it had buried its fangs deep in the professor's youthful leg.

Penner called urgently, "Have you got a knife?" but she could only shake her head. He cursed, tore a tin of sardines from a knapsack, opened it, and used the metal to cut a great gash in the vicinity of the wound. Then he applied his lips.

She winced, stared, and began to see nothing.

"No use," said the professor. "Mamba."

A little later he tried to say something else, but his paralysed larynx only made animal sounds.

Penner, perspiration pouring down his face, leaned over the old man. "What did you say? George, talk to me! Try again! I'm listening."

But there was no life in the twisted lips, no breath even to expel guttural noises . . . She stood there, gun in hand, her consciousness sliding into ever narrowing focus. Penner rose. "We must report this. I'll stay here. Go back, take the car, and fetch the police."

He became aware of the expression on her face. "Do you hear me?"

She spoke then, not in answer to his question, but in tones full of lingering wonderment. "So his name was George," she said.

He tried to grasp her arm, but she shook herself away and stood staring at something in the far distance; in reality, her lids were pricking with the narrowness of her concentration.

She said very simply, "It is calling me," and he felt a flash of panic.

"Wait," he said. "Listen. I know—believe me, I know—just how strong this obsession is with you. But please—concentrate on this—it is *only* an obsession! There is no tyrannosaurus—except in your mind. The professor is lying here dead. You must go back."

She shook her head, and did not know she was shaking it.

"No," he said with decision, "no. You wanted to know yesterday—now I must tell you. I can't let you go on. I'm afraid. Afraid because I . . . love you, Mary."

There was a swirling mist that obscured him; she could only see his eyes. They were very blue and wide apart and intense. Her finger moved, just a slight movement, and then he had a third eye. She was not even conscious of the noise of the shot.

He slid down into the mist and she went forward, stumbling over him, but not knowing she had stumbled.

Sometimes she ran and sometimes she walked, but there was no consciousness of physical weariness when she slowed her pace. There was no consciousness of anything except a pulse in her brain, a single pulse, reverberating, not with pain but with power. And as she went forward, the power grew, slowly exploding into soundless thunder, echoes concussing ever more and more, and those concussions mushrooming into greater beats.

She stopped when she knew she had to.

It was in a glade, and she peered upward expectantly to see what must be there. Her mind was heavy, feathered, and she knew a great sorrow because she could see nothing. Then there was a hint of movement in the trees, a swelling and gasping of the air, and she realized with a sudden flush of triumph that some things cannot be seen because they are too big.

She felt a mighty eye upon her, a red moon, and the beams trembled into her with a knowledge, a certainty of a presence, a consciousness of unhumanity and potent great age.

She called out, "What do you want of me?"

The pulsations in her brain fluttered and boomed telepathically, forced themselves down habitual neural patterns, twisted into her consciousness in the familiar form of words. *I am very pleased you have come.*

She wondered why It was pleased, and even with the thought the answer came, blurting from the pulse in high-toned spasms of power, so that the words they shaped in her brain were ringing echoes in her ears:

I am very, very hungry.

• • •

THE LADY AND THE DRAGON

AFTERWORD

So here is the riddle for this bizarre story: did the tyrannosaurus rex actually exist in this unlikely locale, or was the giant prehistoric monster merely a figment of the apparently rational lady's mind?

A MEDIEVAL ROMANCE
MARK TWAIN

Although Samuel Langhorne Clemens (1835–1910) is justly famous as a great, perhaps *the* great American novelist, with such masterpieces to his credit as *Huckleberry Finn, Tom Sawyer, A Connecticut Yankee in King Arthur's Court* and *The Prince and the Pauper*, it is often forgotten that he was a seminal figure in the history of crime fiction.

The Celebrated Jumping Frog of Calaveras County (1867) was selected by Ellery Queen for his compendium of the 106 greatest mystery short stories of all time, as it told the tale of a stranger who successfully pulls off a great confidence game.

More significant is his semi-autobiographical *Life on the Mississippi* (1883), which contains a complete short story, "A Thumb-Print and What Became of It" (chapter 31), which is historically important because it contains the first fictional use of fingerprints as a method of identification. *The Tragedy of Pudd'nhead Wilson* (1894) is frequently cited as the first fictional use of fingerprints in a detective story novel and was regarded as such a milestone in the genre that it was selected for the Haycraft-Queen Cornerstone Library of important books of detective fiction. While it obviously followed the pioneering short story in *Life on the Mississippi* by eleven years, it is still important because the entire plot revolves around Pudd'nhead's courtroom explanation of the uniqueness of a person's print.

"A Medieval Romance" is, candidly, only a mystery by virtue of its conclusion and its title. It was first published in the Buffalo *Express* in 1870 and in book form in *Mark Twain's*

(Burlesque) Autobiography and First Romance the following year. At least, that is the title on the title page. The title displayed when the story begins is "Awful, Terrible Medieval Romance." It is neither awful nor terrible, hence the shorter title used for this volume.

A MEDIEVAL ROMANCE

BY MARK TWAIN

CHAPTER I.
THE SECRET REVEALED.

IT WAS NIGHT. Stillness reigned in the grand old feudal castle of Klugenstein. The year 1222 was drawing to a close. Far away up in the tallest of the castle's towers a single light glimmered. A secret council was being held there. The stern old lord of Klugenstein sat in a chair of state meditating. Presently he said, with a tender accent:

"My daughter!"

A young man of noble presence, clad from head to heel in knightly mail, answered:

"Speak father!"

"My daughter, the time is come for the revealing of the mystery that hath puzzled all your young life. Know, then, that it had its birth in the matters which I shall now unfold. My brother Ulrich is the great Duke of Brandenburgh. Our father, on his deathbed, decreed that if no son were born to Ulrich, the succession should pass to my house, provided a *son* were born to me. And further, in case no son were born to either, but only daughters, then the succession should pass to Ulrich's daughter, if she proved stainless; if she did not, my daughter should succeed, if she retained a blameless name. And so I, and my old wife here, prayed fervently for the good boon of a son, but the prayer was vain. You were born to us. I was in despair. I saw the mighty prize slipping from my grasp, the splendid dream vanishing away. And I had been so hopeful! Five years had Ulrich lived in wedlock, and yet his wife had borne no heir of either sex.

" 'But hold,' I said, 'all is not lost.' A saving scheme had shot athwart my brain. You were born at midnight. Only the leech, the nurse, and six waiting-women knew your sex. I hanged them every one before an hour had sped. Next morning all the barony went mad with rejoicing over the proclamation that a *son* was born to Klugenstein, an heir to mighty Brandenburgh! And well the secret has been kept. Your mother's own sister nursed your infancy, and from that time forward we feared nothing.

"When you were ten years old, a daughter was born to Ulrich. We grieved, but hoped for good results from measles, or physicians, or other natural enemies of infancy, but were always disappointed. She lived, she throve—Heaven's malison upon her! But it is nothing. We are safe. For, Ha-ha! have we not a son? And is not our son the future Duke? Our well-beloved Conrad, is it not so?—for, woman of eight-and-twenty years as you are, my child, none other name than that hath ever fallen to you!

"Now it hath come to pass that age hath laid its hand upon my brother, and he waxes feeble. The cares of state do tax him sore. Therefore he wills that you shall come to him and be already Duke in act, though not yet in name. Your servitors are ready—you journey forth to-night.

"Now listen well. Remember every word I say. There is a law as old as Germany that if any woman sit for a single instant in the great ducal chair before she hath been absolutely crowned in presence of the people, SHE SHALL DIE! So heed my words. Pretend humility. Pronounce your judgments from the Premier's chair, which stands at the *foot* of the throne. Do this until you are crowned and safe. It is not likely that your sex will ever be discovered; but still it is the part of wisdom to make all things as safe as may be in this treacherous earthly life."

"Oh, my father, is it for this my life hath been a lie! Was it that I might cheat my unoffending cousin of her rights? Spare me, father, spare your child!"

"What, huzzy! Is this my reward for the august fortune my brain has wrought for thee? By the bones of my father, this puling sentiment of thine but ill accords with my humor. Betake thee to the Duke, instantly! And beware how thou meddlest with my purpose!"

LET THIS SUFFICE, of the conversation. It is enough for us to know that the prayers, the entreaties and the tears of the gentle-natured girl availed nothing. They nor anything could move the stout old lord of Klugenstein. And so, at last, with a heavy heart, the daughter saw the castle gates close behind her, and found herself riding away in the darkness surrounded by a knightly array of armed vassals and a brave following of servants.

The old baron sat silent for many minutes after his daughter's departure, and then he turned to his sad wife and said:

"Dame, our matters seem speeding fairly. It is full three months since I sent the shrewd and handsome Count Detzin on his devilish mission to my brother's daughter Constance. If he fail, we are not wholly safe; but if he do succeed, no power can bar our girl from being Duchess e'en though ill fortune should decree, she never should be Duke!"

"My heart is full of bodings, yet all may still be well."

"Tush, woman! Leave the owls to croak. To bed with ye, and dream of Brandenburgh and grandeur!"

CHAPTER II.
FESTIVITY AND TEARS.

SIX DAYS AFTER the occurrences related in the above chapter, the brilliant capital of the Duchy of Brandenburgh was resplendent with military pageantry, and noisy with the rejoicings of loyal multitudes; for Conrad, the young heir to the crown, was come. The old Duke's heart was full of happiness, for Conrad's handsome person and graceful bearing had won his love at once. The great halls of the palace were thronged with nobles, who welcomed Conrad bravely; and so bright and happy did all things seem, that he felt his fears and sorrows passing away and giving place to a comforting contentment.

But in a remote apartment of the palace a scene of a different nature was transpiring. By a window stood the Duke's only child, the Lady Constance. Her eyes we're red and swollen, and full of tears. She was alone. Presently she fell to weeping anew, and said aloud:

"The villain Detzin is gone—has fled the dukedom! I could not believe it at first, but alas! it is too true. And I loved him so. I dared to love him though I knew the Duke my father would never let me wed him. I loved him—but now I hate him! With all my soul I hate him! Oh, what is to become of me! I am lost, lost, lost! I shall go mad!"

CHAPTER III.
THE PLOT THICKENS.

A FEW MONTHS DRIFTED BY. All men published the praises of the young Conrad's government and extolled the wisdom of his judgments, the mercifulness of his sentences, and the modesty with which he bore himself in his great office. The old Duke soon gave everything into his hands, and sat apart and listened with proud satisfaction while his heir delivered the decrees of the crown from the seat of the premier. It seemed plain that one so loved and praised and honored of all men as Conrad was, could not be otherwise than happy. But strangely enough, he was not. For he saw with dismay that the Princess Constance had begun to love him! The love of the rest of the world was happy fortune for him, but this was freighted with danger! And he saw, moreover, that the delighted Duke had discovered his daughter's passion likewise, and was already dreaming of a marriage. Every day somewhat of the deep sadness that had been in the princess' face faded away; every day hope and animation beamed brighter from her eye; and by and by even vagrant smiles visited the face that had been so troubled.

Conrad was appalled, he bitterly cursed himself for having yielded to the instinct that had made him seek the companionship of one of his own sex when he was new and a stranger in the palace—when he was sorrowful and yearned for a sympathy such as only women can give or feel, he now began to avoid his cousin. But this only made matters worse, for, naturally enough, the more he avoided her, the more she cast herself in his way. He marvelled at this at first; and next it startled him. The girl haunted him; she hunted him; she happened upon him at all times and in all places, in the night as well as in the day. She seemed singularly anxious. There was surely a mystery somewhere.

This could not go on forever. All the world talking about it. The Duke was beginning to look perplexed. Poor Conrad was becoming a very ghost through dread and dire distress. One day as he was emerging from a private ante-room attached to the picture gallery, Constance confronted him, and seizing both his hands in hers, exclaimed:

"Oh, why do you avoid me? What have I done—what have I said, to lose your kind opinion of me—for surely I had it once? Conrad, do not despise me, but pity a tortured heart? I cannot, cannot hold the words unspoken longer, lest they kill me—I LOVE YOU, CONRAD! There, despise me if you must, but they *would* be uttered!"

Conrad was speechless. Constance hesitated a moment, and then, misinterpreting his silence, a wild gladness flamed in her eyes, and she flung her arms about his neck and said:

"You relent! you relent! You *can* love me—you *will* love me! Oh, say you will, my own, my worshipped Conrad!"

Conrad groaned aloud. A sickly pallor overspread his countenance, and he trembled like an aspen. Presently, in desperation, he thrust the poor girl from him, and cried:

"You know not what you ask! It is forever and ever impossible!" And then he fled like a criminal and left the princess stupefied with amazement. A minute afterward she was crying and sobbing there, and Conrad was crying and sobbing in his chamber. Both were in despair. Both saw ruin staring them in the face.

By and by Constance rose slowly to her feet and moved away, saying:

"To think that he was despising my love at the very moment that I thought it was melting his cruel heart! I hate him! he spurned me—did this man—he spurned me from him like a dog!"

CHAPTER IV.
THE AWFUL REVELATION.

TIME PASSED ON. A settled sadness rested once more upon the countenance of the good Duke's daughter. She and Conrad were seen together no more now. The Duke grieved at this. But as the weeks wore away, Conrad's color came back to his cheeks and his old-time vivacity to his eye, and he administered the government with a clear and steadily ripening wisdom.

Presently a strange whisper began to be heard about the palace. It grew louder; it spread farther. The gossips of the city got hold of it. It swept the dukedom. And this is what the whisper said:

"The Lady Constance hath given birth to a child!"

When the lord of Klugenstein heard it, he swung his plumed helment thrice around his head and shouted:

"Long live Duke Conrad!—for lo, his crown is sure, from this day forward! Detzin has done his errand well, and the good scoundrel shall be rewarded!"

And he spread the tidings far and wide, and for eight-and-forty hours no soul in all the barony but did dance and sing, carouse and illuminate, to celebrate the great event, and all at proud and happy old Klugenstein's expense.

CHAPTER V.
THE FRIGHTFUL CATASTROPHE.

THE TRIAL WAS AT HAND. All the great lords and barons of Brandenburgh were assembled in the Hall of Justice in the ducal palace. No space was left unoccupied where there was room for a spectator to stand or sit. Conrad, clad in purple and ermine, sat in the premier's chair, and on either side sat the great judges of the realm. The old Duke had sternly commanded that the trial of his daughter should proceed, without favor, and then had taken to his bed broken-hearted. His days were numbered. Poor Conrad had begged, as for his very life, that he might be spared the misery of sitting in judgment upon his cousin's crime, but it did not avail.

The saddest heart in all that great assemblage was in Conrad's breast.

The gladdest was in his father's. For, unknown to his daughter "Conrad," the old Baron Klugenstein was come, and was among the crowd of nobles, triumphant in the swelling fortunes of his house.

After the heralds had made due proclamation and the other preliminaries had followed, the venerable Lore! Chief Justice said:

"Prisoner, stand forth!"

The unhappy princess rose and stood unveiled before the vast multitude. The Lord Chief Justice continued:

"Most noble lady, before the great judges of this realm it hath been charged and proven that out of holy wedlock your Grace hath given birth unto a child, and by our ancient law the penalty is death, excepting in one sole contingency, whereof his Grace the acting Duke, our good Lord Conrad, will advertise you in his solemn sentence now; wherefore, give heed."

Conrad stretched forth the reluctant sceptre, and in the self-same moment the womanly heart beneath his robe yearned pityingly toward the doomed prisoner, and the tears came into his eyes. He opened his lips to speak, but the Lord Chief Justice said quickly:

"Not there, your Grace, not there! It is not lawful to pronounce judgment upon any of the ducal line, SAVE FROM THE DUCAL THRONE!"

A shudder went to the heart of poor Conrad, and a tremor shook the iron frame of his old father likewise. CONRAD HAD NOT BEEN CROWNED—dared he profane the throne? He hesitated and turned pale with fear. But it must be done. Wondering eyes were already upon him. They would be suspicious eyes if he hesitated longer. He ascended the throne. Presently he stretched forth the sceptre again, and said:

"Prisoner, in the name of our sovereign lord, Ulrich, Duke of Brandenburgh, I proceed to the solemn duty that hath devolved upon me. Give heed to my words. By the ancient law of the land, except you produce the partner of your guilt and deliver him up to the executioner, you must surely die. Embrace, this opportunity—save yourself while yet you may. Name the father of your child!"

A solemn hush fell upon the great court—a silence so profound that men could hear their own hearts beat. Then the princess slowly turned, with eyes gleaming with hate, and pointing her finger straight at Conrad, said:

"Thou art the man!"

An appalling conviction of his helpless, hopeless peril struck a chill to Conrad's heart like the chill of death itself. What power on earth could save him! To disprove the charge, he must reveal that he was a woman; and for an uncrowned woman to sit in the ducal chair was death! At one and the same moment, he and his grim old father swooned and fell to the ground.

[The remainder of this thrilling and eventful story will NOT be found in this or any other publication, either now or at any future time.]

The truth is, I have got my hero (or heroine) into such a particularly close place, that I do not see how I am ever going to get him (or her) out of it again—and therefore I will wash my hands of the whole business, and leave that person to get out the best way that offers—or else stay there. I thought it was going to be easy enough to straighten out that little difficulty, but it looks different now.

[If *Harper's Weekly* or the New York *Tribune* desire to copy these initial chapters into the reading columns of their valuable journals, just as they do the opening chapters of *Ledger* and *New York Weekly* novels, they are at liberty to do so at the usual rates, provided they "trust."]

THE MOMENT OF DECISION
STANLEY ELLIN

Having begun this anthology with the distinguished Stanley Ellin, it is our great good fortune that he wrote two riddle stories, so we can end with him as well.

"The Moment of Decision" was adapted to a sixty-minute television show on *The U.S. Steel Hour* in 1961. The lead actor was a former song and dance man who got the opportunity to show what he could do as a dramatic actor. He seems to have passed the test, as Fred Astaire went on to many other non-singing, non-dancing roles.

Other Stanley Ellin works were filmed, notably *The House of Cards* (1969), a Hitchcockian international thriller that starred George Peppard and Inger Stevens, and featured Orson Welles, based on his novel of the same name; *Nothing But the Best* (1964), the dark comedy starring Alan Bates and directed by Clive Donner, based on his short story, "The Best of Everything"; and *Big Night* (1951), based on his first novel, *Dreadful Summit*, directed by Joseph Losey and starring John Barrymore, Jr. *Sunburn* (1979) starring Farah Fawcett was very loosely based on his novel *The Bind*, but Ellin should not be blamed for it in any way.

"The Moment of Decision" was first published in the March 1955 issue of *Ellery Queen's Mystery Magazine*.

THE MOMENT OF DECISION

BY STANLEY ELLIN

HUGH LOZIER WAS THE EXCEPTION to the rule that people who are completely sure of themselves cannot be likable. We have all met the sure ones, of course—those controlled but penetrating voices which cut through all others in a discussion, those hard forefingers jabbing home opinions on your chest, those living Final Words on all issues—and I imagine we all share the same amalgam of dislike and envy for them. Dislike, because no one likes to be shouted down or prodded in the chest, and envy, because everyone wishes he himself were so rich in self-assurance that he could do the shouting down and prodding.

For myself, since my work took me regularly to certain places in this atomic world where the only state was confusion and the only steady employment that of splitting political hairs, I found absolute judgments harder and harder to come by. Hugh once observed of this that it was a good thing my superiors in the department were not cut of the same cloth, because God knows what would happen to the country then. I didn't relish that, but—and there was my curse again—I had to grant him his right to say it.

Despite this, and despite the fact that Hugh was my brother-in-law—a curious relationship when you come to think of it—I liked him immensely, just as everyone else did who knew him. He was a big, good-looking man, with clear blue eyes in a ruddy face, and with a quick, outgoing nature eager to appreciate whatever you had to offer. He was overwhelmingly generous, and his generosity was of that rare and excellent kind which makes you feel as if you are doing the donor a favor by accepting it.

I wouldn't say he had any great sense of humor, but plain good humor can sometimes be an adequate substitute for that, and in Hugh's case it was. His stormy side was largely reserved for those times when he thought you might have needed his help in something and failed to call on him for it. Which meant that ten minutes after Hugh had met you and liked you, you were expected to ask him for anything he might be able to offer. A month or so after he married my sister Elizabeth she mentioned to him my avid interest in a fine Copley he had hanging in his gallery at Hilltop, and I can still vividly recall my horror when it suddenly arrived heavily crated and with his gift card attached, at my barren room-and-a-half. It took considerable effort, but I finally managed to return it to him by forgoing the argument that the picture was undoubtedly worth more than the entire building in which I lived and by complaining that it simply didn't show to advantage on my wall. I think he suspected I was lying, but being Hugh he would never dream of charging me with that in so many words.

Of course, Hilltop and the two hundred years of Lozier tradition that went into it did much to shape Hugh this way. The first Loziers had carved the estate from the heights overlooking the river, had worked hard and flourished exceedingly; its successive generations had invested their income so wisely that money and position eventually erected a towering wall between Hilltop and the world outside. Truth to tell, Hugh was very much a man of the eighteenth century who somehow found himself in the twentieth, and simply made the best of it.

Hilltop itself was almost a replica of the celebrated, but long untenanted, Dane house nearby, and was striking enough to open anybody's eyes at a glance. The house was weathered stone, graceful despite its bulk, and the vast lawns reaching to the river's edge were tended with such fanatic devotion over the years that they had become carpets of purest green which magically changed luster under any breeze. Gardens ranged from the other side of the house down to the groves which half hid the stables and out-buildings, and past the far side of the groves ran the narrow road which led to town. The road was a courtesy road, each estate holder along it maintaining his share, and I think it safe to say that for all the crushed rock he laid in it Hugh made less use of it by far than any of his neighbors.

Hugh's life was bound up in Hilltop; he could be made to leave it only by dire necessity; and if you did meet him away from it you were made acutely aware that he was counting off the minutes until he could return. And if you weren't wary you would more than likely find yourself going along with him when he did return, and totally unable to tear yourself away from the place while the precious weeks rolled by. I know. I believe I spent more time at Hilltop than at my own apartment after my sister brought Hugh into the family.

At one time I wondered how Elizabeth took to this marriage, considering that before she met Hugh she had been as restless and flighty as she was pretty. When I put the question to her directly, she said. "It's wonderful, darling. Just as wonderful as I knew it would be when I first met him."

It turned out that their first meeting had taken place at an art exhibition, a showing of some ultramodern stuff and she had been intently studying one of the more bewildering concoctions on display when she became aware of this tall, good-looking man staring at her. And, as she put it, she had been about to set him properly in his place when he said abruptly, "Are you admiring that?"

This was so unlike what she had expected that she was taken completely aback. "I don't know," she said weakly. "Am I supposed to?"

"No," said the stranger, "it's damned nonsense. Come along now, and I'll show you something which isn't a waste of time."

"And," Elizabeth said to me, "I came along like a pup at his heels, while he marched up and down and told me what was good and what was bad, and in a good loud voice, too, so that we collected quite a crowd along the way. Can you picture it, darling?"

"Yes," I said, "I can." By now I had shared similar occasions with Hugh, and learned at firsthand that nothing could dent his cast-iron assurance.

"Well," Elizabeth went on, "I must admit that at first I was a little put off, but then I began to see that he knew exactly what he was talking about, and that he was terribly sincere. Not a bit self-conscious about anything, but just eager for me to understand things the way he did. It's the same way with everything. Everybody else in the world is always fumbling and bumbling over deciding anything—what to order for dinner, or how to manage his job, or whom to vote for—but Hugh always *knows*. It's *not* knowing that makes for all those nerves and complexes and things you hear about, isn't that so? Well, I'll take Hugh, thank you, and leave everyone else to the psychiatrists."

So there it was. An Eden with flawless lawns and no awful nerves and complexes, and not even the glimmer of a serpent in the offing. That is, not a glimmer until the day Raymond made his entrance on the scene.

We were out on the terrace that day,. Hugh and Elizabeth and I, slowly being melted into a sort of liquid torpor by the August sunshine, and all of us too far gone to make even a pretence at talk. I lay there with a linen cap over my face, listening to the summer noises around me and being perfectly happy.

There was the low, steady hiss of the breeze through the aspens nearby, the plash and drip of oars on the river below, and now and then the melancholy *tink-tunk* of a sheep bell from one of the flock on the lawn. The flock was a fancy of Hugh's. He swore that nothing was better for a lawn than a few sheep grazing on it, and every summer five or six fat and sleepy ewes were turned out on the grass to serve this purpose and to add a pleasantly pastoral note to the view.

My first warning of something amiss came from the sheep—from the sudden sound of their bells clanging wildly and then baa-ing which suggested an assault by a whole pack of wolves. I heard Hugh say "Damn!" loudly and angrily, and I opened my eyes to see something more incongruous than wolves. It was a large black poodle in the full glory of a clownish haircut, a bright-red collar, and an ecstasy of high spirits as he chased the frightened sheep around the lawn. It was clear the poodle had no intention of hurting them—he probably found them the most wonderful playmates imaginable—but it was just as clear that the panicky ewes didn't understand this, and would very likely end up in the river before the fun was over.

In the bare second it took me to see all this, Hugh had already leaped the low terrace wall and was among the sheep, herding them away from the water's edge, and shouting commands at the dog who had different ideas.

"Down, boy!" he yelled. "Down!" And then as he would to one of his own hounds, he sternly commanded, "Heel!"

He would have done better, I thought, to have picked up a stick or stone and made a threatening gesture, since the poodle paid no attention whatever to Hugh's words. Instead, continuing to bark happily, the poodle made for the sheep again, this time with Hugh in pursuit. An instant later the dog was frozen into immobility by a voice from among the aspens near the edge of the lawn.

"*Assieds!*" the voice called breathlessly. "*Assieds-toi!*"

Then the man appeared, a small, dapper figure trotting across the grass. Hugh stood waiting, his face darkening as we watched.

Elizabeth squeezed my arm. "Let's get down there," she whispered. "Hugh doesn't like being made a fool of."

We got there in time to hear Hugh open his big guns. "Any man," he was saying, "who doesn't know how to train an animal to its place shouldn't own one."

The man's face was all polite attention. It was a good face, thin and intelligent, and webbed with tiny lines at the corners of eyes. There was also something behind those eyes that couldn't quite be masked. A gentle mockery. A glint of wry perception turned on the world like a camera lens. It was nothing anyone like Hugh would have noticed, but it was there all the same, and I found myself warming to it on the spot. There was also something tantalizingly familiar about the newcomer's face, his high forehead, and his thinning gray hair, but as much as I dug into my memory during Hugh's long and solemn lecture I couldn't come up with an answer. The lecture ended with a few remarks on the best methods of dog training, and by then it was clear that Hugh was working himself into a mood of forgiveness.

"As long as there's no harm done—" he said.

The man nodded soberly. "Still, to get off on the wrong foot with one's new neighbors—"

Hugh looked startled. "Neighbors?" he said almost rudely. "You mean that you live around here?"

The man waved toward the aspens. "On the other side of those woods."

"The *Dane* house?" The Dane house was almost as sacred to Hugh as Hilltop, and he had once explained to me that if he were ever offered a chance to buy the place he would snap it up. His tone now was not so much wounded as incredulous. "I don't believe it!" he exclaimed.

"Oh, yes," the man assured him, "the Dane house. I performed there at a party many years ago, and always hoped that someday I might own it."

It was the word *performed* that gave me my clue—that and the accent barely perceptible under the precise English. He had been born and raised in Marseilles—that would explain the accent and—long before my time he had already become a legend.

"You're Raymond, aren't you?" I said. "Charles Raymond."

"I prefer Raymond alone." He smiled in deprecation of his own small vanity. "And I am flattered that you recognize me."

I don't believe he really was. Raymond the Magician, Raymond the Great would, if anything, expect to be recognized wherever he went. As the master of sleight of hand who had paled Thurston's star, as the escape artist who had almost outshone Houdini, Raymond would not be inclined to underestimate himself.

He had started with the standard box of tricks which makes up the repertoire of most professional magicians; he had gone far beyond that to those feats of escape which, I suppose, are known to us all by now. The lead casket sealed under a foot of lake ice, the welded-steel strait jackets, the vaults of the Bank of England, the exquisite suicide knot which nooses throat and doubles legs together so that the motion of a leg draws the noose tighter around the throat—all these Raymond had known and escaped from. And then at the pinnacle of fame he had dropped from sight and his name had become relegated to the past. When I asked him why, he shrugged.

"A man works for money or for the love of his work. If he has all the wealth he needs and has no more love for his work, why go on?"

"But to give up a great career—" I protested.

"It was enough to know that the house was waiting here."

"You mean," Elizabeth said, "that you never intended to live any place but here?"

"Never—not once in all these years." He laid a finger along his nose and winked broadly at us. "Of course, I made no secret of this to the Dane estate, and when the time came to sell I was the first and only one approached."

"You don't give up an idea easily," Hugh said in an edged voice.

Raymond laughed. "Idea? It became an obsession really. Over the years I traveled to many parts of the world, but no matter how fine the place, I knew it could not be as fine as that house on the edge of the woods there, with the river at its feet and the hills beyond. Someday, I would tell myself, when my travels are done I will come here, and, like Candide, cultivate my garden."

He ran his hand abstractedly over the poodle's head and looked around with an air of satisfaction. "And now," he said "here I am."

• • •

HERE HE WAS, indeed, and it quickly became clear that his arrival was working a change on Hilltop or, since Hilltop was so completely a reflection of Hugh, it was clear that a change was being worked on Hugh. He became irritable and restless, and more aggressively sure of himself than ever. The warmth and good nature were still there—they were as much part of him as his arrogance, but he now had to work a little harder at them. He reminded me of a man who is bothered by a speck in the eye, but can't find it, and must get along with it as best he can.

Raymond, of course, was the speck, and I got the impression at times that he rather enjoyed the role. It would have been easy enough for him to stay close to his own house and cultivate his garden, or paste up his album, or whatever retired performers do, but he evidently found that impossible. He had a way of drifting over to Hilltop at odd times, just as Hugh was led to find his way to the Dane house and spend long and troublesome sessions there. Both of them must have known that they were so badly suited to each other that the easy and logical solution would have been to stay apart. But they had the affinity of negative and positive forces, and when they were in a room together the crackling of the antagonistic current between them was so strong you could almost see it in the air.

Any subject became a point of contention for them, and they would duel over it bitterly: Hugh armored and weaponed by his massive assurance, Raymond flicking away with a rapier, trying to find a chink in the armor. I think that what annoyed Raymond most was the discovery that there was no chink in the armor. As someone with an obvious passion for searching out all sides to all questions and for going deep into motives and causes, he was continually being outraged by Hugh's single-minded way of laying down the law.

He didn't hesitate to let Hugh know that. "You are positively medieval," he said. "And of all things men should have learned since that time, the biggest is that there are no easy answers, no solutions one can give with a snap of the fingers. I can only hope for you that someday you may be faced with the perfect dilemma, the unanswerable question. You would find that a revelation. You would learn more in that minute than you dreamed possible."

And Hugh did not make matters any better when he coldly answered,

"And I say, that for any man with a brain and the courage to use it there is no such thing as a perfect dilemma."

It may be that this was the sort of episode that led to the trouble that followed, or it may be that Raymond acted out of the most innocent and aesthetic motives possible. But, whatever the motives, the results were inevitable and dangerous.

They grew from the project Raymond outlined for us in great detail one afternoon. Now that he was living in the Dane house he had discovered that it was too big, too overwhelming. "Like a museum," he explained. "I find myself wandering through it like a lost soul through endless galleries."

The grounds also needed landscaping. The ancient trees were handsome, but, as Raymond put it, there were just too many of them. "Literally," he said, "I cannot see the river for the trees, and I am one devoted to the sight of running water."

Altogether there would be drastic changes. Two wings of the house would come down, the trees would be cleared away to make a broad aisle to the water, the whole place would be enlivened. It would no longer be a museum, but the perfect home he had envisioned over the years.

At the start of this recitative Hugh was slouched comfortably in his chair. Then as Raymond drew the vivid picture of what was to be, Hugh sat up straighter and straighter until he was as rigid as a trooper in the saddle. His lips compressed. His face became blood-red. His hands clenched and unclenched in a slow deadly-rhythm. Only a miracle was restraining him from an open outburst, and it was not the kind of miracle to last. I saw from Elizabeth's expression that she understood this, too, but was as helpless as I to do anything about it. And when Raymond, after painting the last glowing strokes of his description, said complacently, "Well, now, what do you think?" there was no holding Hugh.

He leaned forward with deliberation and said, "Do you really want to know what I think?"

"Now, Hugh," Elizabeth said in alarm. "Please, Hugh—"

He brushed that aside.

"Do you really want to know?" he demanded of Raymond.

Raymond frowned. "Of course."

"Then I'll tell you," Hugh said. He took a deep breath. "I think that nobody but a damned iconoclast could even conceive the atrocity you're proposing. I think you're one of those people who take pleasure in smashing apart anything that's stamped with tradition or stability. You'd kick the props from under the whole world if you could!"

"I beg your pardon," Raymond said. He was very pale and angry. "But I think you are confusing change with destruction. Surely, you must comprehend that I do not intend to destroy anything, but only wish to make some necessary changes."

"Necessary?" Hugh gibed. "Rooting up a fine stand of trees that's been there for centuries? Ripping apart a house that's as solid as a rock? I call it wanton destruction."

"I'm afraid I do not understand. To refresh a scene, to reshape it—"

"I have no intention of arguing," Hugh cut in. "I'm telling you straight out that you don't have the right to tamper with that property!"

They were on their feet now, facing each other truculently, and the only thing that kept me from being really frightened was the conviction that Hugh would not become violent, and that Raymond was far too level-headed to lose his temper. Then the threatening moment was magically past. Raymond's lips suddenly quirked in amusement, and he studied Hugh with courteous interest.

"I see," he said. "I was quite stupid not to have understood at once. This property, which, I remarked, was a little too much like a museum, is to remain that way, and I am to be its custodian. A caretaker of the past, one might say, a curator of its relics.

He shook his head smilingly. "But I am afraid I am not quite suited to that role. I lift my hat to the past, it is true, but I prefer to court the present. For that reason I will go ahead with my plans, and hope they do not make an obstacle to our friendship."

I REMEMBER THINKING, when I left next day for the city and a long, hot week at my desk, that Raymond had carried off the affair very nicely, and that, thank God, it had gone no further than it did. So I was completely unprepared for Elizabeth's call at the end of the week.

It was awful, she said. It was the business of Hugh and Raymond and the Dane house, but worse than ever. She was counting on my coming down to Hilltop the next day; there couldn't be any question about that. She had planned a way of clearing up the whole thing, but I simply had to be there to back her up. After all, I was one of the few people Hugh would listen to, and she was depending on me.

"Depending on me for what?" I said. I didn't like the sound of it. "And as for Hugh listening to me, Elizabeth, isn't that stretching it a good deal? I can't see him wanting my advice on his personal affairs."

"If you're going to be touchy about it—"

"I'm *not* touchy about it," I retorted. "I just don't like getting mixed up in this thing. Hugh's quite capable of taking care of himself."

"Maybe too capable."

"And what does that mean?"

"Oh, I can't explain now," she wailed. "I'll tell you everything tomorrow. And, darling, if you have any brotherly feelings you'll be here on the morning train. Believe me, it's serious."

I arrived on the morning train in a bad state. My imagination is one of the overactive kind that can build a cosmic disaster out of very little material, and by the time I arrived at the house I was prepared for almost anything.

But, on the surface, at least, all was serene. Hugh greeted me warmly, Elizabeth was her cheerful self, and we had an amiable lunch and a long talk which never came near the subject of Raymond or the Dane house. I said nothing about Elizabeth's phone call, but thought of it with a steadily growing sense of outrage until I was alone with her.

"Now," I said, "I'd like an explanation of all this mystery. The Lord knows what I expected to find out here, but it certainly wasn't anything I've seen so far. And I'd like some accounting for the bad time you've given me since that call."

"All right," she said grimly, "and that's what you'll get. Come along."

She led the way on a long walk through the gardens and past the stables and outbuildings. Near the private road which lay beyond the last grove of trees she suddenly said, "When the car drove you up to the house didn't you notice anything strange about this road?"

"No, I didn't,"

"I suppose not. The driveway to the house turns off too far away from here. But now you'll have a chance to see for yourself."

I did see for myself. A chair was set squarely in the middle of the road and on the chair sat a stout man placidly reading a magazine. I recognized the man at once: he was one of Hugh's stable hands, and he had the patient look of someone who has been sitting for a long time and expects to sit a good deal longer. It took me only a second to realize what he was there for, but Elizabeth wasn't leaving anything to my deductive powers. When we walked over to him, the man stood up and grinned at us.

"William," Elizabeth said, "would you mind telling my brother what instructions Mr. Lozier gave you?"

"Sure," the man said cheerfully. "Mr. Lozier told us there was always supposed to be one of us sitting right here, and any truck we saw that might be carrying construction stuff or suchlike for the Dane house was to be stopped and turned back. All we had to do was tell them it's private property and they were trespassing. If they laid a finger on us we just call in the police. That's the whole thing."

"Have you turned back any trucks?" Elizabeth asked for my benefit.

The man looked surprised. "Why, you know that, Mrs. Lozier," he said. "There was a couple of them the first day we were out here, and that was all. There wasn't any fuss either," he explained to me. "None of those drivers wants to monkey with trespass."

When we were away from the road again I clapped my hand to my forehead, "It's incredible!" I said. "Hugh must know he can't get away with this. That road is the only one to the Dane place, and it's been in public use so long that it isn't even a private thoroughfare anymore!"

Elizabeth nodded. "And that's exactly what Raymond told Hugh a few days back. He came over here in a fury, and they had quite an argument about it. And when Raymond said something about hauling Hugh off to court. Hugh answered that he'd be glad to spend the rest of his life in litigation over this business. But that wasn't the worst of it. The last thing Raymond said was that Hugh ought to know that force only invites force, and ever since then I've been expecting a war to break out here any minute. Don't you see? That man blocking the road is a constant provocation, and it scares me."

I could understand that. And the more I considered the matter, the more dangerous it looked.

"But I have a plan," Elizabeth said eagerly, "and that's why I wanted you here. I'm having a dinner party tonight, a very small, informal dinner party. It's to be a sort of peace conference. You'll be there, and Dr. Wynant—Hugh likes you both a great deal—and," she hesitated, "Raymond."

"No!" I said. "You mean he's actually coming?"

"I went over to see him yesterday and we had a long talk. I explained everything to him—about neighbors being able to sit down and come to an understanding, and about brotherly love and—oh, it must have sounded dreadfully inspirational and sticky, but it worked. He said he would be there."

I had a foreboding. "Does Hugh know about this?"

"About the dinner? Yes."

"I mean, about Raymond's being here."

"No, he doesn't." And then when she saw me looking hard at her, she burst out defiantly with, "Well, *something* had to be done, and I did it, that's all! Isn't it better than just sitting and waiting for God knows what?"

Until we were all seated around the dining room table that evening I might have conceded the point. Hugh had been visibly shocked by Raymond's arrival, but then, apart from a sidelong glance at Elizabeth which had volumes written in it, he managed to conceal his feelings well enough. He had made the introductions gracefully, kept up his end of the conversation and, all in all, did a creditable job of playing host.

Ironically, it was the presence of Dr. Wynant which made even this much of a triumph possible for Elizabeth, and which then turned it into disaster. The doctor was an eminent surgeon, stocky and gray-haired, with an abrupt, positive way about him. Despite his own position in the world he seemed pleased as a schoolboy to meet Raymond, and in no time at all they were as thick as thieves.

It was when Hugh discovered during dinner that nearly all attention was fixed on Raymond and very little on himself that the mantle of good host started to slip, and the fatal flaws in Elizabeth's plan showed through. There are people who enjoy entertaining lions and who take pleasure in reflected glory, but Hugh was not one of them. Besides, he regarded the doctor as one of his closest friends, and I have noticed that it is the most assured of men who can be the most jealous of their friendships. And when a prized friendship is being impinged on by the man one loathes more than anything else in the world—! All in all, by simply imagining myself in Hugh's place and looking across the table at Raymond who was gaily and unconcernedly holding forth, I was prepared for the worst.

The opportunity for it came to Hugh when Raymond was deep in a discussion of the devices used in affecting escapes. They were innumerable, he said. Almost anything one could seize on would serve as such a device. A wire, a scrap of metal, even a bit of paper—at one time or another he had used them all.

"But of them all," he said with a sudden solemnity, "there is only one I would stake my life on. Strange, it is one you cannot see cannot hold in your hand—in fact, for many people it does not even exist. Yet it is the one I have used most often and which has never failed me."

The doctor leaned forward, his eyes bright with interest. "And it is—?"

"It is a knowledge of people, my friend. Or, as it may be put, a knowledge of human nature. To me it is as vital an instrument as the scalpel is to you."

"Oh?" said Hugh, and his voice was so sharp that all eyes were instantly turned on him. "You make sleight of hand sound like a department of psychology."

"Perhaps," Raymond said, and I saw he was watching Hugh now, gauging him. "You see there is no great mystery in the matter. My profession—my art, as I like to think of it—is no more than the art of misdirection, and I am but one of its many practitioners."

"I wouldn't say there were many escape artists around nowadays," the doctor remarked.

"True," Raymond said, "but you will observe I referred to the art of misdirection. The escape artist, the master of legerdemain, these are a handful who practice the most exotic form of that art. But what of those who engage in the work of politics, of advertising, of salesmanship?" He laid his finger along his nose in the familiar gesture, and winked. "I am afraid they have all made my art their business."

The doctor smiled. "Since you haven't dragged medicine into it I'm willing to go along with you," he said. "But what I want to know is, exactly how does this knowledge of human nature work in your profession?"

"In this way," Raymond said. "One must judge a person carefully. Then, if he finds in that person certain weaknesses he can state a false premise and it will be accepted without question. Once the false premise is swallowed, the rest is easy. The victim will then see only what the magician wants him to see, or will give his vote to that politician, or will buy merchandise because of that advertising." He shrugged. "And that is all there is to it."

"Is it?" Hugh said. "But what happens when you're with people who have some intelligence and won't swallow your false premise? How do you do your tricks then? Or do you keep them on the same level as selling beads to the savages?"

"Now that's uncalled for, Hugh," the doctor said. "The man's expressing his ideas. No reason to make an issue of them."

"Maybe there is," Hugh said, his eyes fixed on Raymond. "I have found he's full of interesting ideas. I was wondering how far he'd want to go in backing them up."

Raymond touched the napkin to his lips with a precise little flick, and then laid it carefully on the table before him. "In short," he said, addressing himself to Hugh, "you want a small demonstration of my art."

"It depends," Hugh said. "I don't want any trick cigarette cases or rabbits out of hats or any damn nonsense like that. I'd like to see something good."

"Something good," echoed Raymond reflectively. He looked around the room, studied it, and then turned to Hugh, pointing toward the huge oak door which was closed between the dining room and the living room, where we had gathered before dinner.

"That door is not locked, is it?"

"No," Hugh said, "it isn't, it hasn't been locked for years."

"But there is a key to it?"

Hugh pulled out his key chain, and with an effort detached a heavy, old-fashioned key. "Yes, it's the same one we use for the butler's pantry." He was becoming interested despite himself.

"Good. No, do not give it to me. Give it to the doctor. You have faith in the doctor's honor, I am sure?"

"Yes," said Hugh dryly, "I have."

"Very well. Now, doctor, will you please go to that door and lock it."

The doctor marched to the door, with his firm, decisive tread, thrust the key into the lock, and turned it. The click of the bolt snapping into place was loud in the silence of the room. The doctor returned to the table holding the key, but Raymond motioned it away. "It must not leave your hand or everything is lost," he warned.

"Now," Raymond said, "for the finale I approach the door, I flick my handkerchief at it"—the handkerchief barely brushed the keyhole—"and presto, the door is unlocked!"

The doctor went to it. He seized the doorknob, twisted it dubiously, and then watched with genuine astonishment as the door swung silently open.

"Well, I'll be damned," he said.

"Somehow," Elizabeth laughed, "a false premise went down easy as an oyster."

Only Hugh reflected a sense of personal outrage. "All right," he demanded, "how was it done? How did you work it?"

"I?" Raymond said reproachfully, and smiled at all of us with obvious enjoyment. "It was you who did it all. I used only my little knowledge of human nature to help you along the way."

I said, "I can guess part of it. That door was set in advance, and when the doctor thought he was locking it, he wasn't. He was really unlocking it. Isn't that the answer?"

Raymond nodded. "Very much the answer. The door *was* locked in advance. I made sure of that, because with a little forethought I suspected there would be such a challenge during the evening, and this was the simplest way of preparing for it, I merely made certain that I was the last one to enter this room, and when I did I used this." He held up his hand so that we could see the sliver of metal in it. "An ordinary skeleton key, of course, but sufficient for an old and primitive lock."

For a moment Raymond looked grave, then he continued brightly, "It was our host himself who stated the false premise when he said the door was unlocked. He was a man so sure of himself that he would not think to test anything so obvious. The doctor is also a man who is sure, and he fell into the same trap. It is, as you now see, a little dangerous always to be so sure."

"I'll go along with that," the doctor said ruefully, "even though it's heresy to admit it in my line of work." He playfully tossed the key he had been holding across the table to Hugh, who let it fall in front of him and made no gesture toward it. "Well, Hugh, like it or not, you must admit the man has proved his point."

"Do I?" said Hugh softly. He sat there smiling a little now, and it was easy to see he was turning some thought over and over in his head.

"Oh, come on, man," the doctor said with some impatience. "You were taken in as much as we were. You know that."

"Of course you were, darling," Elizabeth agreed.

I think that she suddenly saw her opportunity to turn the proceedings into the peace conference she had aimed at, but I could have told her she was choosing her time badly. There was a look in Hugh's eye I didn't like—a veiled look which wasn't natural to him. Ordinarily, when he was really angered, he would blow up a violent storm, and once the thunder and lightning had passed he would be honestly apologetic. But this present mood of his was different. There was a slumbrous quality in it which alarmed me.

He hooked one arm over the back of his chair and rested the other on the table, sitting halfway around to fix his eyes on Raymond. "I seem to be a minority of one," he remarked, "but I'm sorry to say I found your little trick disappointing. Not that it wasn't cleverly done—I'll grant that, all right—but because it wasn't any more than you'd expect from a competent locksmith."

"Now there's a large helping of sour grapes," the doctor jeered. Hugh shook his head. "No, I'm simply saying that where there's a lock on a door and the key to it in your hand, it's no great trick to open it. Considering our friend's reputation, I thought we'd see more from him than that."

Raymond grimaced. "Since I had hoped to entertain," he said "I must apologize for disappointing."

"Oh, as far as entertainment goes I have no complaints. But for a real test—"

"A real test?"

"Yes, something a little different. Let's say, a door without any locks or keys to tamper with. A closed door which can be opened with a fingertip, but which is nevertheless impossible to open. How does that sound to you?"

Raymond narrowed his eyes thoughtfully, as if he were considering the picture being presented to him. "It sounds most interesting," he said at last. "Tell me more about it."

"No," Hugh said, and from the sudden eagerness in his voice I felt that this was the exact moment he had been looking for. "I'll do better than that. I'll *show* it to you."

He stood up brusquely and the rest of us followed suit—except Elizabeth, who remained in her seat. When I asked her if she wanted to come along, she only shook her head and sat there watching us hopelessly as we left the room.

We were bound for the cellars, I realized, when Hugh picked up a flashlight along the way, but for a part of the cellars I had never seen before. On a few occasions I had gone downstairs to help select a bottle of wine from the racks there, but now we walked past the wine vault and into a long, dimly lit chamber behind it. Our feet scraped loudly on the rough stone, the walls around us showed the stains of seepage, and warm as the night was outside, I could feel the chill of dampness turning my chest to gooseflesh. When the doctor shuddered and said hollowly, "These are the very tombs of Atlantis," I knew I wasn't alone in my feeling, and felt some relief at that.

We stopped at the very end of the chamber, before what I can best describe as a stone closet built from floor to ceiling in the farthest angle of the walls. It was about four feet wide and not quite twice that, in length, and its open doorway showed impenetrable blackness inside, Hugh reached into the blackness and pulled a heavy door into place.

"That's it," he said abruptly. "Plain solid wood, four inches thick, fitted flush into the frame so that it's almost airtight. It's a beautiful piece of carpentry, too, the kind they practiced two hundred years ago. And no locks or bolts. Just a ring set into each side to use as a handle." He pushed the door gently and it swung open noiselessly at his touch. "See that? The whole thing is balanced so perfectly on the hinges that it moves like a feather."

"But what is it for?" I asked. "It must have been made for a reason."

Hugh laughed shortly. "It was. Back in the bad old days, when a servant committed a crime—and I don't suppose it had to be more of a crime than talking back to one of the ancient Loziers—he was put in here to repent. And since the air inside was good for only a few hours at the most, he either repented damn soon or not at all."

"And that door?" the doctor said cautiously. "That impressive door of yours which opens at a touch to provide all the air needed—what prevented the servant from opening it?"

"Look," Hugh said. He flashed his light inside the cell and we crowded behind him to peer in. The circle of light reached across the cell to its far wall and picked out a short, heavy chain hanging a little above head level with a U-shaped collar dangling from its bottom link.

"I see," Raymond said, and they were the first words I had heard him speak since we had left the dining room. "It is truly ingenious. The man stands with his back against the wall, facing the door. The collar is placed around his neck, and then—since it is clearly not made for a lock—it is clamped there, hammered around his neck. The door is closed, and the man spends the next few hours like someone on an invisible rack, reaching out with his feet to catch the ring on the door which is just out of reach. If he is lucky he may not strangle himself in his iron collar, but may live until someone chooses to open the door for him."

"My God," the doctor said. "You make me feel as if I were living through it."

Raymond smiled faintly. "I have lived through many such experiences and, believe me, the reality is always a little worse than the worst imaginings. There is always the ultimate moment of terror, of panic, when the heart pounds so madly you think it will burst through your ribs, and the cold sweat soaks clear through you in the space of one breath. That is when you must take yourself in hand, must dispel all weakness, and remember all the lessons you have ever learned. If not—!" He whisked the edge of his hand across his lean throat. "Unfortunately for the usual victim of such a device," he concluded sadly, "since he lacks the essential courage and knowledge to help himself, he succumbs."

"But you wouldn't," Hugh said.

"I have no reason to think so."

"You mean," and the eagerness was creeping back into Hugh's voice, stronger than ever, "that under the very same conditions as someone chained in there two hundred years ago you could get this door open?"

The challenging note was too strong to be brushed aside lightly. Raymond stood silent for a long minute, face strained with concentration, before he answered.

"Yes," he said. "It would not be easy—the problem is made formidable by its very simplicity—but it could be solved."

"How long do you think it would take you?"

"An hour at the most."

Hugh had come a long way around to get to this point. He asked the question slowly, savoring it. "Would you want to bet on that?"

"Now, wait a minute," the doctor said. "I don't like any part of this."

"And I vote we adjourn for a drink," I put in. "Fun's fun, but we'll all wind up with pneumonia, playing games down here." Neither Hugh nor Raymond appeared to hear a word of this. They stood staring at each other—Hugh waiting on pins and needles, Raymond deliberating—until Raymond said, "What is this bet you offer?"

"This. If you lose, you get out of the Dane house inside of a month, and sell it to me."

"And if I win?"

It was not easy for Hugh to say it, but he finally got it out. "Then I'll be the one to get out. And if you don't want to buy Hilltop I'll arrange to sell it to the first comer."

For anyone who knew Hugh it was so fantastic, so staggering a statement to hear from him, that none of us could find words at first. It was the doctor who recovered most quickly.

"You're not speaking for yourself, Hugh," he warned. "You're a married man. Elizabeth's feelings have to be considered."

"Is it a bet?" Hugh demanded of Raymond. "Do you want to go through with it?"

"I think before I answer that, there is something to be explained."

Raymond paused, then went on slowly, "I am afraid I gave the impression—out of pride, perhaps—that when I retired from my work it was because of a boredom, a lack of interest in it. That was not altogether the truth. In reality, I was required to go to a doctor some years ago, the doctor listened to the heart, and suddenly my heart became the most important thing in the world. I tell you this because, while your challenge strikes me as being a most unusual and interesting way of settling differences between neighbors, I must reject it for reasons of health."

"You were healthy enough a minute ago," Hugh said in a hard voice.

"Perhaps not as much as you would want to think, my friend."

"In other words," Hugh said bitterly, "there's no accomplice handy, no keys in your pocket to help out, and no way of tricking anyone into seeing what isn't there! So you have to admit you're beaten."

Raymond stiffened. "I admit no such thing. All the tools I would need even for such a test as this I have with me. Believe me, they would be enough."

Hugh laughed aloud, and the sound of it broke into small echoes all down the corridors behind us. It was that sound, I am sure—the living contempt in it rebounding from wall to wall around us—which sent Raymond into the cell.

Hugh wielded the hammer, a short-handled but heavy sledge, which tightened the collar into a circlet around Raymond's neck, hitting with hard even strokes at the iron which was braced against the wall. When he had finished I saw the pale glow of the radium-painted numbers on a watch as Raymond studied it in his pitch darkness.

"It is now eleven," he said calmly. "The wager is that by midnight this door must be opened, and it does not matter what means are used. Those are the conditions, and you gentlemen are the witnesses to them."

Then the door was closed, and the walking began.

Back and forth we walked—the three of us—as if we were being compelled to trace every possible geometric figure on that stony floor, the doctor with his quick, impatient step, and I matching Hugh's long, nervous strides. A foolish, meaningless march, back and forth across our own shadows, each of us marking the time by counting off the passing seconds, and each ashamed to be the first to look at his watch.

For a while there was a counterpoint to this scraping of feet from inside the cell. It was a barely perceptible clinking of chain coming at brief, regular intervals. Then there would be a long silence, followed by a renewal of the sound. When it stopped again I could not restrain myself any longer. I held up my watch toward the dim yellowish light of the bulb overhead and saw with dismay that barely twenty minutes had passed.

After that there was no hesitancy in the others about looking at the time and, if anything, this made it harder to bear than just wondering. I caught the doctor winding his watch with small, brisk turns, and then a few minutes later he would try to wind it again, and suddenly drop his hand with disgust as he realized he had already done it. Hugh walked with his watch held up near his eyes, as if by concentration on it he could drag that crawling minute hand faster around the dial.

Thirty minutes had passed.

Forty.

Forty-five.

I remember that when I looked at my watch and saw there were less than fifteen minutes to go I wondered if I could last out even that short time. The chill had sunk so deep into me that I ached with it. I was shocked when I saw that Hugh's face was dripping with sweat, and that beads of it gathered and ran off while I watched.

It was while I was looking at him in fascination that it happened. The sound broke through the walls of the cell like a wail of agony heard from far away, and shivered over us as if it were spelling out the words.

"*Doctor!*" it cried. "*The air*"

It was Raymond's voice, but the thickness of the wail blocking it off turned it into a high, thin sound. What was clearest in it was the note of pure terror, the plea growing out of that terror.

"*Air!*" it screamed, the word bubbling and dissolving into a long-drawn sound which made no sense at all.

And then it was silent.

We leaped for the door together, but Hugh was there first, his back against it, barring the way. In his upraised hand was the hammer which had clinched Raymond's collar.

"Keep back!" he cried. "Don't come any nearer, I warn you!"

The fury in him, brought home by the menace of the weapon, stopped us in our tracks.

"Hugh," the doctor pleaded, "I know what you're thinking, but you can forget that now. The bet's off, and I'm opening the door on my own responsibility. You have my word for that."

"Do I? But do you remember the terms of the bet, doctor? This door must be opened within an hour—*and it doesn't matter what means are used!* Do you understand now? He's fooling both of you. He's faking a death scene, so that you'll push open the door and win his bet for him. But it's my bet, not yours, and I have the last word on it!"

I saw from the way he talked, despite the shaking tension in his voice, that he was in perfect command of himself, and it made everything seem that much worse.

"How do you know he's faking?" I demanded. "The man said he had a heart condition. He said there was always a time in a spot like this when he had to fight panic and could feel the strain of it. What right do you have to gamble with his life?"

"Damn it, don't you see he never mentioned any heart condition until he smelled a bet in the wind? Don't you see he set his trap that way, just as he locked the door behind him when he came into dinner! But this time nobody will spring it for him—nobody!"

"Listen to me," the doctor said, and his voice cracked like a whip. "Do you concede that there's one slim possibility of that man being dead in there, or dying?"

"Yes, it is possible—anything is possible."

"I'm not trying to split hairs with you! I'm telling you that if that man is in trouble every second counts, and you're stealing that time from him. And if that's the case, by God, I'll sit in the witness chair at your trial and swear you murdered him! Is that what you want?"

Hugh's head sank forward on his chest, but his hand still tightly gripped the hammer. I could hear the breath drawing heavily in his throat, and when he raised his head, his face was gray and haggard. The torment of indecision was written in every pale sweating line of it.

And then I suddenly understood what Raymond had meant that day when he told Hugh about the revelation he might find in the face of a perfect dilemma. It was the revelation of what a man may learn about himself when he is forced to look into his own depths, and Hugh had found it at last.

In that shadowy cellar, while the relentless seconds thundered louder and louder in our ears, we waited to see what he would do.